SAURIAN

A Novel By
WILLIAM SCHOELL

Encyclopocalypse Publications
www.encyclopocalypse.com

INTRODUCTION

Why *Saurian*? After the relatively more serious tone of *Vicious*, I wanted to do another book that was pure fun and escapism, and which took advantage of my absolute adoration of giant monster movies such as *The Beast from 20,000 Fathoms, Them!,* and *The Giant Behemoth,* movies I watched on television over and over again in my youth. My protagonist also loved these movies, although being older than me he saw them in the movie house. Years later I thoroughly investigated the genre in my book *Creature Features: Nature Turned Nasty in the Movies,* but *Saurian* was my fictional valentine to the genre. There's everything from isolated islands where voracious monsters lurk to Leviathans emerging from the sea or storming across the dark downtown streets of a city in pursuit of prey.

Saurian is a book you either love or hate. If you love the type of movies that inspired it you will get where I was coming from and probably enjoy the novel; if not, you'd better look elsewhere. I enjoyed creating the rather screwed-up characters in this book: Thomas with his difficult parents and traumatic past; his pathetic girlfriend Elsa, who imagines she's a song stylist supreme but is more delusional than anything else; the even more pathetic Samantha, an alcoholic who destroyed a family and may have borderline antisemitic issues. (For the record, although raised as a Protestant I consider myself Jewish as my mother was). And the utterly weird Mistress Dunn, who runs a Monster Society of people who – like Thomas and Samantha -- have had some *very* strange things happen to them. (You might wonder why I gave the Mistress the first name of Eustace? Because I thought it was a *woman's* name, that's why! It's actually a man's name, but y'know, that inconsistency seems to fit in perfectly with one of the weirdest people you'll find in one of my books.)

And then there's Gareth Bronmore, the strangest of all. One could argue that Bronmore takes the notion of metamorphosis – man into wolf, for instance – and takes it to the max!

As for the numerous death scenes in the book: Some people feel there's little point in creating back stories about people who will only be killed a few pages later, but I feel it adds a degree of – for lack of a better word – pathos if you know a little bit about the victims beforehand. Often their deaths have a degree of irony as well.

In any case, *Saurian* was a lot of fun to write, and again the publisher used my original title.

William Schoell
January, 2024

For
Mike Ritzer and Author Tower

SAURIAN

PROLOGUE

North America. 64,000,000 years ago.

It was the largest thing that had ever lived. And it was dying.

In the primeval forest it spent most of its time in the lake or upon its shores. It was a carnivore and had an enormous appetite. In its younger days, it had frequently scouted far from its home for the scent of fresh meat, lumbering after hordes of smaller beasts and larger, more ferocious animals. It also held a distant genetic memory of locking figurative horns with other monstrous reptiles that were almost as big as it was, but that was many, many years ago. It was afraid of nothing and it had satisfied its appetites a thousand times over. No creature could beat it in combat, nor had any mammal yet feasted off even part of its flesh.

But that was before. Now The Beast knew that once the slight flame of life it held inside itself was extinguished, its flesh would feed the scavengers by the hundreds. Its mammoth, bloated body would float up to the surface of the water, and what the fish had not nibbled on, the ticks and larvae would. Then would come the sniveling, furtive forest creatures. It did not like the thought of providing sustenance for unthinking crawling things, but it knew it had no choice.

Now that it had grown old and weak, it rarely left the lakeside. It chose easier prey. Now as it swam beneath the lake, opening jaws wide to take in small fish and plant life that did little to satisfy the ache in its belly, it sensed movement overhead, near the shore, and thought this time it might feed on something more substantial.

It lifted its head slightly above the water. Warm blood! Once it would never have preyed upon mammals without first trying to mentally communicate with them—there was always the chance they were its people—but now it didn't care. They were *meat*.

The Beast knew that it would easily fall should any of the larger carnivores decide to band together and attack it en masse, but these small mammals with their claws and tongues? Even when they hunted in packs they were no match for it. At least not yet. Even in its weakened condition it would make short work of them.

With a powerful thrust of its hind legs The Beast rose up out of the water and headed for shore. It knew just the sight of itself would petrify most of the mammals, making them easier to deal with. It reached the shore, rose up on its haunches, and came crashing down, toppling trees and squashing half a dozen wriggling things under its belly. It left a huge indentation in the soft mud on the shore from which it would later lick the crushed remains of what it had fallen on.

The others were now within reach of its jaws. They screamed and tried to run, but there was never any hope. One flick of its tremendous tongue and it could get several of them at once. A few went down whole, still struggling; others were ground between its jaws until they were a fine, mushy paste easy to swallow. It ate everything—the skin, the bones, the blood.

Nothing was left of the mammalian conclave but one squalling infant creature.

Its tongue went out and sucked up the little wriggling thing, squished it against the roof of its mouth, and let it slide down its gullet to join its kin.

The Beast was still hungry.

It had sinned but did not care. It had eaten mammalian flesh carelessly, possibly eaten its own kind, and it did not care. It had done it before. And if need be, The Beast would do so again.

It thought back to what it had dreamed about its origins, the arrival from the stars of an ancient race who were stranded on this planet, unable to return to their own distant world. The dominant species on this world were gigantic creatures with huge, thundering bodies and tiny, if efficient brains. These aliens, shape-changers, adapted to life on Earth by becoming like the thundering giants. They paid no attention to the rat-like mammals with their pouches and milk glands that darted in futile terror and stupidity among the trees and through the wetlands, eating their seeds and insects, prey to the smaller, less thunderous creatures of the world. The aliens became accustomed to the cooling subtropical climate, the beautiful flowering plants and trees, the shallow sea that divided the huge continent they'd landed on.

And then came conflagration! The bright cosmic fire lit up the heavens, bathed the planet in an eerie red glow and sent a foul burning wind through the jungles and the rivers. Slowly the climate changed. Slowly the thundering giants died, but not the aliens who only *looked* like thundering giants. They survived to inherit what was left of the world. Or so they thought.

For the mammalian population, taking advantage of the death of the giants, began to assert themselves. They rose in great numbers from the ashes, so tiny, so puny, with such fragile, funny bodies. They still walked on all fours, but there the similarity ended. In the days when the thundering giants were dominant, the mammals were just insignificant prey, but now they were slowly growing larger, fiercer, and more cunning.

And much more intelligent than the giants had ever been.

So the children of the children of the aliens decided to change again, to adapt—to *become mammals themselves.*

But many did not want to. The ones who had birthed The Beast had not wanted to. They wanted to remain in their thundering forms, to have the strength of their monstrous bodies and their superior intelligence.

And remain they did.

But as the generations came and went, they were to discover the terrible legacy of the burning fire from the sky that had destroyed the thundering early denizens of Earth. No, it had not actually destroyed them, but its poison had slowly sunk into each cell, removing their ability to transform. They could never return to "normal." They were truly mammal—or truly monster. Even upon death they would stay locked in that form, instead of reverting to energy as they had in the past.

Occasionally a mutant with the power to transform would be born, but they could only switch instinctively from mammal to monster, or vice versa, not into the ancient alien lifeform that had been their spiritual ancestor. One of The Beast's own children was that way, but it didn't like to think of her, out there throwing her lot in with the mammals. Perhaps The Beast had eaten her and not even known it.

The Beast was sad. Had things not changed the scavengers could not have fed upon its corpse; instead it would have returned to the insubstantial state its ancestors had arrived in. But now? Now they would pick its bones the way it had picked and eaten theirs.

The Beast was lonely, too. It had mated many years ago, had watched most of its children grow to look like itself, then watched them wander off into the vast green jungle, to find their own mates, their own domains. They had never returned, nor had it expected them to. It had noticed with dismay that they seemed far more like those early thundering giants of Earth than like itself. With each generation, the beasts-who-were-not-beasts became *more* like beasts, as their intelligence faded and the mammals became ever more dominant.

It had had a long life. The Beast did not want to die but it had no regrets.

It sank down to the bottom of the deep, dark lake and lay in the mud where it died.

64,000,000 years later its bones would be discovered in what would then be known as the state of Arizona.

The Beast was dead.

But its monstrous legacy would live on.

PART ONE
FLORIDA, 1957

CHAPTER ONE

THE BUNCH

His parents wanted him to play with The Bunch.

The Bunch, as they were called, was that motley assortment of girls and boys, around Thomas' age, who lived in the other shacks and houses around the Bartlett dwelling. "Why don't you go play with The Bunch?" Thomas' mother and father, particularly his father, kept asking him. His mother was a little more tolerant, as mothers are wont to be, of Thomas' peculiarities, his desire for privacy, his penchant for games and fantasies. "Can't you play games with other kids?" his father asked. But his mother knew Tommy preferred to be alone, not that she liked it much.

He had no great interest in The Bunch. They seemed strange to him, noisy, unfocused, disinterested in anything but gathering together to play stickball. There were about a dozen members of The Bunch, half of which were always playing somewhere in the area; the other half were sort of associate members, sometimes tagging along with the other six, sometimes not. They scared Tommy. In the back of his mind he wondered if they would accept him. Besides, he could imagine nothing more stupid than standing around aimlessly the way they did, knocking a ball around with a stick, or playing with those silly Yo-yos and Hula Hoops. How could that compare to reading his comic books and monster magazines, to being absorbed in his private nightmare dreams of dark forces and gigantic animals?

How he loved to wander about the house or along the beach, pretending he was hunting down some enormous monster, one of the mammoth creatures that paraded across the color-splashed covers of his comics or thundered across the movie screen at the local theater. Monsters and super-heroes were his universe, the only things he wanted or required.

He knew the members of The Bunch would not understand.

"Tommy!" his mother hollered from the kitchen. "Come get your lunch!"

"I'm coming," he hollered back, knowing he would not stir from his room until he was through with the latest issue of *Amazing Monsters.* The title story was "Brog, The Beast from Planet Bzurax," which sounded like Borax to him and made him giggle. "Twelve years old is too old for comic books," his father told him, but he didn't care. Brog, which looked like a walking eggplant and had long, dripping fangs, had just crashed out of captivity at the space center where the astronauts had brought it in its tiny infant form (six feet) and in the large bottom panel on page seven was picking up an automobile in its claws. Terrific!

"Tommy, I said lunch is ready."

"I'm coming," he said, lying again. He hated to be interrupted in the middle of a good story, and there was nothing worse than reading a comic at the table, with his mother chattering and nagging him all the time. And she never listened to him. When he'd saved up money to see *The Beast from 20,000 Fathoms* a few years ago, he'd not been able to stop talking about it afterward. He'd tried and tried to tell them the plot—fantastic!—but neither of his parents would listen. "You and your monsters," they would mumble, sneering. "I just hope you'll be able to face the real world when you have to."

Who wanted to face the real world? Look at what facing the real world had done to his ma and pa. The real world was a bleak, four room house at the edge of the sea that was constantly in need of repair. The real world was a drunken father who was out of work more often than not. And the real world was a sad-eyed mother who scrubbed floors for a living and looked about a decade older than her 37 years. As for his father, he looked about 20 years older than his 40.

"Tommy, I said lunch is ready. Will you get in here already!"

She was really angry this time. He would have to go. He folded the upper edge of the comic over so he would not lose his place and went into the hallway and down to the kitchen.

She had made him a peanut butter and jelly sandwich. He sat down at the table and began to chew listlessly. He had to remember not to upset them. Next week a movie about giant bugs was coming to the theater and if he couldn't get enough money cashing in soda pop bottles, his usual form of income, he would have to beg them for the remainder. Now and then one or the other of them would take pity on him and give him some change, but they were too poor—or so they said—to give him a regular allowance.

He would have had more chores than most boys, due to his father's perpetual inebriation, had there been more to do around the house. But his parents were not concerned with its neglect. He had to take out the garbage and go to the store— that sort of stuff—but there was no lawn to mow, just weeds and sand, the sand so pervasive it seemed to creep into the house on shoes and the like without anyone noticing. In the wintertime, there wasn't even snow to shovel.

Summers were the worst. Summers were the time when his mother most often threatened to leave and take Tommy with her. But where would they go? he often wondered. He had no living grandparents, no relatives that his mother was close to. Was she speaking to any of them this year? It was so hard keeping up with her feuds.

As he chewed his peanut butter and jelly sandwich, he thought about the possibility of being taken away from the beach, which he loved, and brought to some strange house in a distant town. But why worry? None of his mother's relatives would put them up, not the way his mother treated them. She would scribble angry letters, tear them up, rewrite them, tear them up again, then write them once more and finally mail them. Sometimes, but not often, angry letters from other towns would come in reply. His mother would tear her hair, cry, throw things. "How dare they? *How dare they?*" It was always one thing or another.

* * *

The last big feud had started three years ago when his mother's sister, Aunt Harriet, married a banker in Orlando. The printed invitation had come to his mother with an inked scrawl across the bottom: Please do not bring Martin. We considered your request to have Tommy in the wedding party, but we are afraid we already have four ushers and cannot use anymore, Love, Harriet. His mother was furious.

"I know they never liked your father" she explained. "I can even understand why my own sister doesn't want me as matron of honor or even bridesmaid. But why take it out on a little boy? You should have been an usher, Tommy."

Tommy, who hated weddings anyway, had said, "They already have four. It doesn't matter to me."

"It matters to me! They could have made you the ring bearer. Something. Instead they just shut you out of the wedding. Harriet's only nephew. Just shut you out, damn them. Thinks she's so much better than us 'cause she landed a banker. Well, she liked your father well enough once...before he started drinking. Wanted him herself. Always said, 'Anne Marie, count yourself lucky that man is interested in you. He comes from such a good family.' Ha! She never forgave me for stealing him away. Well, she had the last laugh, but do you think that would satisfy her, do you think it would? Well, it didn't. Nothing will satisfy that woman when she gets the meanness in her. A cold, mean woman, Harriet is. Get no sympathy from her. And don't count on that rich banker husband of hers helping you out either. Damn them!"

* * *

Tommy's mother never drank, and Tommy was glad that she didn't. She was, well, strange enough, hysterical enough, without alcohol, as it were. As she always said, Tommy's father drank enough for the three of them.

Anne Marie Bartlett, nee Anne Marie Rozinski of Summerdale, was a pale, pretty woman who had long since stopped caring about her appearance. She was badly dressed, even slovenly, her unkempt hair falling down to her shoulders in knots and tangles. She wore shapeless housedresses and slippers. In the summer she would walk about in a slip, or just a bra and girdle. She rarely used makeup. Had they enough money to eat well she would certainly have turned to fat, but for now her ribs were showing. She had large eyes, light blue, that always seemed on the verge of tears, a fleshy nose that was a bit too big but not unattractive, fairly full lips and a rounded chin. She'd inherited straight teeth from her mother but they were rotting. Her figure was not bad but nothing spectacular either. It was not helped by her constant slouch, the bad posture that was a result of fatigue and depression and too much housework in other people's homes. Standing tall she would have been five foot seven, but the years were slowly crushing her downward inch by inch.

He had heard the details of her life history hundreds of

times while his father was out on a drunk somewhere. She'd make him a sandwich and sit next to him on one of the battered chairs at the kitchen table and regale him with tales of how Anne Marie Rozinski, who'd had such dreams for the future, had developed into the "old wreck" he saw before him. How "that man" had brought her to ruin. She would refuse—absolutely not countenance —any suggestion that she might be partly to blame, that no one had forced her to stay with Martin Bartlett. Neither would she admit how much she still loved the man.

Once Martin Bartlett had been the "best catch" in Summerdale. His brother Ernest Bartlett was making a name for himself as a noted architect. His father was the politician, Henry Bartlett, and his late mother had been the distinguished stage actress, Lilah Berenson. Martin was being groomed to follow in his father's footsteps and was courting pretty little Anne Marie Rozinski when World War II broke out.

A war record was essential for a successful political career, Henry told his son, even though his influence could have kept him out or gotten him a cushy desk job. Martin volunteered, became an officer, and went off to Europe to fight in "The War to End All Wars." Ernest stayed home and helped the war effort by using his expertise to design more efficient military installations.

Martin Bartlett came back a changed man.

Anne Marie had noticed the change, that certain quiet… madness…in his eyes, but she tried to ignore it. He was her fiancé, heir to wealth and prestige, the answer to every girl's dream. So she married him in spite of those subtle misgivings.

The trouble started almost immediately.

It wasn't just the drinking. It was the *cause* of the drinking —the nightmares, the quivers, the haunted moments when he would just stop in mid-sentence and stare sightlessly at some war memory that he could not even bring himself to share with his wife. He'd seen people die and blown to pieces; he'd shot at men, killed men, lost buddies, been bloodied by spraying offal and body parts. Sometimes he'd just sit there and shake, so badly she thought he'd literally fall to pieces in front of her eyes.

And so the drinking began. At first, it was just to calm his nerves, to help him relax in front of strangers, his father's political friends. No quivering wreck of a man, however, could run for office no matter how distinguished his war record. A man had to be able to push aside all that wartime horror and handle his life with courage, strength and fortitude.

We all went through it, the political bosses said, though most of them had either been too old for the war, had stayed at home giving orders far away from the fighting, or had kept their own sons as far from Anzio and the South Pacific as they possibly could.

But then the drinking got out of control. The drinking made him more nervous, which made him drink more, which made him *more* nervous, and soon he was out of control, nervous and drunk, an eyesore, a slob, an object of laughter, derision and contempt.

When the situation was at its worst, Tommy was born.

Once Henry Bartlett had sympathy and tolerance for his son, but when the boy refused to listen to good advice or seek professional help, when he started running around Summerdale smashing barroom windows, scaring children, and accosting unattached ladies—well, there was a limit to what Henry would put up with. The war had just been an excuse, as far as he was concerned. Sure the boy had had bad experiences like a lot of other men, but why take it out on his wife and child? He had responsibilities, and couldn't measure up to them. He had always been a weakling, Lilah's favorite, a milksop and a fool.

Henry disinherited Martin, apparently never considering how this would only make matters worse for his daughter-in-law and grandson. He had never really cared that much for Anne Marie, and sometimes he thought that had she been a better wife his son might have licked his problems and become a better man. He left all of his money to his other son, Ernest, and washed his hands of Martin Bartlett and family.

Two months later Henry Bartlett died. He had been troubled during his final ill days by his decision, worried about his grandson if no one else, but it was too late; he died before having the opportunity to contact his lawyer and make amends.

Martin's total decline followed quickly. All hope of a political future was over. His brother, Ernest, who had taken pity on him, tried to take him into his firm in some capacity, but Martin never showed up for the interview. He had gone on a three day drinking binge and wound up in Georgia locked up on vagrancy charges.

Anne Marie, who had not been trained in any skill or even given thought to the possibility that someday she might have to work, threw herself on the mercy of her family, for her baby's sake if not for her own. Her parents had both passed away during the war, at least having been spared seeing how their favorite daughter had fallen on hard times. They had been a middle-class couple and had left little savings to pass on to the children. Anne Marie eventually got a check for 300 dollars which Martin cashed and spent entirely on lager. Anne Marie had three living siblings (a fourth had died of influenza in 1928): Harriet, who turned her back on her, secretly pleased at her prettier sister's dismal fate; George, who was in New York struggling as an actor; and Steven, who had tried on several occasions to find his brother-in-law steady employment but received only broken promises, arguments and threats of physical violence for his efforts. He had long since thrown up his hands.

Steven and his wife, Laura, frequently offered shelter to Anne Marie and Tommy, but Anne Marie refused to leave her husband. They sent substantial checks from time to time until Anne Marie got into another one of her feuds, accusing Laura of telling stories about her and Martin to her "snotty rich friends" and implying she had forced her brother to marry her. Not long after, Steve and Laura left town and all Anne Marie ever got from them was an annual Christmas card. Tommy got money for his birthday, which either Anne Marie or his father would appropriate, his father for booze, his mother for food or true confession magazines, which she read for hours on end when she wasn't working.

* * *

So the years went by. They had started out with a lovely house in the nicest part of town, the very center of Summerdale, a wedding gift from Henry Bartlett, but moved farther and farther away from Main Street as the years progressed. It seemed to Tommy that they were always moving; he'd had so many addresses he could barely keep track of them. Houses became apartments became Beachside.

Beachside was the name given to the slum along the south shore. Some of the houses on the shore were mere tin shacks, shanties of corrugated iron, tents of flapping canvas. Some of the inhabitants were like gypsies, pulling up stakes and going inland or out-of-state when the spirit moved them. The hub of the neighborhood was a long series of wooden houses, built upon stilts to let the water flow beneath them when necessary, that had been erected in the early thirties.

There was constant talk about tearing the whole of Beachside down and turning it into a resort so that Summerdale could flourish the way Miami Beach had, but so far nothing had come of it. Nobody cared about Beachside's inhabitants, but there were legalities involved, zoning problems and the like, as long as Beachside was a residential district, it was all above Tommy's head. All he knew was the only reason they lived in a rented house instead of in one of the tin shacks was the money his mother made doing housework for the wealthier people in Summerdale. On occasion, when he was sober, his father would take on heavier chores and at least earn his drinking money and a little extra. Tommy did yardwork, too, but he had to turn over that small pittance to his mother.

The house was one story, with a porch that faced the Atlantic Ocean, and a big window that looked out at the beach from the living room. This room was the largest in the house. Beyond it was the kitchen on one side, and a hallway in the very middle of the house that separated the kitchen from the two bedrooms. The shutters were askew, the steps to the porch were broken, and the porch itself was made of rotting wood beams that groaned or sometimes snapped beneath your weight. The house was furnished with an old sofa, a couple of easy chairs and a table. They had a phone but most of the time it was off because they were behind in the phone bill, so his mother resorted to hate mail when she got angry at the relatives. She sent letter after unanswered letter to brother, sister, brother-in-law. The only one she spared was George, because she knew his circumstances were no better than her own. But at least he was in New York doing something exciting!

The whole house was grim, from its unpainted, dirty exterior to its bleak, drab interior, but Tommy loved it. It was home—his home, their home, his protection from the world.

* * *

"Tommy, what are you going to do this afternoon? I've got to go to work."

On Thursdays she spent the afternoon cleaning up for Mrs. Hampton on Ridge Street. She would get paid today, too. Tommy remembered the movie about the big bugs eating people that he was desperate to see and hoped she'd give him just a little so he could go.

"What do you want me to do?" he said, trying his best to be the good, dutiful son who only existed to act out his mother's every commandment.

"Stay out of trouble. You could bring that dress I repaired for Mrs. Merlvalle over to her house and get what she promised me."

Money! Tommy's eyes brightened at the prospect. Surely he could sneak a quarter or two from the total.

But his mother snatched the opportunity away. "No. Mrs. Merlvalle said she wouldn't be home again from Sarasota until next week.

"Why don't you go play with The Bunch," she said finally, sealing his fate.

"I don't want to," he said.

"Why? I can't understand *why*. Your father and I only want you to have friends. You spend all of your time by yourself. What is it? Are you shy? Can't figure out who you got it from. I'm not shy. Your father's not shy."

Not shy, no sir, not his dad. Drunk people were never shy. Perhaps he should try a drink or two some day. No, his mother would kill him and rightly so, after all they'd been through because of his father's problem.

"Nobody was ever shy in my family. You spend too much time with those silly comics of yours. You've got to get out and have fun."

"I do have fun. I love reading comic books. And I'm outdoors every afternoon."

"Yes, but by yourself, always by yourself. You sneak out of here and go down the beach—yeah, I've seen how you are— just sneak away before those kids catch sight of you. What's the matter? Do they call you names? Have they ever picked on you?"

"No."

"Well, I can't figure you. Such a strange, strange boy. No wonder, with the father you have. Those kids won't hurt you. You have to make friends, Tommy, have to get to know people. People would like you if you only gave them the chance. It's not right for a nice, good-looking boy like you to be alone all the time. Why, next year you'll be thirteen. Dating soon, getting married, having kids."

Tommy was horrified at the prospect.

"Whatcha gonna do, spend your whole life alone? That's not right, not healthy."

Tommy hated it when his mother carried on like this. His father's opinion, pickled in alcohol, could always be disregarded, but despite her pixilated quality, his mother always seemed to talk sense. She seemed to say that he was weird, Martin Bartlett's strange boy, Tommy. Well, someday he'd be a great scientist, a great explorer, and he'd prove that there were monsters in the world. He'd go to Loch Ness, explore South America and try to find a hidden plateau full of prehistoric monsters like in that book *The Lost World* by Sir Arthur Conan Doyle he had borrowed from the library. He'd prove it. Then no one would laugh at him. He'd come back famous and successful. He'd show them all.

Or at least he could always write about monsters for the comic books. That was safer than going out hunting them at any rate.

"Can't understand why you don't make friends in school, either. Bright boy like you. Always get good grades. Can't figure it."

But they both knew why. Kids from Beachside were not fit to be friends with kids from the better parts of town. Every time one of the kids tried to befriend him, their parents would only discourage it when they found out where he lived. Only the shiftless, the dirty, the well-deserved inheritors of failure and poverty lived in Beachside, the eyesore slum of

Summerdale. A lot of the kids in Beachside never went to school at all, hidden prey of the truant officer.

Some of the members of The Bunch, the kids who lived in other houses along "the row," as it was called, of homes-on-stilts in the center of Beachside, went to school, but when he saw them, he kept his distance. They seemed to reek of failure and decadence, to be silly midget counterparts of their shiftless parents. *They* would never get out of Beachside, but Tommy would. Of that he had no doubt. He would get out and come back well-known and wealthy; he would move his parents out of Beachside and they'd live happily ever after.

How could he make his folks understand that the members of The Bunch lacked imagination and ambition, that they were dull and stupid and as hopeless as the parents that birthed them. They belonged in Beachside. Even though Tommy loved his house and the beach it sat upon, he had no intention of staying there forever.

He was not popular at school, but neither was he picked on. He was tall for his age and attractive. Already some of the girls gave him meaningful looks. In a short while he would be returning those looks, with interest. In the meantime, females represented hearth and home and marriage to him, and those things—if his parents were any indication—were to be avoided like a raging case of measles and chicken pox combined.

"I'll tell you what" his mother said. "I'll make you a promise."

He finished his sandwich and lifted his glass of milk up to his mouth. "What's that?"

"I see there's a new monster movie coming next week. Something about giant grasshoppers."

His mother was always surprising him. How did she know about that? She never paid attention to such things. She must have seen the advance ad in the paper at somebody's house.

The Bartlett's themselves never bought the papers, believing it an unnecessary expense. Thank God they still had that old battered TV set which they kept in his room so at least he could watch his favorite shows.

"Yeah" he said. "Big bugs eating people and everything!"

Anne Marie smiled, then laughed, but with love rather than derision. "Tell you what. You go out and play with The Bunch this afternoon, right now, and I promise I'll give you money to see the show out of what Mrs. Merlvalle gives me on Monday. How about that?"

He got out of his seat and went and hugged her. "Please give me the money anyway, but don't make me play with The Bunch."

"Why, honey, you're nearly crying. Do they bother you that much?"

"I'm...I'm scared of them."

"You *are* shy." But it wasn't just his shyness, but what they represented—the hopelessness, the defeat. Why couldn't she see that they just didn't interest him? He hoped she'd melt but instead she turned colder. "Tommy, you've got to get over this shyness or your life will be miserable. You'll get the money to see the movie but only if you go out and play with those children. They're tossing a ball around now, hear 'em? You don't have to play any game you don't want to—I know you're not very physical—but at least go and talk to 'em."

"Do I have to?"

"You'll get no money if you don't."

For just a moment he hated her.

"Go on. Finish your milk and go play. You can't spend the whole summer reading comic books and daydreaming. That movie about the bugs will give you nightmares again anyhow."

"How long do I have to play with them?"

"All afternoon."

"All *afternoon?*"

"Well, at least an hour or two until I get back. Now, go on. I want you out there with them before I leave. Once you see how nice and friendly they are, you'll be glad you did. Why, just yesterday little Suzie Peters asked how come you never come out and join them. They like you, Tommy; they want to get to know you better."

"I'll go out in a little while. I have a comic I want to finish." How he wanted to go back into his room and read about Brog, the Beast from Planet Borax!

"Not later. Now, do you hear me? Out. Out. Get outside. I've got to get going soon."

Dejectedly he headed for the door. "When will you be back?"

She shrugged. "Who knows? After cleaning the Hampton house I have to go look for your father."

"I thought he was helping old Mr. Potter clean his toolshed."

"Yes, but who knows if he ever showed up. If Mr. Potter paid him, you know he headed for the nearest bar or bought a bottle and went off for one of his walks." She snorted. "I'll try to have him home by suppertime. If you get hungry, have a can of beans."

"Okay." He loved beans, luckily.

"Scoot. I have to get going soon."

He headed out the door. He knew better than to bring his comics with him. From his brief past experiences with The Bunch, they'd either deride the comic or pass it around them avidly until it was in a dozen different pieces. Slobs!

For a moment he thought of turning right instead of left and going off to the beach on another of his wonderful imaginary adventures.

But then he thought of the movie about the big bugs and knew he had to go through with it.

* * *

The Man was hungry now, very hungry, but simple food for human appetites would not do. Although his belly was small now, human-small, it was crying out for some enormous sustenance that in his current form he could not even begin to contain.

He would have to change.

He walked down to the ocean. Far to his left was the odious eyesore of Beachside, hidden by the dunes and overgrown patches of prickly weeds. Behind him there was a forest. He sensed, as he could always sense, that no one was about, that no one could see him.

He stripped out of his clothes and strode into the ocean.

Seconds later he had sunk beneath the waves.

Deep, deep under the water, he began to change.

As always, it felt wonderful, like he was coming home, finding his true form, entering a new phase of magnificent existence.

The Man changed into The Beast.

And the hunger grew.

It grew even as The Beast grew.

The Man who was not a man swam through the water as small fish darted out of its way in panic. What did they imagine he was? the diminishing part of The Beast that was still human wondered. Did they even care?

In moments he was several miles from the coastline. It would not do to be seen by anyone in a boat or on shore. He was careful, as always, though he wondered why anyone as formidable as he should have to be careful.

There to his right was movement.

Inwardly, he smiled. It was a great white shark— an enormous one, 15 feet, maybe 20.

Well, it was one predator who was in for a whopping surprise.

If a great white shark could *be* surprised.

As he moved in for the kill, he just shifted his head a little bit, opened his own yawning jaws...

And *swallowed*.

CHAPTER TWO
THE LOST SEA

The Bunch turned out to be not quite as bad as Tommy thought.

There were only five of them playing outside today. Suzanne, who was 11, was a freckle-faced pixie who was short for her age and a little bit plump; she had fiery red hair and dimples. Joey, who was 12 like Tommy, was a skinny, bespectacled kid who always seemed eager to make friends. Patrick, a serious, good-looking, dark-haired lad, was the biggest of them all at 13 and was always dressed in clean, white shirts that his mother futilely warned him not to dirty. Bobby was a short fat kid with a ragged mop of blond hair who seemed the most interested in sports while being physically the least likely to be athletic.

Etta was Tommy's favorite, even though she was less interested in Tommy than Suzanne was. Like Bobby, she was also 12 and had big blue eyes, an intensely pretty face, and a cute pug nose that looked better on her than anyone would have expected. Her dark hair cascaded down to her shoulders in ringlets. Her face was smudged with dirt and she had body odor—not everyone in Beachside was as clean as Patrick Higgins—but Tommy liked her just the same.

Tommy was not as handsome as Patrick, but he was still a fine-looking boy. He had a small, lightly freckled face, even features, blue eyes that seemed sad and penetrating but could light up with joy at the slightest provocation. His light brown hair was worn rather long as his mother hated to spend good money on haircuts but had trouble getting up the energy to cut his hair herself. His devastating smile was enough to make little Suzie swoon and would have that same effect on many people when he reached his teens.

He had gone over to them a little sheepishly, but Suzie had greeted him brightly and the others seemed to take her cue. Joey asked if Tommy wanted to play catch with them, and Tommy said yes even though he didn't. He was gratified to see that none of them were particularly good at it; they all fumbled the ball about the same number of times but only Bobby got upset about it. He was the type who would call a person names if they were no good at something, even though he was hardly any better. But the others just told him to shut up or called him "Fatso," though not unkindly, so his remarks weren't taken very seriously.

By the time his mother left for work he felt fairly comfortable with The Bunch and thought that—while he would have preferred to be reading or chasing imaginary monsters on the beach—the afternoon wouldn't be all that awful. It was nice having kids his own age to talk to, and they were not as hopeless and boring as he'd expected. After they got tired of playing ball they went over to the sea's edge and sat down. Even if the weather had been warmer, none of them were allowed to swim without adult supervision.

"What do you do by yourself all the time?" Suzie asked Tommy.

"I like to read" he said.

"Betcha smart" she replied, pouring sand between her toes.

"I guess so." Not very modest, he thought, but accurate.

"You like to go on walks a lot," Bobby said, picking his nose. "I seen ya."

"I love the beach."

"Didn't you used to live in town?" Etta asked guilelessly.

"Years ago. We, uh, had to move. I've lived all over Summerdale."

"Me, too," Joey said, adjusting his glasses with a thumb and forefinger and staring at Tommy as if he were some sort of heroic idol. "I lived on," he counted off on his fingers, wiggling his body around nervously, "Center Street, Madison Street, Parkinson Place and Sumter Boulevard."

"Boy," Etta said, "have you moved around!"

Wonder if his father drinks, too, Tommy thought idly.

"I can beat that," Tommy said. "We've lived in at least six places. Maybe seven. We moved first when I was just a baby."

Patrick said, "Your father and mine used to work together, Tommy, at the factory in Falmont. Your dad was only there a few days, though."

Tommy reddened. "Yeah." A few days was all he ever could manage on a new job, before his drinking and his temper got the better of him.

Tommy wanted to change the subject. "Anybody want to go for a walk?"

"Where to?"

Tommy shrugged. "Along the beach. Into town?"

Patrick perked up. "Say, I got an idea. Why don't we go to the lost sea?"

"Where?"

"Tommy, you never heard of it?" Suzie said with a wide-eyed gasp.

" 'The lost sea?' No."

"That's only what we call it, what the other locals call it," Patrick explained. "Actually, it's a lake deep inside those woods." He pointed over to where the sand ended and the dense overgrowth of brush and forest began. "It's a couple of miles. I've only been there once, a couple of years ago. There's a trail that goes in there, and it opens out at this big black lake right in the middle of nowhere. No people, no nuthin'. It's got no name, either. It's a long walk, but it's worth it. Wait till you see the old house on the other side of the lake. I swore the next time I went I'd have the nerve to go inside it."

Hidden lakes and mysterious houses. Tommy was more excited than he'd been in a long time. "Does anybody live in the house?" he asked.

"Not that I know of. I asked my folks once, but they said they thought it was deserted. They don't really want me to go there, though, so if we go you'll all have to keep your mouths shut. My folks said a few kids have disappeared around there over the years. Grownups, too."

Although Tommy was appalled by this, it was not enough to dampen his enthusiasm. "What got 'em, you suppose?"

Patrick shook his head. "Don't know. Nobody knows. They never even found any bodies."

Suzie's mouth gaped open again. "A monster, I bet. I bet it was a monster."

"Maybe giant grasshoppers, like in that movie that's comin'," Tommy said, hoping his new-found friends shared his interest in horror films, but their only response was mild laughter.

"What do you say, gang, do you want to go or not?"

Tommy was game, but the others had mixed emotions. Yet it turned out if Tommy was going, so was Suzie and Joey. If Patrick was going, wild horses wouldn't keep Etta away. Bobby tagged along but was not as enthusiastic as the others. Although he liked sports, he hated exercise, and walking two miles was definitely exercise.

As they made their way into the woods to find the trail to the lost sea, Tommy thought again about the missing people and wondered what might have become of them. He felt sorry for them. And he wondered if he were making a mistake, going monster-hunting—maybe for real this time—with a bunch of kids who were no more capable of fighting off a dragon or serpent or wolfman, let alone giant grasshoppers, than he was.

But there comes the time, he thought, when a boy has simply got to be a man.

* * *

Martin Bartlett was thirsty.

He and old man Potter had spent all morning and half the afternoon, it seemed, cleaning up the old fart's garage and toolshed. Or rather, he had cleaned up the toolshed while Potter stood around shouting orders. He remembered when Potter had shown him respect, when the old man, then middle-aged, had been a friend of Henry Bartlett and been properly submissive around his children. But now, all Martin could see was contempt in the old man's eyes, contempt and impatience.

Yes, Martin Bartlett was a drunk, but he was not an idiot. He could understand directions, even complicated ones, but Potter spoke to him as if he were retarded, overexplaining the simplest order the way he would do with a five-year-old. Bartlett had to bite his tongue. He wanted, badly needed, the money the old man was going to give him. He would never get what he needed from his wife.

"Over there, over *there*, Martin," Potter snapped. "Why don't you listen? It goes in the corner and you've put it two feet away."

"Sorry," Martin muttered. "I misunderstood you."

"Well, be more careful. The whole job will go easier if you listen to me. After you've put that cabinet in the right place, I'll show you what I want done with the tools."

Martin realized at one point that some of the tools had once belonged to his father.

It seemed everyone had inherited something from Henry Bartlett except for Martin.

He badly needed a drink. He had stayed sober all last night, somehow, knowing that Potter would have sent him right back home if he dared show up in the morning with even the hint of alcohol on his breath. Potter was so pious. It was as if he hired Martin only so that he could have someone with whom he could indulge in his hidden sadistic impulses instead of kicking his dog or slapping his wife around. The Potters had no children. Potter, with his sunken chest, jowls, crooked teeth and hound dog eyes, the oversized head and slanting body that looked as if at any moment they might topple from the weight of that mean-spirited, misshapen brain, seemed incapable of fathering anything that might manage to last out the night.

Did Potter understand, could he possibly conceive, how difficult this was for Martin? When he was drunk, he could tolerate their contempt and the hardened, sometimes pitying look in their eyes. He could handle it then. But sober like this, spending time with someone who had known him when, who had knowledge of his great, unrealized promise—that was almost too much to bear. All Martin could do was think of the drink that would await him once he was paid. Meanwhile he did his best to avoid looking into Carleton Potter's eyes.

Finally they were through.

"You did a good job, Martin," Potter said, slapping him on the shoulder like he would some feebleminded handyman. Potter got out his wallet, and as he always did, counted out the dollar bills with maddening slowness and solemnity—" five, six, seven"—then finally handed the wad over.

But before he could go, Martin got a lecture.

"Martin, you don't have to be—nobody has to be—an alcoholic if they don't want to be." He could almost see sympathy and concern in the old man's eyes and thought, *isn't life amazing?*

"There's a chapter of Alcoholics Anonymous over in Breton. God knows, it's nothing you're alone in. My cousin Herbert in New Orleans drank like a fish before he died. You owe it to yourself to get help, Martin. You owe it to your wife, your boy." He shook his head back and forth and shoved his lower lip up under the upper one.

Then he said, "Oh, Marty, you could have had such a life, such a fine life. You had everything. You could have been President of the United States. With your father's help and the backing of influential people, who knows how far you could have gone? And" he added, not unkindly, "look at you now."

Potter's sweeping eyes took in the toolshed, the implements, the car, the grease and dirt stains on Martin's clothes. "Make today the first day of a new life, Martin. That money I gave you. It's yours. You earned it, but Martin, don't spend it on drink. Don't Martin. For your own sake. For your son's, Anne Marie's. They're depending on you. Maybe...maybe it's not too late."

Martin tried to open his mouth to say something; but there was nothing to say. Even though he knew the old man was right, he also knew how impossible it would be to change his life at this point. He was 40. The chance for that glorious future had been lost in a haze of booze many years ago. Stone cold sober, day in and day out, night after night, he would have to remember how he had lost it—and that was much more than any man who had served his country admirably and honorably should have to face. But how could he tell old man Potter all this in a way that would make him understand? How could he explain that without drink he would just as soon be dead? At least when he was drunk he entered a world where there was laughter and release and happiness; at least drunk he could think about what he'd done to himself and not begin to cry.

"Thanks, Mr. Potter," he said.

And headed for Chester's Bar and Grill in the northern quarter of Summerdale.

* * *

Anne Marie stood up, stretched and groaned. She let the dust cloth fall onto the table she'd been wiping and sunk down onto the couch beside it. Oh, was she tired! Got wearier and wearier so much quicker these days. Not even 40 and she felt like an 80-year-old.

Speaking of which, Mrs. Hampton's sharp voice shattered the air in the living room. "Don't pay you for sitting down on the job, Mrs. Bartlett."

Anne Marie sat up straight. "Sorry, I got a muscle spasm for a second." She reached behind her and started rubbing where it ached. "Had to rest for just a moment."

Mrs. Hampton was not really 80—60 was more like it—but she eschewed makeup and flattering hairdos and looked much older than her years. She was a bulldog-faced woman with a sturdy frame and a heavy bosom and sometimes wore large glasses that made her eyes seem the size of pot covers. "Muscle spasm, eh? Well, rest for a moment, but then hurry up and finish in here. I'm having the ladies in for tea in half an hour. And you've still the upstairs to do."

"Yes, Mrs. Hampton." She got slowly up to her feet. She was really beginning to hate that old woman. *Don't talk to me like some kind of servant some sort of slave*, she wanted to tell her, but she couldn't—not if she wanted the money the woman paid her to come in and clean once or twice a week, occasionally to cook for Mr. Hampton or serve guests when she had dinner parties. She was Anne Marie Bartlett, she thought bitterly, a member by marriage of what had once been one of the proudest, wealthiest, most prestigious families in town. There was even a Bartlett Avenue on the eastside. But what was left now? Lilah was dead. Henry was dead. Ernest had moved out of town and Martin...? She didn't want to think about Martin.

She should have had a house like this. *She* should have been paying the maid, giving the dinner parties. To think that Anne Marie Rozinski, who had come from one of the town's most respected families herself, would have wound up as a witchy bulldog's scullery maid.

She took up the dust rag again and went over to the piano. It was such a beautiful baby grand. She felt an urge to tinkle the white keys but not while the old woman was watching. "Do a good job, y'hear?" Mrs. Hampton said. "Last time you left dust on the top of the piano." She pronounced it "piannah." "I don't pay you to leave dust on my furniture."

"Yes, Mrs. Hampton."

"And remember to get into the corners when you vacuum. I don't want to have to get out the machine and do it myself after you've gone home. That's not what I'm paying you for."

"Yes, Mrs. Hampton."

"And—" The woman was interrupted by the doorbell. "Dear me, I guess the girls have come a little early today." She moved toward the door.

Anne Marie froze. Some of Mrs. Hampton's friends were women who had known her parents, who had daughters who'd gone to school with Anne Marie. Sometimes she knew the daughters themselves were coming and she worked even harder to get done before they arrived and saw her cleaning house like some common...She could not bear the thought of facing those women, of seeing the smug satisfaction, or worse, the pity, in their eyes.

Anne Marie relaxed. It was only a mailman who'd forgotten a package. She went back to her dusting while the postman and Mrs. Hampton made idle chitchat.

She loved this house; it was almost a joy cleaning it and certainly would have been a joy had it belonged to her. This living room, the beautiful golden wallpaper, polished mahogany furniture, that black shining piano with its glittering white keys, the cushioned sofa with its curlicued patterns and pretty pink pillows, the easy chair in the corner over by the handsome antique loom—everything was so very, very beautiful.

"Mrs. Bartlett! Stop daydreaming, girl!"

"Sorry, I was just admir—"

"And there's another thing." Mrs. Hampton came up and folded her arms across her chest, her face sour and petulant. She sighed heavily, then began. "As long as you're coming to my house to clean, Mrs. Bartlett, couldn't you do something about your appearance? You're a mess, I don't mind telling you. Don't you take any pride? I'm sorry, but if someone works for me I want them to make a good appearance. Do you understand me, Mrs. Bartlett?"

Anne Marie didn't know what to say. Her hand went idly to her head and began twirling a stringy lock of hair that had fallen down to her eyebrow. Had she become that unsightly?

"I'm sure you bathe every day—at least I hope you do or I'd let you go in a minute—but you must do something about your clothes, your hair. I thought about giving you twenty dollars to go buy a decent dress, but then, I got the idea of getting you a uniform, a pretty little maid's uniform. Blue, perhaps. I've talked to some of the other women you clean for about it, and we've all agreed. We're going to chip in and get you a uniform you can wear to work, a nice outfit you can wear in everybody's houses. What you wear in your own house is your own business, but here in our homes—well, that's different. Would you like that, Mrs. Bartlett? We'll pay for it, you needn't worry. And, why, if you fix your hair a bit and use a little makeup, you'll look perfectly fine in no time."

Anne Marie began to cry.

"Why, my dear. I didn't meant to…to offend you. I was only trying to help." The woman made gestures that suggested she wanted to reach out and comfort her but couldn't quite get up the nerve. "I have offended you. My dear, that was the furthest thing from my mind."

Anne Marie pulled a handkerchief from a pocket in her housedress and began to wipe her eyes and nose. "It's all right." She sniffled, drying her tears. "I could have been the queen of this town" she whispered. "I could have been the first lady of this nation."

Then Anne Marie shuffled up the stairs to the second floor and the bedrooms, and as she cleaned she heard the voices of the neighborhood ladies down in the parlor as they sipped tea and ate watercress sandwiches, as they discussed their fine upstanding husbands and their trips to Europe…

…and the pretty blue maid's uniform they would buy for Anne Marie.

* * *

They had been walking through the woods for nearly an hour now. Tommy was getting tired and more than a little fearful that this whole "lost sea." was just the product of Patrick Higgins' imagination. There were far too many mosquitoes to suit him, and the trail was so overrun with spindly bushes, leafy plants and low-hanging branches that it made traveling nearly impossible.

Still, if the others were willing to continue, so was he. They had stopped to rest in a small clearing, leaning their tired bodies against a gnarled and massive tree that sat squat in the middle of the circle. "We're not gonna walk into quicksand or a swamp, are we?" Bobby asked worriedly, slapping a mosquito off his cheek and examining the mushed remains on his fingertips.

"No" Patrick said, sneering. "You know damn well this is only a forest, not a swamp."

"There aren't any gators?" Suzie said.

"This isn't the Everglades," Etta reminded her.

"I went there once," Joey said.

"See gators?"

"Yeah, Suzie. Big ones, too. But there's nothing like that in this forest."

But there might be something like that at the "lost sea," Tommy thought. Something had to do away with those missing people. Possibly a large gator who'd made the lake its home? The thought of those jaws, those teeth, closing in on him, filled him with horror and dread.

"How much farther is it?" Bobby whined.

"It's been a while since I've been here," Patrick said, "but I remember it wasn't much farther past this clearing. Maybe another ten minutes."

"Ten minutes!" Etta complained.

"What's that?" Bobby told her. "We've already been walking nearly an hour."

"Yeah," Tommy said. "We're this close we might as well keep going." But part of him hoped the others would veto the suggestion and force him to turn around and go home.

But they started up again a minute later, entering the trail on the other side of the clearing, slapping away the bugs and pushing aside huge fronds and leafy branches barring their way. The path was very narrow and they had to walk single file. There was a multitude of forest plants and flowers all around them—beebalm mints, morning glories, toothworts, yellow orchids and wild lavender geraniums—and they could hear bird cries and distant planes overhead. Although the branches of the tall trees came together like fingers way above their heads, enough of the bright summer's sunlight got through to bathe the whole green and brown garden in a warm, yellow glow that almost made the forest seem homey. As they walked they continued their discussions of hated school teachers, favorite ice cream flavors, the weirder occupants of Summerdale, and the relative advantages of one brand of TV set over another.

Then, finally, Patrick shoved aside a huge frond in front of them, and there before them was the cold, black, frozen stillness of the lake known only as the "lost sea" The water's edge was only about a foot or two away.

It did look "lost," and it was big. Not as big as a really large lake but a hell of a lot more than a pond. Tommy, pushing his way excitedly through the others, had to squint to either side just to see where it ended, though at this point, at least, the lake was not terribly wide. Too wide to swim, he supposed—it looked to be a good 20 yards from one bank to the other, and Tommy knew how distance over water could be deceptive—but not too far to go if one had a rowboat.

Then he looked up a bit and saw the house.

It looked like something out of those really old horror movies with Boris Karloff and Bela Lugosi that they sometimes showed on TV, movies that had been made even before he was born. It was perched on top of a rise that was situated quite a ways above the water, almost hanging out over the lake. The walls and roof were shingled, and there were bare patches of black tar where pieces had fallen off. There was a porch covered by an overhanging balcony that seemed to be collapsing under its own weight. Cupolas stuck out at odd angles, and the grime-encrusted windows were cracked and yellowed. Beneath the porch was a series of three crooked wooden staircases that twisted precariously down to a dock jutting out into the water. The house was three stories tall, with a high wide attic and possibly a crawlspace.

"Oh, boy," Tommy said. "What a house!"

The others squealed in agreement.

"How do we get over there?" Bobby asked. "Is it safe to swim or are there leeches in there?"

Etta shivered. "It's too chilly to swim," she said. Tommy was beginning to think she was a pain.

"I don't know about leeches," Patrick said, "but it's too far for me to swim, that's for certain."

"Look!" Bobby had spotted something off to the left. There was another dock on this side, a shorter one in even more dilapidated condition with a rowboat tied to the end of it.

"A boat!" Joey said.

Tommy felt his heart race. He *had* to go across, even if the whole place was a little spooky.

"Let's go over in the rowboat and explore the house," he said. "Come on, Patrick. You said you always wanted to."

But now that he had a real opportunity to do so, Patrick wasn't so sure about it. "I...I don't know," he said cautiously. "Maybe that boat isn't watertight."

It hasn't sunk, has it, all the time it's been here?"

Joey suggested they go to the end of the little dock and sit in the boat for a while just to see what condition it was in. But when the little band reached the boat, they realized it might not be prudent for all six of them to sit in it at once. "I don't like the looks of it" Etta said.

"Yeah, Tommy" Patrick agreed. "It may not be safe."

Tommy clambered aboard anyway, hoping to disprove them. He sat down in the middle seat near the oars and stomped his feet, gingerly at first, then harder. "See. It's okay. There's no water in it or nothin'." The small pool in the bottom of the boat might have been made by rainfall. "C'mon, Patrick, I thought you said you wanted to look into the old house this time." He mustered up his courage and added, "What are ya, scared?" He had to remember, though, that Patrick was older and bigger than he was. It wouldn't do to anger him.

Patrick sneered. "I'm not scared, but maybe somebody lives there. And that boat just doesn't look safe. Not for all of us. Suppose we get out in the middle of the lake and it starts to sink? I don't know how to swim," he finally admitted. "And that water looks mighty deep."

"All six of us won't go," Tommy argued. "Just you and me. The others can keep watch. I'll save you if we start to sink. I can swim."

"Nah, it's too risky. Mom will kill me if I come home wet."

It was so frustrating. He could see their side of it, but he'd had such hopes of exploring. It was a once-in-a-lifetime opportunity. To have come all this way for nothing! True, he could always come back by himself some afternoon—an hour's walk or so had never deterred him from getting anywhere before— but he was dismayed at the thought of being all alone in this place. If only he could convince at least one of them to make the trip across the lake with him.

"Doesn't anybody want to go with me?" he said, hands on oars.

Suzie was full of admiration and awe but also wearing a look that told him she thought he was crazy. "Are you really going to row over there?" she said. "What if somebody lives there? They could arrest you for trespassing."

"If anybody lives there, why would the rowboat be docked on *this* side of the lake? Nah. Can't you see that old house is falling apart? It's abandoned, that's what it is. Nobody's over there."

He didn't even try to keep his contempt for them out of his voice. He'd been right all along about The Bunch. They were just a gaggle of ninnies—no guts, no soul, no sense of fun or adventure. Hadn't they whined all the way here like babies? Not one of them —not even Patrick who'd started the whole thing—seemed to have the least bit of curiosity about that forbidding, fascinating structure across the lake.

"Well, if no one will go with me, I'll go by myself." He leaned over to untie the boat and gave it a shove away from the dock.

Suzie attempted to dissuade him. "Tommy!"

"Too late. You all had a chance to go. Now you'll just have to wait for me."

Bobby stole a look at the watch on his pudgy wrist. "Hey, it's getting late. We gotta be getting back now. Tommy, you come back here!"

"We can't wait for you, Tommy," Etta said.

"I'll only be a few minutes," Tommy assured them. "It's not that far away. Wait for me! Don't go without me, please." The sun was still bright and shining in the sky. "We got plenty of time. So wait!"

But a few minutes later, when he was about a quarter of a way across the lake, he realized that he had badly misjudged the distance. This was going to take longer than he'd expected. He turned back and assured himself that the others were still waiting by the dock. Let them amuse themselves while he showed them what losers they all were. They'd never get out of Summerdale with their attitude.

He looked around and had to admit the lake was awfully creepy, and had the kids not been back there watching him he would have been terribly frightened. The water itself was almost supernaturally black. The sunlight that hit it in spots seemed to be sucked away into the inky darkness below. There were bobbing flies and mosquitoes darting across the surface, but apparently no fish underneath to jump up and devour them. No fish, thank God. No gators, no crocs, *no monsters*. He chased away the terrible thought that there was some enormous thing underneath him that might rise up through the murk and pull him under in one fell swoop. He rowed harder and faster. Halfway now. The rest would be a cinch. It had been farther than he'd expected, but not as bad as it could have been. His arms were tired but they'd hold up as long as they had to; he'd rowed a boat in the Summerdale lake often enough. The closer he got to that old house, though, the more ominous and dangerous it looked.

This part of the forest appeared to be almost swamplike. There was heavier vegetation, which grew in clumps and barriers right close to the water's edge all around the lake's circumference and prevented him from seeing what might lay on the land around the lake—knotweeds, thistles, tall rows of rose mallow. And then there was the static fetidness of the solid black unmoving water. The ripples from his oars and the movement of the rowboat were the only motion on the water's glasslike surface. He could see his reflection in the water but nothing else. If there was anything down there in the lake he could not possibly see it coming until it was almost upon him.

He looked to his right and left and could just about see the far edges of the lake. It was much, much longer than it was wide. Weeds and rushes, and decaying surface roots of leaning spidery trees, dotted the shoreline. For a second he had the sensation of being in a long, deep pit full of water and surrounded on all sides by man-eating plants, vines and creepers, slithering, powerful roots that would prevent him from ever again gaining access to the land. He had the disquieting feeling of being out in an abnormal, polluted pool where no man had ever been meant to go, as if this body of water were part of some experiment...full of life-forms that could not exist in nature.

Him and his damned imagination. Too many comic books, too many monster movies, like his mother said. He had to stop scaring himself. This was creepy enough as it was.

He had about a quarter, maybe an eighth, of the lake to traverse—at least the rowboat was holding up nicely—when he wondered how long the journey had taken so far. Ten minutes? 20? That didn't seem like a long time for The Bunch to wait until he realized that he would still have to make the return trip after reaching the opposite shoreline and would need a good half hour or longer to investigate the house. But what was the point in crossing the lake if he couldn't go inside? Would the kids sit still for over an hour?

He turned back to see if the kids were still there—and shuddered.

For the dock was empty.

* * *

Martin Bartlett peeled a dollar bill off the roll and handed it to Chester the barman. Chester was a friend. Chester understood. Chester owned the bar as well as worked it, drinking up most of his profits. Chester was the best friend Martin had in the world. He would serve him when no one else would. Martin Bartlett had never been 86'd from Chester's Bar and Grill on Downy Street.

Until today.

Martin took the beer Chester gave him and took his first fine sip. *Ahhh, good.* Pretty soon, he'd gulp down enough to give him the buzz he required. Then everything would be right with the world, then nothing would matter but keeping the ache in his heart from coming back again.

Chester poured himself a mug of draft and leaned against the bar to join Marty in conversation. He was a grizzled man of 42 with an unshaven face, puffy cheeks, and a flaming red proboscis. His pot belly hung out over his belt to such an extent that it was a wonder it didn't need pillars to support it. His teeth were rotten, and his eyes were blue and beady.

Chester wouldn't say this out loud, but Martin was one of his favorite customers because he reminded Chester that even the high and mighty could fall; so why should he, a mere peon, after all, feel guilty about not amounting to anything? Sure, he took over the business from his senile old man— home now with his wife, who pretended to care for him but when nobody was looking loved to throw lit matches at her father-in-law as he hollered and tried to dodge them in his wheelchair—but the bar was barely breaking even. But he'd not come from a prominent, wealthy family like Martin, had never had his potential or his way with the women. So if Martin, with all his advantages, was down here where Chester was, why should Chester feel badly about being in the same, sorry position? He drank too much because it was the only way he could put up with his wife and father and their hatred of him and each other.

I mean, look at 'im, he said to himself. Martin Bartlett, the war hero, the political contender, son of Henry Bartlett and Lilah fuckin' Berenson. *Now look at him.* There were still traces of Martin's good looks, but the face was too pale and sunken, the eyes too hollow. Martin had a round head with even features and a shaggy shock of light brown hair which he'd passed on to his son, as well as prominent cheekbones, which he hadn't. The great Martin Bartlett was just another drunk.

"Lousy weather," Chester said. "Too cool to take a swim."

"Yeah, yeah."

"But it's hot in here. Ain't that the way?"

"Yeah, yeah."

"Teddy Rochester was in here earlier, askin' about you."

"Oh, yeah?"

The door swung open, and Chester nudged Martin with his elbow.

It was a woman, a looker, slightly off-kilter but not quite inebriated. She wore a black dress and hat that showed off her figure and framed her face attractively. She had red hair, the reddest lips, hips and legs that wouldn't stop and a nice perky ass. She asked Chester to pour her some bourbon and paid with a 20 dollar bill. She took a couple of dainty sips and looked around the place defensively. She seemed to like but not like the way Chester and Marty stared at her and giggled, the way they licked their lips. She licked hers, took out a lipstick and did her lips up until they were smooth like crimson velvet. Was she a hooker?

"You can sit down if you'd like" Chester said, holding his arm out to encompass the whole room, which was a typical faded saloon with battered brown tables, wooden chairs and benches, and old posters on the walls that had long ceased to have any meaning for all but the oldest, drunkenest patrons. There was no one else in the place but the two men and the woman. "Go ahead, have a seat." He didn't like the way Marty was looking at her. Women rarely came into this bar but he'd heard stories. Chester was of the look-but-don't-touch school, but rumor had it that Marty was different.

"Don't you let women stand at the bar?" the lady asked Chester.

"Sure. Just thought you'd be more comfortable."

"I'm fine."

"Suit yourself."

"Give me 'nother beer," Martin said.

Chester handed him one, chucked the empty bottle into the garbage can and tried to take Marty's mind off the woman by engaging him in conversation. It worked for awhile, but a few beers later—and two more bourbons for the woman—it stopped working.

Martin had been staring at the woman's boobs pointedly, rudely, lasciviously, when he suddenly got to his feet and said, "Hell, lady, you are just about the sexiest-lookin' thing to walk into Chester's Bar and Grill in Summerdale in just about twenty-five years."

Chester wasn't sure what the woman was after when she answered, "Thank you, honey. You're not so bad yourself."

At that Martin sauntered down the bar until he was about a foot away from her. "I'd like to lick your..." The rest was indistinguishable to Chester, which was okay with him as he was a decent Christian. He turned around to chuck a couple more of Marty's empty beer bottles in the basket when he suddenly heard the woman holler.

"Hey" she screamed, "get your hands off me, you creep!"

Marty had her in his arms, trying to kiss her. She kept flapping her hands about, trying to hit him in the face. "Ahh, don't be like that, honey," Marty,said. "Give me a kiss. Ain't had one in soooo long."

The woman tried to pull away from him. There was a ripping sound, and the woman squealed in surprise and outrage.

"My dress! You fool! You flaming idiot! My dress, you've torn it!"

Chester thought it would end then but it only got worse. He was coming around to the front of the bar when Marty stumbled and took the woman down with him to the floor. The blessed idiot still didn't know when to let go. She was scratching and clawing, cursing him, but he kept trying to kiss her even as he swung his head this way and that to dodge the blows. They were struggling so hard they bounced across the floor inch by inch until they collided with a table and toppled two of its chairs in a chain reaction that might have been comical under different circumstances. Everytime the woman tried to get up, Marty pulled her down. She'd slap him across the face, but he'd only try harder to kiss her. Then she'd bite him on the hand or arm, and he'd let her go, whereupon she'd get up off the floor again and the whole process would start all over. "Police! Call the police!" the woman shouted.

Chester pulled Marty off of her finally and threw him against the back wall of the bar so hard it took both men's breath away. "Cut that shit out, Marty," he said. "I don't like crap like that in my bar. Think I want to have the police close me down?"

The woman was disheveled but basically uninjured. "Are you all right?" Chester asked her.

"I don't know" she said, running her fingers through her hair in a vain attempt to get the messy locks back into some semblance of order. She dug through her bag for a comb. "I think I might sue."

"Get the fuck out of here, Marty!" Chester said. "And don't come back for a good two weeks if you know what's good for ya." Damned fool carrying on like that. All the stories were true. What was it that made him so crazy around women?

Chester watched Marty stumble out of the door, then turned to the woman and tried to placate her.

But it was all right. She wouldn't sue.

For just as the younger man she'd been waiting for came into the bar to greet her, he recognized who she was—Mrs. Finster of Orchard Lane—and the young guy who was kissing her fervently right on the lips was *not* Mr. Finster.

"I might sue," she said again as they ordered drinks.

But Chester knew better.

* * *

Thomas panicked when he saw the empty dock.

No, they must have stepped back into the shelter of the foliage, that was all. Surely they wouldn't have left him here.

Not after what had happened to those kids. Even grownups had *disappeared*.

He felt a feeling of fear and panic grip him and squeeze him in its ley chilling paw.

They couldn't have left him. They'd just stepped out of sight for awhile.

But he remembered how they'd been hollering at him to come back as he started across the lake. Hadn't he heard them yelling at him even as he got farther and farther away from the dock, but ignored it? And hadn't the yelling stopped a short while ago, when he'd assumed he'd simply gone out of earshot.

They had left him.

Terror ran across him like a scurrying spider, darting up and down his spine and crawling across his stomach. He gasped.

He squirmed, struggled, fought the terror—and finally got

it under control. The terror receded. Be brave, he told himself, be brave.

Maybe this was all for the best. The dock that jutted out into the water below the old house was only a few feet away now. He was much too close to turn back. Besides, he needed a breather and would rather rest on land than in the middle of the lake. Now he could take his time exploring the house and all its treasures. It was still only midaftemoon. Plenty of time to get home, though he wished he had a watch. He tried not to think about the trip he would have to take back across the lake, knowing he was all alone out here, and the long trek back through the woods. And as for those disappearances? Well, Patrick had said those were only rumors, hadn't he? Mere scuttlebutt? Probably no one had ever disappeared here. Maybe one or two kids got lost, that's all. But he knew where the path was, didn't he? He could find his way out of here in no time. He had a good sense of direction and anyway, there was a trail back to Beachside.

The rowboat bumped into the end of the dock, and Tommy reached out to steady and secure it. He hopped out and looked up at the old house.

And shivered.

It was a monster.

Up close like this the house seemed almost alive. It looked haunted, full of goblins and witches and animated corpses that loved to snack on little boys. He wondered if he really had the courage to go inside it. But think of what must be in there! He had to know the house's secrets. He had to go inside it!

His body was literally quivering with anticipation. He imagined walking around through long abandoned corridors and chambers, furniture dusty from disuse, stepping back through a barrier of time into another life, another century, the past. This house was the past, and it was a past that he wanted to enter.

He started up the first flight of stairs at the end of the dock
—It groaned beneath his weight but seemed more or less solid
—and reached the first landing. He stopped to get his bear-
ings, looking about to make sure no one was watching. He
stared across the lake and could see the deserted dock clearer
from this vantage point. Still empty. The kids had really gone
and left him, damn them.

Bunch of creeps!

Still, he supposed he couldn't blame them for wanting to
get home. They had told him they wouldn't wait for him. Pity
he didn't believe them.

Well, the hell with that. He was still going to look around
this place no matter how long it took or how late it got. He
knew his mother wouldn't be back home, dragging his
drunken father behind her, for hours. What was there at home
but silence and emptiness?

The house seemed to call to him. *Come. Come on, little boy.
Enter me. I promise you, you won't be disappointed.*

And Tommy was sure he wouldn't be.

He went up the next set of steps until he reached the
second landing. His back was to the house all the while
because of the angle, and he didn't like it. Then he started up
the third flight and was again facing toward the structure and
feeling safer. He could keep his eyes on it. He smelled a rotten,
fishy smell that seemed to be coming from the house. He
reached the top of the final flight of stairs and walked along
the passage that led up to the porch. *I can't wait I can't wait I
can't wait.* This was better than comic books and chasing imaginary monsters and Brog, the Beast from Planet Borax. *This
was real this was real this was real.*

He stepped up onto the porch and moved quickly toward
the door.

Just as he was reaching toward it, the door opened.

Tommy screamed.

There was a man standing there, a man with pale skin and

deep hollow eyes, a man with a penetrating glare that could melt little boys to little puddles right in their tracks, a man with devil's eyes, and the smell, that godawful smell, was coming from him. Tommy only had time to notice that the man appeared to be somewhat younger than his father, slender, with a long bony face that was neither handsome nor ugly, and a shaggy bang of black hair falling across his forehead. He did not look ill in any concrete way, but nevertheless Tommy sensed something diseased about him.

The man lunged out and tried to grab Tommy by the arm. "What are you doing here?"

Normally Tommy would have stood there and apologized for trespassing— "I didn't know anyone lived here, sir"— hoping his youth and immaturity, his smiling little face and polite, quiet, repentant manner, would get him off the hook, but somehow he sensed it wouldn't work this time. This time he was really in trouble. He pulled away from the man and darted back down the steps, his feet scurrying over the wooden slats, his arms swinging this way and that to help him keep his balance. Twice he almost tripped and would have fallen had he not grabbed a small tree or bush that lined the hill the stairs were built into.

Finally he made it to the dock below and chanced an upward glance. Why isn't he following me? he wondered. He's just standing there on the porch. Why isn't he coming after me? Why wasn't he yelling for Tommy to stop?

Tommy almost got into the rowboat, then changed his mind.

He wants me to take the boat. Then I won't have just trespassed. Then I'll have stolen something that belongs to him. He'll see me take off in it with his own eyes.

Unless he was watching me from the house all the while as I rowed over from the other side of the lake. That really gave him the creeps.

For some inexplicable reason, Tommy just didn't want to go out on the lake again.

He turned around. Earlier he had noticed a narrow path to one side of the dock, almost a continuation of the trail across the lake; it led not upwards but deeper into the woods beyond the house. It, too, was overrun, but passable with effort. He shoved his way in through some tall grass and weeds and was soon racing far away from the house and the man as fast as he could possibly go.

On the porch the man's formerly expressionless face turned cold.

* * *

A while later there were a man and a woman walking along a stream that was now dribbling through a part of those same woods that lay between the old house and the ocean, though far away from the trail that little Tommy Bartlett was running along. The woman was Mrs. Lawrence Finster—Georgia Finster —of Orchard Lane, the selfsame woman who had been wrestled to the ground by a drunken Martin Bartlett in Chester's Bar and Grill. The younger man with her was Louis Ragatto, a local ne´er-do-well who had drifted into town three summers ago and had since made his living tending the gardens of Summerdale's wealthiest—and loneliest—ladies. He lived in a boarding house on Mott Street, where he was forbidden to bring ladies of ill-repute, that is, any woman who would keep company with him. The wealthy housewives he "serviced" would not be seen dead on Mott Street so they had to drive to shady bars and motels all up and down the coast near Summerdale to meet him, places where no one in their crowd would ever go.

Louie was about 22 and he thought he'd done all right for himself with this one, this Georgia Finster. Her husband was a fat, balding banker of 54, but she, at 37, was still a hot vibrant woman with a tremendous set of knockers and a passion in her that could not and would not be satisfied by some pork belly with a prostate problem. But in spite of that, Georgia had these peculiar misgivings. After she'd fixed herself up with bobby pins and such in the ladies room at Chester's and had a couple more drinks with Louie—the woman could hold her liquor, he'd noted with some disappointment—she'd taken him out to her car and driven to a lonely section of highway along Coast Road past Beachside. She'd been all over him like a wildcat, tearing at his shirt, biting his shoulder, planting kisses from his neck to his navel, but when he tried to get her into the backseat she'd suddenly gotten skittish.

"Then suck it, doll," he'd suggested. "Get me so hot, ya do. Suckin' my joint won't get ya pregnant, can't you see that?"

Of course, if Louie attended more to his personal hygiene he might have gotten the blow job he wanted, but he was not one to think of such niceties. Still, Mrs. Finster was not willing to let him leave, either. She grabbed a bottle of vodka out of the glove compartment and took a swallow. That's it, get high, baby. He could always drive the car back to town if necessary. Meanwhile all he wanted was to get laid. It was he who suggested they take a walk in the woods. Deep in the forest away from everyone, Georgia might change her mind and decide it was time to go "all the way."

They followed the little stream so as not to get lost. They'd been walking for a good 20 minutes, while she told him how awful her husband was—even Louie could tell she really loved the man in spite of her protestations—how he gave her things and possessions and prestige and all that, but not the sort of love a young woman like her required. She did not ask Louie anything about his own life or feelings; none of the women ever did. He was there for one purpose only, a gardener keeping company with rich ladies who'd snub him if they saw him on the street, and if he was cynical about it nobody could ever blame him.

Georgia had taken off her high heels and was carrying them in one hand. "I have to rest," she said. "My feet are killing me." She dropped to her feet and leaned her back against a tree stump. She put the shoes and the bottle of vodka on the ground and reached back to rub her shoulder. "That awful man in the bar!" she said for the umpteenth time. "If only you'd arrived when you were supposed to."

"Yeah" he said. "Too bad I got held up. I would have killed the guy for sure." He reached down and flicked his fingers across the bottom of her chin. "Anyone touches my lady."

She giggled.

Yeah, they were "his ladies" while they were drunk and mad at their husbands. Otherwise...

He took a comb out and slicked back his hair, which he wore D.A. style. He had a narrow face with a longish nose, thin lips, and jutting chin. Almost pretty.

Georgia picked a pebble off the bottom of her foot and groaned about the condition of her stockings, as if she couldn't afford to buy a dozen more just like them. The dope should have taken them off in the first place. Pretty soon he swore he'd have *everything* off. She dug into her bag so she could replace the lipstick that had been removed by all their passionate kissing. Louie hadn't bothered wiping it off of himself 'cause his experience with older, insecure women told him there was plenty more where that came from. While she fixed herself up he moved ahead a few yards so he could peer around a large tree on the bank of the stream where the water veered sharply to the left.

And saw this big black silent still-as-glass lake in front of him.

Louie was on the opposite side of the lake from where The Bunch had been, but so far down that he could not see the dock they'd been standing on, and the house, which was quite a ways to his left, was completely out of his sightline. The quiet and stillness of the water was giving him an eerie feeling.

"Hey, Georgia, honey, come and look."

She was taking an inordinate time to answer, and he hoped she hadn't passed out on him. "Coming, honey," she said finally. She was giggling again, but in a different way than before.

Then she stepped out from behind the tree and he knew what she was giggling about, and what he saw made him whistle. "Damn!" he said.

She had removed every stitch of clothing and was wading in the stream. He couldn't believe it. There she was, over 35 and a heavy drinker, but her body was better than a lot of 20-year-olds! Oh, there were a few wrinkles, a few tiny pouches of fat, but otherwise she had a figure a lot of women would kill for. Her extremely large breasts, free from all restraint, jutted out many inches from the surrounding torso, and she had long shapely legs and a nice behind. Now he wanted her worse than ever.

But he knew better than to force it. Who was he, but a bum, a gardener? As always, he'd let her make the first move. She had already made a good start. He started pulling off his shoes, but had to back up a bit so if he lost his balance he wouldn't fall in the water.

Georgia had reached the point where the stream fed into the lake. She was still giggling, holding one hand over her mouth coquettishly and holding the half-empty vodka bottle in the other. "It's time, Louie," she said. "I've...hic...decided it's time." She burped and burst out laughing.

She passed by him where he sat at the lake's edge nestled in between two prickly bushes and started walking into the lake until the water came up to her thighs. The water was so murky, Louie didn't like the look of it. "Don't go out too far, you'll get all muddy."

"Then you'll lick it off" she said. "Hurry up, Louie! Get

your clothes off. Come on in the water with me. I promise you, you won't be sorry."

She had waded out about ten feet off shore when she stopped and turned around to face him. Louie was totally naked now. He could feel his erection growing, feel the desire in him reaching fever pitch. He got ready to step into the cold black water.

Wait a minute! There was something funny happening to the water directly behind Georgia. Something was rushing through it, causing a massive displacement of liquid. Could it be a gator? There was an actual *wave* building, splashing, frothing, gathering height and momentum. In a second it would wash over her, swamp her or worse. He started to call out a warning. "Hey, Geor—"

Oh, my God!

He saw it. He saw what was causing the wave, saw the thing that pushed up, thrust up, through the surface of the water like an enormous fleshy juggernaut and towered above the tiny female prey at its feet.

It was gargantuan.

Georgia hadn't time to turn around. She felt heat like from a furnace, a smothering, oily, loathsome odor, and suddenly everything around her was pitch dark. There came monstrous pain as hard, huge, yellowish things with jagged edges bit into her below her breasts and in the small of her back. She felt herself being sucked up into a hot, red maw coated with a sticky odorous solution and thought...

I'm in a mouth.

And then it was over.

On the shore Louie screeched in disbelief and edged backwards, knowing he had to escape.

But the thing was coming after him.

It was coming out of the lake, pulling its hard, heavy bulk slowly out of the water, and thundering onto the ground like a living avalanche. Behind him, Louie heard trees crashing in its path, felt bits of debris and twisted timber flying over his head. *Have to get away, have to get away, have to—*

Louie ran into a mountain he swore he hadn't seen in front of him.

That wasn't there before, he thought.

Because it *wasn't* a mountain.

It's one of its legs!

Louie was directly underneath the beast.

And then the other leg came down and Louie was squished into an unrecognizable gray-red blotch on the forest's floor.

CHAPTER THREE
BEHEMOTH

"Where can he be? It's way past suppertime. Where is he?"

Anne Marie should have known better than to expect an answer from her drunken fool of a husband. He just sat there, dopey-eyed, in the easy chair, chewing on a chicken leg with spittle and grease streaked across his chin.

She'd started looking for Martin as soon as she got off from Mrs. Hampton's, making the usual rounds. Chester at Chester's Bar and Grill was in an uproar—had thrown the bum out (about time, she thought), but wouldn't say what it was Martin had done to get him so angry. At least she found out that Martin had indeed gone to Old Man Potter's instead of a bar and been paid for his morning's labors. Then she went to Geezer's Tavern on Dunman Street, Ye Olde Harbor inn on Montague Street, and finally Hamman's Bar on Syracuse Lane where she found him nursing a beer with a friend named Sally. Seeing Anne Marie, Sally—who was too fat and ugly for Anne Marie to think of as a threat to her marriage—skedaddled out of the bar and ran down to the pub around the corner. Anne Marie went over to her husband and pinched his left ear between two wiry fingers.

"Time to come home. Supper's ready. Not gonna let you

drink up every last bit of the money Potter gave you. Need money for the boy, you hear me! Need money for the boy!"

Martin, very drunk, tried to brush her pinching fingers, her voice, her very presence, away with his hand, but she would not be deterred. She grabbed hold of him under the armpits and started pulling him out of the seat. "Not gonna let you drink up every last bit of Potter's money when we have a boy who needs it."

"Let's go, you no good drunk," she said, fast losing patience with him. *Maid's uniform, indeed. Why, if I didn't have a husband who drank I'd be bigger and better than all of those upstanding ladies put together.* "Get up, I tell you, or so help me!"

To stop her from battering him about the face and shoulders, Martin finally allowed her to pull him up completely out of his seat. He gave out with a little cry as he toppled over onto the floor. "Get up, you fool! Supper's ready and Tommy is waiting."

The crowd at the bar stood watching this tableau with amusement. Anne Marie heard snickers and giggles, and these enraged her. As she helped her husband up to his feet, where he stood tottering like a flagpole in a hurricane, she turned her anger onto the crowd.

"You think this is all so funny, don't you, you lousy bunch of drunks? You find this all very entertaining, don't you? Well, I'm the one who's laughin', laughin' at all of you, 'cause I'll be there looking down at you when you're lying in the gutter next to my Martin. Take a good look, boys. See your future? See where all your drinkin' will take you? Enjoy, boys, enjoy!" She threw one arm around Martin's shoulder and stumbled with him over to the exit.

One of the men disengaged himself from a crowd in the corner of the bar and offered to help her.

"Get away. I don't need any help!" Then she softened a bit toward the would-be good Samaritan and smiled. "I've done this so often I've gotten used to his weight. I'm even developing muscles."

She'd gotten him home, all right, though she'd had a scare on Montpierre Street where she'd thought he'd upchuck all those beers right in front of two thunderstruck old ladies. But the damn fool had managed to make it back to Beachside without getting sick all over her.

But Martin was the least of her worries. She hadn't necessarily expected Tommy to be home waiting for her—after all, she had ordered him to play with The Bunch and she knew how much he wanted to see that movie she'd promised to pay for—but when he didn't show up by 5:00 as she fussed in the kitchen making dinner, she grew nervous. She turned off everything on the stove, checked to see if Martin was still sleeping it off in the living room, and went outside to look for the other children and see if they knew where Tommy was.

She somewhat knew little Suzie and her mother so she went two houses down and knocked on the Krullers' backdoor. Suzie's mother, a bright-eyed woman with bushy black hair and an overbite, admitted her a moment later and asked if she'd have a cup of tea.

"No time. Making dinner. Is Suzie here? My Tommy was playing with her and the other kids this afternoon, and I wondered if she might know where he is."

Even Suzie's mother seemed concerned. "He isn't home yet?" She called for her daughter to come to the kitchen.

Suzie hesitated but broke down when she saw the stern, worried look on Mrs. Bartlett's face. "He's in the woods. We left him in the woods."

"*Left* him?" Suzie's mother frowned. "Why did you children do such a thing?"

Anne Marie blanched. She had forced Tommy to play with those kids, and all along he'd been right to be apprehensive. If anything happened to him it would be all her fault.

Suzie told the whole story of their trek into the "jungle," as she called it, and how Tommy had insisted, against everyone's advice, on rowing to the other side of the lake. Yes, that sounded like Tommy, all right.

"We couldn't wait for him, Mommy. We'd be late. We *told* him." She started to sniffle. "I like Tommy, but I was scared to go with him." Suzie said she could show Mrs. Bartlett where the path was at the end of the beach.

Anne Marie declined for a moment. It was still light out, and If Tommy had stayed to explore that house he might be home any second. "No, dear, maybe later. I'd better get back and see if he's there."

Back home Martin was awake and hollering for his supper like a pig. Anne Marie ripped a chicken leg off half a cold bird in the fridge and threw it at him. That should keep him for a while. Then she went back to the kitchen to finish making dinner for her boy.

But now half an hour had passed and Tommy still wasn't back. She couldn't seem too communicate the seriousness of the situation to her husband, who was slowly sobering up but was still too drunk to be of much use.

She would give the boy 15 more minutes. Then, before the sun had gone down and all hope of finding him was lost, she would get Suzie to show her the path and would look for Tommy herself.

* * *

Tommy was frightened. He had never had boy scout training, had never had a sober father who could sit him down and show him how to tell directions by looking at the sun or how to survive when you were all alone in the middle of the woods and the day was growing darker. Everyone assumed that he had a good sense of direction because no matter where he wandered on the beach or in town he always made his way home again with time to spare. But he never liked the woods that much and usually stayed out of them. And in the woods his famous sense of direction was really a sham.

The trail he'd taken from the old house had led directly toward the ocean and for a moment Tommy thought he could make his way back to Beachside by walking along the shore. But he was bitterly disappointed when he saw that there was no beach, only a vast piling of large and small rocks that were treacherous to walk upon and were slowly being covered up by the incoming tide. Worse, the edge of land where the rocks ended was an utterly impenetrable mass of weeds, rushes and brambles. What if the tide came completely in before he made it back to Beachside? What if his ankle got caught between the rocks and he had to lie there and drown, no one hearing his cries for help?

Except the awful man back in the woods.

So he had retraced his steps until he reached the point where the trail had curved toward the ocean and now stood there wondering what to do. He could not go back to the house by the lake—in fact, he was in horror of that man suddenly turning the corner and coming upon him helpless in the forest— and could not go back to the ocean. Although there was no apparent path, he wondered if he might go through the forest, around the edge of the lake, and make his way slowly back to Beachside, maybe even go inland after he passed the lake and find that trail he and the kids had been walking on earlier. Still, he knew this forest went on for acres and acres, and there was no guarantee he wouldn't get hopelessly lost.

Then it hit him. What about that stream he'd had to cross earlier; the trail had run right up to it and continued on the other side. What if he followed the stream back to Beachside? Had he passed it again on his way back from the ocean or was it closer to the lake? No, he hadn't gone past it twice or he would have remembered; it couldn't be that much farther beyond this bend.

Five minutes of walking and he reached it. All he had to do was take off his shoes and wade in it—it wasn't very deep and had a soft, lightly pebbled bottom—or walk along the edge, and he'd have a perfect passage out of the woods. He felt elated and relieved.

But wait? What if it only led back to the sea? He'd be right back on those rocks, faraway from Beachside.

Then, he thought, why not go in the other direction? He knew the coast highway was to his left, and the woods did not go past the road. He'd ridden on it and walked along it often enough to know that to the right of the road as you went down to the shore there were only flatlands. That was it! He'd walk along this stream until it reached the culvert that went underneath the road. Then he'd take the road back to Beachside. A much longer route, true, but a safer one.

He took off his shoes and stepped into the water.

Ten minutes later, gratified to see that the stream continued in its diagonal direction, heading inland toward the highway, he stepped out of the water and dried his frigid toes with his handkerchief. It was just too cold. He put his shoes and socks back on and continued walking along the embankment.

Five minutes later he heard a terrible rumble reverberate through the forest.

What was that? Thunder? An earthquake? it sounded like a dozen trees toppling over all at the same time. The very ground he stood on was shaking.

And then, just as suddenly as it had started, it ceased.

Whatever it was, he was somehow sure it had originated from the lake.

His heart beat faster.

He could hardly wait to get home.

* * *

Anne Marie was nearly frantic with worry when Tommy finally walked in the door just as she'd put on a sweater and prepared to go back to the Krullers' house to get Suzie. She embraced him, kissed him, then held him at arm's length so she could scold him.

"You know all about the lake? And the house?" he said, after hearing her mention them during her tirade. He knew she could not possibly know about the man he'd run into and decided it would be best not to tell her.

"Yes, I know. Found out from Suzie. just couldn't resist doing a little exploring, could you? Umm, my baby." She hugged him. "Mama was so worried."

Martin sat there looking stupid in his easy chair, a gnawed bone in his hand, grease and spittle all over his lips.

Anne Martin saw Tommy's look of disgust and threw Martin a napkin. "Wipe your face, you slob."

She turned back to the boy. "Tommy, don't you ever do that again. You had me scared to death."

"You told me to play with The Bunch, and they were the ones who wanted to go see that stupid old lake."

"Yes, yes, I know. Now, we'll discuss it all later. I've got supper all ready on the table and it's getting cold. Wash your hands and then get into the kitchen. Shoo."

She went over the shook her husband, who was nodding off again, and picked the chicken leg up off his lap. "We're eating dinner, Martin, if you can't get yourself together enough to sit presentably at the table, then I suggest you just go to bed. I've no patience with you tonight."

It was like talking to a wall. Martin muttered something and made his way to the bathroom where he'd wash up when Tommy was through.

When Tommy saw his father's reflection in the bathroom mirror he had to stifle a groan. He hated it when his Father was like this—incoherent, stumbling, a ragamuffin.

Martin stood there swaying behind Tommy until Tommy

turned off the faucet and shoved past him. He turned to look at his son with a bemused expression on his face, but Tommy ignored him, went into the kitchen and sat down at the table.

They were having lamb patties again. His mother always apologized when she put the leftover, ground lamb on the table, but it had long been one of Tommy's favorites. He loved it when the patties got all crunchy on the top and bottom, and his teeth would sink into and through the crunchy part and taste that fine soft meat inside.

She handed him a bowl of vegetables, and he had spooned a good-sized helping onto his plate when his father walked in.

Martin sat down at the end of the table and bent his head in prayer. He muttered the words of Grace while Anne Marie snorted. "If you're gonna pray to God, pray that he can put you on the wagon, you horse's ass," she had said on more than one occasion. When he was through, Martin reached out for the platter of lamb patties with a mildly shaky hand and slid them down onto his plate with his hand.

"You slob!" Anne Marie shouted. "Use the spatula!"

Martin said nothing, just picked up his fork and ate contentedly.

Another nice evening at home, Tommy thought.

* * *

After dinner Tommy went into his room to watch TV while his mother sat in the living room reading a true confession story. His father stood outside on the porch smoking a cigarette. Anne Marie had trained Martin not to smoke in the house, claiming it was a disgusting habit. Tommy was glad his parents had little interest in television, so he could watch whatever he wanted—Jackie Gleason, I Love Lucy, My Little Margie, all his favorites. His mother had no patience with the afternoon soap operas (her housecleaning made her miss too many episodes and she lost track of all the plots), and his father was usually too boozed up to concentrate on any program. Dad didn't much care for sports, either, so he had no interest in televised boxing or baseball.

Tommy was watching *I Married Joan* when the trouble began.

It took awhile for it to sink in. He was so used to hearing his parents argue with one another that a raised voice generally didn't register. Sometimes, when his mother got particularly shrill or his father particularly boisterous, he would come out of his room to investigate, but as long as they weren't hitting each other he remained dispassionate.

Tonight the hollering, the sheer volume of their hatred of each other, got so loud he couldn't hear the laughtrack on the TV set.

He got off of his bed where he'd been reclining, quickly opened his bedroom door, and walked down the hall to the living room, looking much older and forbearing than his years. He was usually able to stop the fighting just by putting in an appearance. His mother would say "not in front of the boy," or his father, shamed by his own son's half-pitying, half-contemptuous gaze, would throw up his hands and run out of the house.

But tonight Tommy realized that things had gone too far. His mother was sitting in a chair, crying and cringing, while his father hovered above her menacingly. When his mother started to cry, when sorrow, fear and self-pity overwhelmed her own sense of pride and courage and righteous indignation, that's when Tommy knew his father had somehow, in some drunken fool way, gained the upper hand and delivered the cutting remark that Anne Marie couldn't bounce back from with her usual grace and fury.

"You're not a woman," Martin was hollering. "No woman looks as ugly as you." He was holding an open lipstick case and shoving it toward her like it was a miniature javelin. "How come you never use this no more like most women do?

Why no makeup? Hair's all stringy. You look like shit, lady, *shit.*"

His mother, looking up through her tears, saw Tommy.

"Not in front of the boy."

"Shut up! The hell with the boy. Put it on. Fix your hair. Look like a woman again instead of a sow. Not even forty," he brayed, "and you look older than Spinster Biddies. You look older than a goddamn eighty-year-old!"

"Shut up!" Her eyes were flaming now, the old anger surfacing.

"Put it on, I say, woman! You're my wife. You'll do what I say. I want you pretty, fit to screw with. I can't get it up for no old sow with pale lips and messy hair, you old cunt." He pulled back his free hand and slapped her across the face.

"Martin!"

"Mommy!"

Tommy raced forward and grabbed his father's arm before he could use it to slap his mother again. The lipstick case went flying across the room in a crimson arc. Martin whipped him across the face with the back of the hand and sent him tumbling to the floor.

"Martin! The boy!" She tried to get up out of her chair, but Martin pressed close, keeping her from rising.

"When are you gonna be my wife again, huh? You haven't been my wife since Tommy was born. When you gonna be my wife?"

"What do you need me for? Aren't the drunken whores at Chester's and Greezer's and Hamman's enough for you?" She beat him in the chest with upraised fists. Her tears had dried and all that was left was her outrage.

Martin slapped her again, so hard her head swung to one side and her cheek burned from the force of the blow.

Tommy pulled himself off the floor and screamed, "Leave my mommy alone, you bum, you lousy rotten...leave my mommy..."

Glaring, Martin turned to Tommy and raised a fist.

"Martin! You leave him alone or so help me—"

He turned back to Anne Marie and spit in her face.

"Oh God, you can't do that..." She raised her fists again and beat him in the face, around the eyes, scratching, clawing, battering him with a ferocity that frightened both herself and her husband. "Can't do that to me, you crummy, rotten..."

Even Tommy was scared at his mother's unbridled show of violence. "Mommy...?"

Martin backed up, knocked into Tommy, and sent him sprawling again.

"Out of my way, you little bastard!" He picked up the lamp on the table, wrenched the plug out of the socket, and stood there with it as if wondering whether to throw it at his wife, who was getting up, blood on her fingers, or at his son.

"Leave him alone," Anne Marie said. Martin threw the lamp at her, but she blocked it with her elbow. It fell onto the floor and cracked into pieces. The savagery returned to Anne Marie's eyes. "Why, you bastard, my mother...my mother gave me that, you..." She started hitting him again. One fist sunk past his upraised, sheltering arms against the side of his nose. Blood dripped down from one nostril.

Seeing the blood, Martin went berserk.

He saw Tommy on all fours, rising, and kicked out with his foot so that it hit him on the neck and knocked him to one side. Then he shoved Anne Marie's fists out of the way and grabbed the woman by the hair. "Do that to me, you lousy bitch, dare to do that *to* me!" He pulled her away from the chair while she begged for mercy, pummeling her with his own fists and yanking her hair so hard it brought tears to her eyes. He gave a good wrench on the hair and sent her flying past him until she crashed into a table, cried out in agony, and fell screaming into the floor. Then he lifted his foot and began to kick her— in the chest, in the back, in the face—and she tried desperately to roll out of the way.

Tommy ran over to his mother and tried to protect her with his own fragile body, receiving a few kicks for his effort. Finally his father threw him aside. Tommy ran to the kitchen, picked up one of the chairs at the table, and ran back into the living room. Hoisting the chair as far above his head as his skinny arms could manage, he brought it slamming down onto the back of his father's head and shoulders.

His father's eyes tightened in pain and puzzlement. Who would be attacking him this way? He turned, saw his son holding the chair, preparing for another strike, and tried to grab the chair out of Tommy's hands. Tommy held on for dear life, knowing his father would only use it to batter himself or his mother. Anne Marie got to her feet, ran to the kitchen as Tommy and Martin wrestled for possession of the chair, and came back holding a thick, 12 inch long butcher knife.

"Leave him alone," she said, holding up the knife, her eyes widened as if by bloodlust. "Leave him alone or I swear I'll kill you." She spoke now with a contrasting calmness that made her words seem even more menacing, her intent more diabolical. "I'll kill you, Martin, believe me I will."

Faced with an armed opponent, Martin Bartlett backed down. He let go of the chair but Tommy held it up in front of him warily. Martin wiped blood off his nose and lips with his fingers, stared at his family with disgust, then snorted and headed for the door.

A moment later he was gone.

"I hope he walks into the sea and drowns," Anne Marie said. "He's no good…no good to anyone." Tommy wanted to go and hug her, but she was still holding the knife up in the air as if she would skewer anyone who came near. She definitely looked like she would stab Martin if he came back into the house at that point.

She put the knife on the table where the lamp had been and went over to her boy. "Tommy, are you all right? Did he hurt you, Tommy?"

He let himself be nestled in her warmth and concern. "I'm all right, Mommy." His little face looked up at hers. "Are you all right?"

"Yes, Tommy, I'll be all right. It's not the bruises that bother me, son."

"I hate him."

"No, don't talk that way about your father."

Was he hearing right? After what he'd just tried to do? His mother's face and arms were already turning black and blue, her eye was swelling, and there were bloodstains on her housedress.

"He beat us," Tommy said, sniveling. "Beat us. I hate him!"

"I said don't talk that way. I know he's miserable, but he's your father. He's my husband…"

Tommy rubbed his eyes with his fists. "That doesn't mean he should beat us."

"Well, maybe I haven't been…your father can't help being the way he is. He…"

"He *beat us*, Mommy!"

"Your father's sick, Tommy. He's awful sick. Sometimes I forget how sick he is, and I'm not strong enough to handle it. You marry someone in sickness and health, Tommy. That's what marriage is. Sickness and health, for better or worse. I'm just stuck with it. Your father's sick, and I can't leave him."

Though he tried to understand, it didn't make any sense to Tommy. His father was becoming more and more of a stranger, some slob who came home on occasion and shared their suppers, without once putting food on the table himself. Why did she want him around? He only took and took and gave grief and misery in return. His mother chased him down at a different bar night after night, making sure he slept in his bed instead of a gutter. Why should she care? What had he ever done for them but cause them hopeless misery?

"He's sick, but I love him. God help me, I love him."

"Why?"

"Don't talk that way."

"Why? He doesn't have to drink. He knows what it does to us and to him, but he doesn't care. He could get help, but he doesn't care. He's not sick; he's just evil. He hasn't got a disease; he's just a rotten, scummy bastard..."

His mother's slap was just a soft one, like a kiss in comparison to his father's brutal blows, but it felt worse than all his father's whuppings put together.

Tommy said nothing. He rubbed his face, let the tears fall silently, and went into his room and closed the door.

* * *

Tommy lay in the darkness in his bedroom, having cried himself out and wallowed in a self-pity that no comic book or monster magazine could assuage.

He felt betrayed by his mother's slap.

How could she defend his father, justify his actions? Other husbands didn't beat their wives and children. Other men drank, drank real bad, and they still never laid a finger on their families. He didn't think his father had any disease. What he had was a festering hatred of himself and of his family, a self-contempt that governed his every action, a complete and total lack of self-discipline or manly restraint.

His mother had gone to bed half an hour ago. He was glad she had not tried to apologize or say goodnight, because he was disgusted with her. She belongs here, he thought, shamed for thinking it but knowing it was true. She belonged in Beachside with the losers. She was a loser. Or else why would she stay with a man who drank and who beat her?

Both his parents were losers. And that night he swore that he would never, *never* grow up to be anything like them.

* * *

The Man could not swim from the lake to the ocean. In his human form it was too long a distance; the river ran underground for over a mile and he would have drowned. He could have used diving equipment, he supposed, but he hated its constrictions. Being underwater for such a length of time but being unable to change...no, it would not do.

Neither could he swim from the lake to the ocean in his Beast form. His Beast form was so huge the lake could barely contain it. The rivers were certainly not large enough to accommodate his bulk. He would become trapped in the underground conduits, squeezed into narrow apertures until he was unable to move backwards or forwards.

So he had to walk to the ocean, like some common human being.

He smiled sadly. He had tried, tried so hard to be discreet, to be careful. But that couple at the lake, so close, so easy to just...*change*...and come up from the lake where they were standing. There was no one else around. The little boy had disappeared. He did not often gorge on human flesh, and their tiny bodies—the voluptuous woman's and the minuscule mash of the man's which he'd licked off from the forest floor —had hardly satisfied his enormous appetite. Even when he converted to human form there was still a gnawing inside his belly.

He'd tasted blood again, human blood, and though he had sworn before that he would never again prey on humans he found he had a craving for the sweet meat and stringy veins of rich fluid that ran through it. What were humans, after all, but walking bags of succulent meat and blood? But it would require so many of them to fill his stomach.

Be honest with yourself, he thought. *This "craving" of yours is only an excuse. You've been wanting to do what you plan to do tonight for a terribly long time, haven't you? Beachside has been a thorn in your side for far too long now. Something has to be done about it.* He had hoped for some natural phenomenon—a hurricane, a tidal wave—to just sweep the whole horrid community out to sea, but it hadn't happened. He'd even thought of swamping the slum himself with a few flaps of his tail. But what if someone saw him? What if he didn't get it quite right and there were too many survivors?

No, the trick was to make sure there were *no* survivors.

He would feast on Beachside tonight.

And the ones he didn't devour he would crush.

* * *

An hour after his mother had gone to bed, Tommy's father came back into the house. He could hear him stumbling around. He had probably cadged a drink from someone in the neighborhood, though the neighbors had little patience with him. His father hit his knee on something and cried out. He cursed, spit noisily, then continued toward the bedroom. Apparently he thought better of it, because Tommy heard his footsteps retreating, heading toward the living room again. In the pickled haze that passed for his brain, Martin must have remembered the fight he'd had with his family. He was smart enough to sleep on the couch.

Tommy couldn't sleep but he was weary of thinking about his life and of the grim fates of his parents. He still wanted desperately to get out of Beachside, but now he wasn't so sure that he would come back for them once he was rich and famous. No, he thought, he just might let them rot here. Didn't they deserve each other? The pain of the bruises his father had given him had faded, but his mother's slap was still stinging. He would get out of Beachside and never return.

Satisfied with his decision, he thought about other things. He thought about The Bunch (of losers), which led him to think about the lake, and rowing across it, and being abandoned, and then naturally, he thought about the old house and that awful man who'd opened the door so abruptly and stood on the porch watching him run. He thought of being lost in the woods and following the stream (he tried not to think about the way the earth had trembled) until he reached the coast highway. There had been a car parked at the side of the road, a nice new Pontiac, but it was empty, and Tommy wondered who would leave a beautiful new car like that abandoned. He kept turning back as he walked down the road to Beachside, but whoever owned the car did not appear, at least not while he was looking.

He thought about the dark, sunken, haunted eyes of the man in the house. Perhaps he had not lived there after all; perhaps he was a trespasser himself. In which case, Tommy had run away for nothing. The man might have known all about the house and could have taken him inside and shown him around.

But no, even if the man had been knowledgeable about the house, Tommy thought it would have been less scary exploring it by himself than with that creepy man at his side.

What had happened to the people who'd disappeared out there at the lake? he wondered. How close had he come to disappearing himself? Maybe they had just drowned.

Or maybe that man got 'em.

Should he have told his mother about the man? Or the police? Maybe the man was a murderer and should be locked away before he could kill again.

Tommy didn't know what to do. That guy could have been the one responsible for those people disappearing, assuming anyone had disappeared and it was not just a lot of nonsense.

He was sleepy. Time enough tomorrow to worry about all of this. He turned over on his stomach and shoved his face into the pillow.

Ten minutes later he was still awake. He was strangely apprehensive. What was wrong? Something to do with his mother and father? No. He could hear his father snoring in the living room and was sure his mother had cried herself to sleep, as she often did, in the bedroom next to his own. They were settled in for the night, at least. So what was wrong?

He rolled over onto his back again and soothed himself by thinking about his favorite movie monsters: *The Beast from 20,000 Fathoms* and *The Monstrous Leviathan*. Reptilian creatures from eons past rose up to smash modern cities with a single blow of their massive paws or one burning whoosh of their fiery radioactive breath. He loved the way moviemakers made it seem as if these creatures were really alive, as if there actually were gigantic monsters that could tower above humanity, when he knew they were usually just table top models animated one frame at a time and somehow blended into the action. He'd read all about it in one of his magazines. Imagine! King Kong was only 18 inches tall!

He imagined a huge beast rising from the ocean outside his window, rising, rising, higher and higher, stomping onto the shore, opening its mouth and growling.

He dug down deeper under the cool blue sheet on the bed.

"What would you do if you were walking in town one day," he'd asked his mother countless times, "and you looked up and saw a dinosaur coming up the street?"

When his mother finally got around to giving him a serious answer, she'd said, "I'd probably drop dead in my tracks. Now finish your milk, silly."

He wished he could see a dinosaur. A real live one. Somewhere. Somehow.

For the rest of his life Tommy was to regret that wish.

Completely awake and restless, Tommy got out of bed and went over to the window. He leaned his elbows on the sill and stared out into the night. If he craned his neck a bit he could see the ocean, such a magnificent, formidable force of nature, the waves, the white caps, rolling, slowly rolling onto the land.

He saw something, black, much blacker than the ocean, pull up and separate from the water.

Tommy was transfixed.

The black thing, blacker than black, pulled up, up, stretching to its full height, up, up…

Tommy gasped. It had to be a dream, a nightmare. He wanted to go wake his parents, but he was sure he had to be seeing things. He could not turn away.

The black thing was coming closer, closer to shore. Tommy could see that it walked on four legs, had a long neck and tail, and a massive head.

A dinosaur!

It was coming out of the water. It was huge, huge…

But it was *not* a dinosaur.

Oh, my God!

Tommy saw its face. God, no, its face!

Tommy was too petrified to scream.

* * *

The Man was now The Beast.

The Beast strode onto the land knowing there was nothing and no one who could stop it from carrying out its mission.

It felt like Nature itself in this form.

The Beast looked down and saw scurrying figures, men and women who had been around a campfire, running out of its path, screaming, pointing.

The Beast took care of them simply by continuing to walk. One single stride and it had already gone past them. It bent its head and picked up a few between its teeth, body parts dropping off onto the sand. The Beast's tongue swept out, wiping away blood and gristle. It lifted its feet and stomped the others into the ground before they could escape.

Then The Beast turned toward the houses. It knew it had to move fast.

It simply…walked…through the houses.

The Beast battered the old wooden homes into matchsticks with one blow from its head. It smashed the debris with its feet and swept it aside with its tail. As it went it stopped to nibble on a morsel here or there—little screaming, scurrying things holding babies or belongings.

Hardly anyone, though, had a chance to get out.

After it had reduced the homes on stilts to a pile of shattered beams and pools of blood, it thundered into the tents and huts and shanties by the shore. For a beast so huge it moved quickly. Its neck went up and down, up and down, snacking, feasting, picking up the little squiggling things, consuming them rapidly as they ran helter-skelter, as they screamed in fear and terror, in disbelief. Most were too shocked to even move. The Beast ate as if it were desperately hungry.

Which it was.

The Beast turned and saw what it had done to Beachside and was pleased, though in this form, at this stage, it could not have known why.

Still The Beast was hungry.

It went carefully, but quickly, through the rubble, shoving walls aside with its head, dipping down to pick up a squiggling thing here, part of another one there, gobbling, gobbling. It was so hungry that sometimes it just lifted up whole chunks of debris, wood and all, and popped them and the screaming things inside them into its jaws.

So hungry.

* * *

Tommy didn't know how long he'd been under the house—what was left of it.

He hadn't even time to warn anyone of The Beast, still not sure if what he was seeing was real or just a vision brought on by those slaps to his head. When The Beast had moved out of his field of vision—thought it was so huge it was never entirely out of view—he'd moved from the window and planned to wake up his mother.

But he had just reached the bedroom door when the walls started tumbling. The celling was cracking open, lowering toward the floor, and he had to bend down to keep it from crushing him. He felt like he was in a box that was getting smaller and smaller, and he screamed and cried. He screamed for his mother, but he couldn't even hear himself over the creaking, snapping, shattering sound of the house coming to pieces all around him.

He wanted to go toward his mother's bedroom and save her, but all he could see in that direction was a massive black tower that had suddenly appeared out of nowhere. Where was the rest of the hall? Where was her bedroom? Then he understood what the tower was and was so shocked by the realization that he immediately had to put it out of his mind or go insane.

He'd seen digits at the bottom of the tower.

Then the tower lifted and there was nothing there. Nothing. The tower moved on to the next house.

But the walls and ceiling were still falling. He ran into the crumbling living room and pulled open a trap door that had been constructed in the floor near the entrance to the hallway. He threw himself into the hole just as the celling came crashing down on top of him.

Now he lay crying, struggling, under heavy chunks of wood. Towards the sea, the stilts were still standing; in the other direction—where his mother's bedroom and the kitchen had been—all he could see was a flattened barrier of wood and metal. *Where is my mother? Oh God, what's happened to my mother?*

Suddenly he felt an ease of pressure. Something was lifting the debris off his back, lifting it up through the hole in the floor above him. He twisted around as far as he could and looked up through the hole.

And saw his father.

"Dad! Forget about me. I'm okay. What about Mom?"

Tommy could see the stars above his father's head and open air and a dark scattering of clouds.

His father didn't answer. The man's fingers worked frantically to get all the debris off Tommy's body. He had moved enough so that the boy could reach up through the trap door —when the stars were blotted out by an enormous black shadow above them.

Tommy screamed.

His father reached out his hands. "C'mon, Tommy, I got you. Don't be frightened."

"Daddy! Watch-"

There came a terrible odor, a hot stink of breath and ocean bottom, and suddenly Tommy saw a face behind his father, a face with eyes so huge he could only see one and only part of it at that, and he saw the glistening teeth coming closer, and his father was pulled up and away, snatched away from the hole so quickly and so finally that it was almost as If he'd never even been there.

The face was gone. His father was gone.

Tommy sunk back into the debris below the house. He heard a man screaming, abruptly silenced, but couldn't imagine who it could be or why he should be hollering. What am I doing here? he wondered. He retreated into unreality to save his sanity and his soul.

He smelled that awful odor again, felt that horrible breath, and the remains of the walls collapsed above him and his view of the stars was cut off by crumbling plaster and wood and furniture.

Tommy lay there in the dark below the wreckage of his house and sobbed, wondering why his mother didn't come and awaken him from his nightmare.

CHAPTER FOUR

THE MAN WITH THE EYES

Finally the rescue workers found him.

"Hey, we got a live one here!"

He was pulled out, put on a stretcher, carried along and over the beach until the men reached the road where he was slid into an ambulance.

"Careful. He's in shock."

All the while as they carried him over the sand he tried to think of what had happened, but he had only the dimmest memory. Something had destroyed Beachside.

But what?

He couldn't tell anyone.

At one point he did say: "A monster. A monster."

But nobody believed him—then or ever.

His tears had dried but inside he was sobbing still.

He had been so angry with his parents, had almost come to hate them, had wanted to leave them and Beachside behind and never return.

God had punished him and had sent the devil from the sea to take his parents away. Well he got his wish. He was leaving Beachside. And he never would be returning. Of course, there was no Beachside to return to.

* * *

Everywhere the authorities looked there was devastation.

But what had happened? A freak storm? There hadn't been any storms along the coast. A typhoon, a tidal wave, a fire or explosion?

But the buildings hadn't exploded. They'd *imploded*, been crushed like eggshells from some massive outside force.

The next day they found an odd, gigantic footprint in the sand, but of course it was made by some kids playing practical jokes—funny, as if this was caused by a sea monster, as if this was something to laugh about. (Though the wealthy of Summerdale admitted to themselves if to no one else that they were glad the slum was gone.)

Some people couldn't imagine what else it could have been but a sea monster.

* * *

"Where are all the people?" one of the ambulance workers asked.

"We're still going through the wreckage, remember?"

But even after they'd gone through the wreckage, found several bodies, and one living person, Tommy, they still came up about a 100 people short.

Where did 100 people go?

Tommy could have told them—if he'd remembered.

For he was the only survivor.

Daddy tried to save me and it got him.

But he only remembered in his dreams. And he dared not voice what he saw in those dreams for fear of going crazy.

* * *

As they lifted Tommy's stretcher and put him in the ambulance, he felt a sudden chill run through him. He turned his head to the right and saw a man—he was not a medic, ambulance driver, fireman, or cop —standing nearby. He had a sad, angry, frustrated look on his face.

Tommy did not recognize him, but he did remember the eyes.

The man at the lake. The man on the porch of the house.

And where else had he seen those eyes?

Those eyes even now were boring into his and seemed to say: *Sleep well my prince. So you escaped me. You've earned a good, long rest. There's nothing, nothing you can do to me now. Now...or ever.*

And then the eyes were gone; the man was gone.

In his nightmares Tommy often saw the man and remembered the odd thing he did before he turned his back and walked away from the ambulance.

The man had licked his lips.

PART TWO
FLORIDA, 1988

CHAPTER FIVE

PARMENTER'S SALOON

After what drink did to his father, Thomas Bartlett would never have imagined he'd one day be co-owner of one of the most successful saloons in Miami, much less that he'd be sitting at the main bar on a Friday afternoon enjoying a strong, tasty whiskey sour. Unlike his father, he had no great passion for alcohol and its so-called medicinal properties. He did, however, enjoy a good cocktail now and then, and his favorite bartender, Brian, knew how to make one.

Parmenter's Saloon—the place was named after his business partner Joseph Parmenter—was more than just a saloon, of course, though they did do a great bar business. It also was a restaurant, serving fresh fish and assorted specialties to hordes of hungry customers. Everything about Parmenter's was classy and upscale: the polished light brown wood of the bar with its gleaming gold rail; the spaciously arranged tables with their bright red tablecloths; the big windows showing a view of the water and the boats; the attractive deck outside where couples could stroll with their champagne cocktails. Parmenter's, a huge place, had five separate rooms surrounding a central kitchen, each room with a different decor and ambiance. This bright outer room, which ran the entire length of the building and curved at either end so you could look out of both sides, was the biggest. This was the place Thomas had always dreamed of owning.

Of course, just as every cloud has its silver lining, Thomas' cloud was Joseph Parmenter. He had known and liked Joe for years, but also found Joe too irresponsible and careless to suit his taste. Joe did have one undeniably strong attribute: money. Inherited money, but money just the same.

Thomas had gotten started in the restaurant trade by taking over his Uncle Steven's booming eatery in Riverton after the man had passed away, but soon realized that he had outgrown both the restaurant and the town. He sold the business, moved to Miami, and bought a new, larger place. He knew how to run a restaurant, and the place did well, but it was tiny and hardly challenging. It was not the sort of place that the *nouveau riche* or the "in crowd" would flock to—and for some reason he wanted that, needed it, badly.

Still, it would take much more money than he had to open that kind of place. He had mentioned it idly to Joseph one night—not at all thinking of going into partnership with the man—and Parmenter had suggested doing business together. He put up the extra money, the restaurant had his name, and Thomas could run it with his by now seasoned expertise. Thomas didn't care about the name. Joseph didn't plan on having much to do with the business proper, so Thomas knew it was he, Thomas Bartlett, who would become most associated with Parmenter's in the public eye.

Parmenter's had good food, a nice ambiance, beautiful decor, a wonderful view; before long it was getting favorable reviews and being mentioned in the columns. All Thomas really had to do was be there to oversee things. He had hired an excellent staff, a good manager and assistant manager, a classy maitre d', good waiters—everything couldn't have been better. The only thing that made him nervous was all the friends Joe Parmenter brought into "his place" for free meals. They were always weird, nasty-looking customers in ill-fitting suits, smoking expensive cigars and leaving ostentatious tips that thrilled the waiters and busboys but made them seem as if they were trying desperately to impress. Thomas knew that Joe loved to gamble—he took regular trips to the casinos at Freeport and Nassau and played the horses—and Thomas worried that he might build up the kind of debts that would inevitably put Parmenter's itself into danger. Thomas had no proof that Joseph consorted with hoodlums, but he had his suspicions and hoped he would not come to regret going into business with his buddy.

Thomas left the bar with his drink and went over to sit at one of the empty tables near the big glass walls so he could look out at the bay. The place was not busy at this hour; the lunch crowd had departed and what he called the "Friday Night Outers" would not really begin to appear until well after 6:00 P.M. Still, Parmenter's was never entirely devoid of customers.

He took another sip of that fine whiskey sour—no mixes or any artificial ingredients at Parmenter's ever! —and let it warm its way down his throat to his belly. He had nothing to do today, really. Everything was running smoothly, and he could just relax and watch the water and...

He suddenly arose and went back to the bar.

He could never look at the ocean for very long. He supposed it had something to do with the deaths of his parents when he was 12 and the strange destruction of Beachside, that awful slum they lived in. Not that he remembered much of what had happened that night. Even his parents themselves, what they were like, had receded into a vague, distant memory. He never went into the water and didn't even remember if he had ever learned to swim. Seemed he had liked the water when he was a boy. Now he just thought it was pretty—the lights, the ships, the piers, the people —but always disquieting, as if the blue water and gentle waves hid some terrible secret.

Staring at the water too long made him nervous, and standing on the shore made him break out in a cold sweat.

What did happen that night? A storm, of course. A freak storm came up so suddenly neither coast guard nor meteorologist had time to issue a warning. That was all. A storm, a hurricane, a tornado, a typhoon.

What else could it have been?

He took a few more sips of the sour and shook the thoughts out of his head. It was the past; it was over. In a way, what had happened, as horrible as it had been—all those people crushed by falling buildings, most of them swept out to sea—had turned out to be for the best as far as he was concerned. He had had a miserable, poverty-stricken life with his parents. When his Aunt Laura and Uncle Steven took him into their home, his life improved almost beyond measure, once he got over the pain, loss and trauma. He lived in a nice house in a nice town, had his own comfortable bedroom, a healthy allowance he could spend on almost anything. He lost his interest in comics and monsters, acquired a passion for more adult reading and enjoyed dating the young women his aunt and uncle thought he should meet.

It was a conventional life but a nice one.

In a way it was good he remembered so little of what had happened that night. His aunt and uncle had wondered if he might need professional counseling to get over the shock, but the doctors agreed that he was handling it well, that probing into his subconscious was probably the worst thing they could do. "It's the mind's natural way of protecting and healing itself." they said. "Think of the memory loss as a bandage over a bleeding injury, a new skin healing and growing over the wound." It was a blessing that the whole horrible event was so dim in his mind. He could forget it and get on with his life.

Though sometimes it was hard to forget that he *had*

forgotten something completely—something dark, something obscene.

He had never wanted to build a restaurant so close to the bay, but Parmenter had insisted it was a choice location. Who was he to argue? It had worked out better than he'd ever imagined.

As for his own place, he lived in an apartment in the downtown district of the city. Although it was not that far from the water he had windows that only faced inland.

He had finished the whiskey sour and was about to ask Brian to make him another, when he felt a warm breath at his ear and someone's lips on his cheek. It was Elsa Freemont, his lady friend, who gave him a wink and a smile. "Hi!"

How his late aunt and uncle would have turned over in their graves if they could have seen Elsa. With those fine, upstanding ladies from good families to choose from, he winds up in this casual relationship with a "commie" folksinger. Oh, he'd tried to fall in love with many of those pinch-faced, delicate little heiresses, but it never worked; none of them had truly excited him. Why settle for something safe and dull when life had so much more to offer?

But here he was at 43, still unmarried, still—if he were truly to admit it to himself—alone. Only his ability to entertain himself, to enjoy his own company as he had done as a child, kept him from being genuinely lonely. However, as an adult he had no fantasies to draw upon, no imaginary monsters to hunt for on the beach. Instead he went to bars and parties and social functions, enjoying his role as successful restaurateur and part-time civil leader. He organized events, gave to charities, attended dinners honoring politicians and benefits for assorted associations. He was a wealthy, upstanding, respectable pillar of the community—a middle-aged Miami fixture.

Which made it even stranger that he should be involved with Elsa Freemont.

She was an attractive, some might say sexy, woman of 37, though she looked at least five years younger. She had a thin, long face with big hazel eyes, an aristocratic, upturned nose and thin lips she occasionally made fuller with a slash of scarlet lipstick. Her straight hair was jet black and swept down below her shoulders; sometimes she let it grow almost to her waistline. The hair was always neat, however, kept in excellent condition so that it fairly glistened in the light.

She had no real figure to speak of—though her small naked breasts were more than enough to arouse Thomas' interest—but made up for it by wearing the most attractive and provocative blouses and accessories she could find. The top two or three buttons were always open, and she wore delicate gold chains around her neck. The ultimate effect almost served to make her small bosom an asset. Her long hair, slender waistline, and long, long shapely legs also took men's minds off the fact that she wasn't Dolly Parton. "I know how to dress," she always said, though in truth she only wore these nice clothes when they went out someplace special, "so who needs boobs or makeup?" Today was a bit chilly so she had a light blue sweater on over her blouse, which was buttoned all the way up to the top.

Though his aunt may have liked Elsa's general appearance, she definitely would not have approved of her viewpoints. Elsa was not one of those prim little things who wanted marriage, babies, and a house with a white picket fence. She was a singer, a "good singer," she said, and would settle for nothing less than stardom. Children were not too important to her, at least not now, and if she had any she would expect her husband to take care of them, at least part of the time, while she pursued her career. She used curse words frequently and made no secret that she had lost her virginity at 15 and slept with over 50 men before she graduated college. She had slowed down, she said, in her thirties.

She had joined the socialist party in college, had drifted

away from it in body if not in spirit over the years, and was always going on about police states, military industrial complexes, Reaganomics, the oppressed working people, and other things that seemed indicative of a combination of 60's and 80's paranoia. She wore "Ban the Bomb" buttons, picketed supermarkets that sold the wrong grapes and used the terms "third world" and "raise your consciousness" a lot. She frequently got piqued at what she called Thomas' "social indifference."

"Are you busy tonight?" she asked, and for a second he thought he might be spared the confrontation he knew was coming and dreaded. He was not pleased at the prospect of having to level with Elsa.

"That depends." He smiled. "Are you looking for someone to spend some time with?"

Before she could answer, Brian came over and asked her what she wanted to drink. She ordered a ginger ale with a twist and turned back to Thomas. "I'm going to a party tonight and I need someone for an escort."

"What kind of party?"

"A party given by Walter Langley, the record promoter, on his yacht. Who knows who I might meet there? I ran into a cousin who works for Langely—he's a CPA or something— and he said he'd add my name to the guest list. Even said I could bring a date. How about it?"

Thomas had no other plans. "It's okay with me. What time does it start?"

"Not till late. Ten or eleven. Everett, that's my cousin, says it probably won't get jumping on the yacht until midnight."

As usual, Thomas was agreeable, hoping to please. "We could have a late supper here, take a stroll afterwards, then get to the party whenever you thought you were ready. How's that sound?"

She leaned over and kissed him again. "Wonderful, Tommy! Thanks a lot!"

He knew she was just about to ask him The Question when Joseph Parmenter came in from the kitchen where he'd apparently been chatting with the chef. He clapped a hand on Thomas' back and gave Elsa one of his toothy winning smiles.

Joseph Parmenter was a handsome 46-year-old man with a broad face, a full, neatly combed head of solid black hair, and deep set cobalt blue eyes. He had put on a little too much weight for his five foot seven frame, but disguised his belly with well-tailored suits and flamboyant neckties. He had a strong chin, heavy eyebrows, and a moderately high forehead. His lips and nose were just short of being too full and too broad, respectively. When he smiled he revealed perfect rows of gleaming white caps.

It was only when five foot eight Elsa was sitting down that she wasn't taller than the two male owners of Parmenter's. And when she wore heels, forget it!

Thomas sat there squirming as Elsa opened her pretty lips and bluntly asked his partner, "So, has Tommy asked you about the possibility of my singing here on weekends? What do you think, huh, handsome?"

Thomas recalled what Joseph said when he first suggested the idea. "Give me a break, Bartlett. Just cause she's your girlfriend don't mean she'd bring in new customers. What the hell do we need a folksinger for, huh? A jazz singer, a nightclub entertainer, maybe. But a skinny broad with long hair and a guitar singin' songs about pollution and nuclear reactors? Get wise, buddy!"

Thomas braced himself for Joseph's answer.

"I think it might be just the thing this place needs," Joseph said.

Tommy could barely wipe the look of incredulity off his face.

"Yeah, Tommy, I think this girl of yours might have something, if we work it right. Say, why not let me handle all the details, okay? What does Tommy know about entertainment?"

Elsa smirked and nodded her head in agreement. Joseph put his hand on her shoulder and added, "Let's you and me have a drink together some night and discuss it. You know— how we'll present you, what kind of material you'll sing, what you'll wear. I want to take a personal interest. Tommy, he don't know about these kinds of things, but you'll have to be patient, doll. We're planning a whole line of entertainment for Parmenter's in the fall. You can be one of our first headliners."

"Oooooohhh," Elsa said.

"Yeah. Your name in lights, your picture on a billboard at the door. Hell, we'll even charge a cover. We just got to sit down over drinks one night and work out the details. Maybe in a week or two we'll get together. You got the phone number here. Call me at the office in a week or so and we'll make arrangements."

His hand went down on her leg where he gave her a squeeze quite high above the knee. Then he clapped both Elsa and Thomas on their backs and returned to the kitchen to kibitz.

Joseph was not supposed to be around that much, but since they'd opened he'd been kibtizing everywhere, commenting on every part of the business. Thomas hadn't objected because at least he knew the saloon was more than a tax write-off to Joe, and Joe always let him have his way when push came to shove. But now? Now Thomas thought his friend might have gone a little too far.

Elsa was all excited.

"Isn't that nice, Tommy? Your friend is such a nice man."

"Such a nice sleazeball, you mean."

"What?"

"He's a sleazeball. Please, Elsa, I hope you didn't take anything he said seriously. When I brought you up to him, he was against the idea. Thought it was inappropriate to have a…folksinger…performing in the restaurant. Now, suddenly, he's got all these grandiose schemes and—"

"Maybe he just changed his mind. People do do that, you know, change their minds, he—"

"He practically had his hand up your dress."

"Oh, is *that* what it is." She sat back and took a sip of her soda. "Tommy, give me a little credit. I can spot them coming a mile away. I had that one's number the first time I met him, but I knew if I said anything about it you'd get angry. I know that type of fellow. They've got to flirt with every girl they meet or they don't feel macho. Believe me, I can handle him. He knows I'm going with you. He'd never really make a move on me. If I came on to him he'd turn into a bowl of jello."

"Oh, really? Is that the way it is? Did it ever occur to you, dear, that all that talk of getting together 'over drinks' to discuss your debut at Parmenter's is nothing more than a tub of baloney? Do you honestly think he has any intention of letting you sing in his restaurant? All that talk of a 'whole line of entertainment'—that's the first I've ever heard of it. He never said a thing about it to me. If you go and have drinks with him you want to bet it will be at his apartment, late at night, and he won't give you a definite 'no deal, honey' until after he's kicked you out of the bedroom."

"Thomas! You're so..."

"So honest. That weasel! Making time with my girl!"

"I'm nobody's 'girl.' "

"I know, I know." He wanted to continue the argument, to say a lot more and get some things off his chest, but thought better of it. "Maybe we *should* go to that party tonight, Elsa. You won't be able to count on Joseph Parmenter to help you get anywhere in your career, that's for certain."

She took another sip and licked her lips. "We'll see."

Poor Elsa. She still didn't believe him. Well he guessed she'd have to find out the hard way.

He told Brian to make him another whiskey sour.

* * *

Walter Langley's yacht was certainly impressive.

At 11:15 Thomas and Elsa walked over to the slip at the Miamarina that her cousin had specified. Elsa gave her name to a uniformed employee of Langley's who carried a clipboard of names that he checked off as he stood to one side of several motor launches. Satisfied that "Elsa Freemont and guest" was on the list, he directed them into one of the launches and instructed a man in a red and white striped T-shirt and designer jeans to start the engine. Within moments they were on their way across the water and out to Langley's yacht, which was anchored far out in Biscayne Bay.

The ship was quite large, one of those monstrosities with enough room for several overnight guests, the staff and conveniences of a small hotel, a large dining area, dance floors, and even an indoor pool. The yacht was christened the *Virginia*, probably after Langley's late wife, according to Elsa.

There were so many people on board that Thomas couldn't understand how it would be able to hold anyone else once the party got in gear, and it looked to him to be in full swing already. Once they got on board they were greeted by a handsome young couple, two of Langley's employees, who hugged and kissed them and told them where everything was located. "Welcome aboard," they said. "Have a great time." Then they turned to give the people on another approaching launch their patented plastic grins. "Out-of-work actors," Elsa confided.

Thomas and Elsa made their way past a crowd of people standing out on deck and entered a kind of enclosed ballroom where a crowd was rocking to the hard beat of a live band mounted on a platform in the far corner. "There's a bar near the opposite door," Thomas told Elsa. "Let's go and get some drinks."

"Do you see Walter Langley anywhere?" she asked Thomas.

"How would I know? Until tonight I never even heard of him," he replied. "What exactly does Langley look like?"

"Oh, you can't miss him. Fat and bald with funny eyeglasses."

" 'Funny eyeglasses?' "

"They're his trademark. He always wears funny eyeglasses. I've heard he has about two hundred pairs."

"Charming."

They made their way to the bar and were gratified to see that for the moment there was not a long line for drinks. Thomas ordered a whiskey sour for himself and a gin and tonic for Elsa. She stood sipping her drink and surveying the room. "Drat. I don't see any celebrities."

"Isn't that Warren Beatty over there?"

Her eyes lifted. "Where? *Where?*"

Warren or his look-alike had turned his back and ducked into a semicircle of attractive women. "You just missed him," Thomas said.

As they stood there a while longer, Tom had the impression that Elsa was dying to leave him, to go off on her own and see what "connections" she could make. Not that he blamed her. A man would approach a woman who was by herself a lot quicker than one accompanied by a man—at least while the night was young and the guy was sober.

"Want to mingle?" he asked her, taking her elbow gently. "Explore the ship?"

"Yes, let's explore," she said, a bit too readily. As they moved toward an archway to one side of the bar she craned her long neck and looked this way and that for the sight of a face that might justify their coming here, save her from a night of dreariness.

Thomas felt a sudden surge of pity for Elsa. She wasn't getting any younger, and most of the other women on the boat, all of whom were just as starstruck and stardom bound —at least in their dreams— as she was, were much younger, sweeter things than Elsa. He wondered when it might hit Elsa that she hadn't much chance of hitting the big time. Her type of music was passé, at least in commercial terms, and while she was attractive, she didn't quite have the almost "sluttish" look they seemed to be after.

He had heard her sing a few times in coffeeshops and at parties, and her voice wasn't terrible. It was strong and full of emotion, but she overdid everything—the gestures, the volume, the stridency—so that the ultimate result was more wailing than singing. She didn't caress listeners with her voice; she hit them on the head with a hammer. And her "message" songs, many of which she wrote herself, were equally heavy-handed.

No, no, it was hopeless. If it were still 1960, when she would have been barely reaching puberty, it might have been one thing. But in the 1980's her "sound" was dead. Why couldn't she see that? Oh, she might eke out a living singing at various functions, but become a star? In the 1980's with folks songs? No way.

They walked along a narrow corridor into a large room filled with hors d'oeuvres, banquet tables and another well-stocked bar, Elsa still craning this way and that to see who was on board. Then they went up a narrow flight of stairs to another open deck. There was softer, slower music, playing from loudspeakers, and a few couples were either dancing, holding each other, or necking by the railing. Thomas assumed this was for the older folks on board, and he laughed. At 43 he was older folks, and at 37, so was Elsa, whether she wanted to admit it or not.

He took her by the hand and led her to the railing. They looked out over the open sea, saw the reflection of all the colored lights on the ship gleaming and glistening across the water. Yet, Thomas soon got that odd, disquieting feeling again, as if beneath the beautiful reflection of the colored lights there was only rotting seaweed and garbage, dead fish, *and something dark and huge and dreadful.*

A ferryboat full of people. An enormous head rising from

the water. A woman screaming, shoving her handkerchief into her mouth. Where did that come from?

Then strangely, he remembered. It was a scene from one of his favorite childhood monster movies, *The Monstrous Leviathan,* when the radioactive dinosaur or mutant sea beast or whatever it was attacked a ferry and then stomped its way merrily through London. Odd, he hadn't thought of one of those old movies in years. He'd lost interest, he supposed, as he'd grown older. He remembered how much he'd loved that one, yet the memory of it was so disturbing, as if there was another similar memory imprinted on top of it or underneath it, another memory that was far more frightening than the movie because *it was real.*

"Tommy, you're shaking. What's the matter?"

He shook his head and rubbed his eyes. "Uh, nothing. I just...I drank that whiskey sour too fast. Look, I'm going to find a men's room; I need to take a pee."

Her eyes lit up at the thought of his leaving, or was that his imagination? "Okay. While you're gone I'm going to mingle around downstairs again. I could swear I saw Madonna out of the corner of my eye."

He let her go. She wanted to be off by herself anyway. He'd give her time to make some connections. Yet the thought of her connecting, even sexually, with a total stranger, some spangled, long-haired jerk in the music business, made him far less angry than the possibility of her shacking up with Joseph.

He wandered along the deck until he saw a young man in a uniform and asked him where there might be a restroom. The young man smiled and gave him directions. He had only to enter a room to his right— "starboard"—and take another narrow staircase, and he would find himself in a hallway at the end of which was a toilet in the stern of the ship. Thomas found it easily.

In the bathroom he took a pee and steadied himself. That

first drink here had gone to his head rather quickly. He'd probably drunk it too fast because he was nervous at being among all these rather attractive strangers.

He and Elsa did not really belong here. The crowd was mostly much younger than they were, fancier and freakier. They all seemed very hip, very together.

Of course, he was trying to avoid the subject.

Why am I afraid of the water?

Why did he want to get off this boat?

He hated being on the water. *Hated it!*

He splashed some water from the faucet on his face and dried himself off with a paper towel. He made up his mind that he would go looking for Elsa once and only once, and that was it. If he didn't find her he would leave. Or if he found her happily absorbed in conversation with some "connection" he would leave her to her own devices. He wanted to get off this boat.

Had the waves, that presumably washed the missing denizens of Beachside out to sea, washed over him too, and nearly pulled him off the shore to his death? Was that why he hated the ocean? The sea was fairly calm tonight, but still he was frightened, terribly frightened.

He needed another drink, that's what he needed.

His mother's voice was whispering in his ear. *Sure. Go ahead and turn to drink. Just like your father did. Be a drunken bum like your father.*

But that was ridiculous. He was *not* like his father. He was a very successful businessman. Even with his earlier advantages, his father had never amounted to what Thomas had. He was not a drunk, not even a budding alcoholic. Desperate times called for desperate measures, that's all.

He hated being on this ship, and he wanted another drink to calm his nerves, okay? His mother's shapeless face frowned, but he ignored it.

He went to get another drink.

The nearest bar was a small one set up on the deck with the soft music for the older folks. Some of these older folks— actually he saw no one who was over 45—could get pretty passionate indeed. A man with smooth silver hair and a black eyepatch was nibbling on the neck of his buxom dance partner. And over in one corner a black man and woman were practically performing throat surgery on each other with their tongues.

He asked for a whiskey sour.

Ahh, it tasted good. Not as good as Brian's, but good.

If only his father had been able to control his drinking, he thought, he would have found out what he was missing. All he'd ever had, could ever afford, was cheap pisswater, just lousy, stale, flat beer from Chester's barrels–

Why was he remembering all this?

—or in bottles. Pisswater. With all the alcohol that man consumed, Tommy bet he'd never had a single *decent* drink in his life. He'd been addicted to the ultimate, numbing buzz, and had never learned to appreciate a drink's finer qualities: how good an excellent wine could taste; the sweet, rugged sting of bourbon; snifting and drinking rich, aromatic brandy out of large glass goblets; fruity daiquiris, dry martinis, the sheer sensuousness of a good whiskey sour. Thomas was glad he was able to enjoy liquor without becoming its slave as his father had.

Thomas knew alcoholism wasn't necessarily genetic. He also knew, objectively, that he was neither an alcoholic nor in serious danger of becoming one. But ever since he'd opened Parmenter's by the bay he'd been having more dreams and remembering more of his past (*except* for that night!) and he found himself reaching for a drink more often than he wanted to. He was not exactly in danger of ruining his liver, but he found he needed a tranquilizer more often than he'd ever needed one before.

He went downstairs to look for Elsa.

When he found her, she was standing with a group of several people, clutching the arm of a somewhat portly man with full, feminine lips and a receding hairline. Walter Langley? No, couldn't be. He wasn't wearing "funny eyeglasses."

Elsa smiled when she saw Tommy. That was a relief; he would not be intruding.

"Here he is! Tom, this is my cousin Everett. Everett Sloan, meet Thomas Bartlett."

Cousin Everett turned out to be a pleasant, bubbling fellow with a good sense of humor. "Parmenter's, eh? I've been there. Lovely place, lovely place. Some of the best seafood in town."

Thomas beamed. "You're not a restaurant critic, are you?"

Everett smiled. "You don't need any more rave reviews; every one that I've read has been terrific. And rightly so."

They chatted a bit more, and Thomas asked Elsa, "Seen Madonna yet?"

She smirked. "It wasn't Madonna. Just some broad from New Jersey with a wig and a beauty spot." The silly way Elsa was smiling it was clear she'd had a couple more gin and tonics while he'd been searching for her.

"Let's dance," she said abruptly.

While they boogied to Robert Palmer and Tina Turner songs on the dance floor, he tried to forget that he'd been hoping to ditch her with some handsome record executive. "I hope all this stomping doesn't make the boat sink," Elsa said.

"It was your idea to come here. Meet our host yet?"

She shook her head. "He's supposed to be in one of the cabins with some private guests. He throws these things, then ducks out of sight with a few close friends. Can't say I blame him."

They finished dancing, and Everett shoved another whiskey sour into his hand. He had another one, quickly, afterwards; he had never in his life gotten drunk, or even very high before, and he wasn't sure if he loved it or hated it. It was intoxicating, of course, in every sense of the word. Liberating, too. And…what else? His mother's voice was slowly receding into the din.

Tommy looked around him and saw that nearly everyone was high. A man nearby had some white speckles on his brown mustache. Elsa whispered that a lot of the guests were into drugs. "I don't mix," she said, tapping her glass of gin with her fingers. He leaned up—she was wearing heels—and planted a sloppy kiss on her lips.

"Why, Thomas, are you high?"

He giggled. "Yes. And loving it. No wonder my father got drunk all the time."

"Thomas, you *are* high. You never talk about your father. C'mon, let's dance some more."

The party was really in high gear by 2:00 A.M. The sound of laughter, conversation, boozy giggles and playful screeches all but drowned out the music of the band. Thomas had danced with Elsa, Everett's wife, even Everett at one point, as well as a host of attractive younger women, while Elsa had gone from room to room, deck to deck, starting up conversations with a variety of strangers. She said she'd made a few "connections," collected phone numbers and business cards. "I'll make a few calls next week," she said brightly. "Who knows what will happen?" Wait'll those connections found out Elsa was a folk singer, Thomas thought.

The bunch Thomas found himself in (he thought of another bunch from another time but couldn't recall who they were or what the words "The Bunch" even signified) consisted of himself, Elsa, Everett and Everett's wife, as well as a young man stripped to the waist with a dragon tattoo on his belly, his bride, who had gold hair cropped so close to her scalp that from a distance she appeared to be bald, and two older women who claimed to be sisters and who wore identical bikinis in which they looked rather ridiculous. Wanting to escape the racket and the oppressive heat, The Bunch moved en masse upstairs to the open air where they had some champagne, sang fanny songs, and traded messy, good-natured kisses.

Thomas was having a ball.

He couldn't quite recall the last hour or so, but he did eventually find himself with Elsa and several others riding in one of the launches back to the dock. "Is the party over?" he asked Elsa.

"All over," she said, waving her empty plastic champagne glass and smiling dopily.

They started singing and dancing again in the launch. As it approached the dock, someone gave Thomas a friendly shove and he banged into the side of the boat. He was still laughing as he tottered, lost his balance, and fell over into the water.

"Tommy!"

The water closed over his head.

Black, murky, dragon eyes, terror, mother's screams, father's arms, drunken beatings, blood and death and more blood, the massive tail, the enormous head, the teeth, the eyes, oh God, the face...

He was pulled up out of the water by strong hands and deposited on the pier.

Elsa was bending over him. "Tommy, Tommy, honey. Are you all right?"

"Help me. *Help me!*" he screamed. "Get me out of the water! It's in the water! My father tried to save me! Its *leg!* Got to get out of the water. *Get out of the water!*"

Elsa stared down at him in shock.

Thomas Bartlett had remembered!

CHAPTER SIX
THE TRIP BACK TO SUMMERDALE

Thomas Bartlett turned right onto the exit lane and started on the final leg of his journey into the past.

How long had it been, he asked himself, since he'd seen Summerdale? He hadn't been back since his parents died, over 30 years ago. Three decades had gone by and he wondered what time had wrought to the town he'd been born in. Was Summerdale still there? Had it, too, been washed away with the tide like its poor suburb, Beachside, had been in 1957? Would he recognize any of it, remember anything at all?

He had remembered so much last Friday, the night he'd gone to the yacht with Elsa and fallen off the launch into the water. Somehow the combination of being immersed in the ocean and being inebriated had set off an alarm and broken through the psychic barriers in his head. All these disjointed... memories...came rushing back at him—*memories of something monstrous and inhuman.*

Of course, after being calmed down by Elsa, taken to her apartment where he slept for hours and awakened with an awful hangover, after having coffee, toast and orange juice and looking at things in the cold light of day, he had almost convinced himself that his memories were strictly from old horror films, not from life. Time gave distance to everything; time made everything that had once seemed so sharp and vivid seem suddenly pale and fragile, like his memories. *He saw The Beast through the window again as it emerged from the sea remembered running for his mother's room, seeing the—my God, it had to be the creature's leg in front of him!—the walls falling down, tumbling through the trap door, his father's hand, struggling, struggling to pull him free.* And then?

Something huge behind—no—above—his father, an enormous eye, hot, fetid breath, then...

...nothing. His father was gone.

It had happened.

But it must have happened differently. His memories of the storm that had wiped Beachside off the face of the earth had blended with the memories of the monster movies he loved in childhood and somehow had become absurdly connected inside his mind. That was the only explanation. His father had been snatched away by a wave, not by the mouth of some mythical sea beast. There were no such creatures. They simply did not exist as much as he might have wished they did when he'd been younger. His memory was faulty— part truth, part schoolboy imagination. It was all fantasy, except for the basic, undeniable truth that Beachside had been instantly, utterly obliterated.

Perhaps, once he set foot in Summerdale again, he might start to remember more.

The vague image of The Beast would simply not go away.

He drove his sensible Ford down the road toward town, past motels that had sprung up out of nowhere, vegetable and fruit stands, kids riding bikes and walking dogs. The closer he got to town, the shabbier things became. This was not the Summerdale he remembered, was it?

He sped past the sign: "Now Entering Summerdale."

When he was a child, he slowly remembered that the roads to and from Summerdale had been barren, infrequently punctuated by motels and restaurants. But now he saw a multitude of buildings and businesses on either side of him—gift shops, Carvels, diners, hamburger joints, pizza parlors. What the hell had happened? The population must have multiplied since 1957.

He turned a corner and drove into Main Street.

And realized he'd entered a slum.

It appeared that Beachside had gotten its revenge.

Just one glance told the story. Summerdale was dying. There were more people living there, but the town was in its death throes. The poor people now vastly outnumbered the affluent, so that even the so-called better parts of town were home to what would have at one time been called a "disreputable element." Yes, the poor people had grown in numbers and the affluent had fled, leaving Summerdale in the hands of the out-of-work, the shiftless, the welfare cases, the unemployable. The parks along Main Street, which had once been so pretty, so beautifully kept up with their trimly mowed lawns and luscious flowers, were now wastelands of overturned benches and shattered birdbaths. Garbage was scattered across vacant fields of weeds. Half of the shops in the square had shut down, were boarded up, or had broken windows. Abandoned cars, some of which must have been set on fire at some point, were lining the street.

Summerdale was a slum.

He drove on down the main thoroughfare, having no desire to get out and walk around. What he saw from the car was bad enough.

Yes, the story was obvious. It was a simple question of economics, he supposed. Some towns prospered; others declined. Summerdale had never been home to any strong industries. He remembered how back in the 50's, there'd been talk of building it up into another Miami Beach or Fort Lauderdale, attracting all those tourist dollars, but apparently it hadn't happened. The rich would have gone to the better towns to merrily bask in prestige and elegance. The poor would have done what the poor always did—multiplied, driving out the rich ones who'd stayed behind. The whole town had the look of something that had gone to seed. Poor people had too much on their minds to make sure that lawns were cut, that houses were painted. They were too worried about where the next meal was coming from. The depression and futility first showed on a person's face, then spread out to infect the whole look of the community, the whole physical structure of a city.

Sad but true: Summerdale was terminal.

He kept on driving out to where Beachside used to be and got an even bigger shock.

This time he parked the car along the road and got out on foot.

Where once there had been unobstructed sea and shining sand, there was now only upscale condominiums, a series of huge highrise buildings built for the retired or vacationing. The beach itself had been reduced to a mere sliver between parking lot and ocean. Past the fences that kept out the riffraff, Thomas could see community pools, tennis courts, playgrounds, parks, even stables. He could imagine how much it cost to live here. He looked up at a metal plate attached to the fence near the driveway and read:

WELCOME TO BEACHSIDE VACATION RESORT AND YEAR-ROUND CONDOMINIUMS.

And in smaller print underneath:

BRONMORE ENTERPRISER INC.

Apparently one could either rent for a week or two, a season, or could live there all year. He went over to the gatehouse and received a welcoming nod from the guard who probably assumed Thomas was there to either visit somebody or to inquire as to the availability of units. As he walked he saw green, fresh grass and multi-hued flowerbeds like those that had once adorned the streets of Summerdale.

Yes, Beachside had had the last laugh, all right. Or had it? Everyone who'd once lived in Beachside was dead. The people living here were imposters who probably didn't even know about the disaster of '57. And probably wouldn't care, if they did.

The first building he approached had an office for Bronmore Enterprises off the lobby, but he decided to just keep walking around the grounds. There was nothing left of the community he'd once lived in—no tents, no shacks, no shanties, no houses-on-stilts all in a row facing the sea. No children. None of The Bunch. *(The Bunch?)* Nothing. Everything was gone. There was hardly any beach left, either. He went around the corner of one towering highrise and saw kids and grownups frolicking in the sand and in the water with several lifeguards watching over them.

Beachside had never had a lifeguard.

He felt his eyes tearing, and he knew why. He was thinking of how the value of human life was judged not by compassion, intelligence or worthiness, but by family background and financial status. These rich people got lifeguards; Beachside's original residents had only gotten callousness and death.

He wiped his eyes. Wouldn't Elsa be pleased? He was thinking like her now. They literally had spent hours arguing about the state of the world, he berating her for her naivety and misplaced idealism and she berating him for his affluence and indifference. But when it came down to brass tacks he could see where she was coming from. After all, he had come from nothing, a poor kid with a drunk for a father; while Elsa had actually come from the middle-class. But as Thomas had told her, he had pulled himself up by his bootstraps until he was rich and successful. ("Having a wealthy aunt and uncle as guardians didn't hurt any, though, did it, Tommy?" she'd said.)

Well, why then did he not feel a kinship with these new affluent Beachsiders? He had always hated the original Beachsiders, thought of them as losers, vowed he would go away from Beachside and never set foot in it again. Yet he felt no rapport with these new, wealthier residents.

Still, he had known the original Beachsiders.

But they were dead.

And Thomas was living—the only survivor.

God, how it chilled him. The *only* survivor!

Something hit him then: *The man with the eyes.* Now, what did that mean? He kept getting these odd flashes, which were growing more intense the longer he stayed in Summerdale, flashes of things that made no sense. *The man with the eyes. A lake. A house on a hill with a winding staircase. A trembling in the woods.*

What did it all mean?

He had hoped to remember something this afternoon by walking through the town to the old haunts, strolling along the beach and between the houses as he'd done as a boy. But now there was no point. Nothing was the same. The old haunts were gone. Why bother looking for that candy store on Mott Street where he'd bought his comic books? Mott Street was no longer the same. Why walk along the beach when it really was not the same beach as the one he'd loved so much as a child? Why stay in Beachside a minute longer when it was not the Beachside he remembered?

Funny how things change. The town was now a slum; the slum was Mecca.

He could see what had happened. At first, when

Bronmore's development was announced, the town must have breathed a sigh of relief. Summerdale was saved! They must have thought of all the jobs that would open up, the large labor force the new Beachside would require. But things hadn't worked out that way. Contracts were awarded to out of town contractors. Outsiders were hired as laborers. With its own shops, pools, stable, beauty parlors, barbers and bars, the new Beachside was entirely self-sufficient. The residents and temporary guests didn't even have to leave the grounds. Sure, many of Summerdale's people were hired to work in those shops, beauty parlors, what-have-you, but Summerdale's own shops, its entire downtown district, suddenly found that the flow of tourists and dollars they'd been expecting was nowhere to be found. And with Summerdale's own affluent residents departing the town in droves, the buying slackened off and the economy nosedived.

The result was the death of Summerdale.

He stepped into a coffee shop in Beachside and had a sandwich and a malted. Not as good as the ones he'd had infrequently at Bobbie's soda shoppe on Downy Street (next to Chester's Bar and Grill; good old Chester's), but decent. As he sipped the malted he kept wondering: *the man with the eyes; the lost sea (a black lake); a house with a winding outdoor staircase.* And a pathway through the forest that led to the lake, to the house, and ultimately to the man with the eyes.

Had the man something to do with Beachside's last night of existence?

He paid the check and set out to discover if the path was still there.

* * *

It was there, way up the shore past the new developments, past the sand dunes, behind a tennis court. After 30 years the path was still there. Other children must have discovered it, kept it open, walked back and forth from the lake to their apartments, beating down the brush and the dirt with their feet. Had other kids turned up missing, too, as they supposedly had back in the 50's? Was the house still there?

Was The Man still there?

He couldn't believe how easily he had found it; his memory was really beginning to return to him now. And though he felt some fear and apprehension as he stepped into the woods and began what he knew would be a long, long walk (not that he had anything else to do), he also felt relief that he was walking away, far away, from the ocean and from Beachside.

He felt somewhat foolish walking into the woods wearing good shoes and a pair of nice black slacks, his tan jacket thrown over his shoulder in case it turned chilly, but he was not about to stop now. He had to see if his memory was faulty or not, had to see if at the end of this path there really was a lake and a house—and a man. if that was all true, was everything else true, too?

No, there are no monsters in this world.

He walked.

The forest was cool and a little bit wet from a recent rainfall. He brushed past large overhanging leaves and swatted away mosquitoes (as he had done *that* day) and looked above his head to see branches and leaves and the occasional bird.

Odd—he had forgotten his watch and left it on the dresser this morning. That day, 31 years ago, he had also been without a watch and wished he'd had one. He didn't know how long it had taken, but he arrived sooner than expected. Of course, man-sized strides covered a lot more territory than those of a small boy —though he was not that much taller—and he *had* been here before. He was standing at the edge of a long black lake with tranquil water, standing between two large green bushes that almost hid the water entirely from view until you were practically in it.

He looked across the water and looked up.

There was the house...just as he remembered it?

There was the house...and another and another, and over there, another one, and another on this side of the lake, to his right, and another on this side of the lake to his left...and another and another.

The lakefront was full of houses, not old houses like the one he'd seen 30 years ago—that was gone —but newer houses with white walls and driveways and screened-in porches and kids and dogs and mothers and fathers.

It was another development.

The lake wasn't scary anymore. It was homey. The old house, the forest in the vicinity, had been razed to the ground, and all of these homes constructed. Some were split-level, some were just cabins; others were year-round fortified dream homes with solar panels and metal security shutters. They had come into the woods and turned this spooky wonderful place of nightmares and fantasies into just another garden variety suburb.

Thomas was relieved; Thomas was disgusted. The dock with the rowboat was gone, though some of the homes had their own docks and their own boats or canoes, and in front of one house quite a distance away a bunch of kids *(The Bunch?)* were swimming.

Why was he so disappointed? Because now he would not have the proof he felt he needed, the proof of that old house's long ago existence? He knew there was no point in asking any of the people who lived here about it. Like Beachside, these houses were new to him but they were not really new— they'd been erected, like Beachside, in the early 60's probably.

To think that all that time had passed. It seemed it had only been yesterday he had been rowing across the water to an old house with a porch and winding staircase and a strange man with deep eyes watching him as he ran into the woods.

A lifetime had passed since the last time he'd been here. His lifetime, and so many others.

This explained why the path he was on was still worn smooth after 30 years. Kids who lived on the lake had probably discovered it by accident, discovered that it was a shortcut to Beachside, and hence into town.

He stood there with the sun streaming into his eyes and tried to remember what had happened that day, and he thought he could recall most of it. The Bunch —*a group of kids! Yes!*—had taken him into the woods with them; they'd gone to the lake, and he'd wanted to cross it to explore the old house, but no one had gone with him. He recalled, as if it were something he'd read a long time ago, traversing the lake in a rowboat, looking back to see that the kids had left him behind, going on ahead anyway, running into The Man, running into the woods, following the stream to the coast road, walking home.

His parents had had a fight. He had gone to his bedroom, cried himself to sleep, awakened, gone to the window...

Yes, yes, yes, yes, it had happened...

But it couldn't have...

He sank to his knees, trembling and crying.

And he felt the grief and the rage and the fear all over again for the first time in 31 years.

* * *

The drive back to Miami was uneventful. Thomas did his best to concentrate on the highway and block out the grim and macabre thoughts he'd been having since returning to Summerdale. Such a pathetic waste of a town. He went straight to his apartment and his bed after having a hasty lunch of eggs and salad. He couldn't understand why he was feeling so fatigued, unless it had to do with his depression and confusion that had been brought on by the return—albeit hazy, unfocused, more shadow than substance—of his memories.

He almost wished he had remembered nothing.

Evening came, and he still didn't feel like getting out of bed. He wasn't even sleeping, just lying there in a vague semi-conscious state, frequently changing positions, his mind awash in a tumultuous sea of thoughts and fragments of conversations, scenes from years ago replaying on his eyeballs with seemingly little rhyme or reason.

Now and then he'd see the eyes of a Great Beast.

He woke to the sound of the telephone. Too exhausted to answer, he stayed in bed listening to it ring and ring and ring.

Elsa, probably. Should never have left her alone in Miami with Joseph.

Relax, he told himself. What could happen? Elsa was loyal and faithful, even if Joseph wasn't.

He pulled himself out of bed at midnight to take a leak and have another little snack. Such fatigue was almost frightening. He'd told both Elsa and Joseph that he might be gone for a couple of days so there was really no reason to contact them. Parmenter's would run smoothly without his presence.

His mouth tasted awful, so he went to the bathroom to brush his teeth. As he rinsed his mouth his eyes caught their reflected image in the mirror and he was struck by the sudden realization that he looked rather awful-very pale, hair a tangled mess, strands flying in all directions, hollow eyes, haunted eyes.

He went back to bed. Whether Elsa had slept with Joseph or not seemed terribly unimportant in the light of the things he'd remembered. Perhaps that was why he needed to make it important, to help him make it back to the real world, to forget what he had remembered.

As he wavered on the edges of consciousness, he wondered about the past. Even if a great beast *had* come up on the shore, surely it must be dead by now? Nothing would bring those people back from their watery grave. What was there to do? It was a long, long time ago.

But as sleep finally overtook him he knew he would have to find out once and for all what had actually, truly happened that night in all its terrible and disgusting detail. Otherwise, he'd never have any peace.

For it hadn't been just an animal.

For what kind of animal has that kind of eyes?

Eyes that burned with intelligence and fury, a disarming, cold dispassion.

Eyes like those of the man who watched as he was put into the ambulance.

Eyes that, strangely, terribly, had the touch of something human about them.

* * *

Off the coast of Boca Raton, Sally saw that the boat was getting farther and farther from the shore and she was getting worried. She had only come out on Terence's Sweet Louella with him because he'd promised her he'd not go too far out to sea. She was not crazy, like he was, about the ocean or sailing or anything about the water. Sally couldn't even swim. So she clung to the orange life jacket she wore as if it were a parachute and she were streaming through the air at 100 miles an hour.

She swept her long black hair out of her eyes and hollered into the cabin where Terence was getting beers out of the fridge. "Terence, I think we're drifting too far. Terence, I don't like this."

The boy popped out of the cabin and strode over to her side with an open can of beer in his hand, offering it to her. "What's the matter?"

"The shore is getting farther and farther away." She took a sip of the beer. "And I'm chilly."

"Let's go in the cabin then."

"Uh-uh." She knew better than that. Not only would Terence put the make on her but they might drift miles out to sea without either of them even realizing it. "Can't you drop anchor?" she asked.

Terence let out with a laugh that seemed more like a sneer. "All right. But we're not that far out and there's no current. I like to drift."

"What about the wind?" she reminded him. "Can't that push us out farther than we want to go?"

He shrugged. At 19, Terence was one year older than Sally. She had to admit he was attractive, with his dark, wavy hair and those deep blue eyes. Sally knew she was fairly pretty but wondered what he saw in her. The thought of making love to him one of these days made her feel all tingly inside, but she just wasn't ready yet, and that was that. She had no desire to be just another notch on his belt, although she wondered if he was really as experienced as he pretended.

He was very proud of *Sweet Louella*, which he had saved up to buy with his own money, and which he had named after one of his favorite New Wave rock songs. It was an attractive little thing, she had to admit, 32 feet from stem to stern, painted a pretty green color with the yellow letters *Sweet Louella* done in a fancy script by a professional painter friend of his. Sally had never had the slightest inclination to own a boat, though she guessed some boys felt kind of macho behind the wheel of one. At least he had respected her wishes and kept the speed down as they plowed through the water. The thought of crashing into something, or her falling into the water even with her life jacket on, was enough to send her into a panic.

Terence came back and sat down beside her, snuggling in to rub her cheek affectionately with his nose. She smiled. His breath smelled of fresh beer, but so did hers, and she sure hoped he'd try for a kiss. Instead he pulled away and took another sip of beer. "We won't drift," he said a moment later, wiping his lips with the back of his hand. "Aren't the lights on shore pretty?"

"Real pretty," Sally admitted, letting herself sort of fall sideways until her body was resting against his own. Now if only he'd put his arms around her. Perhaps if she mentioned how chilly it was again? No—then he'd try and get her into the cabin and into one of those bunk beds. And it was too soon for that.

"We're not in the Bermuda Triangle, are we?" she asked, just to make conversation.

Terence snorted. "That's a tub of bullshit. Do you realize how many of those alleged disappearances have been explained away normally?"

"I guess so," Sally said, hating herself for agreeing, when she really felt differently. She had to stop being afraid of what other people thought. Anyway, it seemed to her that the books she'd read on the whole affair were equally inconclusive. One camp would say: "The boat disappeared with all hands. Yes, it was a stormy night that night, but it could have been a victim of the Bermuda Triangle." While the other camp would take the same incident and say, "Well, yes, it's odd that there was no wreckage found and no survivors, no radio messages calling for help—but it *was* a stormy night that night." It was two sides of the same coin, each side saying the same thing but placing the emphasis elsewhere, thereby arriving at opposite conclusions.

It was scary. The thought of just…disappearing like that without a trace.

There was a full moon tonight, and it made the ocean look like a fairyland, like a ghost dimension full of pale wriggling things and the darker shadows they hid in. The aroma of the sea was pungent and almost intoxicating, and the gentle rise and fall, rise and fall, of the waves nearly had a hypnotic effect on her. She looked around her, out at the water, at the calm blackness of the sea, and wondered what might lay hidden beneath that blackness. The lights from the boat glittered across the water but only reflected the surface; they did not illuminate below the surface. Why, something could be down there even now...

She looked over at the vast distance of the ocean stretching endlessly into the night. Anything could be out there.

Then she glanced over at the shore again, with its comfortable lights and houses. But they were so far out...

"Terence?"

"What, babe?"

"Maybe we'd better go back."

He looked at her for a second, and she braced herself for an argument.

"You sure?"

"Uh, yes, I'm...It's spooky out here."

He laughed. "Yeah, I know what you mean. I love it out here myself, but not when I'm alone. Not at night." He sighed and gave her a squeeze. "I'm glad you came with me tonight, Sally."

He was a nice boy, and Sally was filled with that youthful certainty that he would fall in love with her just as she was now sure she was falling in love with him. They'd have a wonderful, long, happy life together.

The next second the boat shook as it caught in a riptide.

"Terence!"

Before either of them had a chance to react, there was water pouring over the side of the boat. It gushed over the railings to engulf them as the boat was *pulled down* from below. Sally screamed. My God, what was happening?

The ship's underwater lights, set in the hull, were still shining, illuminating the scene as Sally felt her breath torn away from her and panic and water filled her to the core. In her last brief seconds she saw that the boat, now fully underwater, was caught in a large conduit with reddish walls, and from those walls there emerged sharp yellow objects that seemed to grow out of the walls and tapered to a point at the end. Terence, struggling, was a few feet away from her, caught, suspended, between two of those yellow, pointy objects.

"Oh, my God, they're *teeth*," she thought as the conduit narrowed and consciousness ended.

CHAPTER SEVEN

GARGANTOSAURUS

Lemuel Harriman had never been more excited in his life.

As he took his shower he repeated names over and over again in his mind. Thundersaurus, Gargantosaurus, Gigantosaurus, Humongosaurus...which was the right one? He wanted to have just the right name when he announced the discovery at the press conference. This could possibly be the find of the century—at least in his field. He had to remember that not everyone was fascinated by dinosaurs.

In 1983 two tourists from Virginia were hiking in the Arizona desert when they stumbled upon huge bones sticking out of a crevice. News of the bones was brought to Harriman, the curator of paleontology at the Arizona Museum of Natural History, but it was not until 1987 that a team of researchers could be gathered together to remove some of the bones from the site. Harriman waited patiently, excitedly, while some bones were retrieved from the ground and measured and scrutinized. Now the verdict was finally in. These bones came from what had to have been the largest dinosaur yet found by paleontologists! A dinosaur of positively stupendous proportions!

It was in the summer of 1986 that the last announcement

regarding the discovery of a new dinosaur had been made. Then it had been Seismosaurus, christened such by the curator of paleontology at the New Mexico Museum of Natural History. Before that, the Supersaurus, evidence of which had been discovered in western Colorado in 1973. Supersauris weighed 60 to 70 tons, was 80 to 100 feet long, and was 25 feet high at the shoulder and 15 at the hip. Seismosaurus weighed 80 to 100 tons, was 100 to 120 feet long, and was 18 feet high at the shoulder and 15 feet high at the hip.

By all indications, this new dinosaur incredibly weighed over 200 tons, was nearly 250 long, and was 80 feet high at the shoulder and 60 feet high at the hip!

Decidedly it was the largest dinosaur that had ever lived.

This one, which Harriman finally decided to christen Gargantosaurus, was quite different in structure from Seismosauris and Supersaurus, which were similar in shape to Apotosaurus (Brontosaurus) and Diplodocus, long, slender, planteating dinosaurs with graceful necks, tapering tails, and comparatively tiny heads. On the contrary, Gargantosaurus was almost crocodilian in shape. It had a much bigger bulk all around with thicker legs, a heavier, shorter neck, a much bigger head and jaw, and a shorter but more massive tail with over 53 vertebrae. Its feet were its largest feature—over 40 feet long—somewhat out of proportion to the rest of the beast, assuming they had not attached the wrong bones to the rest of the skeleton. Harriman and his team were sure from the shape and size of its teeth, some of which had been dug up, that it had to be a carnivore. It was at least 30 times as large as a jumbo African elephant and outweighed a blue whale by 100 tons. No wonder the paleontologists had waited so long, checking and verifying, before letting this out to the rest of the scientific community and the public.

Gargantosaurus!

Sounds like a horror movie, Harriman mused, drying himself off with a towel. Should have just called it Godzilla, though Gargantosaurus walked on all fours, not on two legs like the Japanese movie monster. As tall as Gargantosaurus was, it wouldn't tower over skyscrapers not even while standing on its hind legs.

No, Gargantosaurus was not a fictional monstrosity. Though looking at the artist's conception of it walking about made Lemuel shudder. Imagine having that thing walking about today—and being in its path! Imagine those gigantic jaws, those massive teeth, bearing down on you, opening, swallowing you whole or grinding you to bits and pieces.

As he put the towel back on the rack, he shook his head. He had too vivid an imagination.

Still, what could be worse than being eaten alive?

Knowing it was happening to you, he supposed.

He again wondered if it were possible that some of these prehistoric creatures had managed to survive to modern times. He knew his colleagues would laugh at the notion— they were, by and large, a humorless lot—just as he knew they themselves must have surely entertained the very same thought at some point in time. Imagine! Prehistoric animals alive in the world today! That might explain all those sea monster sightings, the lost ships in the Bermuda Triangle and elsewhere, even the Loch Ness monster.

But no, he shook his head sadly, that was just the stuff of fantasy. He'd leave that sort of thing to his more imaginative cousin, Roderick Thorson, and to all the rather batty, if romantic, cryptozoologists who roamed the world investigating alleged evidence of living monsters.

Besides, would anyone in their right mind really want to come face to face with, say, a Tyrannosaurus Rex?

Or a Gargantosaurus?

He smiled proudly and went into his bedroom to dress.

* * *

While it certainly could not be called the biggest shock of his life, it had to be in the top ten.

Thomas finally got out of bed to go down to Parmenter's, looking forward to having an nice lunch and perhaps a long-delayed chat with his partner, all the while wondering if Joseph had used his absence to make his move on Elsa. When he got to the restaurant he not only knew that Joseph had made his move, but that Elsa had not exactly resisted.

There was a billboard put up on the sidewalk directly outside the entrance.

BEGINNING TONIGHT. LIVE ENTERTAINMENT.

Under an 8 x 10 glossy of Elsa were the words: *For your listening pleasure Parmenter's proudly presents the musical magic of Elsa Freemont.*

Thomas just stood there, staring.

After all the things Joseph had said to Thomas, after all the things Thomas had said to Elsa, Joseph was actually going to let Elsa sing!

That must have been *some* audition, he thought.

As he walked through the foyer and headed for the bar, he realized he was probably more angry at himself than at anyone else. He should have put his foot down and had it out with Joseph, before leaving for Summerdale. He should have made it clear to Elsa that he did not want her meeting with Joseph for any purpose whatsoever. In the first place he should have told Elsa that he himself was not particularly interested in having her sing in the restaurant, but he had passed the buck to Joseph, refusing to tell Elsa upfront how he felt. And this was what happened because of it.

Brian, who had cut his hair in a punk style that did nothing for his rather bony face, looked a bit sheepish as he mixed Thomas a martini. (Whiskey sours for good or indifferent moods; martinis for lousy ones.) Brian probably knew what had been going on. With Thomas out of town, in all likelihood Joseph had hit on Elsa at the bar before bringing her to his apartment to continue the "meeting," to work out "formalities." Did he promise her an engagement at Parmenter's to get her into bed, or offer it to her afterward as a way of saying "thank you?" Elsa could be an extremely good lover when the mood was right. Was Joseph going to appropriate Thomas' girlfriend? And was Elsa meeting Joseph more than halfway?

Thomas had barely finished his first sip of the martini when Joseph walked in the front door waving and smiling. Brian went discreetly to a corner to dry some glasses.

"Hello, Thomas," Joseph said, slapping his partner on the back. He told Brian to give him a cola.

"Hello, Joseph." Thomas decided it would be best to lead into it gradually, checking his temper until he was absolutely sure of all his facts. "Would you do me a big favor, and tell me what this is all about?"

"What's that?"

Thomas indicated the billboard, the back of which could be seen through the window. "That. Elsa. Singing here. When we both know you were dead set against the idea when I first brought it up to you. What happened to change your mind, Joseph?"

Joseph shrugged. "I heard her sing, knew she was a friend of yours and thought I'd do the both of you a favor."

"A favor? For me?"

"She's your girl, right?"

"Is she?"

Brian handed Joseph the cola and retreated to his neutral corner.

"Do you really think it's a good idea?" Thomas asked. "After all your initial objections? Where did you hear Elsa sing?"

"Up at my...at some bar she was in. What difference does it make? She's good. I hired her. I thought it would please you."

"When did you work out...the details?"

Joseph wiggled the swizzle stick around in his glass. "We had a drink. Talked about money and material."

"She does protest songs, you know. Folk songs."

"Well, that's what we talked about. She's gonna do a whole new routine. I told her what I wanted. Nothin' heavy. A little Streisand, some Sinatra. Broadway show tunes. Nice listening music. I told her not to expect much. This is a restaurant, not a theater. But she seemed pleased." He took a sip of the cola and added, "I thought you would be, too."

"Streisand, Sinatra? Show tunes? Is this the same Elsa we're talking about?" But what he wanted to say—what he knew he would eventually have to say—was *have you been making love to my girlfriend*? "I thought we were partners, Joseph. I thought neither of us made a decision without checking with the other."

Surprisingly, it was Joseph who was getting hot under the collar. Out of guilt, perhaps? Nervousness? "You're the one who wanted her here," he said sharply. "She's your chick, not mine. I thought you wanted her singing here. Why should I have to check with you? You brought up the whole idea!"

"You changed your mind awfully quickly, Joseph."

"She's your girlfriend. I wanted to be nice."

"There are ways of being nice and there are ways of being nice. How nice was Elsa, huh? Was she nice? Is that why she's debuting at Parmenter's tonight? Because she was nice to you, you sleazeball?"

"Hey, you got no right to talk to me that way!"

"No right! I got every right in the world!" Suddenly furious, Thomas picked up his martini and threw the glass onto the floor. Liquid splashed out, while the glass, unbroken, rolled back and forth across the floor in a lengthy arc.

Thomas glared at a startled Joseph for a full ten seconds, then stormed out the door.

* * *

Elsa wasn't home at 1:00, 2:00, or 3:00. Did Joseph call her and tell her to rush to his side? Thomas wondered. Finally at 3:00 she answered the phone.

"Hello." She sounded harried.

"It's Thomas. Remember me?"

"Hi, Tom." Thomas looked for clues in her voice but couldn't find any. She merely sounded out of breath.

He wasted no time on formalities. "What's this about your singing at Parmenter's?"

"Yeah. Isn't it great?" But her enthusiasm seemed slightly subdued.

"Is it?"

"Of course it is, silly. I mean, I know it's not a big night-club or anything, but it's a start, right? And I have you to thank."

"Me?"

"Yeah, for bringing up my singing there to Joey. He was crazy about the idea. Did you see my picture out front?"

"Yes, but—"

"I can't talk right now; I'm getting ready. He wants me to sing during the six to eight supper hours. Twenty minutes on, twenty minutes off. Then I'll do a show for the late crowd, just like at a piano bar. I've got this guy accompanying me, a handsome blond pianist. I've got so many things to do. I'm still not sure what I'm going to wear."

Now she sounded excited and happy, and it was a happiness he did not want to spoil, even though he did not see how this could be anything but a disaster. He wanted to ask her what she had done to get Joseph to speed things up, but now was not the time. Besides, there was always the possibility that he was wrong in what he was thinking.

But, of course, he knew he wasn't.

"Relax, El', I'm sure everything will be fine."

"Wish me luck. Wish I could talk longer, but I'm getting desperate. If I don't get just the right ensemble…"

"Wait. What about the material? Did Joseph go over your material?"

"Yes. We talked it all out, uh, over drinks. Don't worry. I know what he wants. Got to go now. Bye."

I know what he wants. Sure, she did. She knew what he wanted and she gave it to him. And she got what she wanted, too.

He hung up the phone and went to sit down on his sofa, leaning over and kneading his forehead with his hands. He felt like he was losing control—control of his life, of his restaurant. He tried to console himself with the knowledge that Joseph was hardly his best friend, and he and Elsa had never become that serious an item, but it still hurt. Did it offend his pride more than anything else? Or did he really care for Elsa? If he didn't, then why make a fuss? Joseph had just acted true to form, after all. Still, it was partly Thomas' restaurant, and he was damned if he'd just sit still while things like this went on behind his back. This wasn't Just something personal now; it affected his livelihood. Although he knew Elsa's voice wasn't exactly bad enough to send patrons running for the exits, he also knew that unless she made drastic changes in her act she would not do much for the business.

He would give her a chance and go to her debut tonight.

After all, it was still his restaurant.

* * *

In Huddington Beach, Florida, Mary Margaret turned the truck onto the road the led out to her father's property and adjusted the dial on the radio. She hated that soul music. Another twist of the dial and she heard a symphony that almost blasted her out of her seat. No way. She had no interest either in that classical shit. She finally got a Jazz station and smiled contentedly. This would do nicely for the 20 minutes or so it would take her to get to her father's property.

Mary Margaret Johnstone was a plain woman of 38 who wore coveralls and had curly brown hair and chubby cheeks. Her father lived on several acres on the outskirts of Huddington that were located about halfway between Miami and Summerdale. He was miles away from town and that was just the way he liked it. Her father had turned into a real misanthrope since her mother had died, letting the property go to seed and living off his pension and social security. It had been a working farm when Mary Margaret had been a child, but as her parents got older and more tired they just didn't have the strength or inclination to keep it up. And Mary Margaret, since she'd moved in with her fella Jim Keller in Sireville, had no desire to work the place either.

Dad didn't care. All he did during her frequent visits was ask when "that bum" of hers was going to marry her, as if he could care as long as she stayed out of his hair and came to see him now and then. He didn't really want her living on the farm with him. He had always liked to be alone, even when her mother was alive, which was part of the reason Mother had never come out of the hospital after the operation and why Mary Margaret had been surprised to see her father mourn her so intensely. But you could never really tell about people.

But that was then. Five years ago. Her father was 73 and in pretty good shape for a man his age. In her mind she could see him now, stepping out of the house, porch door slamming, as she drove into the yard and honked her horn.

But what greeted her this afternoon in reality was an entirely different scenario.

Devastation!

Mary Margaret put her foot on the brake. The truck, raising up dust like a midget cyclone, squealed to a halt half in and half out of the open gate entranceway.

"My God!"

For several moments Mary Margaret just sat there, looking

around, wondering what on earth could have happened. She took in everything little by little.

First of all, there was that flattened metal rectangle lying there at the side of the house where her father's old truck used to be. That couldn't be the truck, could it? It was squashed flatter than a flapjack. She would get out and take a better look in a moment, but for now she concentrated on what seemed to be the bottom half of a dog—her dad's old hound dog, Bellyflop—lying at the edge of the grass to her right. Just the bottom of it. The intestines spilled out of the gaping hole and flies were covering it by the dozens. How could that have happened to a dog?

The chicken coop—Dad still raised some chickens for his personal use only—was now a full 50 feet away from where it used to be, overturned and empty. Even from where she sat Mary Margaret could see the top wall, which was cracked and partly crushed, was covered thickly with some kind of grayish slime. What the hell is that stuff?

All that was left of the garage and toolshed was about one and a half feet of the outer wall. Everything else was gone— no roof, a few scattered implements buried in the debris.

But the most amazing thing, the thing that had set Mary Margaret's mind whirling toward disbelief and incredulity— the sheer impossibility of it!—was what was at the end of the huge, absolutely humongous furrow that had been carved into the ground from the edge of the forest over to what was left of the house.

Lying on top of the debris that had once been the house Mary Margaret had grown up in was a 70 foot cabin cruiser.

Her hand up to her mouth, Mary Margaret got out of the car. How did it get there? There hadn't even been a storm and the shoreline was half a mile away.

Then she thought! *Dad!*

She ran toward the wreckage of the house, cursing the old man for staying alone on this godforsaken property and refusing to sell it. Damn him! He might still be alive if for once in his life he had done something sensible.

The house was totaled, absolutely totaled. There was nothing left of it to salvage. It was just one big pile of shattered debris—chunks of walls, cracked and crushed furnishings—lying underneath a ship that was strangely undamaged aside from the holes that seemed to have been punctured in the side of it as if something had bitten on it.

Bitten on it? Mary Margaret almost laughed at such a peculiar, nonsensical analogy. Still, damn if those didn't look like teeth marks.

"Dad," she called out hopelessly, "Daddy?" Knowing he was buried somewhere under all that debris and that in all likelihood she'd never see him whole and alive again was enough to melt her heart and start her sobbing.

She heard a noise from around the house, muffled, strained, someone struggling desperately to be heard.

"Mmmmmmmary."

Good God, her father was still alive, suffocating under the rubble somewhere! She had to find him; she had to get help. Perhaps she could pull him out of the wreckage herself if he was lying near the surface. Perhaps he wasn't trapped too badly.

The voice kept calling her name and she kept searching. It didn't seem to be coming anywhere from the pile of debris. It sounded like it was farther away, past the house, around the corner, around the back, that is if there had been a corner or a back wall left standing. "Daddy, daddy," she cried, "where are you? Tell me where you are!" She thanked the Lord that against all odds the old fool was still breathing.

Finally she turned to the left and started walking around the remains of the house. Her father's voice cried out plaintively once more and then she saw him.

So that explained it.

She could tell immediately that he'd been drinking. She'd seen him that way too many times before.

When mother had been alive he'd gotten into the habit of taking his bottle and going outside where no one could see him, walking through the woods sipping and sipping till it was pitch dark out and the bottle was empty. Then he'd fall asleep in the woods and stagger home in the morning with his clothes rumpled and dirty and a shit-eating grin on his face. Apparently he'd continued sneaking drinks like that even though there was no one around to holler at him. Nary Margaret felt a tinge of sadness at the thought. He had that same disheveled, dopey look about him now, and he was trying to rise to his feet unsuccessfully from the ground where he lay, which was about ten yards from the shattered wreck of his home.

"Wha' happened?" he said as he saw Mary Margaret approaching.

And then it hit her. The darn fool! Now she would never know what had happened!

For this apparently was the first time her father had seen what had happened to his house and his property.

A dead dog. No chickens. And a cabin cruiser where the house should have been.

And the drunken idiot had slept through the whole damn thing!

* * *

Elsa's debut at Prementer's was not what one would call auspicious.

It was a full house at the restaurant; droves of the hopeful without reservations had been turned away at the door. Elsa had showed up with time to spare looking like a million dollars in a sexy, seductive evening gown and silver high heels shoes. Joseph, busy playing host to the maître d's exasperation, studiously avoided Thomas, who corralled a seat at the bar and nursed a whiskey sour until it was time for Elsa to go on. She spent a lot of time talking to Joseph, thanking him and hugging him, but did come over once or twice to chat with Thomas, too. Deciding not to make her nervous or ruin her debut, Thomas did not bring up what was on his mind. Later there would be hell to pay, he promised.

At one point Elsa said, "I've got a nice crowd for opening night, don't you think, Tommy?"

Thomas almost rolled his eyes. They always had a packed house on the weekends. Did she actually believe everyone had come just to see her? He bit his tongue. At least Joseph had wisely abandoned his idea of charging a cover.

"I hope you've had enough time to rehearse your new material," he said. "This did happen awfully...suddenly."

She puffed dramatically on a cigarette. "Oh, sure. No problem. I'm only doing things I'm like real familiar with. And my pianist knows just about everything."

Something told Thomas that she wasn't going to regale them with her renditions of "People, Witchcraft" or "I Left My Heart in San Francisco". The only material she was familiar with was Bob Dylan, Pete Seeger and some Peter, Paul and Mary, as well as those dreadful songs she composed on her own.

"I even wrote a couple of numbers especially for the occasion," she said.

Thomas almost spit out his drink. "Oh," he said. "That's nice."

Relax, he told himself. Surely Elsa could look around for herself, see these fancy, well-dressed people, and realize that her usual type of song and style of presentation, her whole coffeehouse shtick, would be utterly inappropriate here. Surely she would stick to the safer, less violent numbers in her repertoire. Even she could sing a few pleasant background tunes that people might quietly enjoy while they were eating.

Surely he wouldn't expect people to stop their dining and conversing just to listen to her. How difficult could it be for her to do a nice pleasant tune like, say, "You Made Me Love You" or "Both Sides Now"?

Joseph came over to the bar, still avoiding Thomas, and waited at the other end until Elsa approached him. Thomas wondered if he had told her what happened this afternoon. Probably not. At least Elsa didn't seem disturbed or embarrassed. Was it possible nothing had happened? That he made a fool of himself for nothing?

Then it was showtime. Joseph kissed her on the cheek for good luck, and she gave Thomas a little wave as she went over to the piano they'd set up in the corner. Even Joseph seemed surprised when the lights got dimmer and a spotlight hit the corner. Apparently Elsa had had a little surreptitious chat with one of the staff.

"Hello, ladies and gentlemen, and welcome to Parmenter's." There was a polite, enthusiastic smattering of applause. "I'm Elsa Freemont. Tonight I hope to entertain you musically, and also give you some food for thought to go with your cuisine."

Thomas groaned.

"Some substance to go with your vichyssoise," she continued. "I believe we should all be thinking, concerned, aware people. Aware of our environment, and our children, and the struggles going on all around us. My first number is my own personal composition, entitled 'Love Meat'."

Thomas thought he had heard wrong. Surely she had said "Love Me", not "Love *Meat*". But no, he soon discovered he hadn't been mistaken after all.

The pianist, a tall blond man with a skinny figure and a bright-eyed expression, played a few introductory bars, then Elsa opened her mouth and began to sing. The tune sounded more like a marching song than something appropriate for the dinner hour.

> *"You sit there with your cuts of beef*
> *you hate your lives but you love your meat*
> *while children starve and we must repeat*
> *you hate your lives but you love your meat."*

Thomas put his hand over his face.

> *"Iron chains of poverty*
> *a prison do enfold*
> *but you stuff your face with canapes*
> *and the children, they turn cold."*

Elsa's voice began to rise into that ear-splitting wail of hers.

> *"But as long as your fat little bellies are full*
> *why should you give a damn about the chosen few*
> *you eat your mashed potatoes but the rest is bull*
> *what'll happen when the poor do rise and*
> *they shit all over you"*

There was a shocked murmuring through the crowd. Thomas did not even look over to see how Joseph was reacting, but he could imagine.

Elsa's voice thundered heavily into the chorus:

> *"Well, maggots love meat, too.*
> *Can't you see them crawling on your meat and you*
> *Yes, look at the maggots crawling through your stew*
> *the maggots love meat and they love you, too."*

Finally Thomas dared take a look. Joseph had walked over from the bar and was approaching the piano. Elsa was so "into" her song she didn't see the man coming toward her until he had ripped the microphone out of her hand. Thomas didn't know whether to share Elsa's mortification or his partner's understandable anger. The pianist gulped and stopped playing.

"Heh, heh," Joseph said, his face beaming red with embarrassment and all his teeth showing. "That was Elsa Freemont, our comedy act, I mean, comedy tryout. What a sense of humor that gal has, right, folks?"

"Too bad she doesn't have a voice," someone yelled.

Elsa grabbed the microphone from Joseph, but not before his amplified whisper to her came through the speakers. "What are you crazy? Singin' shit like that? I thought we decided–"

"I do *too* have a voice," she yelled, her loud tones reverberating, shrieking, from wall to wall. "You just don't want to listen. The management..."

More people began to holler now, an occasional obscenity mixed in with cries of "shut up and let us eat in peace" or variations thereof.

"The management of this restaurant," Elsa bellowed, "is oppressing the voice of the people."

"As long as they oppress your voice, honey," a slightly inebriated black lady called out from way in back.

Elsa turned angrily toward the heckler. "Oppressing the voice of the people because they do not care and do not believe." Elsa was manic now, screaming, her face beet red and her eyes nearly popping. "This restaurant is a tool of the fascist Nazi-police state..."

Joseph and Elsa wrestled for the possession of the microphone. The pianist, no longer smiling and bright-eyed, fled for the safety of the men's room. People had put down their forks or drinks and were watching the spectacle with appalled fascination.

"Fascist pig!" Elsa shouted in Joseph's face. "Fascist, I'll..."

She began pummeling Joseph on the chest. Joseph lifted his hand and slapped her.

Thomas got to his feet. Elsa may have been a fool and an idiot but he wouldn't let Joseph hurt her. But as he took a step away from the bar he wondered, judging from the relentless battering Elsa was now delivering to Joseph, if it were not his partner who might need assistance.

He was stopped in his tracks by the following words from Elsa.

"Bastard! Fascist pig!" She shouted at Joseph. "I slept with you to get this job! You told me I could bring my message to the people. Liar! Liar! I slept with you, you pig!"

Thomas, his face pale, got back into his seat, feeling all numb and hollow inside. He picked up his drink and sipped it. He knew the eyes of Dack, the night bartender, were fixed on him but he hadn't the strength to meet his gaze and wallow in the other man's pity. Leave the both of them to hell, he thought. He would not interfere. Let them both make public spectacles of themselves. It was no less than what they deserved.

Still struggling together, Joseph and Elsa backed up into a table and knocked a bottle of wine into somebody's lap. There were screams and shocked gasps from the diners at that table and elsewhere. A woman stood up shouting, "My dress, my dress!" Thomas heard something smash onto the floor and saw the waiters rushing to subdue Elsa before she turned the whole room into a shambles.

But before they reached her he was already on his way out the door.

* * *

Ursula and Stefan loved to take midnight strolls on Marisa Island.

They had a house built on a cliff overlooking the shore. After dinner they would walk off the calories by taking the steep path to the beach. From there they would either stroll along the sand until they hit the edge of the cliff as it curved outward to meet the ocean, or go in the opposite direction until they reached the marshes. Tonight they were walking toward the marshes, holding hands, whispering, basking in shared love and memories.

Stefan put his arm around Ursula and gave her a peck on the cheek. Ursula could feel those vague stirrings inside her and was amazed that time had not entirely dampened them. Stefan was still a handsome man, that was for certain, and she had taken pretty good care of herself over the years.

Stefan and Ursula were both in their eighties.

Ursula was convinced that living by the sea had helped them stay young—fresh sea air, daily swims, lots of walking and light exercise. They were careful with what they ate, but did splurge on calorie-laden goodies occasionally because food was as much a psychological need as a physical one.

Ursula loved living on the island. She loved the year-round generally moderate temperature, the stark whiteness of the glistening sand, the greenery of the grass along the dunes and the reeds and rushes in the marshland. The touch of the breeze on her flesh and the smell of the ocean were intoxicating to her senses.

Earlier, while waiting for dinner to get done, they had sat out on the deck, watching the lights and listening to the music from a yacht sailing several miles off shore. Now Ursula wondered where the ship had gone to. She searched the ocean in each direction for it, but it was nowhere to be seen. Funny how it had disappeared so quickly.

They had walked farther than usual and were about to turn back when Stefan came to an abrupt halt and gave his wife's hand a squeeze. "Honey, look what's out there in the marshes. What is it?"

Ursula's eyes followed his gaze and for a moment her blood frooze. "Why...Stefan...I don't know."

There was something out there in the marshes, something

of great size, and it seemed to be moving. Could something that large actually be moving? It seemed to be in the middle of a pile of other large things that were positively dwarfed by its bulk. Whatever it was, the moonlight glistened off its back but did not reveal the full shape of it; it only offered tantalizing glimpses of something enormous and perhaps saurian in nature.

"My God, Stefan, is that some kind of animal?" She really was frightened now. No kind of animal she had heard of could be as big as she had at first thought this thing was, which meant that they had to be much, much closer to the beast than she would care to be. Her breath rushed out in a gasp of terror. "Stefan...we have to get back. We're too close."

Her husband shook his head. "No. It's not as close as you think. It's just large, that's all."

"What are...what is that all around it?"

"Looks like wood. Debris," he said. He whistled. "My Lord, it's big. I've got to find out what it is."

A sea monster? she wondered. They said if you lived long enough you got to see everything. In her 83rd year was it finally time for her to see an actual sea monster? Goodness! She pulled on her husband's sweater. "Come away, Stefan. I'm scared."

But Stefan stood there watching the spectacle, trying to get a good clear look at the animal—if that's what it was and not an optical illusion—and figure out what it was doing. The neck and head—if it *was* the neck and head—seemed to be going up and down, up and down, like an agitated serpent burrowing for worms. Were there squiggling things being lifted from the ground, from that debris at the beast's feet—or was he imagining even that?

"Stefan, I said I'm scared..."

Stefan forced himself to look away from the animal and got a clear look at a large chunk of the debris in the moonlight.

There was writing on it. He thought of the yacht he and Ursula had watched earlier and shuddered.

Perhaps there had been an accident; perhaps the yacht had gone adrift and needed help. But he had to make sure it was a ship, then he would call the Coast Guard. As for the gigantic thing dipping and rising, dipping and rising, above it, surely that was just another part of the wreckage. The night shadows, the distance, his failing eyesight all added to the illusion. That had to be it, of course.

"Stefan, where are you going?"

He told her to stay put but she wouldn't listen.

He was making his way toward the remains of the ship, sticking to the more solid ground and avoiding the wet patches that might suck him down like a bug caught in a draining whirlpool, when something at his feet sent him sprawling.

He felt out with his hands and found what he had tripped over.

It was a human head.

"Oh God, Stefan." Ursula had come up to him and she put her hands over her face. Stefan had not wanted her to see the grisly object at his feet but she was not looking at the ground nor at him. She was looking upwards.

Up and up and up and up as a towering monstrosity above them seemed to rise toward the very sky, blotting out the moon the stars, and whatever brief future may have remained to them.

Then the monstrosity stopped and looked down.

Ursula saw its eyes peering down at them.

And she got her first good look at it.

This is no sea monster, she thought, it was something much, much worse. Something indescribably evil.

The mouth widened to an impossible width and came down, down…

They say if you live long enough you see everything, Ursula thought.

But the huge, reddish, fleshy appendage that flopped out of the mouth and caught them on it as they tried to run, this huge flying carpet all covered with slime, with its mottled surface of bumps and abrasions that quickly lifted them up and just flipped them into the blackness of the maw behind it...

That was something she would rather not have lived to see.

CHAPTER EIGHT

THE MONSTER SOCIETY

Thomas wondered what on earth he was doing here.

He looked about the hall and thought it was more like an AA meeting than anything else. The 25 or so people sitting in the auditorium with him looked like bag ladies, bums, and mental defectives, people who "saw things" more because they were drunk than for any other reason.

Is this how low he had fallen?

Even now he couldn't say for sure why he had started on this mission of his, this obsessive quest to find out just what had happened at Summerdale years ago. Partly it was a need to satisfy his curiosity. It certainly had been the single most significant event in his life, after all; everything had changed for him after that. Partly there was just a simple need to fill up his time. Several months had passed since he'd broken up with Elsa and he and his partner and former friend Joseph had become mere nodding acquaintances. They let the manager take care of the restaurant while they sought separate pursuits and stayed away from each other. He needed something to fill up the empty days, and as long as he had the free time and the financial wherewithal to indulge himself, why not seek some answers to the most important questions of his life?

The more he thought about it the more he was convinced there was some connection between the nightmarish beast he remembered and the man that stood watching as he was put into the ambulance, the same man who had been in the house across the lake. This was not really a concrete notion—how could it be after all those years, not to mention his selective amnesia?—but it was all he had to go on. If he *had* seen a monster that night, what better way to find out about it than to seek out people who had had similar experiences?

Everyone else who'd been at Beachside that night was dead. Thomas could not contact relatives of the deceased, as he had forgotten the names of Beachside's other residents, and in any case, those relatives had not experienced the nightmare the way he had and would not have the same desperate need. They had already settled for the safe, comfortable explanation of a freak wind, a squall, a hurricane, a tidal wave that had come and gone like a phantom, caused perhaps by a faraway undersea earthquake. They had not seen what he had seen, did not remember what he remembered, and could not possibly be as intensely concerned about it as he was.

At first he used his professional contacts, other prominent businessmen and civic leaders who might be privy to some arcane, esoteric knowledge. He got an introduction to paleontologists at the Museum of Natural History and other scientists and marine biologists who assured him that dinosaurs were long extinct and that other monstrous creatures from the deep were simply the products of fevered imaginations. How could he tell them in the face of their smug, confident complacency that what he had seen had not really even been a dinosaur—something similar, perhaps, but something that was much, much worse, if only he could remember all of the details, but he couldn't.

So he tried other avenues. He went to meetings of people

who believed in or had seen UFOs and alien visitors, hoping against hope that someone's experiences had been at least vaguely similar to his own. Who was to say his great sea beast had not come originally from the stars or even been an alien mechanical construction? But all that these people saw, assuming they had actually seen anything, were spaceships, glowing lights in the sky, little green men with antennae and big teeth, but never any monsters like the kind that had apparently stomped across Beachside.

He went to occult organizations seeking answers in spiritualism, but all he got was an offer to call up the ghosts of his dead parents—for a $2500 fee. He refused. Even if spirits could talk, there was no guarantee their memories would be any better than his own.

Until he came to this meeting of Miami's Monster Society, he had thought the nadir would be the last group, P.I.S., which he referred to as PISS. The initials actually stood for Plesiosaur Investigating Society, which turned out to consist of several fans of "Nessie," Scotland's Loch Ness Monster, who insisted that the sea creature was a plesiosaur, some kind of prehistoric fish, that had survived until modem times. The members got very nasty if you dared to suggest otherwise. P.I.S. was even worse than the group that insisted that the disappearances of ships and planes in the Bermuda Triangle were caused by some kind of mutant vegetation or killer seaweed.

As for The Monster Society, they were his last hope. But as he looked around the room he saw the usual whackos and hopeless cases he had become familiar with in the past few months. These people, who had seen monsters only in their own minds, no doubt, would reduce his tragedy to something inane and foolish, something for their madness to nibble away at like fish nibbling away the brains and faces of drowning victims.

He sat back in his seat and watched as a fat, waddling woman of about 60 approached the lectern they had set up on the stage. Her garments seemed to consist of greasy, odorous tatters, and her face—bulldog dumb—was devoid of sensitivity. She stood there for a moment staring at the audience, then opened her mouth, paused, and finally said, "I seen one. I seen it. Yeah. At the beach. Out at the beach. I seen the monster." She was too inebriated to even articulate this fantasy of hers. Still, Thomas sat spellbound, appalled and hopeful, wishing she had really seen something and could tell them about it with accuracy. Instead she waddled off the stage after a few moments and went back to her seat. These people were hopeless. Why didn't he grab his jacket and get out of here?

He sat there as two more people got up, to tell their stories. A bewhiskered man with a boil on his neck told them he had gone hunting Bigfoot and caught sight of the beast just as it was plunging into a hole in the ground. "It was big, man, really big!" A pale young woman who was so skinny she looked as if a stage whisper would blow her away stood there rubbing her fingertips together and related how she and her girlfriend saw a "big fish" while sailing on the ocean. She would stop now and then to cackle and titter. She gave no description of this big fish but seemed in awe of what she'd seen. In fact, Thomas mused, it had probably driven her to drink. He put his hand over his mouth to stifle a laugh.

At the end of the meeting a woman who had entered from a side door a few minutes before and had been sitting in the front row since then, got up and introduced herself as Mistress Dunn. It turned out that she was the head of the Monster Society. She was a large fleshy woman of medium height in a crinkly black robe-like garment that rolled down in folds to the floor. Her full, broad face had high cheekbones, full lips and big green eyes made up garishly with eyeshadow and mascara. Her reddish-brown hair fell in curls and waves down to her shoulders, making her appear more youthful at first glance, but accentuating her age on second thought.

Thomas took her for at least 55 or older. She spoke with a vague accent which might have been Russian or Romanian.

"I want to welcome our several newcomers to The Monster Society," she said. "Forgive me for my late arrival, but I was unavoidably detained. I'm sure our secretary, Miss Smith, did an adequate job of handling things while I was gone."

There was a scattering of applause as Miss Smith, an elderly woman with jug ears and a build like Olive Oyl's, got to her feet and took a bow. Then Mistress Dunn continued. "If there is no one else who wishes to come up, as I'm sure Miss Smith suggested at the beginning of the meeting, and share their stories with us, may I then tell you a little more about our society?"

No one protested, so she continued, "As its name implies, the Monster Society is dedicated to the pursuit and discussion of monsters, any kind of monsters, and is for those of us who have actually seen these creatures and have been held up to ridicule because of it. The society is a place where all of us can come and tell our stories without having to endure the scorn and intolerance of others. We publish a monthly newsletter which relates our members' experiences and also run news items regarding worldwide monster sightings. In every issue there is an update of 'Nessie,' one of our favorites."

A man sitting not far from Thomas raised his hand. "Must you have actually seen a monster yourself before you can join the society?"

Mistress Dunn smiled, and Thomas had to admit it was a pleasant smile. "No, actually we'll be glad to take your ten dollar annual dues even if you haven't been so blessed. This organization is open not only to people who have seen monsters, but to people who wish they *might* have seen one." Some of the audience laughed appreciatively and nodded their heads.

"We are not only a support group for those who have stories that no one else will believe, but we also wish to investigate these strange animals and beasties that so many of us have actually seen. Frankly we are without the financial resources to do much more than contact professionals, not to mention monied individuals with a sense of curiosity and adventure, and try to work some gentle persuasion on them. But one day, we hope to do more, to launch our own investigations into the wonderful world of the monstrous and unknown. Until such time as that we exist to serve our members with this forum, a place to talk about, to dream of, and ponder the strange lifeforms out there that so few among mankind have seen or even believe in. *We* believe. We are here for those of you who believe, too."

When the audience applauded Thomas found himself joining in. The woman was like a trained stage actress, reading what might have been a prepared speech but doing it in such a way that it almost seemed natural and spontaneous. He saw intelligence in her eyes and wondered what she was doing here with these loonies and why she had even founded an organization that she must have known would attract weirdos by the dozens. Miss Smith had earlier said that it was a slow night due to the rain. How many members did this organization have?

"May we break for refreshments?" Mistress Dunn suggested, folding her hands as if in prayer. "Afterward we can go into the next room and split up into groups to discuss various...well, whatever you wish." She shrugged, smiled again and made her way down off the stage. What a character.

In the back of the hall a table had been set up with coffee, cookies, fruit cake and brownies, and several jugs of wine. The members rushed toward the food—so quickly that Thomas was nearly trampled—as if some of them hadn't eaten in a week. He contented himself with a very tall glass of rather cheap white wine.

Why didn't he just leave? Surely he wasn't as lonely as some of these people undoubtedly were?

For some reason he felt an urge to talk privately with Mistress Dunn, to level with her, find out if she were actually as sane and canny as she appeared to be. For the moment she was surrounded by several members, who nodded their heads obediently and deferentially as she spoke, allowing cookie crumbs to drop out of their mouths and onto their clothes or the floor without even noticing or caring.

Finally, as the others drifted off into private conversations among themselves, he found himself standing next to her, his wine glass empty. She nodded at him. "Hello."

He held out his hand and took hers, it was warm and slightly moist. He dropped her hand and said, "My name is Thomas Bartlett. Do you mind If I ask you a few questions about your group?"

"Be my guest," she said. She took a sip from her coffee mug.

"How long has this group been active?"

"Several years," she replied. "See our pamphlet on the literature table in the next room? It has all that information." Then, as if to be conversationally polite, she continued, "We started out by meeting in each other's homes. Then one of the members, who owned this building, left it to us in his will, and we've been here ever since."

He looked her straight in the eye. "Are any of these people's stories true?"

She paused before answering. Was her voice lower and did her eyes dart about the room, or was that his imagination? "Yes, I believe so. In some cases. As I'm sure you've noticed, the society does attract its share of...well people in Miami, in any big city, are lonely, Mr. Bartlett. If coming here and saying they saw some formless mythical monster gets them a little company and conversation, free cookies and coffee, who am I to turn them away? They don't really do any harm."

"Aren't you afraid they might frighten away people who have really...seen something?"

Her eyebrows lifted. "Have you really seen something, Mr. Bartlett?"

He wanted to tell her. How badly he wanted to tell her. "Yes," he said finally, "I have. It happened a long time ago and it's something I'll never forget. I came here for that reason. Not because I'm lonely and not because I needed coffee and cookies." He looked around the room, anything to avoid her brilliantly penetrating gaze. "But I wonder if there's any point..."

He turned back to her abruptly. There was no one else about, so he whispered, "Why did you start this group? What do you get out of it? Surely the dues aren't enough to...?"

She smiled. "You *are* getting personal, Mr. Bartlett."

He reddened slightly, like a schoolboy in front of his fifth grade English teacher. "I'm sorry, but—"

"But I *can* tell you that my late husband left me well-fixed and I did not start the society for financial reasons, as you have already surmised. Let me also say that I, too, can sometimes be lonely, and I, too..."

Thomas found himself losing patience. Suddenly full of unreasoning anger, he snapped *"Did you ever see a monster? Did any of these silly people ever see a monster?"*

Her face was an indecipherable mask. "You don't have to have seen a monster to become a member, Mr. Bartlett."

He waved his hand at her in disgust. "That's not an answer, and you know it."

"Why don't *you* answer me?" the woman said sharply. "Tonight, privately, after the others have gone, why don't you tell me what you saw?" Her face looked concerned now, vaguely agitated, anxious, even demanding. "I might be able to help you, Mr. Bartlett. There's more to this society than meets the eye." She drained her coffee mug in one slurping gulp and put the mug back on the table. "If you have actually seen something, I want you to tell me all about it. In fact, I insist."

He shook his head, gestured helplessly. "I can't hang around these people…"

"Some of 'these people' have seen things, Mr. Bartlett, whether real or imaginary I cannot always say. But these people have nowhere else, no one else, to turn to. No one who will listen. Did it ever occur to you that some of these people are the way they are *because* of what they might have seen? Just as you are the way *you* are?"

"What do you mean by that?"

She tapped her head with her forefinger. "The eyes, Mr. Bartlett, the eyes. I can always tell by the eyes. They don't have on fancy suits like you do, and they don't have your obvious breeding. But look at their eyes and look in the mirror and tell me if you don't all wear the same perplexed and haunted expressions. Some of them are too far gone to help. But you, Mr. Bartlett? Perhaps you have a chance." She leaned in closer and whispered. "Tell me what you saw, Mr. Bartlett, for I'm probably the only person in this city who will actually believe you."

She began to walk away, toward the adjacent room where the others were waiting. He could see tables, people gathered in clusters to discuss God knows what, but whether it was for this odd woman's amusement or her edification he was not sure. Before he could speak, she turned back and said, "You can wait until we're done here, or call me at my private number." She stepped toward him and handed him a business card.

"How much will this consultation cost me, Mistress Dunn?" he said coldly.

She stopped in her tracks and looked both a little sad and highly insulted. "Nothing, Mr. Bartlett," she said. "Nothing but some of your time."

And then she was in the other room, and Thomas was all alone in the hall.

* * *

The following day Lemuel Harriman got off the bus and looked about for his friend. The terminal was bustling with parents and kids and chattering groups of people saying hello or good-bye or wandering around looking like little lost puppies. Finally he spotted Roderick behind an obese couple who were hugging each other farewell and called out his name. Roderick turned, saw him, smiled and waved. A few moments later the two men were greeting each other warmly.

Harriman's cousin Roderick was a big man of six foot two with a barrel chest, large muscular arms, and thick salt and pepper hair cut almost to the scalp. His features were large and rubbery and he wore a beard which was always neatly trimmed. In contrast, Lemuel Harriman, curator of paleontology at the Arizona Museum of Natural History, was short and dapper, with a pencil thin mustache but no other facial hair nor indeed a strand of hair anywhere on his head, which was completely shaved even on the back and sides. He wore horn-rimmed spectacles and had a hearing aid. His features were delicate, particularly as compared to his cousin's. Both men were in their early fifties.

"Honestly, Lem," Roderick said, "You are the only man alive who would take a bus all the way from Arizona."

Harriman smiled. "It was dreadful, just dreadful, but I made it." He absolutely refused to fly and wouldn't take trains either since he'd once barely survived an Amtrak derailment. He beamed up at his cousin. "Rod, you look good, very good. All that fishing and sunshine and sea air must be good for you."

Roderick went "achh" and snorted. He still had a touch of a Norwegian accent. "I don't know about that. My doctor tells me to take it easy, not to swim so much, not to sail so much, too strenuous, and all that. I feel like a little old lady. About all the exercise I get is taking walks on the beach. You should see my gut"—he pinched himself at the belly—"so much flab it makes me sick."

"It doesn't show," Lemuel said truthfully. "You're in fine shape. Still look like you could wrestle a bear to the ground."

Roderick Thorson—nicknamed "Thor" in his college football days—had been a Mathematics teacher at a local college until three years ago. He got a heart attack from a combination of genetic factors and overactivity and decided to make some radical changes in his lifestyle. He had enough money to retire early and teach only occasional weekend or evening seminars, instead of a full roster of classes, and spent much of his time doing research for friends, associates and paying clients while bemoaning the fact that he couldn't get out and do the robust things he used to do. Truthfully, Lemuel suspected that it was Roderick himself and not his doctor who imposed the strict regimen; the heart attack had nearly finished the man off and Lemuel knew his cousin had no desire to follow his late wife Gladys into extinction. Lemuel himself had never been married, claiming to be too set in his ways.

Roderick lived in a reconverted farmhouse in Hillsboro Beach, about 35 miles from Miami. He drove a foreign sports car, that seemed far too small for so vast a man, but was just the right size for his more compact cousin, Lem. As they drove Lemuel mused that this visit was long overdue. He and Rod had always been good friends, sharing similar interests. Lemuel had almost loved Gladys as much as Rod did. There was no competition or strain between the men, no family feuds, no quarrels, no bitterness. Kind and conversational and friendly, Roderick was a relaxing man to be with. Their mothers had been the Evebar sisters of Orlando. Patti married a Norwegian, and Willona a Jew.

"These past few months have been busy for you, haven't they?" Roderick asked. "Since your discovery of Gargantosaurus, eh?"

Lemuel rubbed his chin. "Yes, they have been. But I didn't 'discover' Gargantosaurus. I only named him."

"Still, it's quite an achievement, even an honor. I'm very proud of you." He turned to look at him briefly. "And there's no doubt now? The creature did exist?"

Lemuel nodded. "Gargantosaurus, as we call him, did indeed walk the earth almost sixty-five million years ago. As far as we can tell those bones date back to the very end of the rule of the dinosaurs. Almost an entire skeleton has been assembled from the bones found in the desert. The activity around the museum has been beyond belief—reporters, biologists, paleontologists from around the world, magazine writers, columnists."

"It must be very exciting."

"Yes. So exciting I need a rest."

"Well, you'll get plenty of rest during your visit, don't worry." He turned into a small narrow lane that wound sinuously through lush green farmlands punctuated with motels and gift shops and said, "You say this Gargantosaurus was the absolute largest dinosaur that ever existed?"

"Absolutely...until we find the remains of something bigger. When they discovered Supersaurus and then Seismosaurus, they thought they had found the biggest. Perhaps somewhere out there in the desert an 'Even Bigger-osaurus' is waiting to be discovered —who knows?—but I doubt it."

Roderick whistled. "And you're positive that nothing like that could still be existing in the 1980s somewhere?" He had a wistful tone that Lemuel recognized, the hopeful siren song of the dreamer, the foolish it lovable romantic.

Lemuel shook his head. "Unlikely, I'm afraid. Why do you ask?"

"I haven't told you, but there have been some strange things going on around here."

"Strange things?"

"Yes, well…we're almost home. Why don't we wait until we get there? I'll make you a nice drink and we can talk."

Lemuel smiled. Roderick sure knew how to pique his curiosity, even after all these years.

Upon arrival, the farmhouse was as charming as Lemuel remembered it, though since Gladys died it had lost some of those feminine touches—flowers on the windowsill, new curtains, new wallpaper every few years—that she had brought to the place with love. It was two stories high, with a front and back porch, a barn-garage to the right, and a vegetable garden out in back which Roderick toiled in almost every afternoon. Lemuel was dismayed to learn that Rod's Scottish Terrier, Yippie, had passed away last year.

They had settled in the handsomely furnished den with two strong martinis in goblets when Lemuel turned to his cousin and said, "So…about these strange events you were mentioning…"

Roderick relished having a good story to tell his cousin, and Lemuel could see from the expression on his face that this was better than most.

"The neighbor of a former student of mine," Rod began, "lives in Huddington Beach up the coast. Name of Johnstone. Well, his entire house was destroyed several months ago. He had to go live with his daughter and her boyfriend." He chuckled. "And my student tells me they're all going crazy with *that* arrangement. Anyway, you'll never guess what happened to Johnstone's house."

Lemuel took a sip of the martini which was excellent. He shrugged. "A storm, a fire, a bolt of lightning?"

"None of those. It was a ship."

"A ship?"

"Yes. A cabin cruiser, which somehow flew a half of a mile inland from the ocean and literally plowed across the grounds and into the house. It's lucky no one was killed."

"How on earth did it happen?"

Roderick shook his head and laughed. "Who the hell knows? The most popular story among the children in the neighborhood was that a sea monster picked the ship up in its teeth, carried it on land, and simply threw it at Johnstone's house."

Lemuel tittered along with his cousin. "Kids. They would come up with a crazy idea like that."

But then Roderick stopped laughing. "There were puncture holes in the ship's side like teeth marks, Lemuel. I saw it for myself."

"You're crazy."

Roderick shrugged. "I know. It is crazy. I don't believe it was a sea monster any more than you do, but what the hell could it have been? There was no storm that night, not even a wind. The sea was calm. How did the ship get there?"

"What about the owner, the crew? What did they say?"

"Ahhh, that's just it. When I said no one was killed I meant no one on *land*. The Coast Guard found out that there had been at least nine people on board that cabin cruiser, but all of them are missing and presumed dead. It's been months. None of them were on the wrecked ship, and none of them were ever found at sea or anywhere else." He paused. "They did find a human leg on the boat, though, but that's about it."

Lemuel grimaced.

"And that's not the only strange thing that's been happening. There have been even more lost ships and shipwrecks in this area of the country than usual. This is no Bermuda Triangle curse or rumor, mind you; it's fact. The Coast Guard has reported that this is one of the worst years for sea tragedies in their history. A yacht with thirty people aboard was found adrift in the marshes on Marisa Island, everyone missing except, again, for a few severed body parts. Houses along the eastern coastline have been destroyed in the night, and animals, even people, were found crushed to death. No one has added it all up, of course, or admitted that it's more of a mystery than people would care to believe. It started about the time you made the announcement of Gargantosaurus and has gotten worse ever since."

Lemuel turned the martini glass in his hand impatiently. "Roderick, surely that was only a coincidence. The fact that the bones of a 'new' prehistoric creature that lived millions of years ago were found in Arizona can hardly have anything to do with shipwrecks and coastal tragedies in present day Florida. Rod, the Gargantosaurus, along with all dinosaurs and sea creatures of that era, is extinct."

Roderick waved his cousin's misinterpretation away with a gesture. "Of course, Lem, I wasn't suggesting there was a connection. I just mentioned it as a point of reference, time wise. Listen, these incidents may well be isolated tragedies and nothing more, but I've seen some of the devastation and I think whatever is responsible is something large, very large. Of course not a Gargantosaurus. Still, might it not be possible that some large marine animal could be responsible, some freak of nature, a genetic misfit, a prehistoric leftover of some kind?"

Lemuel had had similar discussions with Roderick. In spite of Rod's practical demeanor and solid, substantial background and profession, there was one area in which he was totally illogical and fantastic. And that was sea monsters and prehistoric animals. Even as a kid, Roderick had been enthralled with them. It was funny, because it had been Lemuel's interest in dinosaurs and paleontology that had inspired Roderick's fascination in the first place. But whereas Lemuel had turned his passion into a profession, Roderick had subordinated it into a hobby that bordered on obsession.

Roderick left his seat and came back with a scrapbook in which he collected numerous clippings. The scrapbook had grown larger. "You've got a lot more material in here than last time, haven't you?" Lemuel said as his cousin handed him the book.

"Lemuel," Roderick said, "this isn't the same scrapbook you've seen before. This is a new book. And every single clipping in this file has come from papers during the past few months."

Lemuel turned the pages quickly at first, then slower, as he couldn't help but react to what he was seeing. Page after page after page of items were about shipwrecks—impossible ones such as the cabin cruiser on the farmhouse—missing sailors and yachts, a car parked on the beach that had been flattened by something tremendously heavy with a necking couple still inside it. There were odd, horrifying incidents, many of which made no sense and had no seeming explanation, it was like thumbing through a paperback copy of *Ripley's Believe It Or Not* Animals torn in half, whole houses with families swept away during the night, small boats sucked out of sight while only a mile or so off shore. True, many of these tragedies were explainable in rational terms—boats did sink and people did drown every day—but far too many of them resisted such comfortable assurances.

When he was through with the scrapbook, Roderick handed him a picture which he said he had taken himself. "I hired a helicopter," he said. "Wasn't half as expensive as I thought it would be."

The picture was an 8 by 10 and very clear. Lemuel realized that it was a shot of that crushed car with the couple, probably still inside, but taken from a different angle than the one in the paper. The car was squashed so flat no one could have survived. The photograph had been taken from directly above, and showed that the indentation or hole the car had been found in was actually...a *footprint*.

Lemuel gasped. He had seen that kind of footprint before.

Was it, could it be possible? No. Not in a million—65 million—years. He looked up at Roderick.

"There's something else I have to tell you about Gargantosaurus," Lemuel said.

CHAPTER NINE

SAMANTHA

Thomas stepped into the foyer of the apartment building on Dubin Street and looked for the name Clark in the listings by the intercom. Bradford, Carney—ah, there it was—Clark. Apt. 6W. He pressed the button and waited to hear the voice come out of the little box at the side. Instead the only answer was the sound of the buzzer indicating that the door into the building proper had been unlocked from upstairs.

Although he had not stayed for the rest of the meeting of The Monster Society the previous night, he did call Mistress Dunn at the number on the card the following afternoon. "I'll be in town tonight," Mistress Dunn told him, "at the apartment of another of our members, one who will be most interested in hearing your story. Why don't you meet me there, around seven? We'll have a little supper and some wine."

"Are you sure it's all right with this…?"

"Samantha? Samantha Clark. Of course, it's all right. I've told her all about you. She'll be very pleased to meet you."

"Well if you're sure."

"I'm sure. Seven, all right?" She paused and then added, "I knew I'd be hearing from you again, Mr. Bartlett."

She hung up.

Which brought him to this tacky, rundown apartment building, one of those old rent-controlled monstrosities with about 20 apartments to each floor and narrow pea-green painted corridors with low ceilings and dim overhead lighting. He could hear children bickering and smell food burning through the thin walls and was glad he didn't have to live here.

He rang the bell at 6W and waited for someone to answer. Finally he heard approaching footsteps. The door opened a crack and a slender face peeked through. "Mr. Bartlett?"

"Yes, I'm to meet Mistress Dunn here."

"Yes. Eustace is here already. Please come in." She pulled the door open wider and admitted him, giving him a tight if pleasant smile. Samantha Clark was a woman in her late thirties or early forties. She was almost painfully thin, with drawn features and pale dry skin. She had wide, thin lips, heavily lidded brown eyes, and faded auburn hair that fell limply down to her shoulders. Her nose was long and narrow, and her chin a pointy knob on a small eggshaped head. Thomas took her to be about five foot three. She might have been attractive had she paid more attention to her appearance and put on something other than that shapeless housedress that reminded Thomas too much of the outfits his mother had always worn.

She closed the door and escorted him down a narrow corridor. The hallway opened up into a small living room which was tastefully furnished and looked as if it had been recently and hastily put in order. He could see a kitchen to his right, and a small bedroom and bathroom to his left. Mistress Eustace Dunn sat primly in the center of the couch against the far wall below the window. She was holding a glass of white wine.

"Bring Mr. Bartlett some wine, Samantha," she said. She

spoke as if she were addressing a beloved servant who had been with her family for years and was almost a part of it. The directive did not seem to rankle Samantha who disappeared into the kitchen abruptly.

Thomas could barely keep a sardonic edge out of his voice. "Hello, 'Mistress' Dunn."

"Call me Eustace, please."

Thomas moved toward her but did not hold out his hand. "Frankly, I was wondering where this 'mistress' business comes from. Is it to impress some of those lonely people we were talking about last night?"

Eustace laughed. "Hardly. It's a long story. Anyway, I'm an old woman and I'm entitled to my peculiarities. Sometime all will be explained to you. But first things first."

He took off his jacket and draped it neatly over the back of the sofa, then sat in a hard chair that had been set up across from it. There was a table in between with crackers and appetizers on it. He chose something that tasted of cheese. "Let me guess. First you want me to tell you what I saw, is that it?"

The older woman nodded. "That's about it, Mr. Bartlett. Crudely put, perhaps, but accurate." She let out with a charming giggle, which made Thomas wonder if she were on her way to being intoxicated. Mistress Eustace Dunn. Lord, what a handle! He had to be crazy thinking she was any less loony than her constituents.

Samantha came back into the room and handed him some white wine in a water glass. He took it and thanked her. "How long have you been a member of the Monster Society?" he asked her. He decided as long as he was going through with this he might as well get "into" it and have a few laughs if nothing else.

Samantha had a soft, low voice, that he had to strain to hear, with a tiny bit of an accent in the background—upper-crust, Bostonian, Thomas wasn't certain. It was a thin, clipped voice, but sweet. "A year or two," she said. "Mistress Dunn was very helpful when I came to her and told her of my experiences." She gave the older woman a heartfelt look. "She was the only one who really believed me."

"What happened to you?"

Samantha looked at Eustace again, helplessly, then back at Thomas. "I...I don't want to talk about it."

Thomas was about to assure her that he'd keep an open mind—after all, who of all people was more likely to understand?—when Miss Dunn interceded. "Mr. Bartlett. Samantha doesn't like telling her story to strangers. She doesn't want to be laughed at, you see."

Thomas felt like hooting. "But isn't that what you expect me to do? Tell my story to strangers? Risk being laughed at?"

"There is a difference, Mr. Bartlett. Don't deny it. You came to us because you needed to talk about your experience with someone sympathetic. Samantha has already found a sympathetic ear. She doesn't need you, but you need us. Why not brush that chip off your shoulder, accept us for what we are, eccentricities and all, and just tell us what you've come here to tell us. It will simplify matters all around."

He finished the wine in his glass in a couple of gulps, then wiped his lips with his fingers. "I warn you, if you people are charlatans..." He spoke more to himself than to them. "...I'll feel like a fool for even speaking to you."

Eustace Dunn's eyes narrowed coldly. "We are not charlatans, Mr. Bartlett, nor fools. Drop your tiresome preconceptions. Maybe we can help you."

He got to his feet in a rush of frustration and helplessness. "The likelihood of that is...What happened to me is so *incredible*...If I only knew that one of you had honestly had a similar experience..."

Samantha suddenly reached out and took his hand. "What did you see?" she said. There was a look of great pain, almost desperation, on her face. "Tell us!" She looked down at the floor and shook her head. "It can't be worse than what..." Then she looked up again. "Tell us, Mr. Bartlett, please?" It was as if she needed to hear what he had to say more than he needed to say it.

He looked at her hand, which was still clutching his, and Samantha self-consciously let it go. As Thomas slowly dropped to his seat, she looked away.

"All right, all right. You win. I'll tell you."

And Thomas began to finally unburden himself.

* * *

Roderick was cleaning the supper dishes as Lemuel walked off his dinner outside. Roderick's pot roast wasn't as good as Gladys' had been, even though he followed the same recipe, but it was still mighty tasty. He was glad Lem had enjoyed it. It was good having company. Since Gladys' death and his own semiretirement Roderick was a lot lonelier than he cared to admit.

He finished drying the dishes and went back into the den for a moment to look at the drawings Lemuel had taken out of his suitcase earlier. He picked the first one up in his hands and, looking down at it, couldn't help whistling out loud again.

So that was Gargantosaurus, or at least one person's view of it.

It was an artist's conception of what the animal might have looked like those millions of years ago when it walked the earth. The size, of course, was enormous, dwarfing even an elephant, that had been sketched in for comparison at the side. The head itself was many, many times larger than that of a full-grown man. It walked on all fours but was capable of rising up on its thick, powerful haunches if need be. It was reptilian in nature, like some overgrown lizard, and had a tremendous sweeping tail that could probably smash a house apart with one stroke. The mouth was open and showed row after row of gigantic slashing teeth. Its feet, all of which were the same, divided in the front into three clawed toes; a fourth claw, which could grip tight or slice apart the hardest ground, grew straight out of the back of the foot. It was that foot that had gotten Lemuel so agitated before dinner.

The imprint surrounding the crushed car was the approximate size and shape of the footprint of Gargantosaurus.

Of course it had to be an incredible coincidence, nothing more. The whole thing had to be a hoax, an elaborate joke. Dinosaurs did not walk the earth in 1988!

But Roderick remembered how upset Lemuel had been when he admitted that the artist's conception was not entirely accurate. "He was thinking in traditional, conventional terms," Lemuel explained. "After all, this was a dinosaur, as far as he was concerned, and he had drawn plenty of them before. So he can be forgiven for making certain—alterations? adjustments? When he drew the head, he drew it as he himself thought it must have looked. He made it look more reptilian— and who can blame him? But the skull bones we reconstructed at the museum indicated that the head was extremely unusual. Saurian in nature, basically, but flattened, more angular, a bit less...beast-like. In addition to its reptilian features, the head had certain qualities similar to an ape's, or I dare say, a human's."

Roderick gulped. "Gargantosaurus had a human skull? An ape's?" He indicated the drawing. "This doesn't look anything like King Kong."

"No, not quite. Gargantosaurus is nothing like the legendary movie ape, I assure you. It's basically a dinosaur, of that there's no doubt, but we've never come across a skull quite like this one's before. The discovery of Gargantosaurus has thrown a lot of what we know about prehistoric animals out the window. Its size alone is like nothing we've ever seen."

He handed Roderick another slip of paper. "Forgive the crude drawing. I'm not very good, I'm afraid. But this is what I think Gargantosaurus *actually* looked like."

The body was basically the same, of course—the feet, the four claws—the head was a reptilian head, yes...

Yet it had a *face*, a face that glowed with intelligence, a face that was almost, in some vague, terrible way, somewhat human, or at least mammalian, like a man-lizard out of a child's comic book.

"The shape of the skull from the bones we reconstructed indicate *this*. Something reptilian, but at the same time *between* human and reptile. I realize the human part is only how I perceive it because I *am* human; I mean, human beings, even primates, didn't exist until millions of years after the end of the Cretaceous period when the dinosaurs died out. Perhaps it might be better to say the skull has an alien, unrecognizable quality about it. In any case, it's different from any other dinosaur's that ever lived."

Roderick didn't know what to say.

They had continued the conversation during dinner. "Has anyone ever seen the beast that might be involved in the mishaps in this area?" Lemuel asked him.

"Nobody alive," he replied. "You must remember, Lem, nobody is admitting to the existence of a beast. It's just a theory."

"But that footprint...the car? How did they explain that?"

Roderick wiped gravy off his lips and said, "You think anyone is just going to accept that a dinosaur walked out of the sea and stepped on an automobile parked on the beach? It must have run across some of their minds—kids' minds, the more imaginative policemen's—but there's no proof. No one has *seen* anything."

"Or at least lived to tell of it."

"Exactly."

Lemuel chewed his meat thoughtfully, then asked, "Rod, do *you* think it's a sea monster?"

He nodded. "Yes, I do."

Lemuel put his fork down and leaned back tensely in his seat. "The footprint is so similar. Let's face it, it's exactly the same as the kind of print Gargantosaurus would make. How is it possible? I should make calls, phone colleagues. To think a *living* one is running amuck in the ocean even as we first learned of the existence of one in prehistory. It just doesn't make any sense."

Lemuel banged his fist on the table. "Rod, I need to talk to someone in authority—Coast Guard officials, policemen, anyone who may have investigated these incidents and gathered information."

"Who?" Roderick said. "Who do you think besides me is keeping a scrapbook? I have lots of free time. I can sit around dreaming about sea monsters, taking notes, making comparisons, but the authorities have their hands full as it is just with day to day business. All these different officials don't have time to sit down and discuss the facts with one another."

Lemuel would not give up so easily. "Surely, someone must have come to the same conclusion as you have, or at least admitted to the possibility?"

"Maybe. But I couldn't tell you who."

The two men grew silent.

Roderick had just put the two drawings of Gargantosaurus back on the table when Lemuel returned from his walk. "See anything unusual?" he quipped.

Lemuel chuckled and rubbed his palms together. "No, thank goodness. But I did have time to do some thinking."

"And what have you decided?"

"I've decided that you're going to drive me out to that spot where the crushed car was found."

Branton Beach was about a 15 minute drive from there.

Although Roderick's farm was not that close to the ocean, he shuddered at the thought of that huge thing, Gargantosaurus or whatever it was, stomping inland and in short order—considering its size and the length of its strides—arriving at his own place. "Yes, I can do that," he said. "When do you want to leave?"

"Immediately."

Roderick went to get his car keys.

* * *

By the time Thomas had finished his story he was crying.

"So there you have it, ladies. The whole sorry, strange, incredible mess. And I don't expect you to make heads or tails out of it, 'cause I sure can't. But that's it. That's what I remember. Correction! That's what I *know* happened that night, as sure as I know I'm sitting here talking to you now. So, go ahead and laugh at me if you want to. I don't even care anymore."

But Eustace and Samantha weren't laughing. "You say you don't remember any specific details?" Eustace asked. "You don't clearly remember what the creature looked like?"

He shook his head. "Not specifically, no." He did seem to recall one peculiar, terrible detail, but he decided to keep it to himself. The ladies were probably thinking he was crazy as it was, though he could not imagine why Eustace should have such a queer, knowing look on her face.

"I don't remember exactly what it was or what it looked like. It was a monster, a sea beast, like—but not like-some kind of dinosaur. Anything more than that…It's just been too long; my memory is too hazy."

Mistress Dunn reached out toward his chair and gave his hand a gentle, sympathetic pat. "There, now. It all happened a long time ago. It's dreadful—your parents, those poor people—but it's over."

He said in a cold, weary voice, "You don't believe me, do you?"

Eustace lifted her head appeasingly. "On the contrary. I do believe you. I believe in sea monsters. I believe that strange, abnormal things can suddenly appear out of nowhere. I believe in tragedy."

"That's not what I meant! Oh sure, in some silly abstract manner you believe in witches and monsters and goblins and demons, but you don't really think my story is true, do you? Even the way you're looking at me now—like I'm some pitiful, deranged creature."

"Why, that's all in your mind," she snapped. "We're not looking at you that way at all."

All in your mind. For a panicky, despairing moment he wondered if everything he "remembered" about that night had been just a dream, a childish fantasy, all in his mind. Perhaps the reality was worse. But what could be worse than having your father snatched away in the jaws of some primeval monstrosity right before your very eyes?

"It *did* happen," he said firmly.

Samantha had sat there quietly, spellbound, as he told his story, and not said a word until now. "I believe you," she whispered. "I know what you're saying is true. I've seen the monsters myself."

Before he could ask her to explain her cryptic words, she burst into tears, covered her face with her hands, and ran into her bedroom. He could see her sprawled across her bed, still sobbing, out of the corner of his eye.

Mistress Dunn motioned for him to stay seated. "She'll be all right. She gets like this frequently. Samantha has had a very tragic life."

"What was it she saw?"

"I'd rather she tell you herself when she's ready. That way her story will have more veracity for you. Only one who has actually experienced the unknown can talk about it with any degree of...passion."

"Do you believe her story?"

"Of course I do, just as I believe yours." Again, he saw that queer look in her eyes. "I know your story is true, Mr. Bartlett. There's no doubt whatsoever in my mind." She paused, as if holding something back that she wanted to say to him, then added, "I could read your face as you spoke and see the truth of it in your eyes. In the first place, why would you come here and lie to us? What purpose would it serve? I told you I recognized that haunted look—the look of those who have witnessed the unknown and spend the rest of their lives trying to accept it or deny it or explain it to themselves, the look of honest, searching bewilderment. Your coming to me was healthy. It's just that...?"

"Just what?"

She wrung her hands and frowned. "I wish you had remembered more of what the creature looked like, something of its...peculiarities. I know your story is true. What you mistook in my eyes for condescension a moment ago was merely weariness, Mr. Bartlett. You're not the first person to have seen creatures, harmful, murderous creatures that kill without compunction or remorse."

"It was just an animal," Thomas said. "You make it sound like some kind of evil criminal."

"I think it was," she said, but wouldn't elaborate. She nodded her head several times quickly. "Yes, I do believe you, Mr. Bartlett. For one thing, what else could have been responsible for the destruction of Summerdale?"

"Beachside, actually. It was a district in the town of Summerdale."

"Yes, yes, of course, I remember." She pulled a pen and pad out of her bag. "These facts can be easily checked. Oh, I don't mean I'm checking up on *you*, Mr. Bartlett. I just want to look into the official records of the accident. Sudden storms, tidal waves, yes," she chuckled darkly, "all the usual tomfoolery, the specious explanations for the inexplicable that they always come up with." She at least made a show of jotting down the data he'd given her, then shoved the pad and pen back into the bag.

"Yes, it will be interesting to read all the rationalizations for this Beachside tragedy. I had heard of it, actually, but I'd forgotten. I'm very, very glad you came to me. I wish you had remembered more, but this should be...quite useful."

Useful? What the hell was she talking about? "What are you, writing a book?" he asked her, trying to fight off his feelings of paranoia and mistrust.

"No, no, Mr. Bartlett, relax. I'm taking this far more seriously than you imagine." She sat back and studied him for a moment. "What would you prefer?" she asked. "That I just stare at you in awe, wide-eyed like some schoolgirl, nodding my head and muttering about monsters the way some of the more pathetic members of the society would? Would that make you feel better? Would that help you take me more seriously? I have already said that I believe your story, but I won't just take your word for it, and why should I? Would you? I doubt it. Normally, the next step, if I am to be of service, would be to investigate what you've told me, to check the papers, the records of the incident, to find out if a district of Summerdale named Beachside was indeed destroyed in 1957."

"It was," he said icily. "You said you'd heard of it yourself."

She looked him straight in the eyes. "Yes," she said. "Actually I've known of this incident for quite some time now. But there have been so many strange incidents over the years —and this *was* over thirty years ago—that I needed to refresh my memory. I believe the mysterious destruction of Beachside has become quite famous in certain circles. Would you be interested or amazed to know, Mr. Bartlett, that I had wanted to talk to you, the only survivor and eyewitness of the tragedy, some years ago but couldn't trace your whereabouts? It appears when you were a boy you were swept out of town and taken to parts unknown, by relatives, I presume. I tried to track you down years later but couldn't."

"Are you telling me you've heard of me?"

"I didn't recall your name last night, of course. It's been some time since I tried to find you, but it started coming back to me a while ago when you mentioned Summerdale. Of course you have to be that little boy who survived. You went through a trauma perhaps worse than Samantha's."

"What happened to Samantha? Did *she* see this thing?"

Eustace seemed unwilling to give out any more information than she had to. "Not quite. Something…related. As I said, I'll let her tell you herself later if she cares to." She got up slowly. "But for now I must be going. Samantha!" she called spiritedly. "I'm leaving. Dry your eyes and say goodnight. Mr. Bartlett wants to stay and talk to you." Clearly Eustace would not put up with any of Samantha's nonsense. Thomas didn't know if Mistress Dunn was utterly insensitive or if she had been through this so often she'd simply determined the only way to snap Samantha out of her misery was to ignore it.

Before Thomas could say anything, Samantha appeared in the doorway of her bedroom. Her eyes and nose were red, but the tears had stopped. "I'm sorry, Eustace, it just got to me." She looked apologetically at Thomas. "Forgive me, Mr. Bartlett. As you've probably guessed," her expression turned slightly bitter, "I'm not the most stable person in the world." She pulled a tissue out of a pocket and wiped her nose.

"Really," Thomas said. "I don't think I should stay if Miss Clark is upset."

"Nonsense. What she needs now is someone to talk to, someone who's experienced the unknown as she has. Stay, Mr. Bartlett. Talk to Samantha."

"Wait! What happens now? What can your society do for me?"

"That's entirely up to you, Mr. Bartlett."

He raised his eyebrows. "Meaning?"

"Meaning that the society is supposed to be a support group for people such as yourself. Why do you think I wanted you and Samantha to meet? As for the rest, I said I will look again into this Beachside incident—not to confirm your story, but to see if we can find some answers for you. You do want answers, you know." She said softly, "All of us do."

"Do you think you can find these answers?"

She smiled sadly. "I won't make any promises. In the meantime, take comfort in the fact," she indicated Samantha, "that you're not alone. Not anymore, Mr. Bartlett." She headed for the door.

"Wait. I have one more question."

"Yes?"

"Have *you* seen any of these monsters?"

She smiled. "When you're ready, Mr. Bartlett, I'll tell you a little story. Until then let me have the prerogative of holding on to some of my secrets. It's all I've got left, after all."

Samantha started whining. "Eustace? What about dinner? I invited you for dinner."

"Mr. Bartlett looks like he has a good appetite. He can eat my share. Fatten him up a bit; he can stand it."

"Eustace!"

"Samantha, dear." She came over and gave her a peck on the cheek. "I really must be going. Have a nice supper with our new friend here. You two don't need me to compare notes. Get to know each other better."

Thomas had the feeling Eustace was playing matchmaker, and he wasn't quite sure how he felt about it. On the surface Samantha seemed not to be his type at all, yet there was something vulnerable and appealing about her. He wanted to comfort her and console her. In fact, he wanted to pick her brain.

Then the peculiar, enigmatic Mistress Eustace Dunn was gone, and Thomas was alone with Samantha.

"Do you like manicotti?" she asked.

Thomas smiled. "One of my favorites," he said.

* * *

This whole thing was giving Roderick the creeps.

He had driven Lemuel over to Branton Public Beach as he'd requested, but at this hour, in such cool weather, the shore was deserted. For a few days after the tragedy—after the authorities found the crushed car and discovered that two youngsters had been inside it—the beach had been packed with throngs of the morbidly curious. Eventually, when one official theorized that the car must have been crushed in the press at an automobile junkyard, then towed to the beach and abandoned, prospective monster and mayhem hunters got discouraged and went away. The "footprint" it was in was so large that its shape was not immediately distinguishable to anyone standing in it or near it. When its shape was finally seen from overhead, mashed down in the hard, wet stand near the shoreline, the authorities suggested it had been scooped out by a mischievous group of youngers who had come upon the car after it had been left on the beach by whoever killed Sally Rogers and Edward Begler.

Most of the print had been washed away by this time, the tides rolling in, filling it, covering it completely. There wasn't much left for Lemuel to see, but at least it was low tide. There was still an impression in the sand, only its shape was less distinct.

There wasn't much light left in the sky, and Rod hoped Lem would hurry. He did believe in sea monsters and did not want to be caught on the beach after dark.

The beach along the coastline stretched out in either direction for miles. Elsewhere on the shore big hotels had been built practically right up to the water's edge, but here that wasn't the case. Coupled with the vastness of the sea in front of him, the beach gave Roderick a feeling of impenetrable, hopeless loneliness. Behind him he could see the lights of houses and motels and cars driving down the highway. But if he stared straight ahead into the ocean it was possible to imagine he was caught on an alien beach on an abandoned planet, the only living soul in the world.

Lemuel hurried across the sand to the spot where the impression was, Roderick barely keeping up with him. He watched as Lemuel stepped into the indentation and started looking around. By the time he reached the footprint Lemuel was over at the far end of the impression—it was about 40 feet long, 20 feet wide, and almost three feet deep—bending down over what could have been the imprint of a gigantic clawed toe. Roderick shivered.

While Lemuel took pictures with his special night camera, Roderick turned about and stared back out at the sea. Just the thought of some enormous thing rising up out of the waves and striding malevolently out of the water was horrifying. What did happen that night? Had it been a hoax? Or had Gargantosaurus or one of its relatives decided for some reason to walk up on the land and trample everything in its path? And why only *one* footprint? Why did it go back in the water, and where did it go after that?

It was a breezy night, and he was chilly. He closed all the buttons on his sweater and wished he had brought something warmer. There was a jacket in the car, but he did not like leaving Lemuel alone—as if Rod could do anything to save his cousin if a monster did decide to rise out of the deep.

"Lemuel," he said, "what do you think? Could this whole thing be a hoax? News of Gargantosaurus with initial sketches were in all the papers. Some kids could have come out here.

The sand was wet, easy to shape with a spade or shovel. It might have taken some time, but still..."

Lemuel held out his arms. "Look how big this is. Who do you suspect—an entire football team working through the night? Besides, it's so perfect, so exact, even what little of it is left." He shook his head. "No, what you suggest is too incredible. And to do it down on the ground without guidance or the right perspective." He ran his hand back across his shiny bald head. "As for that picture you took, Rod, exactly when did you go up in the helicopter?"

"Last week. The same morning the print was found. I told you, I hired a helicopter just for something different to do, seeing as I can't do much of anything else anymore, and had the pilot take me for a long scenic ride. Anyway, I was snapping pictures like crazy the whole time, finally using that camera Gladys bought me before she died. I didn't even know what this here was when I was shooting it, only that it looked peculiar. By the time I got the pictures developed and had this one enlarged, I'd heard the news story about the crushed car and realized what I'd photographed. By that time, other people had done the same thing."

Lemuel was excited. "Don't you see? What jokester, no matter how devious, could have made such a perfect footprint while working on the ground? In that picture of yours, the shape is precise, the proportions perfect. And in the dark, too, in the middle of the night? I think it would have taken a whole team of surveyors using complicated instruments to get the measurements just so, wouldn't it? The footprint in that picture of yours is just too perfect." Roderick got the impression that Lemuel was trying to convince himself more than anyone else.

The wind swelled up suddenly, and Roderick felt terribly cold. Was Lemuel saying that Rod's suspicions were confirmed, that some gargantuan sea beast was wreaking havoc here along the Florida coast? If so, then what were they doing out here on this beach?

"I think we'd better go," he told his cousin.

Lemuel stood up straight and looked out at the ocean. "Just a minute." His face was glowing with enthusiasm. "To think—a living Gargantosaurus. It's just incredible!"

This was not like his more rational cousin Lemuel, to jump to conclusions so quickly. That was Rod's style, not Lem's. "Lemuel," Roderick said to him, "you still can't be certain. Aren't you the one who for years has scoffed at my foolish notions, my 'scrapbook of monsters,' as you called it? A crushed car, a footprint..."

Lemuel turned to him abruptly. "And what about all the other inexplicable events? The cabin cruiser on top of the farm with the teeth marks in it? Eh?"

"Those punctures could have been made by anything." He gestured helplessly. "Lemuel, I got a little carried away. I wanted to believe, so I rejected rational explanations."

Lemuel pulled himself up to his full height and glared at his cousin. "What are you saying, Roderick? That now that your theory may well be correct, you're afraid? Is that it? Are you afraid, Roderick? Or have you been lying to me, deliberately exaggerating?"

Roderick had never seen Lemuel so angry before. "Lying, Lemuel? Never! Everything I told you is the truth. But a professional man like you can't just jump to conclusions, no matter what has happened. You have a professional reputation." His shoulders sank and he moaned. "The truth is that I wanted to believe in this sea monster, but I don't want to believe in it anymore. Yes, Lem, I'm scared. Scared for everybody."

Lemuel snorted. "Bah! Stop acting like an old woman. Here we are, possibly on the verge of the greatest scientific discovery of this century, and you stand there quivering like a schoolboy. You of all people should be thrilled at the possibility of the existence of a living prehistoric animal."

"There's no need to yell, Lemuel. Now can we please get out of here?"

Lemuel gestured in disgust. "Bah!" he repeated, like some caricature of a mad scientist on the late show.

As they made their way back to their car Roderick was glad it was growing dark because then his cousin couldn't see his red face or the tears welling at the corners of his eyes. "Thor" Thorson was much more sensitive than his appearance suggested; since childhood he had hated to be yelled at. And his cousin was so mad at him. Why? Because Roderick hated the idea of a sea monster coming out of the ocean and killing people? He felt awful.

It was one thing when it was a safe, romantic fantasy, a silly preoccupation with a Loch Ness type of creature who stayed in his watery burrow and bothered no one. But *this* was something else again. It had never really hit him until now. Why was his rational friend Lemuel getting so upset about all this? Surely a man of science would have to see more evidence before arriving at such a blatantly risky verdict.

But as they reached the car and he slid behind the wheel he thought he knew why this was so important to Lemuel. As Lemuel had said earlier, he had not really discovered the remains of Gargantosaurus, or even pieced them together. He'd only named the creature. But this was a chance to do so much more, to win the approval and admiration of his colleagues. He needed this monstrous sea beast to be real and alive, needed it like a junkie needed his fix.

Neither of them spoke as the car pulled away from the side of the coast road where it had been parked. Roderick broke the silence a few moments later. "Anyway," he said, "it's getting dark now. There's nothing left to see."

Lemuel only grunted.

"What should we have done? Stayed there all night?"

"Afraid of your own shadow," Lemuel muttered.

"Afraid? You bet I am." Stay calm, he told himself. "This Gargantosaurus. Is it carnivorous?"

Lemuel nodded. "Indubitably. And it was probably endothermic—hot-blooded—which meant it had to eat lots of meat to generate its own heat."

"And its home was the ocean?"

"Like other dinosaurs and animals it's equally at home in the sea or on land. But unlike many of the large sea creatures of the prehistoric era, it *is* a dinosaur."

"How did one get as far inland as Arizona?"

"The topography of the world was quite different back then," Lemuel explained impatiently. "Much of the desert was originally under water."

"Yes, yes."

"Any more questions?"

"Just one."

"What is it?"

"This beast—that may have crushed the car, and been responsible for all those other things in my scrapbook—do you honestly believe it could be a living Gargantosaurus?"

"Yes."

Roderick thought of all the times his cousin had scornfully dismissed the possibility of living dinosaurs, citing facts and arguments and physical laws against it. "But how, Lemuel? Why now? Why here? It's too much..."

"Of a coincidence? Yes, it is."

Roderick shrugged. "Then...?"

Lemuel scratched the side of his nose. "I can't explain it."

"You're not going to rush into something..."

"No, of course not." Lemuel sighed heavily and ran his hand across his forehead. "Rod, I'm sorry. I got so upset. It's just that, without even realizing it, you built up my hopes, then seemed to be...backstabbing...I mean backsliding." He sighed again, briefly. "God, I'm tired. Rod, please forgive me, okay?"

"Sure."

"It's just that out there on the beach, in the twilight with that vast ocean right in front of us, it seemed as if anything were possible

"Yes, I know," Roderick said and shuddered.

* * *

It was midnight and Barney Weiler was running wild.

He had hit every bar in the small Florida town of Panamonte, then got behind the wheel of his car and drove back to the shanty where he lived. He almost cracked up half a dozen times, then screamed out defiantly and joyously at the top of his lungs when in some dumb lucky way he managed to survive. Now his truck squealed and shook belligerently as it pulled up to the dilapidated piers and shacks that made up Weiler's Fishing Station.

Weiler made a good living renting boats to tourists or the occasional local, who wanted to do a little fishing. He had everything from canoes to speedboats. He sold tackle and souvenirs in one of the shacks out on the main dock and even had a little snack bar in another shanty on the shore. Yes, it was a good, easy living, that was for sure. He had nothing to complain about.

But every once in a while he needed some female companionship, which was hard to come by as Weiler was 63, five feet four, and weighed over 230 pounds. So he got into his truck and drove into town where he drank too much out of frustration. Tonight was no exception. He grunted as he stumbled out of the truck, tripped over an empty beer bottle at his feet, and fell right over onto his belly.

Think I'll just lie here, he thought. It was too much trouble to hoist himself up and walk on his squat, shaky legs to his bedroom in the shanty. Nothing seemed to be broken; his fat had protected him. He'd just put his head on top of his arms and go to sleep right there like a baby.

Half an hour later he was abruptly awakened.

Something was there in the boat yard, something big and dark, and it was smashing apart the rowboats. *What the hell is that?*

He was sober in an instant. Good God, one of the larger boats had just risen 15 feet up into the air and been thrown, simply hurled, into the woods at the edge of the fishing station. It broke apart into at least a dozen pieces.

"My God!"

Barney stood there in disbelief as another boat went flying out of the water and into the trees. Then another! It was almost as if the destruction was planned and methodical. What the hell could be doing it?

Then the water directly in front of the dock he was standing on parted and the engineer of this destruction was right there before him, at least part of it—a neck and head rising like a fleshy, angry monolith from the ocean.

All Barney could emit from his suddenly constricted throat was a little gurgle. He tried to run but couldn't; he was too petrified to move.

He was staring into an eye that was bigger than he was.

And the eye was staring back.

A dim part of his brain recorded and nearly rejected the fact that if that one single eye was *that big*, then the whole beast itself must be...

Then the thing sat up in the water. Boats all around it were instantly shattered into splinters, and Barney saw his whole life and business falling down around him in bits and tatters.

And the eye was now many, many feet above Barney's head.

Barney looked up, transfixed. His bladder burst, releasing a warm, pungent stream of beer-piss that ran down his legs and collected in a puddle at his feet. He could feel his bowels begin to open.

The Devil. It had to be The Devil. There was no other possible explanation. *God help me. God help me!*

Then the sight of that horrible face above him was blotted out as an enormous hand/paw/claw came rushing down out of the sky.

Barney screamed.

The hand crashed down. Blood and urine intermingled and dripped between the slats of the dock even as the dock itself burst into pieces.

The Great Beast lifted its appendage, stuck out its tongue.

And licked Barney off its hand.

CHAPTER TEN

ATTACK OF THE REPTILE
MONSTERS

Thomas had not intended to spend the night with Samantha Clark. It had been the last thing on his mind, in fact. True, he had not slept with a woman since his abrupt and final break up with that nutty Elsa, but he had always been a man of comparative temperance and moderation. Casual, boozy sex was not for him; he could wait until the right one came along. But the evening progressed and evolved in such a way that their sleeping together was almost inevitable. If nothing else, both of them had the need.

It started almost at once, right after Eustace Dunn left. Samantha went to check on dinner, poured him a little more wine, then excused herself as she went to the bathroom. When she came out a little bit later, not only were her tears completely dry, but Thomas saw that she had applied rouge and lipstick to make her face less pale and more appealing. She'd run a comb through her hair. Then she snuck into the bedroom somewhat self-consciously and came out dressed in a lovely skirt and blouse Instead of that awful housedress.

Thomas was flattered. Is all that for me? he wondered. He hadn't had a woman primp for him in quite some time, and it certainly made a difference. Samantha would never be a raving beauty, but her appearance had improved perceptibly. Even just the change of clothes would have worked miracles. And the expression on her face was so warm and tender, so desperate for approval, and so sympathetic. He saw things in her that he had barely been aware of before.

She checked on the dinner again, then sat down on the sofa across from his chair and smiled. "Sorry again about my little spell back there."

"That's okay. I gather what happened to you was as bad for you as my experience was for me. You've got nothing to apologize for. If a person can't shed a few tears in their own apartment…"

She laughed.

"Anyway. If you'd like to tell me what happened later, I'd be glad even honored, to hear it." Already the wine was going to his head.

She nodded. "Maybe later."

While they ate dinner, which was delicious, and had more wine, he asked her how she had come to join the Monster Society. "I mean, how did you learn of its existence?"

"I read about it in some magazine. What happened to me…happened many years ago. About ten years ago, actually. Nobody seemed able to help me; no one believed me. I knew there'd be a lot of crackpots at the society, but…"

He rolled his eyes heavenward. "Brother, are there!"

She smirked in agreement. "Yes, there are quite a few. This fat lady called Amanda who swears she has a rat as big as a dog living in her attic." Her laugh was infectious. "And Squinty, this weird old guy with funny eyes who hardly ever talks to anyone. And others."

She stopped for a moment, then said, "But at least they listened; at least they didn't laugh at me. Mistress Dunn said she would investigate for me and try to prove to everyone— everyone outside the society, that is—that I wasn't insane."

"Is that what people thought?"

"Wait'll you hear my story. Even you might think I'm crazy."

"I doubt it."

"Anyway, I found myself searching through the membership—not only people who came regularly, but even stragglers—looking for anyone who had had a legitimate experience, as we had. Not that I had much luck, at least confirming anything. I don't know why I did it. I thought it might help, I guess, and in a way it has. I've been less...lonely."

She got up from the kitchen table abruptly and went to a cupboard over the stove. "I'm not really crazy about wine," she said. He watched her take down a bottle of vodka, pour a great deal of it into a water glass and throw in a couple of ice cubes. Did he make her all that nervous?

As she sat back at the table with her drink, which she put behind a bottle of salad dressing as if she were hiding it, he asked, "How has Mistress Dunn's investigation been coming along?"

"Oh, she's done more than I ever expected. Contacted lots of people, professionals, and scientists. She has money and connections, you see. But she hasn't turned up anything that might prove my story one way or another. It's not her fault. She tried."

"What does *she* get out of it?"

Samantha only shrugged in reply.

As dinner progressed the conversation switched from the society, Mistress Dunn, and prehistoric monsters to matters less esoteric. Samantha said she worked as a clerk typist for a temporary employment agency. "I've been there for years. I don't actually work at the agency. You see, they send me out on assignments to different places. I can take a few days off whenever I want to. My parents left me quite a bit of money, and I don't pay much rent. I wind up working only about six or seven months out of the year."

"I have a lot of spare time, too. I'm a restaurateur."

He told her about Parmenter's, and she said that she had heard of it.

They talked awhile longer about favorite restaurants and life in Miami—a little personal history, but nothing heavy—and Samantha stood up and got herself another vodka, less surreptitiously this time.

She held the open bottle out toward Thomas. "Would you like some?" she asked.

The wine he'd consumed had made him so pleasantly light-headed, so supremely capable of relaxing and enjoying this unexpected evening—as he had not enjoyed an evening or anyone's company in such a long time—that he didn't want to lose the feeling. The wine was all gone. "Okay," he said, "but do you have anything to mix it with?"

"Uh-huh." She opened the refrigerator. "Let's see. Orange juice, grapefruit juice, tomato juice. Hell, I've even got prune juice."

"I think grapefruit juice will do."

"A greyhound. That's what it's called. One greyhound coming up."

The drink was a bit sour, but the more of it he drank the better he liked it. He licked his lips. "Good."

"Slowly, now. Vodka can sneak up on you."

Feeling silly, he said, "I'll be careful. Wouldn't want you taking advantage of me." The minute he said it he regretted it, but Samantha laughed and laughed.

"I'm sorry I've got no dessert. Neither Eustace nor I eat any."

He patted his belly. "I try to avoid it myself."

"Bosh. You're in great shape." She took a large slug of her vodka. "Why don't you relax in the living room while I clear the dishes?"

"You want help?"

"No. I'm just gonna pile them in the sink and let them soak."

They were both high, he could tell, and he reminded himself to slow down on the drinking and watch his behavior. He was not as experienced a drinker as Samantha obviously was. He didn't mind getting high now and then, but God help him if he became like his father.

His father!

He had a flash: *"I've got you, grab my hand,"* *His father. The trapdoor. Debris. Screaming.*

Then it was gone.

He held his forehead for a second and calmed himself.

A few minutes later Samantha came into the living room and sat beside him on the couch. Drink had made her personality come alive; her face had lost its haunted, hangdog look, its dour passivity, and it seemed spritely and animated. Thomas was finding her increasingly attractive, but whether it was because he was high or she was high, or both, he wasn't sure.

When she offered him another greyhound he hesitated for only a moment. Yes, he was getting a little drunk but so was she, so she'd hardly care or notice if he made a slight fool of himself. Anyway, it felt good. He was comfortable. He could handle it. "I will have another," he told her, thrusting out his glass. "Damn, that was good."

"Good," she said, taking the glass and rising to her feet. "And I think I'll have another, too." As she went into the kitchen she muttered something cryptic into a singsong manner, "I was hoping you'd say no but I'm glad you said yes." Was she running low on booze? he wondered.

But no, she brought the bottle and grapefruit juice back with her and put them down heavily on the table, and he could see that there was plenty of vodka left in the bottle, more than enough for both of them. As they sat and talked and giggled, laughing about Eustace's silly name and the whole nitwit Monster Society, as they forgot their troubles, Thomas almost matched Samantha drink for drink. Finally, after she poured herself another vodka, without ice, this time, he held his hand over his glass as she tried to pour him another one. "No more. Let me rest a bit. I'm getting…high."

"Good," she said. She leaned toward him and planted a quick kiss on his lips. "I like it when my men are high. I like it when I'm high, too. God, I love to be high, don't you?"

Thomas hiccuped. "Excuse me. High's okay. But I don't wanna be d-drunk."

"Party pooper. I can get you a soda."

"Nothing. Maybe later." He was quite high, but not sick, though he knew he'd have a hell of a hangover in the morning. His words were beginning to slur and he felt dopey and probably looked it, too. Samantha was very high but in better control of herself. It was as if she could turn it on or off at will, silly one minute, restrained the next. Samantha's face loomed in again, and this time her mouth was opening and his mouth was opening, and they were caught in a deep sloppy kiss that seemed to go on forever. Thomas felt that certain stirring in his groin. Samantha leaned against him, her small breasts rubbing against his chest, and he enfolded her in his arms. They pulled out of the kiss, pulled in again, and then were suddenly in the throes of that ageless, conscienceless passion made up of one part sex and two parts alcohol. "Bedroom," she muttered out of the corner of her mouth, her lips still tight against his own. "Let's go bedroom."

In the back of his mind he wondered if this was a good idea, but he wanted her and didn't want to displease her. Women had always been able to wrap him around their little fingers. Oh God, I'm high, he thought. But he knew he'd have no problem getting it up as he could feel his erection hardening already.

Which brought him to this point, lying at her side in her bed, their passion spent, both satisfied from the animal act, drowsy from booze and food and frantic exertion. Had it been good sex? He couldn't tell or remember. It had been so quick, so desperate, so frenzied. The end result, though, was that it had felt good, and he supposed that that was all that mattered.

He was still high, but in control. The food had soaked up much of the alcohol, and she'd been niggardly passing out the vodka, saving most of the bottle for herself. She was putting it to her lips now, and he was tempted to ask her if he could have a swallow.

"You like your vodka, don't you?" he said, leaning up on his elbow, facing her as she lay on her back with her head upon the pillow. Some of the vodka was spilling onto her bosom and he bent down to lick it off.

"I like that," she said. He stopped, lifted his head, and smiled.

"Yes, I do love vodka," she finally replied. "In fact, I live to drink. I mean, *love* to drink."

For a moment he just blinked, "Just as long as you don't overdo it. I mean, it's okay to go off on a toot now and then, just not every night. Like my father did."

She turned her head to look at him. "Your father was a drunk?"

"The town drunk. A real hard case. I can hardly remember when he wasn't three sheets to the wind."

"Poor guy."

"Ah, don't feel sorry for him. All this talk of disease and heredity and all that shit and those silly people going to AA meetings and telling themselves that it's not their fault 'cause they're just sick. Sick, my eye. Bunch of losers. Damn drunks. And they never shut up about it once they've reformed." He snorted. "Gotten some backbone is more like it." The moonlight from the window fell against a corner of the room beyond the bed, and he saw a desk, with photographs and clippings of some kind taped to the white wall behind and on either side of it. "What are those clippings?" he asked. But she didn't answer.

"Damn drunks," he continued. "I'm tired of their self-justification. Just a bunch of weaklings without courage or character and the strength to say no. Hate drunks."

Samantha snuggled down deeper into the mattress. She was very still and quiet for a moment. Then flatly she stated, "I'm a drunk."

"No, I mean, seriously. We were just partying."

She continued her confession. "I party all the time. That's why I don't work so much. I'm too hungover to go into the office." She lifted the now empty vodka bottle. "I go through more of these a week than you could imagine."

"Really? But–"

"I'm a drunk. An alcoholic. I even went to AA and the whole bit. Can't stay on the wagon, though. Just weak, I guess. Like you said."

"God, Samantha, I didn't mean—"

"It's okay, Thomas, it's okay. I'm not sure I don't agree with you. I guess a lot of us are weak. I didn't intend to drink tonight, but I did. Knew it would make things easier. First it was just going to be some wine—just one glass, that was all—and then I thought I'd have a teensy refill just to keep you company. But then I got this craving. You were so attractive, and the night was going so well, and I can be so shy and so awkward when I'm sober…"

He refuted her softly, "No, no," though of course she was right.

"…so I got out the vodka and…you know why I offered you a glass? Not because I was being a good hostess, but because I figured if you had a drink it would give me an excuse to have another and another just to keep you company. After that, I didn't care anymore. I swear I didn't plan to drink tonight. But I did. So you see what a mess I am? A drunk. Just like your father."

Before he could say anything—God, what could he say?—
she got out of bed and turned on the light switch. She went
over to the desk in the corner and held out her arms to take it
in. "This," she said, "this is my shrine, my altar." He could see
it was covered with pictures of a family, possibly Samantha's
family, a clean-cut husband type with a pipe in his mouth, a
pretty wife with dimples, two cute children about nine or ten
years old and a dog. He was too far away to see what the clippings on the wall said, but he could tell they had been taken
from newspapers.

"I could say I started drinking because of what happened
to me—what Eustace loves to call my encounter with the
unknown—but actually I used to tipple a bit even before that.
What happened to me made it worse, I suppose. I was driving
home from a bar one night five years ago when I had a little
accident. I ran into a car with four people inside. *These* people.
The Allen family. I made it, but they didn't." She paused for
what seemed like a long time and added, "Would you believe
even that didn't get me to stop drinking? Four people, a whole
family, dead because of me, and I still couldn't stop drinking. I
was in the hospital for months. Dried out, desperate for a
drink. I wanted to die, wanted to drink myself into oblivion.

"DWI and vehicular manslaughter laws were more lenient
then than they are now. I lost my license, paid a fine, spent a
little time doing community service. Joined the religious nuts
at the AA. The whole bit. As if any of that could compensate
for what I'd done."

She pulled herself up a bit and wrapped her arms around
her body as if she had a chill. "One day I woke up and realized that it had gone too far. A whole family was gone, wiped
off the earth, because of my drinking, and I had to stop it once
and for all. I became obsessed with finding out everything I
could about the Allens. I got pictures of them—don't ask me
how, half the time I was drunk, even then—made photocopies
of the stories in the papers about the accident. I was hoping

they'd turn out to be hateful people but they were really nice. Mr. and Mrs. Allen were only in their thirties. The children… were children. He was a lawyer and she was a part-time registered nurse. Unlike me, they'd made something of their lives. And I'd taken all that from them.

"I framed the photographs and hung the clippings on the wall and made this desk a shrine, an altar, my 'remember why you must not drink, Samantha' corner. Every morning when I woke up, the first thing I saw would be the Allens, the clippings about my accident, about how I destroyed them. I told myself never, ever, to let myself forget."

She sunk down into the wooden chair in front of the desk. "But now look at me. Still drunk. Still drinking. Just as weak as ever. I can't drive anymore, I tell myself, even if I got my license back. I can't be a menace on the highways. No one will ever die again because of me. So it's safe. Why not take one more drink just to ease the pain and loneliness? Why not, Samantha? Anything to wipe away the faces of the Allens as they keep staring at me and hating me and—God help me—forgiving me from the grave."

As she sat there weeping, her head hanging down, her body collapsing in on itself, Thomas tried to make sense out of what he was hearing and of his conflicting feelings. He was appalled, he was repulsed, he was touched, he was concerned, he hated her, he loved her, all of these and none of these, and it didn't help that everything that was happening and was being said had the quality of a dream about it, a sense of distance, due to the alcohol in his system.

He got up and went over to her side, touched her shoulders. "Samantha, stop. I'm sorry. Samantha, whatever happened was a long time ago. It's over. I'm sure you didn't mean…" But inside part of him wanted to say, "Get up, you stupid drunk, and get yourself together. Kill four people and you go on drinking! What kind of stupid, helpless, hopeless wreck of a woman are you?" He wanted to slap her face and make her cry some more, wanted her to do penance for every drunken, stupid thing that she and his father—and he?—had ever done. "Samantha, please. It's over now. What happened was a very long time ago."

She looked up after a moment, tears still streaming down her face. "Do you want to hear it?" she said. "What happened? You might as well. You've heard everything else."

He had been referring to the automobile crash, the tragedies, but apparently she had thought he meant the "encounter with the unknown" she had yet to speak of. He moved away from her and sat down on the edge of the bed, facing her. "Yes, I'd like to hear it. If you think it might help."

She wiped the tears away from her eyes and cheeks with the back of her fists. "It happened in 1978," she started. "My fiancé Harold and I decided to go sailing for a few days with some friends, do some fishing, go swimming, get drunk." Her eyes flicked in his direction for a second. "Even on the ocean I'm a character." She put her hand on her cheek for a moment. "Anyway, we left West Palm Beach and made our way toward the Bahamas. Our friends were not exactly what you'd call experienced sailors. Harold and I assumed that the captain and his wife, a rather dippy couple named Reuben and Fanny Koerner, had some idea of where they were going and what they were doing, but I think all they really wanted to do was show off their new cabin cruiser. It was a beautiful boat, I'll grant you that. Anyway, it wasn't long before we ran into a storm.

"It seems Reuben and Fanny had never checked to see what kind of weather lay ahead. But they had this summer home on one of the tiny islands northeast of the Grand Bahamas and the Great Abacos. There were only about four other houses on the island and a dock with a boathouse and storage shed. Reuben had even had an automobile shipped over some months before so he could tool around the dirt roads on the island in his Cadillac. What a bigshot! We hadn't planned on arriving at the island for a couple more days at least, but he thought it would be safer for us to head for and hole up on the island until the storm was over. It hadn't started raining or anything yet, but we could hear thunder in the distance and the clouds were positively black. I'll never forget when we finally pulled into the little harbor and got off the boat and Reuben told us to wait a minute and stepped into the storage shed that I guess all the residents could use."

* * *

Summer, 1978. Halliday Island.

"Wait a minute. I'll be right back," Reuben said. Again Samantha could not help noting with distaste how repulsive he looked with his belly straining against the material of that loud Hawaiian shirt. He combed what was left of his hair, just a few black greasy strands, across his bald scalp and always had a smelly stogie hanging out of his blubbery lips. He was a short fat disgusting man with a face that looked like a backside.

His wife Fanny was almost worse. She was a blowsy brunette around 45 who thought she was 20 years younger. She had high cheekbones, pointy chin, her long hairspray-stiff tresses curling upwards and outwards as they hit her collar-bone. It would take a cannonball to mess up that awful hair-style. She wore a tight black tank top, tight tan shorts (she had ugly legs whether she wanted to admit it or not) and hideous thick white spangled bracelets around her wrists. Pink high heels completed the ensemble.

Samantha had been throwing daggers at Harold the whole trip. She loved Harold Myers—though her late parents would turn over in their graves if they knew she planned on marrying a Jewish man—but she could abide few of his friends or relatives. Fanny and Reuben were a vulgar, loudmouthed couple, and she planned on telling Harold that when she was alone with him. He should have known better than to drag her along on this outing, the whole purpose of which was for "Rube" and "Fan" to show off their latest acquisitions. What a vulgar, vulgar couple! Samantha swore she was not anti-Semitic, but she clearly *still* had issues.

The other couple were also Jewish, at least the husband, Allan Bergman, was, but they were the nicest folks you'd ever want to meet. Allan's wife, Betty, had once been Protestant like Samantha, but had converted to Judaism when she got married. Allan was a dear, a nice-looking, quietly masculine man with blond wavy hair, a winning smile, and glasses. He was tall and broad-shouldered but had a wonderfully sensitive face and charm to spare. Betty was almost half Allan's size, a wispy, sweet thing with thin lips, a button nose and big brown eyes. She was wearing her hair in a ponytail today and always wore a lot of bright red lipstick.

Samantha's Harold was a tall, slender man with curly brown hair, big ears, glasses, and what she thought was a very sexy Paul Newman kind of nose. He looked too skinny in his bathing suit, though; she liked him better when he put on his clothes. She loved him very, very much.

Samantha and Betty were the youngest ones there, in their early thirties, and had become instant friends. Fanny tried her best to insinuate herself into the duo—"just us girls, huh?"— to make it a trio, but Sam suspected Betty didn't like the woman, either. Fanny was totally devoid of warmth. Then they all heard the toot of a car horn and suddenly Reuben drove out of the wide open doors of the shed at the landing in the most vulgar purple Cadillac that Sam had ever seen. It even had cattle horns on the hood.

Fanny and Reuben were in their element, showing off the car, proving they were so rich they could afford to keep an extra Cadillac locked away on an island for a goodly part of the year. "C'mon, everybody. I'll drive us all up to the house."

The six of them piled into the automobile, and Reuben, still chomping on his "ceegar," honked the horn again and took off.

Samantha had to admit the island was beautiful, with lush greenery, beautiful plants and flowers. Not even Reuben and Fanny had ruined it yet. They passed one house—a split-level monstrosity done up in pseudo-Japanese style that overlooked the ocean —and continued on to a higher level of the island. Soon they were surrounded by an extravagant purplish-green tropical forest. Samantha could hear birds chirping, and she took a deep breath to fill her lungs with good clean air instead of the smell of Reuben's stogie.

The dirt road began to incline upward rather steeply, and Samantha could see Reuben and Fanny's summer home up at the top of the hill. The forest gave way to a long stretch of lawn that rolled all the way up to the house. From a distance the lawn looked magnificent, but up close one could see the brown patches and dead grass baking in the hot summer sun. Reuben hit the horn again.

"Stop doing that,"' Fanny screeched. "I have a headache."

"Tony wasn't down at the dock, so I figured he might be up at the house checking things out for us." He chuckled. "Thought I'd give him a chance to put our booze away."

Fanny sighed and explained that Tony was the year-round caretaker whose salary was divided up and paid by the four tenants. "He doesn't expect us for two or three days," she reminded her husband. "We probably won't even have any lights."

"I can work the generator," Reuben said. Fanny grunted.

The house looked more like something you'd see in Beverly Hills than on a tropical island. It was one story, with stucco walls, tiled walkways, large glass patio doors, a large oval swimming pool, and a deck in back that hung out over the cliff which itself led down to the ocean. Fanny assured them that it had all the modern conveniences and that the pantry was stocked with plenty of food and liquor. "If it rains, we'll party," she said.

It did rain. For two straight days. The men ran about battening down the hatches as the wind howled, trees overturned, and dirt and pebbles spun through the air. Tony was nowhere to be found, not at his small cabin which was located near the landing, nor at any of the other houses. As there were still no phone lines, Reuben had to drive around looking for the man and came back so soaked, disheveled and freezing he went straight to a hot bath and stayed there for practically the rest of the evening.

The group made the best of it. Fanny made casseroles and martinis, and they played bridge and parcheesi. After a few drinks Samantha found that she was beginning to like Fanny, who was a good sport and a perfect hostess; she eventually won over Betty, too. Reuben was likeable enough in his rough crude way if you didn't take him seriously. Samantha did her best to shed her affluent waspish pre-conceptions—all of which Reuben only perpetuated—and treated herself to another vodka and tonic. She and Harold cuddled on the sofa when the others went to sleep.

On the third day the sun came out and the clouds disappeared. There was not even a hint of rain or humidity. To celebrate, Fanny broke out a bottle of champagne which Samantha guzzled as if it were oxygen and she a suffocating scuba diver.

None of them sensed that they were no longer alone on the island.

The group decided to stay one more day and night on the island and then set sail at a leisurely pace for the mainland. Plenty of time to soak up the sun and the bourbon. The six of them went about in a state of perpetual semi-drunkenness and, noticing that that bitch Betty was being affectionate with other men besides her own husband, Samantha simply had another vodka and tonic.

The first bad sign was when Betty and Allan, walking off their dinner, found Tony's personal sloop cracked and muddied, full of water and washed up in a lagoon on the south side of the island. "Doesn't mean he was in it," Reuben said.

"Then where the hell is he?" his wife protested. "If he was out there during that storm…"

"He would have known better. I'll take another look for him before I radio the Coast Guard from the ship."

They didn't know that Tony, who hit the bottle to make the time go faster, had sailed to a tiny adjacent island to kill some hours and had been stuck there when the storm broke.

He had been sailing back to the island after the rain stopped when he became the first victim of the island's malignant visitors.

The second bad sign was when Reuben never returned from looking for Tony.

The dirt roads were so muddy from the rainfall that he didn't want to take his Cadillac; instead he went off on a bicycle the Koerners kept in the garage. Cursing, Fanny took the Cadillac anyway when she went to look for Reuben. When she came back the car was filthy and she was sobbing. She had found the bicycle but not her husband. The bicycle had been crushed, as if placed in a clothespress, and was lying in a puddle of blood. There was no sign of Reuben.

"There, there," Samantha said, "he probably just injured himself a little. He'll be all right, I'm sure."

"But where is he?" Fanny whined, pressing her fingers to her lips.

The last bad sign was when three-quarters of the search party never returned, either. Allan, Harold and Betty went with Fanny in the Cadillac to search the area where she had found the bicycle. Samantha stayed in the house in case Reuben showed up. As she stood on the deck looking out at the sea, she thought she could hear strange thundering noises in the trees on the lower part of the island but convinced herself it was only the wind.

Fanny and the Cadillac came back an hour later. She was hysterical, her arms and legs scratched and bloodied, mosquito bites all over her face. She and the others had split up, she said. There was a big path through the woods not far from the bicycle that looked as if a herd of elephants had gone through it. Allan and Betty and Harold followed it to look for Reuben while Fanny drove along the road to the other side of the island, hoping to come upon Reuben, possibly dazed and injured, disoriented, walking in the wrong direction. She came upon one of the other four houses, a small, comparatively flimsy cottage that had been literally torn to shreds, apparently by the high wind velocity of the storm. There were odd large footprints in the mud, though, several times the size of a man's, and a lot of blood all over the ground.

"It gave me the creeps and I panicked," Fanny said. "I got back in the car and drove back to where I'd dropped off the others. I followed them inland, calling their names..."

She dropped her face into her hands. "And then I heard this terrible screaming. I saw something coming for me through the trees...I couldn't see what it was, but it was enormous. And I think it got them." She sobbed and shivered like a sinner facing final judgment.

Samantha slapped Fanny's face. "Get a hold of yourself! What did you see? Be rational! You didn't just leave them stranded, did you?" But Sam knew it wasn't so far away that the others couldn't always walk back to the house if they had to.

"I was scared, so scared," Fanny chattered. "I want my Reuben, I tell you. I want my Reuben."

And Samantha wanted Harold. She poured off a stiff drink for Fanny and another for herself. *I think it got them.* Thank goodness she wasn't sober.

Fanny was no help; Samantha would have to take things

into her own hands. What first? It was growing darker. Take the car and go look for the others? Stay here with Fanny? What? She decided she would take the car, but first she would fortify herself with another little drink. Of course that story about "screaming" in the woods and something "enormous" was a lot of bullshit. Stupid Fanny probably panicked when she saw a mouse.

It was a good thing Samantha took that drink or what happened to Fanny might have happened to Samantha.

"I need some lotion for these bites on my face," Fanny said absurdly, still thinking of her appearance as her life was seemingly tumbling down around her. Shocked by whatever had really happened to her, she had retreated into the deceptive security of everyday normality. The lotion she wanted was in her purse, which she'd taken with her out of habit and left in the car. She went out the front door to get it.

Samantha saw the whole thing from the kitchen window as she was opening a tray of ice cubes.

Fanny, dressed in that same ridiculous outfit she'd worn when they arrived at the island, was bending over the side of the car to pick her purse up off the seat. Just as her fingers touched the purse, something crashed out of the trees and bushes to the right of the driveway. At first Samantha thought she had to be seeing an optical illusion. The beast she saw was really just a small thing actually, and it was crawling across the window pane, and—it was silly, really—because of the odd perspective it just looked as if it were big enough to swallow Fanny whole.

And then it swallowed Fanny whole.

Fanny probably had time only to see the shadow fall across her, sheathing the Cadillac in darkness, when the lips opened and the tongue slurped out and she was pulled up and off the ground, pulled right out of those pink high heels of hers. Fanny was engulfed by heat and spittle and sucked up into a maw, caught between those thick slimy lips, and eaten.

It was like a lizard swallowing a bug.

Samantha saw the lips of the beast moving, moving.

My God, it's chewing her. The ice cube tray fell out of her hands and dropped into the sink, freeing its contents. Samantha's stomach almost did the same.

The thing that Samantha saw was about the size of a bus. She couldn't exactly describe it, but she would have said it was a big lizard, like an overgrown iguana, with a long body and tail, four fat legs, a large head that grew straight out of the torso, and no neck to speak of. It had lidded eyes that blinked steadily and seemed to be swimming in a gelatinous concoction.

The thing turned toward the house.

But that wasn't the worst thing; it wasn't even that Samantha saw several more of the monstrous lizards strolling out of the forest and heading in her direction. The worst thing was her realization that what that monster did to Fanny it had probably done to Harold and the others.

She ran out of the kitchen, as if shutting the beasts out of her sight would somehow send them out of existence, and kept telling herself this was only a drunken fantasy. What she saw through the kitchen window had never even happened. She went straight to the vodka bottle on the living room table and lifted it to her lips. The problem wasn't that she was drunk; the problem was that she was not drunk enough. Was this what they called the D.T.s—*please God, let this be a halluci-nation, big lizards instead of pink elephants, please*—or had she suddenly lost her mind overnight?

This whole thing had to be a dream.

She finished the bottle of vodka and took a peek out of the kitchen window.

The lizards were still there, only closer. They were sort of playing with the Cadillac, tearing it apart. One of them was bleeding from an injury on the side and had to keep fending off the carnal blood-lusting advances of the others. They were hungry, all right. And a nice human morsel was just waiting for them nice and helpless inside the house.

It was getting dark very fast, Samantha noted hysterically, still in a state of disbelief. The day had passed quickly. Perhaps the lizards would go to sleep when night came. Perhaps they would go back to the sea where they must have come from. She was sure it was the storm that brought them.

When the wall came tumbling down in the next room, Samantha ran to the hallway where Reuben had shown them the trap door that led to the attic and the roof. She pulled it down—it had a folding wood staircase built right into it—and hastily climbed upward. She could hear more walls crumbling, hear things falling to the floor, toppling over, furniture being cracked and crushed and glass shattering everywhere. She was so drunk she was ready to pass out, but she knew that if she did she'd never survive.

She hunkered down in the narrow attic and held on to a hammer that some workman had left there as if she were a baby, and it, the mother. She tried to keep the walls from quivering by focusing on one spot and one spot only on the floor. The creepy thing was that as they tore the house apart to get at her the reptiles made no noise. Not a sound, not a bellow. Nothing.

When she heard movement directly below her, she panicked. The house might literally crumble around her, which would send her flying directly down into the mouths of those animals. She saw the little window that led out onto the roof and ran over to it. Dropping the hammer she thrust herself through the narrow aperture and pulled herself out into the night.

Lying flat on the roof—it was vibrating so much she felt as if she were on the wing of a plane a million miles up in the air —she lifted her head and chanced a peek. She felt the light crackling of shoulder and neck bones as she stretched up and tried to see what was happening.

She saw that the house was no longer surrounded by several lizards.

There were more like several dozen.

Samantha whimpered. She prayed to God and she spoke to Harold and she screamed silently for her mommy and daddy. Stay low! Keep your head down! If only she could stop her head from swimming! If only she could wake up!

They couldn't see her, but surely they could smell her. Or was the wind in the wrong direction? Half of the house had been completely demolished, but luckily the part she was on was still standing, albeit shakily. They had poked their loathsome snouts into the rooms to seek out victims but had found none.

It was a miracle! The reptiles were retreating, moving away from the house. She watched them as they slowly lumbered down toward the sea and slid almost gracefully off the beach and below the waterline.

In a half hour or so they were gone.

Samantha collapsed.

* * *

Thomas thought Samantha had collapsed but she had only thrown herself onto the bed so he could hold her. "I managed to climb down, get to the boat and use the radio to call the Coast Guard." She laughed mirthlessly. "I tried to see their side of it. By the time they got there it had started raining heavily again, washing away the blood and the slime and the footprints. All they saw was a hysterical, half-insane woman who had booze on her breath. I screamed at them to look at the house, at the car, to tell me where the others had disappeared to. 'It was the worst storm this area has had in a long time, lady,' they told me." Samantha's fists clenched some of her hair and started twisting it, as if she needed to inflict pain on herself to dissolve the memory.

"Those fools almost had me convinced it was the storm, the wind, that crushed those houses–'inferior building materials' they said that my fiancé and friends got blown off the island—do you believe that?—*blown* off by the storm and were lost at sea. I told them that no one disappeared until after the storm was over, but they thought I was crazy, driven mad by grief and alcohol and by being trapped alone for so many hours. No one would believe me. Monsters, I told them, it was monsters, and what the monsters did to one island they can do to another!

"But of course they never did. All those big green lizards never showed their noses anywhere after that. Not ever. Which did not exactly make my incredible story any more believable."

Her body shuddered for a second as she inhaled deeply, then let the air out in a weary yet violent rush. "I wanted to stay on the island. I wanted to keep looking for Harold. I knew what must have happened, but if I survived there was always a chance that he did, too. I ran away from them half a dozen times and had to be dragged kicking and screaming onto their boat. They sent search parties out to scour the island—six people gone, after all, including the caretaker—but they never found them, not a one.

"So here I am, years later, still mourning that fine man I was going to marry. Still haunted by what happened. Trying to imagine what his death must have been like for him but not capable of conceiving it. Was it quick, was it painless, was it over before he knew what hit him? I can still see Fanny through that kitchen window and I think there was time for her to realize, without really comprehending, what was about to happen."

He held her in his arms and kissed her face and her neck. "I'm sorry, I'm very sorry," he keened softly. "You're not alone. I also lost my parents to the impossible. I know how much it hurts. I know how easily it can drive you crazy if you let it."

She looked up at him through her tears and said desperately, "Why won't anyone believe us, Thomas?"

He didn't answer because they both knew neither would have ever believed the other's story had they not gone through something similar themselves.

"Sometimes I think it was all a drunken fantasy, after all," Samantha said. "That the Coast Guard was right."

"But you know they weren't," Thomas said.

She nodded.

It was almost daylight. She went to make them a pot of coffee. He vowed to himself to help her stay on the wagon if she asked for his help. It was an awful lot to take in in one evening. Her story. Her tragedy. The Allens' tragedy. Her alcoholism. His concern and affection for her. Or was that just the alcohol in his own bloodstream speaking?

She had said the monsters on that island were as big as buses.

The monster that had wiped out Beachside had been much, much bigger than a bus.

Had Samantha encountered the infants and he the adult? He now believed more than ever that what had happened to him had been real.

Eustace Dunn knew something about all this, of that he was sure.

And one way or another he would force it out of the old woman if it were the last thing that he did.

CHAPTER ELEVEN
EMISSARIES

When Roderick got out of bed in the morning he found
Lemuel on the phone frantically dialing numbers. The whole
living room bristled with the little man's energy. He had a
coffee cup in one hand and a cigarette in the other and was all
agitated and busy.

"Lemuel, is something wrong?"

Lemuel scratched his bald pate with his fingers. "Is something wrong, the man asks. No, nothing is wrong. Everything
is right, Finally right, after all these years."

The bad feeling that Roderick had been having since last
night was quickly intensifying. He had been a fool to imagine
that the evening's episode was only a minor, temporary
relapse. He should have realized, at least been prepared for
the possibility, that it was the beginning of a major seizure.
But who would want to imagine such a thing? He had so
hoped Lemuel's visit would be a pleasant one—two old
friends, two cousins, enjoying each other's company, having
good conversations, maybe getting drunk once or twice,
easing each other's loneliness. Instead...?

Just because Lemuel had been all right for years didn't
mean he couldn't have a relapse. Anything could set it off.

And coming on the heels of the discovery of Gargantosaurus, when Lem was bound to be in an agitated state to begin with...Why couldn't he have kept his big mouth shut?

"Lemuel, who are you calling?"

"Sssssh, I'm speaking to someone!"

Yes, it was the same, just the same as before, that nervous, almost belligerent, intensity. Roderick put his hand out and slammed it down, cutting the connection.

"Idiot! What did you do that for? I was talking to CBS!"

Roderick mustn't let his temper get the better of him. He had to remember he was dealing with a sick man. "You can call me all the names you want, Lemuel, but this is my house and my phone and I want to know who you're calling. Something's not right about this and you know it. Tell me what's going on and tell me now!"

Lemuel's eyes narrowed as he glared with hatred at his cousin. "You're getting in the way of science, Roderick. You're trying to stop me from getting ahead. You were always jealous, always—"

"Shut up, Lemuel! Tell me who you're calling!"

Lemuel's eyes widened as if in long-delayed triumph. "The press, Roderick! The TV channels and the newspapers! The networks may not want me, but..." he tapped a piece of paper at the side of the phone that he had scribbled numbers on, "...by God, the local people do. I'm calling everyone. I'm going to make an announcement of staggering proportions."

"Not about...the beast?"

"Yes, the beast, the monster, the one and only Gargantosaurus. *My* Gargantosaurus. Alive! Today! Alive, I tell you! I was going to let you share in my victory, but now I think I'll let you wallow in the background where you belong."

"Lemuel, you can't do this. You yourself said you needed to do a little more investigating, you had to talk to people and consult with experts—"

"Experts! I am an expert!"

"You're a curator, you're not a—"

"Get that contemptuous tone out of your voice, Roderick. What have you been all your life but a second-rate math teacher. I *am* an expert. I know what I saw on that beach, in your photo, and I'm telling you—"

Rod snorted in anger and pointed a finger at his cousin. "You still need more proof, Lemuel. You'll be a laughing stock. They'll all make fun of you. Without any proof, they'll think you're a crackpot."

"Proof? I'll give them proof." Lemuel went into the den, Roderick following, and grabbed up the folder of clippings that Roderick had collected. "Here's your proof! Explain these. Explain these, I ask you!"

Rod tried to grab the file away but was unsuccessful. "I know, I know...but we still have to go about this scientifically! What happened to your objectivity, Lemuel, what's—"

"Scientific objectivity doesn't get anyone anywhere. Passion is what counts. Passion and belief in the unbelievable. If you think I will stand by while somebody else announces the existence, in 1988, in modern times, of a living Gargantosaurus, you are mistaken. Bah!" The folder slipped out of his fingers and the mounted but loose clippings inside fell all over the floor and furniture like outsized chunks of confetti.

"Lemuel careful!" Roderick bent to pick up the clippings nearest his feet when he saw Lemuel heading out of the den. He rushed ahead of him and barricaded the exit with his body. "Stop, Lemuel! You're going nowhere. Not until we talk. Not until you calm down."

"Get out of my way, buffoon."

"Don't call me names, Lemuel. I'm trying to save you, to help you, to keep you from making a terrible mistake. Sit down on the couch and listen to me, or I swear I'll never let you out of this room!

Lemuel stamped his feet comically. "Roderick!"

"Do I have to lift you up by your armpits and throw you there—or will you go under your own volition?"

Seeing that the man meant business, Lemuel went over to the couch and sat down. Roderick, cracking his knuckles as he always did when he was tense or upset, moved away from the door and went over to Lemuel's side. He stood before him and sighed deeply. "Lemuel, it pains me to have to bring this up, but you have to face the possibility that what you're feeling, the excitement you're going through, isn't real."

"The beast *is* real, I—"

"I'm not talking about that! I'm talking about your...manic behavior, Lemuel. We both know this has happened before—once when we were boys, another time in college, when you were in your thirties and then again a decade later. It's happening again, that's all. You're blowing this thing way out of proportion. You've having another...episode."

Lemuel quieted down, and for a moment Roderick was sure he was considering his cousin's words, absorbing them and realizing the truth of what Roderick was saying. Roderick could read the pain and torment and confusion in his friend's haunted eyes, but then that intense, frightening, out-of-control look was back and Roderick knew it was not going to be as easy as all that.

"You once were told you would have to spend the rest of your life on medication," Roderick said, "but when years went by without an episode you stopped taking it, didn't you? Instead of calling the papers, the TV stations, Lemuel, you and I both know you should be calling a doctor. You're a manic depressive, Lemuel, and this whole Gargantosaurus thing has sent you flying into the manic stage."

Roderick kneaded his chin for a moment and continued. "You're not looking at this thing calmly and objectively as you usually do. Maybe there *is* a sea monster, but if there is you must prove it scientifically and not go about half-cocked calling newspapers and issuing statements. It's much too soon for you to do that."

Roderick flapped his arms up and brought them down against his sides. "You are not yourself today, Lemuel. I'm afraid my enthusiasm over this whole monster thing has affected you and brought on another attack. I want to take you to a doctor. When you're well, when you're calm again, we can investigate this Gargantosaurus proposition of ours together, objectively and thoroughly, and come to some well-researched and documented conclusions." He stared at his cousin and watched carefully for his response. "How about it, Lemuel?"

Lemuel stared back at him for a moment, conflicting emotions and reactions playing across his features, and for a second Roderick was positive he had gotten through to him.

Then Lemuel jumped to his feet, brushed past him, and ran back into the living room.

"Get ready!" he shouted behind him. "The press conference has been called for twelve o'clock!"

* * *

Mistress Dunn had agreed to see both Samantha and Thomas that afternoon. They had gone back to bed after having some eggs and decaffeinated coffee and not gotten up again until 2:00. Samantha had told Thomas that she, too, had always felt Eustace was holding something back, though both admitted that all they had to go on was intuition. Mistress Dunn seemed to have some additional information, and together they would go to her and demand to hear what it was.

Samantha made the call to Eustace and was overly polite. She and Tom would like to see her that afternoon. Eustace told them to come out to her house in Key Biscayne at 4:00 P.M. "I look forward to it," Eustace said.

Although Samantha had consumed about twice as much

alcohol as Thomas, she was not as hungover as he was, but of course there was no possibility of her driving. Thomas felt too queasy to trust himself with his car, so from her apartment he called a limousine service he had used in the past and made arrangements for them to be picked up at her door. In the meantime he used her shower, swirled some of her toothpaste around in his mouth with his finger, and got dressed in his clothes which were rumpled but not odorous.

The limo drive took the Rickenbacker causeway out to Key Biscayne. When they reached Crandon Boulevard Samantha directed the driver to the house. Samantha previously had been to Dunn Manor, as she referred to it, but Thomas and the limo driver were impressed. It was one of those very old limestone mansions with a large veranda, gables, turrets, sloping roofs, bay windows, the works. It was three stories high. Eustace had a large lawn in front, and there was a lush forest on both sides and in back of the house. It was a bright sunny day and rather hot.

Two Dobermans came rushing up, barking, as Thomas and Samantha got out of the car, but a gardener or houseman quickly whistled them back to his side. "Pleasant creatures," Thomas quipped as they walked up the drive to the house.

A stubby German woman with apple-red cheeks and a dimple in her chin opened the door for them and led them into a parlor—that was the word she used—where Mistress Dunn would "receive" them. Apparently the servants had been conditioned to play out the same medieval fantasy that Eustace herself, judging from her manner and her outfits, seemed to be embroiled in.

The parlor was a large, cluttered room with lavender carpeting, thick purplish drapes, and reddish wallpaper. Talk about garish, thought Thomas. There were bookcases against every wall, and magazines, papers, tomes, and parchments were overflowing on coffee tables and piled on top of chairs. There was an old-fashioned velveteen settee against one window, and Tom and Samantha settled comfortably against its cushions.

Mistress Dunn came in a moment later and greeted them. "Hello, hello! Oh, please, don't get up. Make yourselves at home, please. I've already instructed Marthe to bring us some tea and pastry." She sat down across from the settee in a large arm chair that looked older than she was. She sighed heavily and stretched her arms out along the arms of the chair. "Now what is it you wanted to see me about?" she asked.

Thomas did not mince words. "We came here to hear the truth."

Eustace looked uncomfortable for a moment and her fingernails began unconsciously scratching the arms of her chair. "The truth?" she said.

Samantha, taking over from Thomas, leaned forward and said, "Eustace, last night Tom and I had a long, long talk. Both of us had extraordinary experiences and are the worse because of it. I've long thought that you...somehow you knew more about these experiences and others like it than you've let on. Thomas has the same feeling. Call it intuition, if you want. Eustace, I really think it's time you told us who and what you are and why what's happened to us concerns you so much. I think it's time you leveled with us. Both of us."

Eustace sighed again and settled back in her chair. "Yes," she said. "Yes, I suppose it is time."

She had no chance to go further before someone brushed through a beaded curtain that covered an archway in a far corner of the room. "Oh...Mother, I didn't know you had company."

"Franklina, come in," Eustace said. "Sam, you've already met my daughter, of course. Franklina, I'd like you to meet Mr. Thomas Bartlett."

The young woman came over and shook Thomas' hand. It was hard to determine her age, he thought, anywhere from late teens to mid-twenties. She wore glasses, frames white as pearl, and had a pendant at the end of a necklace hanging down over her pink blouse. She wore a modest green skirt and brown loafers. Tom surmised she was about five feet eight.

She was not an unattractive woman, but she carried herself strangely and her face was a bit peculiar. Her cheeks were very heavy, almost jowly, making the lower half of her face wider than the upper. Her nose was a dainty little stub in the exact center of her face. The forehead was high and broad, and she had perhaps the largest green eyes he had ever seen. She wore her hair cut short in an attractive, if quaintly old-fashioned manner.

But her most disconcerting feature was her mouth. When she opened her thin, wide lips to smile, he saw what at first appeared to be a great deal of dental work, but quickly realized weren't braces at all. It was as if she had twice as many teeth in her mouth as most people—rows of them—and they seemed sharp and pointy.

"Sit down, Franklina, and get acquainted. Marthe is bringing up some tea." The young woman moved some books off a chair beside a large rectangular table near the settee and sat down primly with her hands in her lap. She looked for a moment like a very young girl home for the summer from some exclusive, if sheltered, prep school.

Sweet though the girl may be, Thomas did not want to spend the afternoon chatting with Franklina and her mother. If the old woman was trying to stall...

"Have no fear," Eustace said, calming him before he could say anything. Just then the German housekeeper swept in carrying a tray with cups and cookies and a big old pot from which issued clouds of steam. "Here we go," Marthe said merrily. "I'll just put it down on the table here and you folks can help yourself. Oh, Franklina, I didn't know you were here. I'll just get a cup for you, too, dear."

Franklina held up her hand. "I don't want any tea, thank you, Marthe."

"All right, dear." She addressed the group as if she were the hostess in a restaurant. "Call me if you need me, please." Then she went out the way she'd entered.

"Franklina," Eustace said, "our friends want me to tell them everything I know about the society and its purpose, and why I'm so interested in monsters."

Franklina perked up. Or did she tense? "Are you going to, Mother?"

"Yes, I think it's time."

"If you're sure," Franklina said.

"I'm sure, dear. I told you last night about what Mr. Bartlett told me. And you've known Samantha's story for quite some time now. I suppose we really must return the favor."

Franklina said nothing but her eyes were guarded.

Eustace got to her feet. "But first let's have ourselves some fortification. Tea, anyone?"

They had settled in with their cups of tea and their little pastries when Eustace resumed her seat and began what Thomas could not help but think of as her performance.

"Now I'm going to tell you a story," she said, "a story besides which your stories will seem like the very height of normalcy. I don't expect you to believe me at first, but at least try to keep your minds open as you listen. I ask you to grant me the same tolerance that I granted you when you told me your experiences."

She took a deep breath, sat up straighter in her chair, and leaned a bit forward as she began.

"Many millions of years ago in this world's prehistory, representative—emissaries you might call them—of an alien race were stranded on Earth."

Thomas groaned and looked away at the wall.

"Mr. Bartlett. At least common courtesy should not be such trouble for you to manage."

"I was wrong, Samantha," he said. "This silly woman doesn't know a damn thing. Aliens. Prehistory." It wasn't like him to be so rude, he knew, but there was a limit to his patience, after all.

"You came to me with a story of a sea monster," Eustace reminded him, "and I believed you. Won't you at least let me *finish* my story before judging?"

"Then I need some more tea," he said, getting to his feet and pouring himself another cupful. It was strong and aromatic and tasty.

Mistress Dunn continued. She told how these aliens, stuck in a hostile, prehistoric environment, used their natural powers of metamorphosis to better adapt to life on Earth. "They were shape-changers; they had the ability to mimic the form of any living creature or even become new kinds of creatures. They could grow to any size, large or small, acquire any shape no matter how unusual. Naturally, as the dinosaurs were the undisputed rulers of the planet in those days, they decided to turn into a variety of similar giant reptiles."

Samantha gasped.

"But as the centuries passed, the dinosaurs died out and earth had a new master: the mammal. Mammalian forms were far weaker, in a physical sense, than that of the dinosaur, but they had become the dominant lifeform. Reluctantly, the descendants of those original emissaries gave up their monstrous reptilian forms and turned into mammals, then, as the centuries went by, primates, and eventually, the most intelligent of all mammals, man. Or more accurately, the alien-mammals' descendants—along with those of ordinary mammals—eventually became humans through the simple evolution."

"What did the aliens look like originally?" Thomas asked.

Eustace shrugged. "Who knows? That has been lost to us."

He rubbed his lip. "I see."

She explained that some of the aliens' descendants refused to give up their tremendously powerful physiques; they became the dragons, sea monsters and scaly serpents of legend.

Thomas smirked. "I suppose next you'll be saying these aliens are the ancestors of the Loch Ness monster."

Eustace smiled. "Yes, I've no doubt the mysterious Nessie is the direct descendant of one of those, shall we say, renegade aliens. The aliens who remained in monster form—at least monstrous to us —can live much, much longer than mammals. That was not true of the vast majority of aliens who elected to turn into mammals. They largely become mammalian in all ways, including their life span. Most of them eventually forgot their peculiar origins and mated with ordinary mammals, until the strain was practically lost.

"But the aliens who remained monsters had it far worse. True, they lived longer, but eventually they found themselves regressing mentally. The dinosaurs, by human standards only, were rather dumb, though not as stupid and lumbering as we like to believe. The alien-monsters eventually became just as dumb. They're large, rather pathetic freaks of nature who instinctively shun contact with humans, hiding in their holes and lakes and caverns. It's ironic. Their ancestors had wanted to remain in their gigantic forms because of power, but they finally became utterly powerless, not the rulers of this world but only the basis of its shadowy legends. Occasionally a human will see one—out in the ocean at night, deep in a jungle—but they run and hide and will never be captured. They lost it all, you see."

Thomas leaned forward and spoke bluntly. "The monsters that attacked Beachside and Samantha's island didn't run and hide. They made their presence known, believe me."

"Ah, yes," Eustace said. "I think that poor Samantha happened to get caught in a genuinely freakish occurrence. The minute she told me her story I knew she had encountered a very rare colony of alien-monsters, dumb as mules but large and dangerous, who had probably been driven inland by the storm and starvation. It hardly ever happens. You've heard of seagulls getting lost in a fog and invading a town, and perhaps that other true incident when polar bears descended into an Alaskan village to hunt for food? Very, very rare occurrences. Those reptile monsters went back to the depths of the sea and went about their business. They were not really malevolent, just hungry. It's very infrequent that you'll hear of such large numbers of them converging. Occasionally a colony will become too large, and the population is whittled down by starvation or cannibalism; the silly beasts eat each other, you see, but only as a last resort. I don't doubt such things have happened in the past. It might explain a lot of this world's unsolved mysteries, but there have never been survivors, like Samantha, before. Luckily, she was downwind of them. They don't like to spend too much time out in the open. Instinct, as I said. They were hunted down by man, their numbers greatly reduced, in ancient times."

Thomas saw that Samantha was weeping. The old witch had disturbed her with her stories. "Stop It! You're upsetting Samantha."

Eustace expressed concern. "I'm sorry, dear. I didn't mean to. I thought you would like to know that what happened to you, as horrible as I'm sure it was, was not a dream or a joke or something impossible. I would have told you sooner had I thought it would have brought you any comfort, but as you can see...I can assure you that I honestly did my best to find someone or something that could validate your story, for your own peace of mind, if nothing else."

Thomas put his arms around Samantha and let her huddle in his warmth for a moment. Franklina was staring at them but he couldn't tell if it were with pity or contempt. He looked at her mother. "And I suppose the beast that wiped out

Beachside and killed my parents was one of those aliens, too? Another freak occurrence?"

Eustace cocked her head a little. "I've told you about the aliens that became monsters, and I've told you about the aliens that became mammals. But I haven't told you about the aliens that become *both*.

"I think It's time I told you about the *hybrids*," she said as she bit into a cookie.

* * *

The man stripped off his shirt in preparation for his predinner shower. He turned the water on—it always had to run awhile before it got good and hot the way he liked it—and then flicked on the TV set. Might as well watch the news while he was waiting.

One of those interchangable TV newswomen with the earnest voices and the pretty blonde hair sat behind a desk in a studio. "Ordinarily," she said, "we would file this story under the lighter side of the news, but considering the large number of deaths and disappearances up and down the Eastern Florida coastline during the past few months, as well as the destruction of property in this area, anyone who says they can connect those assorted incidents and may also have an explanation for them, has to be taken seriously, at least initially."

The Man's attention was riveted. He forgot all about his shower.

"This afternoon a man by the name of Lemuel Harriman, curator of paleontology at the Arizona Museum of Natural History, called a special press conference at the home of a friend in Hillsboro Beach. A few months ago, Harriman provided the name for a new species of dinosaur, Gargantosaurus, whose bones were dug up in the Arizona desert. Now he claims there's a sea monster on the loose. Tracey Bevens filed this special report. Tracey?"

The screen now showed another bland cutesy female reporter, this one a brunette with chubby cheeks and bangs. She was standing at the back of what appeared to be a living room full of folding chairs and several unprepossessing individuals who were walking about aimlessly. "We're at the home of Roderick Thorson, a retired math teacher. Thorson's friend, Lemuel Harriman, made an astounding statement today. We're going to get reactions to that statement in just a moment, but for now let's roll the tape and see what Mr. Harriman had to say earlier this afternoon."

Over the next few minutes the TV showed a short bald man with a mustache pontificating on Gargantosaurus. He claimed that a living specimen was swimming off the coast of Florida and had left its footprint—he held up a photo and sketch and compared them—on top of and around a crushed automobile on the beach at Branton.

The Man cursed. *It was the wrong spot that was all. The Beast had taken one step on shore and dimly realized it hadn't gone far enough down the coast. The Beast had never even realized that car was there. It had taken one step and returned hastily to the ocean.*

When the fool was through with his announcement, Tracey Bevans returned to the screen. "That was at noon. Since that time a number of people, reporters and scientists, have come to talk to Harriman, some to encourage him, but most to sharply criticize."

She shoved the camera in front of a scholarly bearded type who had obviously been waiting, prepared, out of sight at her side. "Joseph Martell, Professor of Paleontology at Florida University— what do you think of Harriman's claim?"

He shook his head and positively bristled with outrage. "I think nothing of it, Tracey. The man is hysterical; the man has no proof. The crushed car and footprint were dismissed as a prank several days ago. I don't feel he has any basis in fact whatsoever. A living Gargantosaurus? I'd sooner believe Godzilla had jumped off a movie screen and was shopping for a nursing home. It's absurd!"

Next came a much younger man, slightly effeminate, with a skinny face and body and a thick pair of glasses. "I am Chet Minnow of the Florida Monster Watch, and I am here to say 'Right on, Lemuel Harriman!' We of the Monster Watch have known for years that something was out there, something monstrous, and now Mr. Harriman has stepped forward with proof. I hereby christen this creature Gargoyle the Magnificent!" He added that the Florida Monster Watch had all of two members and had been in existence for only half an hour.

It was always the same. Professional men and women disagreed, thought Harriman was too hasty, jumping to conclusions on insufficient evidence. The only ones who supported him were teenagers and cretins. Harriman's employers in Arizona had issued a carefully guarded statement—not discrediting him, but hardly supporting him, either.

The Man smiled.

Still, Harriman could be a danger. The Man knew what fools these people could be, how they loved to hunt down whatever they didn't understand.

Harriman was getting much too close.

The Man thought he would have to pay a call on this Lemuel Harriman—once it was dark and the rest of the world was sleeping.

CHAPTER TWELVE
HYBRID

"The hybrids? What are they?" Thomas asked Mistress Dunn.

She wiped her lips with a napkin and said, "A hybrid, as its name implies, is a combination of alien-monster and alien-mammal. Nowadays a hybrid is a man or woman, descended from the alien emissaries, who is capable of switching at will from human to monster form. Most have died out by now. As you can imagine, they are extremely dangerous. A human mind in a monstrous body? Think what they could accomplish if they wanted to. The only thing that keeps them from being too dangerous is the fact that when they revert to saurian form, although they still retain some of their human consciousness and memories, their animal instinct takes over. Instead of men they become beasts. At least, in most cases."

"You see," she continued, "as the years passed both the alien-humans and alien-monsters lost their natural ability to change shape. But a few—a very few of both species—retained the ability and passed it on to some of their descendants. Whatever hybrids exist today, however, were probably born as humans."

Although Thomas couldn't understand why he was taking any of this nonsense seriously, he said, "Let me get this straight. You said most of the aliens changed into mammals and their descendants became human like the rest of us did. As for the other aliens, they've remained monsters all these years. Forgetting these hybrids for a moment, let's back up a bit. When these aliens first came to Earth, when they took on the shape of dinosaurs, were they stuck in that form?"

"No, no," Eustace explained. "Until they lost the ability to shape-change, the aliens were never stuck as you put it, in any one form. But the process of metamorphosis was excruciatingly painful and time-consuming; their whole mass and size had to undergo an extreme and shattering transformation. They could not flip back and forth from one form to another very quickly or very often like, say, a werewolf in the cinema. Once they changed they had to remain in that form for quite some time. Of course, the aliens lived much longer than ordinary humans so it didn't seem such a stretch to them. But once they adapted to their new earthly forms, whether mammal or monster, they had no reason to change to anything else or to revert to normal. They got used to themselves and each other as saurians or mammals, as the case may have been; it's that simple."

She bit into another cookie and smacked her lips. "But as I was saying, these hybrids, or mutations, if you will, not only retained the ability to shape-change, but were able to do it with much less pain and in a far shorter time than before. In fact, they did become like the werewolves of Hollywood, able to flick back and forth with relative ease whenever they wanted to. In the olden days they were often thought of as witches, warlocks, and sorcerers, even Gods and Goddesses. They would walk among men as humans and then swoop down in the night in their monstrous bestial forms to attack or devour those same humans, anyone who offended them or got in the way of their quest for power. In medieval times whole European villages were in thrall to these mutants, who ruled and terrorized, plundering at will."

She finished what remained of the cookie in her hand and wiped her lips again. "Which brings me to the present. You asked why I started this society. The answer is simple. It's because many years ago I suspected that at least one of these hybrids was still in existence and that it was using its shape-changing ability for malevolent purposes as its ancestors did. I believe it was this same hybrid who destroyed Beachside in 1957 and was also responsible for other unexplained tragedies in Florida over the years, including the frequent ones during these past few months."

She looked straight into Thomas' eyes. "I know what you've been thinking, Mr. Bartlett. That I'm crazy. That this whole long story is crazy. But think for a moment. You did see the beast, didn't you? It did destroy your home and your parents, didn't it? It did happen. If what happened to you is the truth, then why can't everything else I've been saying to you be the truth, also?"

He didn't reply. For during the past few minutes he had been thinking just the same thing.

"Another thing, Mr. Bartlett. The beast you saw—was there not something peculiar about it? These aliens did not turn into dinosaurs, they turned into creatures *similar* to dinosaurs— enormous, reptilian animals that resembled the terrible lizards in all ways but one. Their eyes and their skulls, retained some of their actual race's quality—something alien. So did the mammals later on. And the hybrids, whether in mammalian or monster form, retained a bit of both as well as the barest hint of their original alien physiognomy. Tell me, Mr. Bartlett, did not the monster who destroyed your home have something just a bit human about the eyes, the face? It was a reptile, yes, but didn't the face glimmer with intelligence?"

Thomas was trying to absorb it all, everything she had told him and particularly what she was saying to him now, when he realized with a start that he was trembling. He was reliving it, seeing that face, suspended above his father's, again, seeing it as it came swooping down to...

"God, yes! Yes! Its face, its eyes. Something *human*..."

Samantha held Thomas the way he had held her earlier. "It's insane, it's insane," he kept repeating, "the whole thing is insane."

Franklina got up calmly as he ranted and quickly poured him another cup of tea. The beverage seemed to have tranquilizing properties like a witch's brew. When he'd quieted, he said, "If everything you say is true, which it might as well be considering everything else that's happened, how can you explain that paleontologists never uncovered the bones or fossils of those creatures; how come archeologists haven't come across their ancient camps, or spaceships, or—"

Mistress Dunn held up her hand to silence him. "First of all, how do you know they didn't? Man can't always recognize what's in front of him, you know. Besides, there are several other things to remember. The aliens reverted to their own original forms upon death, and broke down into a boneless type of energy that dissolved and left no traces. There was nothing left for paleontologists to discover. Once they became incorporated into earth society, whether as monsters or later as mammals, they had no camps as such. As for their original camps or the spaceships they came in, who knows what they might have looked like or consisted of? We're talking about a completely alien culture, a totally unique lifeform that we could barely relate to or understand. At least, not on their terms.

"As for the sea serpents, the dragons, the alien-monsters that came later on—or their descendants, I should say—when they died, like their latter-day human cousins, they remained in their adopted forms. They looked like monsters—or prehistoric man—because that's truly what they had become. How could archeologists or paleontologists distinguish them from the real thing? For all intent and purposes they had *become* the real thing."

"But you said, they looked different, human or alien or—"

"When they were alive, yes. Their eyes for instance. As for their skulls and bones, remember scientists can only approximate the appearance of prehistoric creatures given the tools and fossil remains at hand. Some of these men and women may have noticed peculiarities in the skulls or bones of these ancient men and beasts; others, compensating for their lack of raw material, would have assumed the finished, living creature conformed more to what they expected it to, to what they already knew about dinosaurs or primitive man. Everything is a question of subjective interpretation."

"Speaking of early man," Samantha said, "why didn't the alien-humans, as you call them, with their infinitely superior intelligence, build up huge cultures and societies? Couldn't a race that had come from the stars have completely taken over?"

"And why didn't they ever go back?" Thomas said. "I can't understand how such superior intellects could ever be stranded on Earth or anywhere else."

"A simple lack of raw materials," Eustace explained. "Our world was composed of different elements than theirs. And as for your queries, Samantha, how do you know humans with the repressed but pure alien strain did *not* take over? Think of all the inexplicable but complicated accomplishments of early man, all the great cultures and societies that did develop, and who do you suppose might have been responsible for them? And as for wanting to go back where they came from...well, that could explain humankind's continual fascination with space, our perpetual quest for the stars. Perhaps in some deep instinctive way there are those of this world who do want to go back to their point of origin."

Thomas said, "It's all rather disillusioning. These aliens

were apparently responsible for everything from the space program to the discovery of fire."

Eustace shook her head. "Not necessarily. Real humans may well have been responsible for most of Earth's accomplishments. Anyway, by the time the alien-mammals' descendants evolved into human beings, I would imagine they were indistinguishable from, and no smarter than, other humans." She looked oddly pensive for a moment. "Aside from something deep in the alien-mammals' genes, their subconscious, perhaps, that only they were privy to.

"But I still must tell you more about our renegade hybrid and the purpose of this society, which, as you've probably guessed, is to ferret out the mutant before he or she can do any more harm to innocents. I've devoted the past few years of my life to determining the identity of this creature, its *human* identity. I knew that most people who saw these beasts or had strange encounters either kept silent for fear of being thought crazy, or even had become slightly unhinged because of the incidents. Some of the crackpots and weird people who show up at our meetings are not all crazy. However, with the exception of people such as yourself, Mr. Bartlett, most responsible, professional, reputable individuals do not go around telling other reputable people about their—what is the term?—off-the-wall experiences. But over the years—although it has been an almost insurmountable task to plow through the many false reports and find even a kernel of truth— loonies and reputable people alike who have had legitimate experiences have come to the society to unburden themselves. Just as you did.

"It was just those loonies who often gave me the best information, who had *really* seen something important and were crazy enough not to keep quiet about it. A serious, intellectual society would not have worked, Mr. Bartlett. So I called myself Mistress Dunn and paraded about in these robes of mine and created the kind of atmosphere I thought necessary.

I did not wish to alert the hybrid, who may have lived and operated in this area.

"You see, why should he or she feel threatened by anything as absurd as my silly little monster society? A serious, thoughtful, substantially endowed and recognized organization made up of members of the professional and scientific community might have garnered more publicity than I desired and alerted him or her to my true purpose. I let a few condescending stories about our group appear in the paper, of course, but that was only to help spread our reputation as a bunch of crackpots, to attract more crackpots, who, as it sometimes turned out, were not really crackpots at all. Clever, wasn't I?"

Sure, she was clever. And shrewd. Or simply insane. Thomas didn't know what to think anymore.

"Eventually my plan worked. And I have to thank you, Mr. Bartlett, for your unexpected appearance reminded me of the Beachside destruction, which I had nearly forgotten about. Things have been busy enough lately as it is. When I did a little checking up, it all came together. I think I now know our renegade hybrid's human identity."

"Wait a minute," Thomas practically shouted. "I just can't absorb this. You're telling me that the gargantuan beast that attacked Beachside is somehow capable of transforming itself into a mere human, a tiny human being? All that weight and mass and tonnage can be compressed into a shape that must be one hundredth of its size? I can buy everything else you've said, but *this*, this just doesn't make sense."

Eustace leaned back heavily in her seat and rubbed her eyes. "Again I must remind you we are dealing with a being that carries the pure strain of an alien race in its blood. If you want hard scientific explanations you'll have to go to a physicist. All I can tell you is that it has something to do with energy being converted to mass and vice versa. It takes on energy to grow in size, then expels that same energy to grow smaller. The flesh, if you can call it flesh, twists and stretches, undergoing a transformation on the genetic level itself. The individual cells multiply or diminish at an incredible rate, mutating even as they grow or shrink in size. Thus the hybrid becomes an entirely different organism. But why am I going on talking in earthly terms about something that is entirely unearthly? Think of it as magic, Mr. Bartlett, hmmm? Sorcery. The supernatural. Whatever you want to call it. The end result is the same. A Man becomes a Beast and a Beast becomes a Man."

She gestured impatiently. "But enough of that. What I have to say now is more important."

Franklina interrupted, speaking for nearly the first time since she'd entered the room. "Mother, is it true? Have you finally figured out who the hybrid is?"

"Yes, my dear. The evidence is unmistakable." She got up and pulled out a file folder tucked under a few heavy books at the corner of the large table Franklina was sitting next to. Eustace returned to her seat and opened the folder. "There's no possibility of error, I feel. All that's left is for me to get close enough to the man to make the final judgment." She began sifting through papers and clippings in the folder. "This hybrid has only become very active during the past year or so," she said. "Between the time of Beachside's destruction, for which I'm sure it was responsible, and 1987, it was relatively benign. But there's been a method to its madness. And *that* has been the monster's undoing.

"During the past few hours I've gone carefully through my files and clippings and removed any and all material that may, by any stretch of the imagination, have had a rational explanation. I also disregarded those incidents that occurred between 1957 and 1987 for the time being, except incidents related to me personally by the society's members, although I've no doubt they would only add to the veracity of my claim. I concentrated mostly on this past year, when there has been an alarming increase in peculiar occurrences." Her eyes lit up. "And I saw a pattern emerging. At first I couldn't figure out what, if anything, all these tragedies and accidents had in common. But when I refreshed my memory on Beachside, checked it out, something hit me and everything else fell into place. Then I made a few phone calls regarding these more recent events, and got the information I required."

She held up a clipping. "Huddington Beach. A farm destroyed when a cabin cruiser was dropped on it! A certain corporation had been hoping to buy the land from the owner, a Mr. Johnstone. Now, of course, he's more than willing to sell to them."

She waved another clipping. "A series of bungalows in Merrimonte smashed to pieces one winter evening. This same corporation as before wanted to build a hotel in that area. Needless to say, the owner sold out and moved back to Chicago. He had insurance, but he was understandably freaked out by what happened to his property while he was attending his sister's wedding in California.

"And this one. The home of one Paul Jerrolds was destroyed, completely obliterated, one night back in April in Darvannah. No storm, no winds, no fire, no explosives. Jerrolds and his entire family and weekend guests were presumably killed. Only one body—or part of it, rather—was ever found. Jerrolds had long since been an outspoken opponent of the business methods of the head of the aforementioned corporation.

"One more—though there are plenty of others-just to make my point. Just last evening a small fishing station owned by one Barnard Weiler was completely destroyed, also at night, and its owner snatched off the face of the earth with no apparent explanation. Do I have to add that this same corporation I've mentioned previously wanted to take over the operation and expand it into a small resort and retirement village? Weiler wouldn't sell.

"The list goes on and on. No explanations. Just lots of theories and lots of policemen and officials shaking their heads in puzzlement. People are either killed or disappear or they're so spooked that they pick up stakes and move. The corporation always gets its way."

Thomas and Samantha spoke simultaneously.

Sam: "Which corporation?"

Thomas: "What corporation would employ a monster to do its dirty work?"

Thomas gave Samantha a squeeze. "Ladies first."

Eustace gave them a tense smile. "The answer to both your questions is: Bronmore Enterprises, Incorporated."

The name was familiar to both of them. "I've heard of it," Samantha said. "It's been buying up and building on half of Miami."

Thomas was stupified. "I can top that. I've met the corporation's owner, Mr. Gareth Bronmore himself."

And then in a flash Thomas remembered something else, remembered his trip back to Summerdale and the new community that had been erected on the site of the original Beachside. He saw the sign on the fence next to the gate and recalled the writing that was on it.

Bronmore Enterprises, Inc.

"Oh my God," he said.

The pattern fit.

"And you're saying that someone in the Bronmore Corporation is this hybrid?"

"Not someone," she said. "Gareth Bronmore! He's the one who most benefited from the Beachside tragedy, as well as all these others. All one has to do is pick up a magazine or newspaper to realize how ambitious and ruthless the man is. My spies tell me that his underlings and associates are simply not in the same league. Besides, some of them weren't even born when Beachside was destroyed, and that's the key."

"But Bronmore...he's this old man. I've met him at events over the years, in Miami..."

"He wasn't always old. In his terms he's still just middle-aged. And as dangerous as ever."

"But to think I've met the man, chatted with him. He seemed a little old, distant, but charming and pleasant. A wealthy man and an ambitious one, yes, but a great help to the community. He's singlehandedly developed old neighborhoods and removed eyesores and given vast amounts to charities."

"No doubt."

"And *he* destroyed Beachside in '57?"

Eustace nodded. "Yes. Undoubtedly for the same reason he destroyed all those other places. Beachside was where he got his start. That development alone made him a millionaire many times over and put his corporation on the map. With everything on the property wiped out and washed away, it was much, much easier for him to buy it all up and start building. Years sooner, of course, than had he gone through normal channels. In the same way, and for similar reasons, he has suddenly begun a massive campaign up and down Florida's eastern coastline."

"But all those people...It's murder!"

"The man is a monster in every sense of the word," Eustace said. "He thinks he's better than the rest of us, as well as bigger."

Thomas felt his hands forming fists. "The bastard murdered my parents! Maybe they were drunks and losers, all of them, but they didn't deserve to have *that* happen. I could kill him for what he did!"

Eustace nodded. "Which is precisely what must be done."

Samantha's head shot up in astonishment. "You're talking about murder!"

"It's what he deserves, isn't it?" Thomas snapped. "The only question is how do we—how do *I* do it? I mean, he's a very prominent businessman. I can't just walk up to him and kill him, not if I don't want to spend the rest of my life in prison. And I sure as hell can't tackle him *after* he's changed into a monster."

"No, of course not. But there *is* something you can do. You can confirm that he is the man we're after."

"I thought you said you were—"

"Ninety-nine percent sure. But I want to eliminate the one percent of doubt. And as long as you know him, there's a way you can do it for me."

"How?"

"Get close to him and feel his back. Hybrids almost always have enlarged spines, almost humps, on their backs. He would wear clothes to disguise it, of course, and compensate for it in his walk and how he holds himself. Just walk up to him—it doesn't matter how you do it—and make sure he has that hump."

"I can do that," Thomas said, amazed at how quickly he'd become convinced that all this lunacy was real. "In fact, I can do it tomorrow night."

"That quickly?"

"Yes. The Chamber of Commerce is having its annual dinner dance, y'know, to give out awards and hold elections. I should be able to get right beside him at some point during the evening. He always attends these functions." He looked at Samantha. "Sam, will you be my date? I think I'm gonna need some moral support."

She hesitated, and he couldn't blame her. After all, this was not her battle anymore.

"Look," he said, "I know It's really not your problem. Bronmore had nothing to do with your fiancé's death, with what happened on that island, as Eustace told us, but—"

"That's not it," Sam said. "I've just been trying to take it all, in, that's all."

"Do you believe Eustace's story?"

"Yes, I do. After what I saw on that island, you bet I do! And I'm going to help you, Thomas. It may not bring Harold or the others back, but consider it my contribution in the war against the aliens. Though I have to tell you that I'm scared. What's to prevent him from turning into a monster right in the middle of dinner?"

"Very unlikely," Eustace clucked. "True, he's so huge no one could do him much harm, but his cover would be blown. And even a hybrid doesn't want to spend the remainder of his life as a beast. So I think you'll be safe there, dear."

Thomas asked the question that had been on his mind ever since this bizarre conversation began. "Eustace, how do you know so much about these aliens?"

She looked at Franklina and the two of them shared a smile. "Some people have been blessed—or cursed—with retaining their genetic memory of the aliens. I won't say any more than that. But I do want to add, that once you've made the confirmation, you are to retreat and do nothing further."

"But what about Bronmore? What about killing him? He's not a human being, he's a..."

Again Eustace shared a smile with her daughter. This one was tinged with a hint of regret and bitterness.

"Never mind. We shall take care of Mr. Bronmore. Franklina and I know how to deal with a hybrid."

"But how?"

Eustace put a finger up to her lips. "Later," she said.

In a short while Thomas and Samantha bid adieu and left the mansion. Now Thomas knew why Eustace and Franklina had seemed so otherworldly. Surely some of the alien-humans had kept their blood pure over the centuries and resisted mating with normal humans. They had lost their shape-changing abilities but not their memories of the past. Perhaps Eustace actually remembered a lot more than she was saying —what the aliens looked like originally, for instance—but found it prudent not to tell him. Although they could not truly be called aliens because they had been born on this planet, he sensed both mother and daughter were not of this world.

For surely Eustace and her daughter would not have known so much about the aliens unless they were their direct descendants.

* * *

It had been a very hectic day, and Roderick was exhausted. There had been cameramen, reporters, paleontologists and scientists, neighbors, police officers, even an ambulance and paramedics for an overweight monster lover who'd mistaken indigestion for a heart attack, and Roderick thought if he had to look into the face of one more wide-eyed innocent stranger he would puke.

It was after midnight, but Lemuel was still up, working on an article he was going to prepare for some journal (which would never accept it) and *Us* magazine (which probably would). He not only wanted the respect of his reputable peers, but also wanted his name and picture splattered across the front page of every paper, tabloid and fan magazine in the country. Lemuel was obsessed.

He walked out of the den where he had appropriated Roderick's desk and typewriter and slapped one hand into the other. "Paper, more paper!"

"In the cabinet above the stereo," Roderick said wearily.

Lemuel the lion went back into his den.

Roderick was too tired to fight or to reason with his cousin anymore. All he could do was sit back, watch the sparks fly, and wait until his little friend wore himself out. He loved the man and would have to be there to save him from his despair when he returned to normal and realized he'd turned himself into one of the biggest laughing stocks in the country.

Roderick had lived through these episodes before and knew how they peaked and waned, and how crushing it would be for Lemuel when it was over. Suddenly, in the midst of his agitation and hysteria, he would deflate almost visibly, go to his room, and not get out of bed for hours, even days. Part of him would realize what he had done during his manic stage and be depressed over that. But much of the mood swing would simply be caused by the illness itself, and he'd not be upset over anything in particular. It would be when he came out of the depressive stage and could face the world more or less sanely and realistically that the full extent of his actions would hit him. Left to his own devices, the shock and embarrassment might snap him back down into another, even more severe depression, one he might never recover from. Lemuel had tried to kill himself at least once before that Roderick knew of. Or he might pull himself together as he also had done before, and go on.

Roderick listened to the clattering of the typewriter's keys and felt such sadness. Poor Lemuel was ruining his life and his career. Would the museum even want him back after what happened? He knew there was no point in trying to snap him to his senses; it had gone too far. Lemuel would only yell at him, stomp his feet, and throw things. Roderick could deal with the man only if he stayed out of his way. Otherwise, Lem would get belligerent and Rod would get belligerent and they would simply wind up screaming at one another. That was not the answer. If only Lemuel had stayed on his medication!

He couldn't believe it this afternoon when Lemuel actually went ahead with the press conference in spite of Roderick's protestations. For a moment Roderick actually thought that things might be all right. So many representatives of the media had showed up, and apparently there had been much concern over the sea and coastal tragedies that he himself had been studying, for everyone was curious and excited. For a moment he thought that Lemuel's story might be taken seriously. After all, Rod himself still believed (if with considerable reservations) in a sea monster, and Lemuel could be right that the beast was a living Gargantosaurus. But once the professional people Lemuel had called gave their scathing, educated opinions to the news reporters afterward, Roderick knew that his hopes had been without foundation. Why hadn't Lemuel consulted with them first before going public? The Gargantosaurus, assuming it existed, had probably returned to the undersea grotto that spawned it to remain there forever. It might never put in another appearance, something that was necessary if Lemuel were ever to be exonerated. Rod wasn't sure which was worse—the monster's staying away or its coming back!

Poor, poor Lemuel!

The phone hadn't stopped ringing all afternoon. Most of the calls were either from the media or from nutty members of quickly formed monster-watching societies who had gotten Rod's number from information. He would have to get a new unlisted number if this kept up.

He looked at his watch again. Quarter to one. It was time to go to bed. Roderick had been afraid that Lemuel might enter the depressive stage that evening and had wanted to be awake and there for him when it happened. He knew Lem would need his love and support then, and would easily agree to go to a doctor or hospital for treatment. But it was rare that Lem would wear himself out that quickly. Anyway, it looked as if Lem would be up half the night, and it wouldn't do either of them any good if Roderick were also exhausted in the morning. He just couldn't keep his head up any longer.

He'd spent some time cleaning up after the reporters. Once he'd accepted that Lem was going through with it and there was nothing he could do to stop him, he decided he might as well cross his fingers, make the best of it, and make the whole thing as painless and professional as possible. He'd borrowed folding chairs from neighbors, made huge pots of coffee, called a caterer to deliver pastries and little sandwiches— anything to make Lem look like less of a crackpot. Of course it hadn't worked. When it was all over there were plastic coffee cups scattered over the floor and furniture, cigarette butts, bread and pastry crumbs mashed into the carpeting, cigarette burns on the sofa's upholstery, and little puddles of soda, beer, and coffee on the rug and kitchen linoleum. Disgusting pigs!

Bed. He had to go to bed. He simply couldn't keep his eyes open any longer.

He could hear the sound of the wind whistling through the trees outside the house and Lemuel typing in the den. And something else, some other sound.

A tremor? Was the whole house vibrating—or was It only his imagination? He thought he could hear something like a footfall, *a tremendous footfall.* But of course he had to be mistaken.

"Lemuel," he shouted. He had to remember Lemuel's hearing wasn't the greatest.

Another one, another tremor, like a giant was walking on the earth.

Like a giant...?

Boom. The cabinets rattled; a tea cup fell to the floor and shattered.

Boom.

Something—*my God—* something was coming this way, from the direction of the ocean.

BOOM.

The whole house was shaking now.

BOOM.

Earthquake, it has to be an earthquake...

But earthquakes didn't go

BOOM.

It would only take a few strides, just a few strides for something that large to walk from the sea to the farmhouse, just a few

BOOM

strides.

BOOM

The walls were shaking, cracking; Roderick could swear the floor was beginning to buckle just from the force of those approaching gargantuan footsteps. A painting slipped off the wall and a cabinet was tipping precariously, spilling Gladys' figurines and china. A lamp toppled off a table.

"Lemuel!" he screamed.

Lemuel had stopped typing. The wind had stopped howling. There was only

BOOM

BOOM

BOOM

getting louder and closer and louder and closer until—

Lemuel screamed.

—everything faded to black.

CHAPTER THIRTEEN

GARETH BRONMORE

The whole neighborhood was awakened by the footfalls, but no one saw the creature that had made them.

No one but Roderick, that is.

Luckily the area was not heavily populated and the buildings were quite widely spaced. Even so, dozens of people and homes were destroyed. The Beast had plowed across several acres on its way to Roderick's house, smashing through a trailer camp, a small closed amusement park, and the newly erected Happy Sky Sun 'n' Fun Holiday Cabins, most of which had been occupied by tourists. No one survived. Along with the trail of devastation it left in its wake, there were several more of its footprints in the loose mud and wet sand near the beach where it had come ashore.

Roderick wondered how the authorities would pass this off. With more of their glib and facile explanations, he supposed.

There was one advantage to being so small compared to a creature of those proportions. It couldn't see you way down at your level if it wasn't looking for you, if it wasn't looking right at you. At the last possible moment, as he could hear the rush of misplaced air that meant the foot was coming down right on top of the house, Roderick jumped through the window, rolled down the incline in the back of his house, crashing uninjured into a clump of thorny bushes.

As he lay there in the bushes looking up at the house, his urine spread through his underwear and wet his pants and legs. He shivered in shock and terror. He looked up and saw the beast tearing the house apart, stepping on it repeatedly with its tremendous feet, mashing poor Lemuel down into the crawl space underneath and doing it all with a silence and exactitude that was unnerving.

And the face! Just as Lemuel had described it. Not human, but with a vague human awareness. Reptilian. Horribly ugly. Yet magnificent and breathtaking. And so evil.

In a matter of seconds Roderick's home was reduced to a great big pile of splinters and sawdust, smeared into the ground and spread out about his property as if it had been nothing more than substantial than a dollhouse of papier-mâché.

Then the thing turned around and went back the way it came, its booms, like thunder, receding the father it got.

Still Roderick lay in the bushes.

He was still there in the bushes when the police came in the morning, shivering and crying and screaming about the monster.

The part of his brain that was still sane kept saying to itself that poor Lemuel was right all along. And there was the proof, as big as life and twice as scary; there was the proof, walking all the way to Roderick's house as if to present itself for approval! There was the proof, the monster—the Gargantosaurus—just climbing out of the sea and literally walking to Lemuel's doorstep. The proof had come to Lemuel but what good could it do Lemuel now? Now that Roderick was sure the poor fellow had been right after all, Lemuel was dead.

Lemuel had been exonerated by being killed by the very proof he needed.

They couldn't laugh that off, could they? A man declares a dinosaur is alive in the 20th century, and the very same night he's stomped to death by some horror from the ocean.

Roderick was not in serious physical condition but he was suffering mental trauma. Despite this he had visitors at the hospital, which the nurses tried to curb. He told the probing reporters that Lemuel was dead and what had killed him. Then there was a woman who'd apparently lied to the nurses and said she was a relative. She told him her name, something peculiar, and said to call her when he was able. Her card was on the table beside the bed. Another one of those idiotic monster societies, he bet. But a man, a nice, normal-looking man in a business suit, who said he was Mr. Barton or Mr. Bartlett or something like that, had been with her and he had seemed decent and sensible. "We believe your story," he said. "Your friend was killed because he knew the truth. If you want to find out what that truth is, please call us. Either of us. My name and number's on the back of the card. We can help. We can help you get over this. We can help you get even."

And then they were gone.

Get even.

He liked the sound of that.

* * *

Gareth Bronmore woke up with a headache, as he often did. He stretched, pulled himself out of bed, and went into the bathroom. As usual, he splashed water on his face and studied himself in the mirror. What he saw staring back at him was a man who appeared to be in his sixties and who might very well have once been handsome. He had gotten better looking as he got older, his gaunt frame and hollow face filling out, becoming less cadaverous. But now, in his 121st year of existence, time was catching up with him. No one, not even those closest to him, would have believed he'd been born in 1867.

The dark hair was mostly gray now, but it was still thick, brushed back off his forehead and cut short at the back and sides. The face was long and narrow, with a high forehead, a Roman nose, and firmly set mouth with a full, pensive lower lip. The edges of his lips hung down in a perpetual sneer or scowl except when he was smiling. He had a strong chin, which made him seem determined, and his penetrating steel-gray eyes were deep set.

He had a nice night, he mused. The hired girl he'd brought up to the penthouse in the Bronmore building, where he resided, had been pretty, even elegant. He'd plied her with liquor, kept the lights low so she'd not get a good look at his peculiarities, and had his way with her. He'd paid her and dismissed her, all in an hour's time.

It was as he was drying his hands that he remembered what else he had done last night.

Idiot! he screamed at himself. Have you no self-control? After the girl left, he'd still been a bit giddy from the wine he'd consumed, and he'd taken the private elevator down to the chamber below the building where there was an underground channel to the ocean he'd had specially constructed. He'd been consumed with thoughts of that ridiculous fool Lemuel Harriman. He had found out that afternoon where Roderick Thorson's house was located and fixed the location in his mind; he'd sent someone out to take pictures of it under some pretext and memorized its quaint, pastoral appearance.

But he had not intended to do anything about Harriman so soon after the man's press conference; it would only add weight to the curator's dubious story. But once he'd entered the water and the change began, once The Beast with its bloodlust had taken over, there was nothing Bronmore, The Man, could do. Lemuel Harriman was doomed.

He shook his head with disgust and left the bathroom. He

would check out the afternoon papers for news of Harriman's death and the destruction of Thorson's house later on. Now he was not in the mood. Besides, who could do anything to stop him, after all, he who was probably the most powerful "human" in the world?

As he had his first cup of coffee and some toast in his fully modernized kitchen, looking out over the city from one of the huge picture windows he had installed in every room, he felt a slight tinge of remorse. He was a ruthless businessman, that he had to admit, but he would not apologize for the way he did business when his competitors and everyone else around him would do the same to him and worse. But in his rational, human moments he could still not quite condone the spilling of blood; it was The Beast side of him that acted upon his subconscious impulses and let him do things that in his Bronmore identity he might often have found appalling. Oh, there were some people whose deaths he would not lose sleep over; he was after all above petty human laws and morals, wasn't he? He was not really a human at all, and anyone blessed with his gifts and abilities could certainly not feel guilt for using them for his own ends, as anyone else would. But sometimes he wished The Beast would exercise more self-control and let him go about things his own way, in his own good time.

He went into the living and dining area, stylishly decorated in blue and gray, with high tech video and stereo equipment and even computers, and sat on the sofa looking out the window. He thought back over the years, all the years, and wondered if he had ever made a mistake as bad as the one he might have made last night. He remembered how it all began...

* * *

The Bronmores had been an influential Summerdale family back before the turn of the century when he was young, his father being a prominent realtor and land owner. Almost every day he and his father would go swimming together in the ocean. One afternoon his father led him farther and farther away from the shore, driving him forward and egging him on, until Gareth finally screamed in fear and exhaustion. How would they ever manage to make it all the way back to shore? His father said, "Save yourself, Gareth. If you stay human you'll never make it; you'll drown. Save yourself." And lo and behold the son began to change, to mutate, out of instinct, just as the father changed, and soon they were swimming back to shore together as saurians, transforming back at the last moment so that they could emerge from the sea as humans. To Gareth it had been the most natural thing in the world. Couldn't everybody do that?

But his father sat him down later and told him that they were very special, and if people knew of their abilities they would hunt them down and kill them out of fear and jealousy, hating anything that was different.

"But we're bigger than they are," Gareth protested.

"Yes, and outnumbered, too," his father said sadly, and told Gareth how once there had been many more of them, and how most of their cousins, the great sea beasts of legend, were just plain dumb animals as incapable of independent thought as they were of metamorphosis.

His father showed Gareth how to feed when in his Great Beast form (which at the time was much smaller than his father's), how to swallow sharks, to pluck whales or tuna from their schools and devour them when he would be large enough to do so on his own. "You must never consume man," his father told him. "That is a sin. Never, ever, eat human flesh."

Gareth laughed. "It would take so many of them," he said, and his father laughed with him.

But things changed the summer of 1880. Hybrids, as Gareth's father told him they were called, needed to make the transition into beast form and back about twice a year only, but for some reason Gareth needed to do it much more often. If he didn't change, he would lose sleep, have nightmares, undergo an alarming personality change. Gareth's father could not always accompany the boy and was afraid to have his son, still comparatively small even in his beast form, out in the ocean alone on such a frequent basis. He was afraid one day he might be spotted.

So the elder Bronmore bought some property deep in the woods at the edge of Summerdale, hired plenty of brawny workers, and had a large, ornate house erected. He built no roads; all the equipment was carried in painstakingly through pathways in the brush. He had the ground scooped out and enlarged the lake that was already there.

In a few months the house and lake were ready, a place where Gareth could go when the "beast fever" infected him; he had his own pool to swim in and his own house to shelter him when he returned to human form. Eventually Gareth discovered the underground channels in the lake that ran into the ocean, but quickly grew too large to use them.

Gareth would never forget the first time he ate human flesh.

His father had stocked the lake with all kinds of fish, which Gareth snacked on during his more or less monthly visits to the house, but his appetite was so voracious. One day he sensed movement in the water above him, saw legs kicking, and the hunger lust came rushing through him until he was completely under its control. He swooped up from the bottom of the lake and engulfed the wiggling white thing in his mouth. When he had swallowed it, he saw another white thing rushing toward the shore with desperate strokes.

In his beast form, human beings were just another kind of prey, another type of meat, to him. He could not say when he realized that the wriggling white things were human. Was it after he devoured the boy who raced to get away? Or before? Had he eaten the first victim's companion because his father had said to never let anyone see him? Had he been getting rid of a witness?

In any case, he made the mistake of telling his father. His father's eyes grew wide; he slapped him and hit him and knocked him down the stairs at the top of which they'd had their encounter. "Sinner! Sinner! I told you! Would you eat me if I were human and you were beast? Would you have devoured your own dead mother?"

Gareth tried to explain, but it was no good. "We're not normal," he cried. "We're not human beings, even if mother was. I didn't mean to kill them, but my beast side only saw them as food. I'm sorry, father, I'm sorry!"

His father, who was very old by any standards, died a few weeks later. His heart just stopped in the night. To think such a literal giant should ever succumb to the simple scourge of human age and weakness.

Afterward, Gareth spent a lot of time in the house in the woods while still actually living in his father's large house in the northern end of town. He avoided the lake until he could stand it no longer. Soon the lake grew too small for him. He had to walk from the house to an abandoned spot at the beach, then dive into the ocean to become the enormous monstrosity his beast form had developed into. He did, however, continue to go to the house for privacy and meditation frequently; he'd follow the stream bank from the road while in his human form. He tried to stick to a diet of fish and crustaceans, but without his father to scold and torment him, to remind him, soon he was committing sins again. He didn't ask for wandering strangers, for children, for lovers, to come uninvited to his lake. But when they came, when he saw them —it got to a point where the taste of human flesh was so exquisite that even in human form he was hardly able to control himself—he would rapidly transform and gorge himself on his victims.

Each time he devoured human flesh he swore it would be the last time.

He broke this vow continually.

There were rumors over the years—about the lake, the house, his youthful appearance-but nothing was ever found and hence nothing was ever proved.

And then there was Beachside.

He had thought of using his saurian form to wipe away the eyesore and slum and everyone in it—his beast-thoughts had infected his human-thoughts and caused him to think of humans as prey even when he was walking among them—but he had not really intended to do so. Not really. Or so he told himself. But once he turned into his beast-form, his subconscious bestial side took over, and there was just no stopping it from happening.

A whole community destroyed. All those people dead.

His belly felt full for weeks.

He loved it, and he hated it.

Still he had formed attachments to other humans. He had friendships and love affairs; he developed guilt. What, he asked himself, if that pretty girl he was dating or that banker who'd kindly invited him home for supper with his family inadvertently became one of his victims? He began to see humans as other than prey and felt horrified and guilty over what he'd done at Beachside, even though it helped to make him not only a business success but a millionaire many times over.

He would never do it again, he vowed, swearing that he really meant it this time.

It was strange to be the way he was, to be constantly split in two conflicting directions. He was human; he was not. He was equal to other people; he was superior to them. People were friends, neighbors, associates, lovers; people were food.

As the years went by, he used the money he made from the Beachside project, invested and multiplied many times over, to turn Bronmore Enterprises, Inc. into one of the biggest developers in the state. He soon outgrew Summerdale, which aside from his project had turned into a disaster area, and moved his base of operations to Miami. No project was too big for him, too demanding or challenging. His comparatively small outfit soon grew into one that required an entire floor instead of an office, three floors instead of one, a whole small building Instead of a few stories, and then finally, the Bronmore building itself which he erected in 1967, one of Miami's largest and most beautiful structures.

Outwardly, to all intents and purposes, he was simply a businessman, admired by some, hated by others, one of the movers and shakers of the city. He avoided long-term relationships, much to his regret; he had too many secrets. He employed female companions to satisfy his lusts of the flesh, which had not diminished with age. In spite of everything he was a lonely man.

For the first 90 years of his existence, he had stayed in Summerdale, a shrouded, mysterious figure; associates undertook his day to day duties, and he told himself he was secure and content and satisfied. But after the Beachside incident, something broke out inside of him and he knew he had to make the second half of his long, long life more meaningful and exciting than the first half. So he did.

Each month, as usual, he would take to the sea but was careful to steer clear of land or ships. Now and then, in spite of his precautions, he'd be spotted; now and then his subconscious took over the bestial side and forced him to do things he later regretted and tried hard not to remember.

But it wasn't until a few months ago that things really started to get out of hand.

Bronmore Enterprises, Inc. had a serious new competitor, The Reddington Corporation. It's not that the success of

Reddington would have necessarily driven Bronmore out of business, but Bronmore hated the idea of being "number two." He also had a strong personal dislike of Jeremiah X. Bishop, the man who ran Reddington. It was a matter of pride. As he grew older and more tired, Bronmore felt a need to prove himself, a need to hold onto his self-image as superior to each and every other man, as invincible in all things—bedroom, boardroom, ocean. His human side would sulk in frustration whenever a property or project would elude him, when someone wouldn't agree to sell, when they sold to someone else, when things at a prospective site were moving too slowly. Then his beast form would take over and settle everything in a much faster and more permanent fashion.

It was happening more and more often. And the bloodlust had grown so strong that Bronmore took to the water much more frequently than once a month, sometimes two or more nights in a row. He could sneak right up close to the coastline by sticking low to the ocean floor, stretching out to his full length with his belly scraping the bottom. He tried to avoid naval installations and submarines, but when he couldn't he would confound their sonar by frequently switching sizes so they assumed their equipment was malfunctioning. He rarely left witnesses, but when he did it was unlikely anyone would ever believe what they had to say.

In the morning he would have dim memories of attacking ships and coastal houses, just to satisfy his appetites, which had become almost insatiable. Just as his need for human sex increased with age, so, too, did his need for human flesh. The two drives, the two hungers, were merging, and that was scary.

One night, while making love to a buxom blonde with long legs and hazel eyes, he had felt a need to devour that was so acute it nearly overwhelmed his urgent wish to ejaculate. He had come very close to transforming right there in the bedroom, had almost destroyed his own penthouse and risked exposure, just to have a forbidden taste of that woman. Since then he had learned to control himself.

He loved being The Beast and satisfying his secret cravings and appetites but it was as Gareth Bronmore, The Man, that he could safely be the object of so much awe and admiration. Gareth was his first identity, and one that he did not intend to lose.

He got up off the sofa and turned on the TV in the living room. He flicked from channel to channel looking for news reports. He found a news program but they were talking about some South American revolution. He could swim down there and restore order in no time, he thought. Seriously, as big as he was, he was still vulnerable to weapons, to science, to the increasing technical sophistication of Man. He knew he had to be careful, as his father had told him.

How funny, he thought. Eons ago, when faced with the decision of becoming mammal or remaining monster, some mad egomaniacal mind like his own had chosen to stay in the form of a great beast that Lemuel Harriman, millions of years later, had dubbed a Gargantosaurus. The strain had run down through the ages, rare but now extinct, and the form he and his father took after metamorphosis was indeed, as Harriman surmised, that of the Great Beast. Harriman and his associates hadn't realized that not only had they not discovered the bones of an actual dinosaur, but that the bones they had found did not date quite as far back as the last days of the giant reptiles. The dinosaurs had already been destroyed by the great cosmic conflagration that occurred when a star exploded too close to the solar system. The entire Earth was bathed in radiation that radically affected the climate and served to wipe out the dinosaurs gradually while affecting mammals slightly and aliens not at all—except to strip them of the ability to shape-change, even to change back into their original otherworldly physiognomies. Hence, instead of dissolving upon death as they had before, alien-mammals and alien-monsters alike decomposed in a more natural fashion. The remains found in the Arizona desert had been of a post-catastrophic alien-descendant, as indeed many remains of prehistoric beasts discovered elsewhere had been.

The carbon-dating process, when applied to items that were eons old, could only be so accurate. It wasn't uncommon for it to be off by a million years or more. And the process would also have been affected by the fact that those old bones had not exactly been the same as other fossils, though humans could hardly have been expected to have recognized their unusual properties when they'd been buried underground for so long a period.

Bronmore chuckled. If modern man only knew which of his favorite dinosaurs had actually been created by the aliens, and that the end of the age of dinosaurs had occurred slightly before contemporary scientists assumed, he would be amazed. Many of the aliens adapted the same kind of form while others were individualists. Gareth had no doubt that whoever had first assumed the shape of Gargantosaurus had been as individualistic as they came.

And individualistic as he was.

He sighed. There was a price for everything.

Loneliness, for instance. It had caused him to seek out others of his kind. Part of him could not bear to think he might be the only one of his unique species left, but how could he tell who others might be? There was no test, no immediately visible sign or condition. He went to all kinds of ridiculous gatherings, organizations full of occult freaks, UFO enthusiasts, fanatical lovers of Nessie, but all he ever came across were crackpots. There were groups in Miami for bingo lovers, feminists, atheists, singles and gays, but no number to call, no place to go, to meet other hybrids. Gareth Bronmore could not be seen haunting these halls of weird, haunted people, but, in disguise, he hoped to someday come across someone who was like him, or at least knew of someone who was.

Take that Monster Society for instance. Most of the members were ninnies and cretins, but he somehow sensed a kinship with its leader, that Mistress Dunn. He remained on his guard, of course. He had not told her who he really was. Slowly he had been accepted into their outfit—in his disguise they thought him harmless and slightly demented—and slowly he would divest them of all their secrets. Some of the members might have seen—might even be— others of his kind!

In the meantime he would determine once and for all if Eustace Dunn was friend or foe.

And God help the old bitch if she were foe.

* * *

Samantha looked almost ravishing. She was wearing a long blue gown, pearl earrings, and a lovely necklace. She had washed her hair and pinned it up in an attractive style that framed her face and showed off her slender neck. Her makeup was tasteful and subdued. They had been at the dance half an hour and she had drunk nothing stronger than ginger ale. Thomas leaned over and kissed her on the cheek.

She smiled. "What's that for?"

"That's just 'cause you look so nice."

They were standing in one corner of the large banquet hall, which had been decorated with colorful streamers and posters. A band was set up in another corner, with about one quarter of the room set aside for dancing. There were tables full of hors d'oeuvres and a full open bar where people were milling about. The other half of the room was full of round tables, six seats each, where guests would be served dinner. The end of the room was dominated by the dais. Once, when Thomas had been an officer in the Chamber of Commerce, he would have sat there, but he had been neglecting such activities since opening Parmenter's. Perhaps it was time to get back in the swing of things. No, not while Gareth Bronmore was still breathing. First things first.

Could it be true, though? That was the question he had been asking himself over and over again since yesterday. It was not rational. He was not rational. But then, he reminded himself, neither was what happened to Beachside. For the past few hours he had been existing on sheer nervous energy, walking around like a stranger who had borrowed his body, proceeding as if there was no question in his mind that Eustace's theory was true.

That's why, when he had seen that late night news report about Lemuel Harriman and the Gargantosaurus, he had called both Samantha and Eustace and excitedly told them the news. But the way the press made fun of the man! Eustace was right; nobody took these things seriously.

They decided to go have a talk with Lemuel Harriman. For one thing, Thomas wanted to get another look at those drawings Harriman had held up at the press conference, but which the camera had never shown in close-up. But they soon discovered it was too late; Harriman was dead. Thomas learned that Roderick Thorson, the man Harriman had been staying with, had survived and been taken to the hospital in Pompano Beach. But Thorson had been too doped and depressed to speak coherently; all they could do was leave their names and numbers and hope he'd get in touch.

Which brought him to this present crisis. Was Bronmore really a hybrid, a man who could in some incredible fashion turn into a monster, bigger than anything else that had ever existed? And if he was, could Thomas bring himself to kill him?

Eustace had said that contemporary hybrids—what few there were—were born as humans. What would a hybrid born in saurian form from a saurian mother be like if by chance it were to switch to a human form? Probably a hulking, mindless moron full of animal rage and confusion. And had any more of those aliens ever returned to the Earth, perhaps to look for their long lost comrades? Were they here even now?

And then there was no more time to think about anything.

For Gareth Bronmore had just walked into the room.

There was a cluster of friends and business associates already going over to greet him as he waved and strolled confidently toward the bar. Thomas would have gone over to him immediately, too, but they were really only nodding acquaintances and it would have looked funny. Bronmore would probably recognize him but would need to be reminded who he was. Not that the reverse was true. Bronmore had the kind of striking appearance and determined stride that stayed in one's mind. Tonight he had on a handsome if loosely tailored suit that might have served to disguise his small lump. Thomas found it so hard to believe. Despite his intimidating presence, Bronmore was just an old man.

But what if he were something more? What if Bronmore had been responsible for the horrible deaths of hundreds of people over the decades? Would any court ever convict him? Should Bronmore be allowed to walk around with impunity, to never pay for his crimes against humanity? Thomas knew what the answer to that had to be—No!

He owed it to his parents, to Beachside, to Lemuel Harriman and the dead of Hillsboro Beach to find out the truth about Gareth Bronmore. As incredible as it seemed, if it were the truth, he had to know it!

"Bronmore looks so normal," Samantha said. "Just an old man. Nice looking. Tall. Could he have really done the things Eustace said he did? God, Thomas, can he really do what she says?"

"That's what we're going to find out. Come on."

He went over to Bronmore on the pretext of introducing

Samantha, feeble as it was, but it was impossible to get near him. Everyone was sucking up to him, basking in his wealth and privilege, kissing his ass. All it would take would be for me to clap him on the back hail and hearty-like and squeeze, Thomas thought. Samantha and Thomas traded nervous glances. At this rate the cocktail hour would be over before he had a chance to get near him, but he couldn't just start shoving people aside. He didn't know the man very well, after all. If Bronmore were young and handsome Samantha could have pretended to be a little tipsy and infatuated and gotten close enough to hug him, but he knew that wouldn't work under the circumstances. Besides, there was simply no getting near the man.

Thomas went back to the bar to fortify himself with another drink. He would just have to wait for an opening. He'd never have a better opportunity to talk to Bronmore than now. Once the dinner was served and the presentations and speeches begun, it would be next to impossible. It was highly unlikely that they'd be placed at the same table, given the power seating he knew these affairs went in for. And he was sure Bronmore would be surrounded by even more people as he made his exit than he was right now. Their only chance might be if Samantha somehow got Bronmore to dance with her once the dinner and speeches were over.

It was too late; everyone was heading toward their seats. Bronmore had a busty young woman on one arm, and another older gentleman whispering in his ear. Thomas couldn't just go up and feel the guy's back from behind. He would have to wait until another opportunity arose. He was wondering where Joseph Parmenter was when he remembered that his partner was off on another business trip this week.

"Now what'll we do?" Samantha said.

"We wait. C'mon. Let's go find our seats."

Their seats turned out to be not far from Bronmore's, who was closer to the dais than Thomas and was separated from him only by one other table. Bronmore's right side was facing him. Thomas wanted to converse with Samantha, to at least keep her entertained in case this whole thing turned out to be a fiasco, but his mind was too preoccupied. But she kept touching him and smiling at him and letting him know that it was okay; she understood. She surprised him with her ability to converse socially and intelligently with the other people at the table, a couple of whom Thomas had met before.

The food was served. Thomas tried to relax and enjoy it but as he began to chew the boeuf bourguignon all he could think about was Bronmore and what he'd done. The noodles were like human innards; the meat like human flesh. Would Bronmore be satisfied with beef, with cattle? Weren't human beings his cattle?

He looked over at Bronmore and saw him lustily cutting his meat and stuffing chunks of it into his mouth, chewing it carefully. *My God, my parents are part of that man. He gobbled them up, consumed them; their blood and their flesh became part of his blood and flesh, their cells part of his cells.* His parents had provided him with sustenance, with fuel, just as the beef on his plate was doing now. He thought of their bodies, their bones, being snapped between giant jaws, cracked between teeth, limbs severed, blood gushing out and dripping down...

"Thomas, are you sure you're all right?"

"I'm feeling a little..." He pushed his plate to the side. He couldn't eat any more. He made an "I'm okay" sign with his fingers. He finished the drink he had and held his arm up again until the waitress came, then ordered another.

Samantha said nothing; she just looked at his glass hungrily. She needed some artificial courage herself but they both knew why she couldn't have it.

I've got to do something, he thought, before I overdo it and get drunk and sloppy and blow the whole thing. I've just got to do it! But how?

Occasionally someone would go over to Bronmore's table,

stand at his side, and lean down to chat briefly or just say hello. Why couldn't Thomas do that, too? Still, most of the man's back was supported by the back of the chair. Thomas had to get his hands right there, and if he went over while Bronmore was seated, it would be a wasted effort.

The first speech was over quickly and was relatively painless. They had wisely decided to spread them out during the evening. A course would be served, and someone on the dais would either step forward to present an award or to talk. Then the band would play two or three songs and people would dance. Then the next course would be served and more speeches made. "Samantha," Thomas said, throwing down his napkin, "let's dance."

It was a slow number, and he was able to hold her close, the way he wanted to. She had dabbed on a little perfume, and he loved the fragrance. Why was he beginning to care about this woman, this drunk, this murderess—and was it healthy for either of them? All he knew was that this was not the time for either one to be asking questions or making commitments. Who knew if they would even be alive when this was over? If it were ever over.

He had thought that in the cold light of day he would be disgusted by Samantha and what he'd done with her while under the influence. The old Thomas Bartlett certainly would have been. But he was a different man now, one with a purpose and a need, and Samantha was part of that purpose and that need. And a steel bond had been forged between them when she told him her story, which he had somehow never doubted. Something had happened in the dark, in her bedroom, that had stripped each of them bare for the other to peruse, and he momentarily felt closer to her than he did to anyone.

The band switched to a livelier number, a fair approximation of Tina Turner's "Break Every Rule". Though most of the dancers pulled apart and began to gyrate sexily to the faster rhythm, Thomas and Samantha remained together.

"What are you going to do?" she asked him.

"I don't know. Wait for a good opportunity, I guess."

"Thomas?"

"Yes?"

"Thomas, I never thought I'd be saying this, but…is there something I could do? Does the old man have a weakness for dissipated middle-aged women?"

He pulled her head up sharply and looked at her. "Don't talk about yourself that way."

"Forget that," she said impatiently. "I meant what I said. Can I do it, do you think? Somehow get close to Bronmore?"

"No. I want to do it. It's not your responsibility. Besides, you've never even met him before; it'll make him suspicious." He hated the idea of anything happening to Samantha and the intensity of his feelings surprised him. "I'll figure out a way," he said. "It's still early yet."

"Thomas?"

"Uh huh?"

"I just wanted to say, I like you. I like you a lot. I…I hope you'll be careful." She hugged him very tightly then, as if he were her rock, her shelter in the face of loneliness and madness, and he could see that she was crying. He hugged her back just as tightly and tried to keep his own tears from falling. Once he started crying, he knew there'd be no stopping. Not if he thought about poor fucked-up Samantha, what had happened to his parents, what had been done to both him and Sam by forces beyond their understanding…and by one evil son of a bitch!

"Samantha, wait!" He pulled away.

"Tom, what is it?"

"Bronmore's getting up. It looks like—"

She saw. "Oh, Thomas, he's leaving!"

"No. No, he's not leaving. He's going to the men's room, I

hope. I guess even hybrids have to respond to the call of nature. I'd better do it now."

In his hurry to get to Bronmore he left Samantha standing on the dance floor by herself; he had to catch up to Bronmore in the hallway.

Just as he had traversed the ballroom and turned into the corridor toward the rest rooms, he saw Bronmore on his left, disappearing into the men's room.

Thomas walked to the men's room, pushed open the swinging door, and went inside.

There was no one else inside the men's room but Gareth Bronmore, standing before a urinal. Thomas went and stood beside him at the next urinal, unzipped his pants, and pretended he was taking a pee. Thomas imagined Bronmore growing, growing, popping out of his clothes and rising, colossus-like, to the ceiling, crashing through it and reaching down through the falling debris to crush him in a massive hand.

"Uh, Mr. Bronmore, how are you?"

Bronmore hadn't even bothered to see who'd come in, he was that supremely sure of himself. At the sound of the other man's voice he looked over at Thomas. "Oh, hello, Mr..."

"Bartlett. Thomas Bartlett."

"Oh, yes, of course. Of Parmenter's Saloon."

"That's the one. You've got a good memory."

He winked. "Yes, I'm happy to say. And it's been a big help to me over the years, let me tell you."

Such a charming gentleman, Thomas couldn't help but think. As usual, his suit was expensive, rather thick for such warm weather—the hump?—and he wore that same strong, spicy cologne he always favored. To cover up the stench of The Beast?

Bronmore was shaking the drops off; Thomas would have to wait until it would seem natural for him to clap the other man on the back. Have to go through the charade of urinating and washing his hands.

The two men again by the sinks, discussed the party and the food. Thomas prayed no one else would enter and get in the way.

They were getting ready to leave the rest room. It was now or never. He had to get into position somehow.

Suddenly the door opened; someone was coming in. Bronmore slipped out between Thomas and the new arrival. "Talk to you later, Bartlett," he said.

Thomas got past the intruder quickly and moved rapidly down the hall until he was beside the older man. He had to engage him in conversation again, so he said the first thing that came to mind.

"You built that beautiful Beachside development down in Summerdale, didn't you, Mr. Bronmore?" He moved in close, put his arm up around the other man's shoulders, slowly slid it down then farther down.

Bronmore smiled. "Yes, that was many years ago. My first major project, in fact."

Thomas' fingers grazed the man's suitcoat, explored, pressed down.

"I used to live in Summerdale. When I was a boy."

"Oh, really? So did I." Yes, Thomas thought he remembered now. There had been a developer named Bronmore, hadn't there? He must have been the one. Coincidence? No.

Thomas' hands pressed down harder on the material, could feel the flesh of the back underneath it. Could feel the-

"Yes, Mr. Bronmore. As a matter of fact I'm the only survivor of the tragedy of 1957; you remember...when Beachside and everyone in it was swept out to sea overnight? Quite an occasion."

—bone, the big thick spine, much thicker, wider, than an ordinary man's, like a hump! He grabbed it and tightened his fingers around it, just to make sure.

Bronmore pulled back. "What are you doing?" He moved away from Thomas in anger.

Thomas feigned innocence. His hand dropped. "Sorry!"

Bronmore continued to back away from him; his eyes were furious and somewhat frightened. He was trying to hold something back.

There's something about their eyes.

His eyes were almost glowing in that peculiar way they did when he was frustrated and outraged, glowing the way they had when Thomas had first seen him on the porch of that house, the way they had when Bronmore had watched him being placed into the ambulance. *The way they had when he bent down to pop Thomas' father into his mouth.*

And in that instant Thomas could tell that Bronmore had remembered *his* name, and who *he* was, too. Bronmore had finally recalled the name of the little boy who'd survived his attack that distant night, the little boy who had gotten away from him twice.

Bronmore kept glaring at him, backing away, remembering, and Thomas felt a chill that was colder than anything he'd ever felt in his life.

Bronmore turned on his heels and went back into the banquet hall.

CHAPTER FOURTEEN

SAMANTHA'S FRIEND

"More coffee?"

Roderick Thorson drained the coffee in his cup and handed the cup to Thomas. "Yes, please. That was good. You would not believe how bad the coffee was in the hospital."

Samantha smiled. "We're so glad you've recovered so quickly."

But Thomas wondered if the man had really recovered the way he was stammering and shaking, the nervous way he drank coffee and smoked—as if making up for all the years he'd said he'd gone without caffeine and cigarettes—the brief crying spells he had over his dead cousin, Lemuel.

Much to Thomas' surprise, Thorson had called Thomas' apartment and asked him to pick him up at the hospital. "I'm going to take you up on your offer," Thorson said. "To get even." Since Samantha had spent the night after the banquet at his place, Thomas decided to bring her along. Eustace Dunn did not answer her phone, so they couldn't get in touch with her. Roderick was waiting for Thomas in the lobby, looking about so surreptitiously that they wondered if he had been officially released. It was a short drive back to Thomas' apartment.

"I couldn't stand the hospital another minute," he told them now. "I wanted to be home, in my own bedroom. There was nothing physically wrong with me aside from some bruises and scratches so the hospital couldn't make me stay. Then I realized that I have no home. I have no bedroom. Everything is gone."

He wiped his eyes and his shoulders shook with his effort to hold back the tears. "Luckily, I have my fine friends, people I used to know at the university. One of them is somewhat my size, and he brought me these clothes to wear." Which explained why the shirt and pants were such a tight fit.

"What do you think you'll do now?" Samantha asked, handing the man another donut while Thomas poured the coffee. The big fellow seemed to be starving.

He shook his head wearily. "I don't know. This one couple who were friends with my late wife have a guest house they've offered me free of charge until I've rebuilt my home, and I guess I'll take them up on it."

"I'll be happy to drive you there afterwards," Thomas offered.

"That's good of you. Thanks." He took a sip of the hot coffee, then blew on it to cool it. "But I wonder if my insurance will cover all of this. What, I wonder, will the investigators decide wrecked my house? Unknown causes? I may never get a penny. I suppose I could put up a shack or sell the property. I know it's valuable. Maybe I should accept that it's time to move someplace else, some other city." He took another sip of coffee. "There's nothing left for me in Florida."

Samantha and Thomas looked at each other helplessly, but said nothing.

Roderick put his cup down on the table. "I was going to settle in at these friends I mentioned earlier, but I couldn't wait to talk to you. I still can't understand why you believe my story. Have you actually seen this Gargantosaurus yourselves?"

"I have," Thomas told him. "As soon as I found out what happened to your house I knew what must have been responsible."

Thomas was now positive that Bronmore was The Beast. He and Samantha had left the dinner immediately after his confrontation with Bronmore and called Eustace. She had said only that she would be in touch. Samantha and Thomas had spent the night talking about how and whether or not Thomas should murder Gareth Bronmore—before Bronmore killed Thomas. They had reached no conclusions.

The TV was on at low volume in the background. The media was still having a field day with the story: *Man claims existence of giant monster; man's house is destroyed the next day.* Thomas could hear the anchorwoman's voice: "…cut a swath of destruction leading all the way from the sea past several other farms, houses and developments, and up to the ruins of Thorson's house. Lemuel Harriman is still among the missing."

An official was interviewed on camera. "Yesterday the only apparent survivor of this destruction told us an incredible story about a sea monster, the Gargantosaurus that Harriman claimed was swimming in coastal waters. Do you think Thorson's story could have any validity whatsoever?"

The official smirked. "When we get to the bottom of this," he said, "and we will, it won't be any sea monster that's responsible."

"Then you think all the destruction was due to natural causes of some kind?"

"I'm sure that will be our determination once the facts are in."

"Do you think each disaster—the destruction of the Thorson house, the Happy Sky Sun 'n' Fun Cottages, the amusement park—is unrelated, or do you think all this destruction has only one cause?"

"As I said, that will be determined once the facts are in."

"Thank you."

Thomas got up and switched off the set. Rationalizing idiots!

"So that's the way it is," Roderick sighed. "Not only have I lost my house and my best friend, but everyone is going to think I'm crazy on top of it. Why couldn't someone else have seen the beast and lived to tell of it?"

Samantha twirled a piece of hair absently and looked downcast. "Join the club, Mr. Thorson. We've all been in it."

Thomas said, "We told you at the hospital that we had some answers for you, but I have to warn you, Mr. Thorson, they're going to be awfully hard to swallow."

"After what I saw the other evening? Hardly."

Still, Thomas knew that Thorson wanted to get even with what he probably assumed was a mindless sea creature for stomping his life to pieces, as if he were a modern Captain Ahab. How would he feel when they told him the astonishing truth?

Thomas and Samantha exchanged glances again. "Okay," Thomas said. "Here we go."

And they told him everything they knew about Gareth Bronmore—the alien emissaries, the monster-aliens, the hybrids, the corporation, the coastal tragedies that had benefited Bronmore Enterprises. Roderick had no problem believing every word of it. He told them he had seen the human cast of the monster's eyes, the 90 percent reptile/10 percent human head and face, just like in the sketch Lemuel made, which was now lost in the mashed debris of Roderick's house. He knew, he said, that their explanation was no more insane than any other someone else might come up with.

"Mistress Dunn claims she knows how to destroy The Beast, but she hasn't told us." Thomas indicated the phone. "And we can't get in touch with her until she comes home and answers her phone."

Roderick fixed Thomas in a steady, pointed gaze. "You and

I both escaped from Bronmore," he said. "Probably the only ones who ever have. You and I are going to have to destroy him."

Samantha put her face in her hands and moaned. "God, I could use a drink."

"I think we all could," Thomas said.

* * *

Samantha was at her own apartment getting ready to go out to dinner when she heard the downstairs buzzer. Thomas? When she had left his apartment, leaving the two men to discuss strategies by themselves, she had said she would meet him at Parmenter's for dinner. Perhaps he had decided to pick her up instead. The intercom had been broken for weeks. She pressed the button that would open the door for him and went to primp a bit in the mirror.

How her life had changed during the past couple of days! Everything was moving so damn fast, not that that was necessarily a problem. Perhaps if things were moving slower she'd have time to be alarmed by it all. As it was, she found it hard to deal with anything that was happening. She remembered how she had barely escaped from those lizards on the island, and the thought of that giant Gargantowhatsiz coming out of the sea and chasing after her—when she was sober yet—was enough to make her crazy. She just couldn't conceive it. She believed Eustace and she believed Thomas, and yet part of her didn't believe any of it. It was safer, saner, that way. Anything else would drive her right back to the bottle.

She hadn't had a drink since the morning after the night she'd slept with Thomas. She had wanted one and wanted one still, but she would resist with all her might. She was falling for Thomas, as absurd as that seemed after such a short period, and was sure he was falling for her. She knew she wasn't worthy of him, but the least she could do was try to stay off the sauce and hope he didn't notice her many faults. Though she supposed if he could get past her alcoholism and her slaughtering the Allen family, maybe he wouldn't be much bothered by comparatively trivial imperfections.

She felt like she "had a fella" for the first time since Harold. Slow down, she said to herself as she put on the pearl earrings he admired. You've only known the man three days. But they'd spent practically every hour since then together, made love again—both sober, both revealed in their true, imperfect natures and not repulsed by the other nor disappointed—and it felt so damned good. She felt real hope for the first time in ages. Maybe she could put everything behind her. She knew where the monsters on the island had come from and could accept that Harold had fallen victim to a force of nature, however peculiar. It was tragic, it was terrible, but there was no one to blame.

As for the Allens, she would keep their shrine in her room and devote her every waking hour to being and staying sober; she would get in touch with anti-drunk driving organizations and volunteer to do what she could to save lives. She could never fully atone for what she had done to that poor family, but she could accept that fact and go on, trying to make something good and positive out of what happened and to prevent it from happening to others.

The only sour note in all this was that terrible Bronmore business. It just could not be real, she thought. She felt very uncomfortable when they talked about rubbing Bronmore out, just killing that old man as if he were a monster. But of course he was a monster, wasn't he?

She just didn't know what to think, so she'd not think about it at all. Maybe it would all go away. Mistress Dunn could just wave her wand and make Bronmore or The Beast disappear.

She heard the doorbell. Thomas had arrived upstairs. Think about all this later, she told herself.

As she went to admit him she realized with some dismay that the apartment had already fallen back into its normal state of clutter. What would he think? Why hadn't she cleaned? This was a drunk's apartment, not a sober woman's. And his own apartment had been so neat and tidy, so beautiful. Well, she thought, he might as well get used to the fact that, drunk or sober, I'm a slob.

But she was also far beneath his social station, too, wasn't she? Sure, she had come from an affluent background, but that was many years ago. Now her fortune had to be carefully nurtured—which was why she lived in this dump instead of a decent place—bolstered with the occasional part-time office job, in order to last out half the next decade. She felt part of her hope receding the closer she got to the door.

By the time she opened the door she looked much the way she had when she had first peeked out at him the other evening. Only the man she was peeking out at this time wasn't Thomas Bartlett.

She almost said "Squinty?" before she caught herself. Many of the members of the Monster Society called the man out in the hall Squinty, because of his peculiar eye condition, but his real name was Paul and she didn't want to offend him. She opened the door to admit him. "Paul? What are you doing here? I didn't even know you knew where I lived?"

He pulled a wrinkled piece of paper out of his pocket. It was a notice for an open house she had held for the society members last year with her address on it. Squinty hadn't come but apparently he had planned to, for he had taken the notice and kept it.

She thought that Paul might have been drinking and she was about to turn him out when she remembered her earlier vow to help others like her, though she didn't know if Squinty had a car or even knew how to drive one. "Come in, Paul. Is something wrong? I have to go out in a few minutes, but I can chat for a little while."

Paul was a tall, slender, unshaven fellow, probably in his fifties, who always wore a gray coat, grimy pants, and a pale yellow shirt. He also had big boots on his feet. No one knew where he lived or what he did. He told everyone he had once seen a monster but never elaborated. He was harmless, even kind of sweet. Samantha had always assumed he made his infrequent trips to the society primarily for the cake and coffee.

She had never really taken a good long look at him before but as he sat down in the chair across from the sofa she realized that he was not unattractive. He was just another lonely old soul, an old sot who might even be homeless for all she knew. She didn't think he had formed any attachments to others in the group. Sometimes people talked in front of him about all sorts of things as if he weren't even there.

She settled on the sofa. "What can I do for you, Paul? Want a cup of coffee?" She remembered that the last time she had had a conversation with him at a meeting she had been quite high, maybe even drunk. Had she made him some promise, formed a boozy bond with him that she could not even bring herself to remember? "I'm sorry. I keep no liquor in the house." Which was a lie, but she didn't want to get either of them started.

Paul had a rather raspy voice, "I just...I just need to talk, Samantha. Sometimes I...sometimes..."

"I know," she said. "I know." It's a cruel, cold world out there, all right. Look at how many fucked-up cases there were. And now they had to contend not only with muggers and junkies and cancer and the threat of nuclear catastrophe, they had to worry about 250 foot carnivorous monsters, too.

She thought he could use a drink, to get him going, but none for her. She excused herself, poured him some Scotch—strength! Samantha—and even made him a sandwich. She put it all on a tray and deposited the tray on his lap. "Enjoy," she said.

While he ate he told her a little bit about himself. It sounded like he was making up the details as he went along, though Sam had no reason to suspect he was lying. Widower. Unemployed. Lived off the state and handouts. Had a small room in a crummy residential hotel, one of the few left in Miami. Samantha got this feeling that Paul wanted to ask her something, something specific, but he just didn't know how to phrase it, how to arrive at it. It was as if he were hoping she did it first, as if he were waiting for her to bring up the subject. Maybe he didn't even remember why it was he had come here.

She looked at her watch; it was getting late. She would have to keep talking and hope that something she said would spark his memory.

"We had a nice meeting last week," she said. "Got a few new members. Uh..." What else could she say? She wished he'd hurry up and finish that sandwich, but maybe he wasn't hungry.

"Who?" he asked.

"What's that?"

"The new members," Paul said. "Who were they?"

"Oh, well, I don't recall all their names, Paul. There was quite a lot of them. You should have been there. Will you come next week?"

Paul put down the remaining half of his sandwich. She looked at the one round bite mark his mouth had left in the bread. He was looking at her. "Was one of them Bartlett?" he said. "Thomas Bartlett?"

How did he know that? She could have sworn Squinty hadn't been at that meeting. "Why, yes, Paul. Thomas Bartlett. Do you know him?"

Paul nodded slowly. "I've known him for quite a long time, Samantha." Odd. She could swear his voice was changing, becoming deeper, more resonant, less hoarse and scratchy, more intelligent. Paul reached a hand up to his head and removed his battered brown hat. "Such a long time. In fact, you might say we're old friends."

He was beginning to get on her nerves. And why the voice-change? Had he been using a fake voice all this time? "Really?" she said. "He's never mentioned you. Perhaps he doesn't know you're in the society." She believed she had only mentioned Paul's nickname to Thomas anyway; even she didn't know Paul's surname.

"No, he doesn't, but he will. If you tell him." He was leaning forward in his seat, pushing the tray aside carelessly so that any moment it might topple to the floor.

"Say! Paul, be careful..." She reached out for the tray, but his hand was faster. He gripped her wrist and pulled her closer toward him as the tray and its contents clattered onto the rug.

"What were you and Bartlett doing at the Chamber of Commerce banquet last night? Tell me!"

"What?" How did he know that? "Stop It! You're hurting me," she said.

"Tell me, woman! I saw you leaving with him, don't deny it. I want to know what he was up to."

"Who...who are you?"

A terrible, sinister smile came over his face then, and for a moment he looked like a mischievous, sadistic devil who promised fun and games to children but really loved to rip their limbs off. "I'll show you," he said.

In the next instant Paul's face began to change, the flesh sort of shimmered, folded in on itself, just slightly, and so slowly that at first it was barely even perceptible. And then Samantha could see what was happening. The nose was becoming less broad, the eyebrows less heavy, the skin tone and the spotted complexion were becoming smoother, yet at the same time more lined. Paul was becoming an older man.

These were all only subtle, cosmetic changes, but the ultimate effect was amazing. Squinty lost his squint; his eyes were bright and alive and full of menace. Paul now looked like another person, someone who resembled him but was altogether different. Samantha knew then that Paul had never been real; he was just an identity this man had assumed months ago and now sloughed off like a serpent shedding its skin. *How could anyone do that?* she thought. And the answer to her question formed quickly in her brain. *He can if he's a metamorph. He can if he's an alien. If someone can change into a gargantuan monster, how much trouble would it be for them to shift their features ever so slightly to disguise their normal appearance?*

Last night she had never gotten a very clear, close look at Gareth Bronmore, but she was sure that that was Paul's true identity. He had been spying on them all along.

Samantha felt sick to her stomach-cold, panicky, horrified.

Gareth Bronmore was in her apartment.

She shuddered.

"Will you tell me what I want to know?" Bronmore said. "Tell me what you and Bartlett were doing at the dinner?"

"Tom was invited," she said. "I was his date, that's all. What more do you want from me?" Try as she might she couldn't wriggle free from his grip.

"Don't play games with me, woman. That's not what I meant and you know it. How much does Mr. Bartlett know? About me? Tell me!"

"You're Gareth Bronmore, aren't you?" she said. "And everything Eustace Dunn said about you is true!"

His eyes flared and his head snapped backward momentarily. She knew she had said too much.

"What did the old cow tell you? What did she say about me?" He twisted her arm painfully and she gasped, twisted it and dug his fingernails into her flesh. "What did she say?" Oh, God, it hurt so much. Samantha was afraid he was going to tear her arm off. And he could do it, too.

"She said you were a hybrid, a descendant of alien emissaries. That you could change—into a monster. That you were responsible for all the death and destruction along the coast-line. That you were a murderer!" And then something broke inside of her. She thought of Harold's horrible death and the tragedy of her wasted years and of the reptiles that had caused it. She knew this man was just another cruel, devouring reptile and she hated him. She gathered up all her courage and spit right in his face.

Bronmore wiped away the spittle and dropped her arm. She held it, rubbing all the sore spots. Now what was he going to do? Kill her?

But Bronmore somehow seemed less angry than before, even satiated, for now. "So I was right all along. There is much more to Mistress Dunn than anyone suspects. I wonder if she's as much a threat to me as she'd like to imagine. I suppose Bartlett was looking for my hump last night, wasn't he?"

Samantha whimpered. "Y...yes."

Bronmore rose to his feet. "I've gone to great pains to keep my back out of sight all my life, knowing it might brand me as a..." He stopped and shook his fist in the air. "Bartlett got away from me. Twice, he got away. Uncanny luck, or some-thing more?" He muttered the rest to himself. "It was as if he knew better than to row across the lake to get away from me, as if he knew I'd only dive into the water and change. I wanted to stop him at first; he might have seen me in town and recognized me. But then I realized that he saw me do nothing incriminating, so what does it matter?"

He spoke louder now, but Samantha still didn't think he was talking to her. "I didn't even learn who he was until the papers had the story about Beachside. I recognized him as they put him in the ambulance, of course. I couldn't resist going there in human form just to admire my handiwork, to make sure I'd left no witnesses. My father told me never leave any witnesses. No, no, he didn't say that, but he meant it. I know that's what he meant."

He lifted his head and started laughing. "Oh, it feels good to confess to someone, to let someone know who I am and what I can do!"

He was crazy. Talking to himself. Not making any sense.

Bronmore stopped laughing and turned back to Samantha. "I'm a lonely man, Samantha. I've seen that same loneliness in your eyes. You were one of the few in the Monster Society who befriended me, befriended 'Squinty.' Yes, I know that's what they called me. 'Paul' liked you, you know; I liked you." He leaned down and began to stroke her arm. "I still do. I'm sorry I hurt you, very sorry. But you see...I had to know." His touch felt like sandpaper.

He sat down beside her on the sofa and stared at the opposite wall. "God, it's not fair. I didn't ask to be like this, the only one on this planet to be like this. You call me a monster, but I'm only acting naturally for one of my species. What would you do if you had the power, if you could tower over everyone and everything? Would you sit at home and watch TV and eat your supper and let yourself be trampled and ground under by superior numbers? Don't you think I realize, that my human half realizes, the horror of what I've done? But I'm not human, Samantha. Why don't they realize that I'm not human? I'm an animal. Part of me is bestial. I can't always control what The Beast does. I can't always stop it. I can no more control myself or my appetites than a killer shark. I am what I was born to be. A hybrid. Why hate me for being different? I didn't ask..." He sighed deeply.

She could almost feel pity for him, understand that if you hated him you might as well hate a man-eating lion, a shark, any carnivore that ate flesh not out of spite or maliciousness but because that was only its nature. She could almost pity him were it not for the fact that unlike the lion or the tiger, he had a human side and a human mentality. He knew what he was doing, knew that it was wrong, had, in fact, just admitted it to her.

"I do hate you," she said. "You kill innocent people. You say you like me but you'd eat me, too, wouldn't you? You're worse than those lizards that got Harold. They were just dumb, hungry reptiles. They didn't know any better. But you do know better. You *know*."

He grabbed her by the shoulders and shook her. "No, you're wrong. Won't anybody listen? Try to imagine being like me, Samantha. Torn and twisted into separate directions, like having two identities. I can't help being the way I am, acting the way I do."

"It's every person's responsibility to control the beast," she said. *Sure, Samantha, sound so righteous, the Allens called from the bedroom. Is that why they had to pick us up with tongs and put us into 17 different specially marked bags?*

Shrugging the aural hallucination away, she continued. "It's your responsibility to control your urges, to make sure your human mind is dominant over your bestial side. Everyone has to do that. Or you really will be just a beast, a murdering animal. I know how it is to give into those weak, self-indulgent impulses, to allow yourself to hurt yourself and others, to hurt strangers or people you love. I know. Someone with your power—why, your responsibility is a hundred times greater. I gave in and I killed four people. When you give in you kill hundreds. You can't give in, you have to control—"

"But Samantha, I told you! I'm not a human being!"

"You are! You *are* human. As long as you're sitting here talking to me you are human. You say there's no one left who's like you. Well, if that's true, turn your back on your beast side and accept your humanity. You won't be as lonely as you say you are if you accept it. Look at all the things you have, the things any ordinary human would give their right arm for—money, power, an empire—and that's not enough?"

She saw the shallow, impervious look on his face and knew she wasn't reaching him. And it made her furious. She slapped him in the face, pushed him aside, and jumped to her feet. She wasn't scared of this sick old man. He could do nothing to her here. She wasn't scared, and her lack of fear surprised her.

"Go ahead and change," she said, backing up toward the door. "Smash the building, crush me to death, a mere mortal female. Go ahead! Or fight it and accept that you're a man. Because if you don't, I hope they do kill you. I hope Tom and Thorson and Mistress Dunn make sure you're the very last of your kind!"

She knew she had said too much, but it was too late to take it back.

He got to his feet slowly, his eyes fairly crackling with unharnessed anger. "Kill me? Tom and Thorson? Why, there really is a conspiracy, isn't there? You really do mean to kill me, the whole lot of you. And you expect me to just stand by and let you do it. No, my God, no. I won't allow it. I'm not ready to die!"

He moved faster than she would ever have expected, grabbing her and hurling her away with such force that she wound up sprawled on the floor outside the kitchen. Her arm hurt so badly she thought she would scream. She twisted around and tried to rise. She grimaced. For the moment she could barely stand on her ankle. "Tell me what you plan to do," he said. "Tell me—or so help me!"

"I wouldn't tell you even if I did know!"

And then, before her disbelieving eyes, he calmly and quickly removed his clothing until he stood before her naked.

Bronmore began to change. He spread out his arms and took deep, deep breaths, then exhaled them. With each breath his stomach ballooned and stayed expanded, until the next breath made it even larger. Concurrently, his arms and legs began to thicken. The penis between his legs hung down like a bull's.

He was expanding and expanding, his head getting bigger,

taking on a vaguely reptilian cast. The hump on his back was enlarging, pushing upward, while curving and arching downward at the same time, forcing the front half of his body toward the floor.

Bronmore transformed into his intermediate form, which was so big that it literally filled the living room. If Samantha hadn't been prepared for it (as much as anyone could be), she would probably have doubted the evidence of her own senses. She wouldn't have known what to call or how to describe the creature that had taken Bronmore's place.

It was basically humanoid but stood hunched over like an elongated ape. It had a thick heavy neck that supported the largest, ugliest head she had ever seen. The head was pale and hairless, with a snout that was similar to that of primitive man's. The mouth opened to reveal four gigantic serpentine fangs in front and rows of small pointed teeth behind them. The hunched over body was a large misshapen lump of mottled flesh and bone. The legs were short and chunky, also hairless, ending in feet with four claws. The arms were comparatively thin and long and also had four clawed digits. There was a long rubbery grayish tail swishing behind the legs, and a monstrous appendage in front that Samantha didn't want to think about.

In the back of her mind Samantha rapidly computed the thing's dimensions. It was 15 feet long from tail to snout, eight feet wide, and eight feet tall while it was hunched over, but if it stretched to its full height it might reach 12 to 15 feet. The massive head was as large as an executive's desk, and one of those fangs, in front of the mouth, was about one and a half feet long, if not longer.

She had never seen nor imagined in her wildest nightmares anything like it. Bronmore had changed from human to this monstrosity all in the space of 30 seconds. She could not recall individual details of the metamorphosis and didn't want to.

The monster thrust out its head and tried to snare Samantha on its fangs. She ducked into the kitchen where she hoped it couldn't reach her. Luckily her ankle was only mildly sprained and already her arm was feeling better. Then the thing began to butt its head against the wall between kitchen and living room.

Crash! A few thuds and hairline cracks started forming. A few more, and plaster fell from the ceiling and the wall began to buckle. Dishes fell off the counter; the cabinet doors opened and spilled their contents. Cans and glasses and silverware tumbled onto the floor. Samantha's high-pitched screams resembled the wall of an ambulance.

She knew Bronmore could get much bigger, but he—It—seemed satisfied at this size, which was bad enough. A few more butts with its head and she'd be at its mercy. She hadn't been frightened before, or so she thought, but that was before Bronmore had actually demonstrated what she'd been told he could do. Now she couldn't understand how she was managing to hold it together in the face of such terror and absurdity.

She had to get away. Bronmore might grow even larger if she escaped, but she was counting on his fear of exposure to prevent that.

She wanted him to return to normal size where she and the others could deal with him. For he had become her enemy, too, and she, his.

She thanked God she hadn't been drinking. It would have slowed her reflexes and made her too courageous and too foolish. She peeked out from the end of the wall that divided living room and kitchen and saw that Bronmore's size was actually a disadvantage. The monster was so big it could hardly maneuver in such close quarters. Her apartment was a mess. Her paintings had been cracked by the beast's bulk scraping against the walls, and the furniture lay in ruins beneath its feet. There had to be a way out of this.

As larger chunks of plaster rained down on her head and the wall tilted downward at an alarming angle—she'd be crushed like a bug if he kept it up— she grabbed an empty vodka bottle, a can of volatile stain remover, a dishtowel and matches, and rapidly made herself a makeshift "Molotov cocktail," She felt like a commando on a battlefield. The pain in her arm flared up again while she worked, but she ignored it. She poured the stain remover in the vodka bottle and stuffed in the dishtowel. Once the end of the dishtowel was set on fire, she grabbed the bottom of the bottle, jumped out from behind the dividing wall, and chucked the bottle into the monster's open jaws.

There was no way the beast could have backed away or dodged it; there simply wasn't room. The bottle flared and exploded in its mouth, and the beast howled in agony. In reaction to the pain its head reared up toward the ceiling and it backed up against the bedroom wall. The ceiling smashed upward and cracked in a dozen places, but otherwise remained intact; the bedroom wall was completely shattered.

Samantha saw her chance. While the thing had backed away and was preoccupied with the fiery torment in its gullet, she ran past it and down the hall to the door.

She thought she felt its breath on her back and hoped it was just an illusion. The door was just a second away. There!

Her fingers reached out to grab for the doorknob. She made it!

She didn't bother with the elevator, but ran toward the service stairs and went down them faster than she had ever thought humanly possible. Her ankle was throbbing in outrage but she knew she had no choice.

She was constantly aware that there was nothing to prevent Bronmore from changing into his Gargantosaurus form and smashing up the whole building and its surroundings in the hopes of somehow killing her. But surely he would know she might still manage to survive, as Thomas and

Thorson had. She was counting on him leaving, sparing the building, and coming after her. She didn't know where to go or what to do. She didn't want to lead him to Thomas, but both he and Thorson had to be warned. Eustace, too. He knows. And he's angry. And he's coming after you.

She reached the lobby and headed for the street. As she opened the door she saw a cab pulling away from the corner. "Wait!" she screamed. "Wait!" Tom could pay the cabbie when they reached the restaurant. Surely the four of them could put their heads together and figure out what to do.

As she got in the back seat of the cab and looked behind her she almost expected to see the building collapsing from within, windows shattering, people falling out, walls crumbling away to reveal the evil at its center, the humongous lizard at its core.

But, as she had hoped, Bronmore returned to normal.

For as the cab pulled away she saw him walking fully-clothed out of the building, his eyes, thank God, facing in a different direction.

I'll go to Parmenter's, she thought.

Thomas will know what to do.

* * *

Bronmore stood outside on the street and pondered his next course of action. Where will she go next? he wondered. To her lover's side? Of course. He had checked the address of Thomas Bartlett's apartment; it was, unfortunately, too near the center of the city. But wait…she had said she was going out. Where else would she go but the restaurant her lover owned.

Bronmore chuckled. He remembered. He would go to Parmenter's Saloon. Parmenter's *by the bay!*

CHAPTER FIFTEEN

THE BEAST

What was keeping Samantha?

Thomas kept looking over to the entrance to Parmenter's or through the glass window to see if she was walking down the street, but there was still no sign of her. He checked his wristwatch. Almost half an hour late.

He looked across the table at Rod and smiled. "If she's not here soon we'll go ahead without her. I'm hungry, aren't you?"

Roderick nodded. "Yes. It was awfully nice of you to invite me to dinner."

"My pleasure," Thomas said. But he was not too sure of what Samantha might think of it. This was supposed to have been a date, a romantic dinner for two; he was going to take a table in the more dimly lit backroom, away from the water, and sit with Samantha by candlelight. But a table in the brighter front room was more appropriate now that Rod had joined them. It was a slow night, past the peak period, and many of the tables were empty.

He had only been polite when he asked Rod if he wanted to dine with them, not expecting the man to say yes. He'd thought he would have preferred being driven to the home of his friends so he could get himself settled in their guest house. But when he said yes, Thomas couldn't exactly rescind the offer. It was as if Roderick wasn't about to let go of anyone who actually believed his story about the monster attacking his house, as if now that he had met a kindred spirit he had to cling to him for fear that Thomas might vanish once his back was turned. Thomas was his only link to sanity.

Roderick had stayed in Thomas' apartment long after he and Thomas could not reach any solid conclusion what to do about Bronmore—and had looked so lost and lonely that Thomas hadn't the heart to turn him out. If a dinner in Parmenter's would cheer him up, it was the least Thomas could do for him.

From what Thorson had told him, Thomas assumed that the existence of the Bronmore-Gargantosaurus was the man's greatest fantasy and nightmare come to life. He had readily accepted their incredible story because he was only one step removed from the impractical, romantic, gullible members of the Monster Society himself. He had dreamed of monsters all his life, and up until now at least, had fervently hoped they were real.

Thomas raised his hand and the waiter came over. He ordered another Bloody Mary and a Scotch and soda for Roderick. Then he got to his feet. "Excuse me a moment. I'll be right back. I want to try Samantha's line again and see what's keeping her."

As he walked to the phone in the corridor near the men's room, he thought back to the terrible confrontation he'd had with his partner Joseph just half an hour ago.

He'd walked into Parmenter's with Roderick, left him nursing a drink at the bar, and gone into the restroom. Joseph was there and appeared to be washing his hands at the sink. On either side of him were two heavy-set mafioso types who had apparently been leaning on him. Joseph's face was stark white except for the right side which was red and swollen. One of the mean-looking characters rubbed his fist and gave Joseph a significant look. They walked past Thomas and left the restroom.

"What the hell was that all about?"

And Joseph told him that everything Thomas had most feared was coming true—gambling debts, I.O.U.s, the whole bit. "You know who owns most of this restaurant," he whined, splashing water on his sore and bruised right cheek. "They do, that's who. Their bosses. There are more crooks running Parmenter's than slot machines in Atlantic City."

Thomas exploded. "You bastard, this was half my restaurant!"

"It ain't now. If I can't pay up, if we can't pay up, they're gonna take it away. Or kill us."

"How could you get us in this mess? This was our restaurant, not just yours." Had Joseph not looked so defeated and weary, so petrified already, Thomas would certainly have taken a swing at him. "Bastard!"

Joseph told him the amount they needed, which was astronomical. Thomas felt so ill he had to lean against the sink for support. "My God, what will we do?" Joseph did not reply.

A moment later Thomas said, "Let them take the restaurant, damn it. I don't want to be in business with a creep like you any more." He headed for the doorway. "And Joseph...I hope they do kill you."

He walked out of the bathroom so overflowing with hatred and regret he could barely stand it. In one sense, everything about Joseph, the crooks, and their hold on Parmenter's, seemed quite trivial up against the menace of Gareth Bronmore. Yet, he was having trouble worrying about a hybrid when his whole life and livelihood seemed to be crumbling all around him.

He took Roderick over to a table and made strained

conversation with him while they waited for Samantha. Roderick merely assumed he was upset about Bronmore. After awhile they grew silent; Roderick had his own grim thoughts to keep him company.

Now as Thomas dialed Samantha's number, he hoped she'd show up at the restaurant soon. Maybe she could cheer the two sad sacks up a bit.

Everything was so strange and unreal. If they did lose the restaurant, which seemed likely, he'd have to try and get out of it as financially intact as possible. He had considerable savings. He would have to consult his lawyer immediately and see what he could do. He'd bring Joseph up on charges, but he had to be careful. Organized crime was involved in this, and even he knew that those people didn't play fair.

He was wondering what in hell he was really going to do when a recorded voice broke in to tell him there was trouble with the line. He dialed again but got the same message. He hoped nothing was wrong. When he couldn't get through a third time, he asked the operator to try, but she had no luck, either.

When he returned to the dining room and began walking toward the table, Samantha suddenly rushed into the restaurant and approached him. She threw herself into his arms and started sobbing.

"He's after us," she said.

Thomas knew who she meant.

Had he been wondering what else could go wrong, he would have had his answer.

* * *

Out on Biscayne Bay Bronmore lay on the deck and rested, breathing in and out, getting his strength back, while the man knelt beside him and asked if he were all right. Of course he was not all right. Would he be here, like this, naked, caught in nets and hauled aboard the boat like some common flounder? Would he have been in his human form, considering his consuming rage and purpose, if he were all right?

"Must have tried to kill himself," someone said. "Surprised he lasted this long."

"How did he get all the way out here?" someone else wondered. "We're miles offshore."

Someone with a more authoritative voice told the men to back away, and soon this new figure was kneeling beside him, holding his head up by the neck, poking and probing. "Are you all right, sir?" It was a beefy brown man with a Spanish accent and concerned brown eyes. "Get a blanket for him; he's freezing."

It wasn't the cold air bothering him, but he couldn't tell them that. If only they would leave him alone so he could rest. "I...I'll be all right," he told them. "Fell off a boat. Was treading water—long time. Just let me rest; I'll be all right."

"Don't worry, old-timer, we're heading into harbor now. We'll have you in a hospital in no time."

One of the men looked up at the sky. "Boy, are we gonna have a storm!"

Bronmore had headed right for the water as soon as he left Samantha's apartment. He'd found a deserted pier, stripped, entered the water and changed to his intermediate shape immediately. He transformed completely as soon as he was far enough out to sea...but something happened. He was too tired, too nervous. He tried not to make his changes back and forth—human to intermediate, back to human, back to intermediate again, then to monster—too quickly. This time it had taken its toll. He had found himself reverting to human form while he was miles out at sea, unable to change back to his saurian incarnation. It was all the tension, the stress, the panicky feeling that things were closing in and he had to rush to resume control.

He could have survived on his own—treaded water, the

way he'd told these men he had, until he was able to switch to the intermediate phase—but when he saw this trawler (or rather when they saw him) he figured he could get his strength back quicker if he allowed himself to be taken aboard.

Well, he still had tricks up his sleeve. Even if he couldn't regain his saurian form this evening, there were still things he could do to hurt Samantha and her friends. Had Mistress Dunn told them about all of the hybrid's abilities? Did Mistress Dunn even know of them herself? He thought not. Surely he had some secrets. He would have a surprise for the whole lot of them, those miscreants who dared try to wipe him off the face of the Earth. He would take care of them, all right!

But he sensed it would not be necessary to use his more mystical abilities. He felt his strength returning.

They had carried him into a cabin on deck and left him alone on a cot under a blanket. Better to do it while they were still relatively far from the harbor.

Part of him wondered if what he was planning do to was smart, if it was really safe, but he didn't care. It was time the world, the whole world, knew of his existence. Try to kill him, will they? Once he destroyed anyone who knew of his metamorphoses, he could safely switch back and forth from monster to human whenever he needed, and dominate these pitiful humans both as Bronmore and The Beast. Why hadn't he thought of it sooner?

It's time, he thought a few minutes later. *It's time, I can tell. This time I won't have to switch back until I'm ready. It's time.*

First he changed into his intermediate phase, like he had at Samantha's apartment, which didn't take very long to do. He would shift his mass as his body parts swelled and expanded, as he gathered up energy and power from the air and the atoms all around him. His head grew large, the jaws widened, the fangs grew, the teeth multiplied. The neck swelled outward until it was several times its normal size. The torso lengthened and thickened and stretched, and his legs grew as fat as tree trunks. His five human toes were enveloped by the rapidly swelling flesh, and four clawed digits, one on the back of the foot, took their place. His arms grew long and thin and his five fingers were also absorbed by the wave of tissue until four more digits and claws popped out. He stood hunched over, his back scraping the roof of the cabin and his head hanging slightly lower.

Just then the concerned brown man with the Spanish accent opened the door to the cabin.

Before the man could scream, Bronmore slashed out with his claw.

He tore at and sectioned the man's body—that first swipe alone had taken half the head away—and greedily flipped the pieces into his mouth. He sucked away the blood and swallowed the skin. Bones cracked between his teeth and he ground away all the meat, every last strip of flesh, before sucking out the bone marrow, too. He crunched the bones between his jaws and let the tasty white powder fall down his gullet.

The man was consumed in a minute and a half.

Ahhh, good, thought Bronmore. He had been fortified. More energy. He felt better than he had in hours. If he had been able to devour that Clark woman at her apartment he would never have had his weak spell in the water. Bitch! His mouth still burned! Good food was always the answer.

Now it was time to complete the transformation.

Changing into his beast form was always moderately painful—it took longer and required vaster amounts of energy, more shifting and dividing of tissue—but he could handle it. He had handled it all these many years; he would handle it now. He prepared himself, took deep breaths and began.

All the individual processes, the changing of each body

part, happened concurrently. An oozy substance dribbled out of the pores and hardened into skin, which emitted more ooze, which in turn hardened into more skin. The whole process was repeated over and over, the skin constantly thickening and expanding, until Bronmore grew from a ten ton creature to one that weighed over 200 tons! His head continued to balloon until it alone was roughly the size of 20 large bull elephants, and its eyes as big as buses. Rows of yards-long teeth popped out of the gummy tissue inside the mouth as the fangs of the intermediate stage receded. The ears and nostrils of The Beast were mere rounded indentations in the skin and the face had no actual lips.

The legs and arms thickened and became similar in size and shape although the two front legs, formerly the arms, were somewhat longer and had more relative maneuverability. The claws grew until they were 1000 times the size they had been in Bronmore's intermediate form. The neck was short and massive, while the tail became an elongated chunky appendage that was almost as heavy and powerful as one of the legs. The torso had puffed and pulled out, stretched, until it was no longer hunched over or compressed, as in the intermediate phase, but was spread out over 250 feet. The skin was a tone between dark red and black, slick with oil, smooth in some spots and bumpy in others. In this form Bronmore would walk on all fours.

Bronmore was now a Gargantosaurus, the largest beast that had ever lived, the most powerful animal in the world.

The mere act of metamorphosis wrecked the trawler. The Beast's head shattered the roof of the cabin as its legs tore through the decks and holds. Men were crushed beneath the oozing flesh as it expanded. The tail whipped out and flattened anyone too slow to get out of its way. The giant claws sliced through screaming sailors and littered the water with body fragments. The thousands of fish that had been caught that day were devoured by The Beast in one hasty swallow.

Nets, wood, and metal went flying everywhere as the boat fell apart under the weight of the creature.

As The Beast dived down into the ocean beneath the shattered remains of the trawler, it turned its head this way and that to pop a drowning seaman or two into its mouth. It needed sustenance, energy, strength to do what it had to do, what Bronmore wanted to do. Man and Beast were now fully merged and obsessed with a terrible, raging objective.

The trawler was lost at sea with all hands aboard.

Then with one thrust of its powerful legs, The Beast turned inland and headed toward the lights and the people, and those who would seek its nonexistence.

In just a few strokes it would be there, the city at its mercy.

A mercy he did not care to indulge in.

* * *

It was so dark outside it might as well have been midnight. Thomas could hear thunder in the distance and saw the occasional lightning bolt illuminate the sky. The streets had grown dark under the storm clouds. He expected it would pour any minute. He sipped his third Bloody Mary, picked at the food left on his plate and thought back to Samantha's excited entrance almost two hours ago.

He had paid off the cab driver and taken Samantha to the table. She'd been so hysterical she barely noticed that Roderick was sitting with them. She told them what happened at her apartment. "What will we do?" she said.

Thomas tried to remain calm as he asked the waiter to bring their menus. "We eat dinner is what we do. We sit here, try to relax, have a nice drink, or soda, and put some good food in our bellies. Then we can think clearer."

"But what if he comes here? What if he transforms?"

"We're safe until it's dark," Roderick interjected. "He's always struck very late at night or early in the morning. He won't try anything with so many people, so many witnesses, about and awake."

Thomas thought that Roderick was probably right. Bronmore would have nothing to gain by attacking them now. He couldn't even be sure they were here. Thomas felt uneasy, as usual, being this close to the water. Still, he would not run away. He did not believe Bronmore would change his pattern and come crashing down onto the city where thousands of people, many of whom might survive, could see him. Besides, if he were to run it would be admitting to himself that the whole fantastic story was true, that Bronmore's abilities were for real and the man had to be murdered. And despite what had happened at Beachside, and what Samantha had just told him, he just wasn't ready for that yet not completely.

But that was then, two hours ago. This was now. The skies were dark, threatening rain, and the crowds had left the waterfront for home. Parmenter's was practically deserted. It was only 10 o'clock but it might as well have been the witching hour. And Thomas began to think that perhaps they were wrong in assuming Bronmore would not attack in front of witnesses. He could kill all the witnesses, Thomas thought, remembering Beachside, when over 100 people had filled Bronmore's belly and not deterred him from his purpose. And while this was a city and not a small town slum, it was still in a comparatively deserted area, especially at this hour.

Thomas looked over at the bar, where a dour-faced, frightened Joseph sat consuming one martini after another. Wonder what he'd say if he knew we're facing an even greater threat then those friends of his in the syndicate?

"I'm finished," Samantha said, pushing her plate with its remains of cheese cake to one side. "Maybe the three of us should go..." She stopped short and leaned back in her seat, grinning strangely. "I almost said go back to my apartment for coffee. I have no apartment. God knows how I'm going to explain it to the landlord!"

"We'll worry about that in the morning. You can stay with me if you like. As long as you need to." *Forever, if you want.* He thought a moment and added, "You, too, Roderick. I have a guest room you can use. I can drive you out to your friends in the morning."

"Uh, that's kind of you." He looked at Samantha for a second. "But I don't want to intrude."

Thomas managed a smile. "Stay in the guest room and you won't be intruding."

They agreed to leave Parmenter's and take off for Thomas' place. Thomas left a large tip on the table and took Samantha by the hand. "Let's get out of here."

Samantha was still worried. "Do you think you ought to tell everyone to go home early? Just in case?"

He checked his watch. "It's closing time in a little while, but I suppose you're right."

He was wondering how to phrase it, how to deal with Joseph's curiosity, when he felt a sudden sideways shove and wondered who'd bumped into him. Then he realized that not only he but the waiter, Sam, Roderick, and everyone else in the dining room were sprawling to the floor or tumbling all over each other! Crying out, Joseph flopped backward off his chair, and Dack the bartender went rolling completely over the counter.

It's happening.

Thomas had barely gotten off an "Is everyone all right?" had just managed to pick Samantha up off the floor, when the whole place shifted toward the sidewalk as if it were in the middle of an earthquake.

Bronmore definitely had changed his pattern.

The few customers and staff in the place began screaming and heading for the exits. Chairs and glasses were knocked over in the rush. There was a groaning, snapping noise and chunks of the ceiling began hurtling down to the floor, crashing onto and flattening tables and serving carts. Thomas saw that both Sam and Roderick were frozen in horror, too scared to even save themselves. He had to get them out of here.

He gave Roderick a push toward the door and said "Move!" Roderick still seemed vague and confused, but he obeyed. Thomas was about to follow, dragging Samantha behind him, when he saw that Joseph, drunk, had climbed back on his chair at the bar and seemed too disoriented to save himself. He hated the man, but he couldn't let him die.

Thomas pushed Samantha after Roderick and hoped she would snap out of it and run out into the street as fast as her legs would take her. Thomas tried to reach Joseph, but it was difficult getting through the crowd of busboys, kitchen staff and patrons from the other dining rooms that raced to get out as Parmenter's collapsed around them. Beams and huge chunks of masonry were falling down from the ceiling, and shards of glass sprinkled the room as the windows cracked and popped out entirely.

There was another shove—The Beast literally slamming its bulk into the building—and Thomas went sprawling. Joseph reached out his hand to grab the bar and managed to hang onto his seat. The bartender had long since fled with the others.

Thomas pulled himself up off a semiconscious woman in an evening gown. He had helped her to her feet when a man appeared out of the dust and debris to take her in his arms and carry her out. He watched the good Samaritan for a second, then continued on his way. More chunks of plaster and wood came flying down, smashing to pieces on the floor. What had once been a chic, expensive restaurant now looked like a condemned building that had been hit by a wrecking ball.

Thomas was only a few feet away from Joseph, who was still clinging drunkenly to the bar counter. All the bottles had tumbled off their shelves, and there was a strong alcoholic odor permeating the room along with the stench of the dust and the burning smoke. Thomas thought he could see fire erupting in the kitchen. He prayed that everyone in the rear had managed to make it through whatever exits they could use in time. One outer wall had completely crumbled, and Thomas could see the harbor lights and feel the cool breeze from the ocean through the gap. *And something else. Something dark and enormous.* He knew if he stopped to think about it he would be terrified and helpless.

There came another shove, and he fell backwards over a long wooden beam that had landed on a table and punctured one of the windows. He struggled to right himself. All he had to do was grab Joseph and get out of there.

But then there came another crash, a wrenching, ripping groan of wood and metal—a whining, earsplitting wail that sounded like all civilization was being gutted—and much of what was left of the ceiling fell abruptly into the dining room. Thomas was pinned beneath another beam which had just barely missed shattering his legs; luckily the table behind him had taken most of the impact. All Thomas could do as he struggled on his back to get his legs out from under the beam was look upward helplessly. And he knew what it was that had torn the gaping hole in the roof.

God help him. This was The Beast of his nightmare; The Beast of his memory, The Beast that had murdered his parents and destroyed Beachside. He could feel its breath, smell its foul odor, see its eyes glowing, as they came closer and closer. Its color was the color of dark, dried blood, and it was, if anything, even bigger than he remembered.

From what Thomas had seen through the hole in the wall earlier, he imagined most of The Beast's body was still in the water outside; it had hunched itself up and used head and front legs to pound against the restaurant. With most of its heavy bulk still in the bay, The Beast's front legs could do little but tap the back walls; otherwise they would have completely obliterated the restaurant with just a few blows. Obviously the creature was reluctant to leave the water.

And now it was digging its head down into the debris, catching sight of him, trying to stretch and lower its neck until it could grab him with its teeth and consume him.

Thomas stared up at the death's head that was the monster's face. Yes, it was a reptile. Yes, it was a man. Yes, it had a face, a semi-human, semi-reptilian countenance that leered and chuckled and grinned with its lipless mouth like a devil. A massive claw reached down through the debris where the head could not reach and Thomas strained to escape from under the beam.

Everything was abnormally quiet and still in the restaurant, except for Thomas, struggling to get away before that claw could come any closer. The Beast strained and stretched, but still Thomas was out of its reach. It would have to pull itself farther out of the water if it wanted to get him, and Thomas prayed that it would stay where it was. He knew the only thing preventing The Beast from tearing the whole building apart—which it could easily do if it came on land— was that it didn't want Thomas to be lost beneath the debris. Oh no, that would not do. It wanted to pop him in his mouth, to chew him and swallow him and make sure this time he was dead. *Cheated me twice, boy, twice. But you're not gonna cheat me again. Not this time.*

The Beast was actually salivating over its approaching feast, its victory. Great gobs of odorous, viscous spittle dropped out of its open mouth and plopped down and over Thomas like gigantic raindrops, spilling across the floor and the broken tables. The Beast was licking its chops, savoring its meal. Thomas was no bigger than the size of one of the monster's teeth, but he was a morsel the creature coveted like no other.

Ironically, Thomas was too small for The Beast to grab with its claw, even if it could reach him. The monster itself was about five times the size of the enormous restaurant, and its oversized feet were nearly as big as the one room. There was no way the creature could successfully grab anything as tiny as Thomas between those thick, greasy digits and claws.

Thomas tried harder to squirm free. If he fainted, if he lapsed into unconsciousness from pain or dread, he would die. The only thing that kept him from passing out was the knowledge that this was no dream, no safe fantasy he could turn his back on, but something terribly real and physical. It had substance.

Yet anything with substance could be fought. Somehow, it could be beaten.

The monster's eagerness was its undoing. The spittle greased Thomas' legs and the lumber he was pinned under until he was able to slide out from under his prison. The whole room was warm, stinking from the monster's horrible breath.

In shock, Joseph still sat on his stool, staring at the spectacle from the miraculously undamaged bar as if his universe had gone tilting sideways into a crazy alternate dimension; there was nothing he could do but watch. Thomas made his way over to the bar, twisting through the wreckage, trying to hold his breath against the smoke and grab Joseph and get out.

But the monster sensed his intention.

There was another wrench as another wall fell down somewhere, and The Beast pulled itself up farther from the water. One of its front feet came down…

…came down on top of Joseph!

One second Joseph Parmenter was there, dumbly watching Thomas' progress, the next there was nothing but a thick dark tower in his place.

The tower! The tower that crushed his mother's bedroom. The tower with the digits.

The Beast could have squashed him or reached down for him, but to torment him it had crushed Joseph instead.

The foot was lifting, its claws making a futile grab for Thomas. Thomas did not want to see what was left beneath the foot—though the true horror was that there was nothing there to see. Joseph Parmenter was just a blotch on The Beast's paw now, a blotch the Beast would lick off at its leisure.

The foot was almost as big as the room! The very next step would crush Thomas and everything around him. The only thing in his favor was that The Beast could not move very quickly; each movement, in fact, seemed to take a lumbering eternity.

As Thomas crawled over the debris toward the exit, he saw that he was in the very center of the shadow of the tremendous foot, a shadow that was widening, growing, as the foot came closer and closer. How could he hope to get away? If this step didn't get him, the next one would. And there were three more feet besides this one.

The foot just missed him. He could feel the very tip of one claw scraping away the back of his shirt, bloodying him, sending sharp stabs of blinding agony through his body. But he was still alive and in one piece. He stumbled out onto the street where Samantha and Roderick were waiting. Everyone else, seeing the monster towering over Parmenter's, had fled the area.

"Get moving!" he screamed, grabbing Samantha and pushing her ahead of him. Which way should they go? If they chose the wrong direction they would wind up crushed beneath the monster's feet. And he could tell from the wretched cacophony, the mashing, whoosing sound behind him, that it was following him, pulling itself up out of the water. What was left of the restaurant crumbled to the ground and died, just fell to pieces in a welter of snapping wood and disintegrating masonry. The other buildings on either side of Parmenter's had so far suffered only minor damage, but by the time The Beast managed to pull itself out of the bay, that would no longer be the case. Already some walls were starting to crack and quiver.

Thomas pushed his two companions toward his car. As they piled inside he grabbed his keys out of his pocket and hurried to start the engine. He tried not to think about what would happen if The Beast should step on the car while they were in it. His trembling fingers inserted the keys and he prayed. The engine started.

He had a flash of himself as a little boy, asking his mother, "What would you do if you saw a dinosaur walking up the street?"

Well, pretty soon the whole city would have an answer to that question!

His first thought was to drive as faraway from the bay as possible, but in spite of his terror he was reluctant to have the creature follow him into the city's densely inhabited areas. He would not have that many deaths on his conscience, not when he knew that The Beast really just wanted to kill him. Or would it be satisfied with nothing less than the flesh and blood of thousands of innocents? Did it now think itself strong enough to destroy a whole living city instead of one slumbering neighborhood?

He drove down the street outside the ruins of Parmenter's, heading for Biscayne Boulevard. He could swear he could hear the first footfall as The Beast came on land, the roar of water cascading off its back. Where to go? On the west side of the boulevard there were tall hotels and office buildings—too many people. Then he got it. He would go right into Bayfront Park which had 62 acres with wide walkways he could drive on! He prayed that in this lousy weather the park would be empty.

"Where are you going? "Samantha said, so hysterical she could barely get the words out. Roderick was shivering in silence from his second close escape. Thomas was amazed the two of them had even managed to stick close to the restaurant, particularly when he doubted if either had expected to see him alive again. He couldn't blame them for not going back into the restaurant to get him. What could they have done?

"If it's going to follow," he said, pressing down on the gas pedal until the car raced along as fast as it could possibly go, "I want to stick to the bayfront." He didn't think The Beast would want to be caught too far inland, away from an easy escape into the water, but he could be wrong. The only slim advantage they had was that the creature was so big and heavy it could not possibly walk very fast. But then, at that size, it didn't have to.

They were driving along at 90 miles an hour past benches and statues, pools with fountains, lovely tropical gardens. Trees simply whizzed past the windows. Roderick hung out the back shouting at the occasional pedestrian to run for his life. Even over the sound of the engine they could hear the BOOM BOOM BOOM of the monster's thudding footsteps. It was coming after them, crashing through the trees and making the earth itself tremble. Thomas wondered if there were any point to their trying to escape, even in a speeding automobile. At that size the monster's strides were so huge it would catch up to them literally any second. The thought of that tremendous monstrosity behind them in the dark somewhere, so huge, so relentless, so large and heavy its footfalls sounded like thunder, was enough to drive him senseless. There was no escape. How could he ever have imagined there was? Why couldn't he accept it? That might as well be God behind them! The sky had opened, and God was walking the land and crushing all nonbelievers.

Roderick put his hand on his shoulder. "Slow down," he said.

"What are you, crazy?"

"Listen. That sound."

Thomas could hear it, like a tidal wave, a huge, splashing

sound as if a battleship had been dropped into the ocean from 50 miles overhead.

"Pull over. I think it's gone."

Thomas did not want to slacken his ferocious pace, but he knew he would have to stop eventually. He had driven right through the park and into the tiny warehouse and pier district on the opposite end. He stepped on the brake. The car began to slow down until he was driving along at a gentle cruising speed. In another moment he hit the brake again and pulled over to the side.

Thomas parked outside of a deserted warehouse, and they quickly got out of the auto. He hated the idea of being on foot but he had no idea where The Beast was in relation to the car and knew he couldn't get out of its way if he didn't know where it was. But Roderick was right. All they heard was silence. They saw nothing towering above or behind the warehouses all around them.

Thomas shuddered. It would be just like Bronmore to blend The Beast's dark body into the shadows, to hold his breath, flatten down against the ground like a building or miniature mountain and wait for them to walk up to it. Or it could jump back out of the bay right down the block and be on top of them before they knew what hit them. He could simply not stop trembling.

"It went back into the bay?" Samantha said. "That was what we heard, wasn't it? The splash when it went back into the bay? But why? Why did it leave us alone?"

"Who knows?" Thomas said.

They could see the devastation it had left all the way from Parmenter's to about halfway through the park—trees flattened down to nothing, statues and fountains crushed to rubble. There was a foot or so of water that had been displaced from the bay covering everything. Thomas only hoped it wasn't covering any bodies.

Why did it retreat when it had them?

Samantha looked as if she were about to drop dead from the experience. "What do we do now?"

Thomas looked at his bleeding arms and chest, not to mention the wounds on his back, and noted the hysterical condition the others were in. "We get some medical attention," he said.

And then he fainted.

Samantha looked at if she were about to drop dead from the experience. "What do we do now?"

Thomas looked at his bleeding thumb and chest, no to mention the wound on his back, and noted the frightful condition of the others. "We've got to find medical attention. Be safe."

CHAPTER SIXTEEN
FINAL CONFRONTATION

"Are you all right? Are you all right?"

Someone was slapping his face, gently maybe, but it irritated him. He started waving his arms in the air to get rid of the slapping hands, then opened his eyes. He saw three hazy faces above him: Samantha, Roderick and Eustace Dunn. How did she get here? And behind her—was that Franklina? Damn creeps! How did they find them? Why hadn't the old witch and her creepy daughter left him alone? If It weren't for her he wouldn't have practically molested Bronmore at the banquet the way he did; he wouldn't have agitated The Beast into coming after them. He was coming back to consciousness, his bitter, inappropriate thoughts fading, replaced only by confusion and pain.

Rod stopped slapping his face and handed him a shot glass full of bourbon. Thomas took a sip. It burned and it didn't help at all. He shook his head and handed it back to Roderick. "Enough," he said.

He sat up and discovered he was on a bench in a booth in the back room of a dingy bar and grill called Harry's on Ermine Street. He saw an open door directly opposite the booth through which one could enter the bar proper. Aside from three beefy sailors or longshoremen at another booth, the back room was deserted, and all the rest of its booths and little round tables empty. Although they had done a good job of refurbishing it—wooden plaques and pictures on the walls, bright yellow tablecloths—they hadn't quite succeeded in disguising the fact that the bar had once been a couple of offices. For a dump, it wasn't bad. At least they kept the lights down low.

Thomas pulled himself up until he was sitting at the table. Roderick and Eustace sat down across from him, their faces full of concern. Samantha and Franklina had sat down at a round table next to the booth. Franklina was staring off into space, and so was Samantha—except Samantha had a drink in her hand and Thomas could tell from her spacey expression that it wasn't her first.

"What happened?" he asked.

"You fainted," Roderick explained. "We carried you in here and over to the booth. We didn't think you required an ambulance, as you kept reviving periodically and your injuries looked worse than they are."

Thomas tried to remember. Apparently his shirt had been shredded, because all he was wearing on top was the light jacket Roderick had borrowed from his friend before leaving the hospital. "I hurt all over," he said. "I have blood on me. Spittle." *The saliva of The Beast*

"We're all bloodied and injured, but not severely. There's time for us to go to a hospital and get a thorough checkup. I think you passed out from shock and exhaustion, the sheer terror of what you'd been through. Of all of us, you came closest to dying in there."

Thomas shivered and remembered. Already it had the quality of a nightmare, something that never had happened, the mind's way of dealing with the unbelievably dreadful, he supposed.

He looked at the old woman, who was studying him.

"How did you get here?" Turning to Roderick, he asked, "Did you call her?"

Eustace answered for both herself and Thorson. "No, Franklina and I were already in the city. When neither you nor Samantha answered the phones at your apartments, we decided, since we had to have dinner anyway, to drive to the restaurant and talk to you if you were there. We arrived just in time to see the three of you pile into your car and drive off. We didn't understand your haste until we saw the Great Beast come out of the water and follow you. We drove out of its path, just in time, but it wasn't interested in us."

Thomas thought he would have been if he had known who it was.

"Minutes later, we saw it plunge back into the ocean and swamp half the waterfront. We continued on in our own car, using the regular highway, and drove around this district until we saw your auto parked out front. We walked inside just as they were depositing you at this booth."

Just then a beer-bellied man with a red monk's fringe and mustache came over and asked, "Everything all right here? He gonna be okay?"

"Yes," Roderick told him. "He's much better now, thank you."

"What was he—hurt in the explosion? Somebody said there was an explosion. I hear across the park all the buildings have been blown apart like they were matchsticks. Most of my customers went over to watch the firemen."

Roderick looked at the others and waited for a reaction. "We don't know what happened," he said finally. He handed the man his empty shot glass. "Bring me another. And whatever the ladies are having."

Eustace and Franklina ordered sodas, while Samantha held up her empty glass and requested more vodka. Thomas couldn't meet her eyes. But for now, at least, her drinking was the least of their problems.

Once the bartender was out of earshot, Roderick added, "I don't know how I'm going to pay for these. My wallet's in the wreckage of my house in Hillsboro Beach."

"Let me handle it," Eustace said.

Before Roderick could say thank you, Thomas was hissing, "Surely *somebody* saw the monster. Surely they aren't going to pass off the destruction of Parmenter's as an explosion."

"Of course not," Roderick said. "Too many people in the restaurant and the street saw the monster. The story will get out, don't you worry, but all that the authorities and curious spectators saw were crushed buildings and fires. The Beast's stampede through the commercial area outside the park did start a number of small fires and minor explosions, according to what the bartender told us earlier he heard on TV. Unless people have seen The Beast for themselves, it's better for the moment to let them assume that's the explanation."

"Do you...do you think everyone got out of the restaurant in time?" Except Joseph, of course.

When none of the others answered him, Eustace decided to speak up. "You must hope so. The rescue workers can't be sure until they've gone through the whole building. Let's keep our fingers crossed."

"Why did it go back to the sea? It could have smashed this whole town apart and everyone in it if it wanted to."

Eustace smiled grimly. "It's old. The Beast Is old; The Man is old. Bronmore has his limits whether he wants to admit it or not. He won't be changing back to a beast again this evening."

Thomas remembered how he had assumed The Beast wouldn't attack Parmenter's and been wrong. "Are you sure?" he asked. "We're still only a block from the water. What if he..."

Eustace laid her hand gently on top of his own. "If he does decide to change, Thomas, there won't be any place that's safe, believe me." She looked over at her daughter. "But we'll know." Franklina's eyes were still blank; she was still staring at the wall and her body completely rigid in its seat. "My daughter will know. She's tracking him now."

"Tracking him?"

"Franklina has special gifts. She sensed somehow that The Beast would attack moments before it did, but of course she could not be positive. Later, she felt it change from Beast to Man. Now she is tracking the man—mentally, if he comes here, as I think he will, we will hopefully have some warning."

He knew better than to question her story or her daughter's psychic ability. Everything else she'd said had been true.

"You think he'll come here…as a man, I hope?"

"Yes."

"Good. Then I can kill him."

"Let Franklina and me take care of that. We've spent many, many hours thinking up our plan, arguing on the best way to go about it."

"But…"

"Killing him won't be easy. Neither will be staying alive. Even in his human form Bronmore has what you might call supernatural powers. All that energy he draws into himself to convert to the mass of The Beast? Well, he can also draw in that energy and use it for other purposes."

"Shouldn't we get out of here then?"

Franklina spoke out loud abruptly, shrilly. "There's no point," she said. She was still holding her head and body in that odd, stiff manner and now her eyes were closed, too. "He knows where we are. And he's coming. It worked, Mummy. He sensed me tracking him and locked onto my mind. He's coming here."

Thomas started to rise. "Come on."

"Remain!" Eustace said. "You've trusted me up to this point—trust me now. We're safer inside, believe me. Bronmore will remain human but we can't be sure what else he'll do. It's time, Thomas, time to pay him back for everything. The last stand, you might call it. Or he'll just hunt us down wherever we go at his leisure."

She leaned back and lifted her head proudly like an ancient queen who knew her reign was over but would not give up until after one final fight and would, as always, comport herself with dignity. "We'll sit and we'll wait, Thomas. We'll let him make the first move. And we'll strike when the opportunity arises. No more running. Not any more."

Thomas was beginning to get an inkling of what made the woman tick. "I think you hate Bronmore even more than I do."

She said nothing for a moment, then she nodded. "Yes, I do. I've hated Gareth Bronmore since before I knew who he was, since that night eighteen years ago, when I was carrying Franklina, that my husband and I went sailing on his ship, the Windward. My husband Frank and I were very much in love. I've never met anyone like him. I was down in the cabin while he was out on deck. Suddenly, the whole ship shuddered, and I tumbled around in a dread. I stumbled to the deck where I found Frank prostrate, crying out about a monster he had seen in the distance. Then I saw it, too, in the moonlight. I saw its face."

Her eyes narrowed coldly, and she spoke with an intense, burning loathing. "Bronmore doesn't like witnesses. He carelessly had risen to the surface for air and been spotted. He struck us again from below, just a casual bump, and the ship fell to pieces all around us. He didn't stay to see if we had drowned or not. I assume his belly was full. We were beneath contempt. He didn't care about me, Mr. Bartlett, or my husband, or the child I was carrying. He didn't care about the years of love, the bond between us, what we felt for one another. But although my husband drowned and I nearly lost the baby, another ship came by soon afterward and I was rescued. I didn't much care without Frank. If it weren't for the child…

"So I dealt with my loss and my pain by dedicating my life to finding the creature. I had seen its face and I knew it was a hybrid, that it was a renegade and evil. As you've undoubtedly guessed, I'm sure, Mr. Bartlett, I come from a long line of alien-descendants, and somehow have the genetic memory of their past. But now isn't the time to explain it."

She folded her hands and studied them for a moment. "But it was Bronmore's fatal error to leave me alive, even more than not killing you or Mr. Thorson. For he didn't know that the baby I was carrying—"

She hadn't time to finish. For at that moment, Franklina got up out of her chair and screamed, "He's here!"

Thomas, Rod and Eustace went over to the window. Samantha started shivering and clung to her drink as Franklina backed away, eyes widening.

Thomas saw a taxi drive up to the bar. A man got out moments later as the taxi pulled away. The storm had finally broken and the street was windswept and rainy. Even so Thomas recognized the stance and bristling energy of the man who stood on the opposite sidewalk looking in on them, eyes glaring like spotlights in the dark.

"Bronmore!" he said.

* * *

Bronmore smiled.

There they were, the fools, watching him from the window. Thought they could get away from him, eh? Well, they were sorely mistaken.

He had thought he had been crashing after them—in such a rage that his mind was dominant and had willingly blended with The Beast's—when he realized that he was expending a great deal of energy in what might be a purposeless pursuit.

For one thing, he could not be sure Bartlett was in that car in the park; he hadn't seen him get into it. He'd assumed so from the way the car zoomed away. For another, he could see that they were nearing the end of the park and from there could turn in any direction, duck around any corner or down any side street, leave the car and hide in a cellar or sewer, and miraculously survive his thrashing and crashing about simply because they were out of sight or too small to be noticed. Why smash a city, *his* city, apart just to kill one person?

The Beast was also experiencing a great deal of pain, and he was afraid he might revert to human form right in front of witnesses. So he retreated, dove into the bay, wrecking ships and docks, stomping poor, slow unfortunates in his way. Then he swam in his intermediate form to the pier where he'd left his clothes. A simple matter then to hail a cab and go home to plan, to regain his energy.

But then he felt something, a pinprick at the back of his brain. Someone—someone like him?—was tracking him, surveying him, and he was as curious as he was annoyed. But if they could home in on him, could he not do the same to them? He locked in on their psychic aura and brain waves, and instructed the cabby to take him back to the waterfront.

And there they were, cringing inside, imagining that now that he was human they could take him. Well, he would show them how wrong they were.

The food he consumed in his bestial form was almost immediately converted to a type of energy, most of which he expelled during normal activity and the rest when he trans-formed back to human. He needed more energy now—and quickly. He spread out his arms into the storm and let its energy come to him, let it fill his body and electrify his every cell and membrane. His eyes grew larger and brighter. He would not absorb this energy and use it to change, instead he would expel it and use it to finally rid himself of the noisome gnats who dared to judge and attack him.

* * *

The first thing that happened was that the temperature began to rise.

"Why is it getting so hot in here?" one of the sailors said. "Hey, Manny, turn down the heat for cryin' out loud!"

Manny came in with the drinks. "I didn't do anything."

"I'm going out there," Thomas said. "He killed my parents, wrecked my restaurant, murdered Joseph. I'm going to kill him with my bare hands."

"No!" Eustace indicated that Roderick should help her restrain him. "No, Mr. Bartlett, you mustn't go. He could strike you down with a thought. If he wants to play with us, let him play with us. Let him use up his energy. Then it's Franklina's...then it's our turn."

"Say, it really is getting hot in here," Manny the bartender said, putting the drinks they'd ordered on the table. Samantha grabbed her double vodka hungrily and started gulping it. Franklina had become stock still again, and was staring into space, her face determined, brave, perhaps a little frightened. She looked much too young and frail to amount to much of a threat to Bronmore.

Manny called to the others at the window. "Say, is something wrong, folks? Is—ouch!"

The table where he'd had his hand resting had turned red hot; he pulled his hand away with a start just as the three sailors and Samantha jumped out of their seats. "Hey, what is this?" one of the men hollered.

In spite of the open window, the air in the room was quickly becoming close and stifling. Thomas felt the sweat pouring off his forehead. Eustace looked pale and faint, while Roderick was drenched in perspiration. "He's trying to cook us alive," Thomas screamed.

The soda or beer on the hot table and in the sailors' booth began to boil and sizzle, frothed over out of their glasses and dripped onto the table where the liquid disappeared in a puff of smoke.

Manny's face was beet red. He grabbed at his collar. "Hot, too hot." He stumbled and two of the sailors made a grab for him. Franklina stood frozen by the table where Samantha was crying and screeching, "Leave us alone leave us alone oh please God leave us alone."

The temperature seemed to be up to 110 degrees in the room—the walls and windows were even hotter, burning to the touch—when the impossible happened.

The wall above the booths began to melt, to ooze. The paint was running down, and little bubbles appeared in the concrete behind it, bursting and leaving tiny pockets on the surface. From these pockets dripped a gummy, runny substance that was the color of flesh. Before long there was a broad circle of this substance on the wall, about six feet high and four feet across. It was directly over the booth where Thomas had been sitting. Roderick stepped away from the window where Thomas and Eustace stood thunderstruck; all of them were struggling for breath in the steaming atmosphere.

"Samantha, move away!" Thorson thundered. The table she was standing by was right in front of the circle of ooze on the wall. She jumped at the sound of Roderick's voice and stepped to the center of the room near Franklina. Behind them Manny was still supported by two of the three sailors. The third was coughing into a handkerchief, watching the fleshy circle in astonishment as it bubbled and expanded.

Soon the flesh had protruded a foot or so from the wall. It was taking shape, becoming something—a *face*—taking on features.

Bronmore's face was taking shape in the ooze, only it was more obscene and distorted and hideous than ever. It grew out farther from the wall, taking on more and more substance as the ooze collected in the folds and lines that made up the features. The mouth was slowly opening as the head stretched and pulled and tore away from the walls, which was beginning to take on hairline cracks like a windshield hit by branches.

Then, before anyone was prepared, the huge misshapen, hairless head pulled out from the wall and started stretching across the room. Thomas pushed Eustace toward the door and into the corridor next to the bar, while Franklina woke up out of her spell and headed rapidly for the same spot from where she'd been standing. "I tried to stop him, Mummy, I tried. But he's so powerful!" The two sailors supported the heavy bartender between them and raced to get out of the grinning mouth's way, their coughing companion following behind them.

Roderick wasn't quick enough.

Before he could get away from the table where Samantha had been sitting, the stretching, thickening lips of the head closed around him and pulled him up and into the widening maw. He squealed. The hardening teeth inside the maw bit down, chomped on him, until blood spurted from a dozen puncture wounds. "Aghhhhh. Help me!" Roderick's earsplitting screams reached an unbearable pitch.

Samantha tried to pull him out of the mouth even as it pushed farther out of the wall, but soon she realized it was hopeless. She turned away in futility just as Roderick was sectioned by the dismembering teeth and sucked down into the blood-red throat, which was now nearly as long as the room was wide. The closed eyes of the head had fully formed and opened as the now empty mouth emitted a horrible triumphant chortle.

Thomas, Eustace and Franklina were out in the corridor that dissected the bar and grill and were waiting for the others to join them so they could slam the door behind them. The two sailors supporting the barman managed to make it inside and collapsed. Although Samantha had had a comparatively small quantity of vodka, she was pretty high due to her hasty consumption. She stumbled and fell to the floor directly in the path of the growling, stretching ooze-head. Before Thomas could go in the room and get her, the third sailor went back, picked her up, and threw her hastily through the doorway and into the corridor.

"Hurry!" Thomas screamed to the man.

But before the sailor could get through himself, the door slammed shut of its own volition.

"We've got to get him out of there," Thomas shouted, struggling with the doorknob. The sailor banged helplessly and furiously on the glass window set in the door. "Get me outa here," he screamed. He was too confused to think of running to the window in the front of the room.

Thomas saw that inside the room where the man was trapped with the monstrous head just a foot or two behind him, the temperature had started dropping. Ice was rapidly forming on the window, and the trapped man's breath was turning to mist. Freezing, he stopped banging on the door and began slapping his sides with his arms. He turned to see how far away the mouth was, and Thomas' eyes went with him.

The head had stopped expanding, growing out of the wall, as soon as the room grew cold. The fleshy ooze that it was composed of now gathered on the sides of it and ran over until the neck had spread out from one side of the room to another. The ooze-flesh hung down in tremendous wrinkled flaps and folds. The head sunk back into this mass until the gooey substance formed a long wide solid wall. Even as the trapped man became coated with icicles and frost, the solid wall the ooze had formed began moving closer, expanding outward, to crush him.

Samantha pushed Thomas aside. "It's my fault," she said. "I tripped because I was drunk. He saved me. We can't let him die—not again, not again." She keened in a softer voice, "Not like the Allens."

Her fists pounded against the glass which had become brittle from the cold. Cracks began to form and this encouraged her. She beat on it harder and harder until finally the glass shattered and her wrists broke through.

The solid wall of ooze-flesh had now almost traversed the entire room. Thomas could see there was barely time to save the half-frozen sailor, but Samantha was determined. He tried to hold her back but she wriggled out of his grip.

She knocked out all the glass with her bleeding hands and thrust herself through the opening before Thomas had a chance to stop her. She went into the room, pushed the man, so stiff he could barely walk, out through the opening, and tried to follow him to safety. But it was too late. She was crushed by Bronmore's expanding ooze-wall herself.

"Samantha!"

The ooze-wall was beginning to crystalize as the temperature dropped to normal. Bits of it fell onto the floor and dissolved. The sailor's friends saw to him, while Thomas pulled Samantha's bloodied body through the hole in the door. He lay her gently down on the corridor floor and knelt beside her, holding her and crying.

Franklina was back in her trance state. "That's two," she said.

Eustace gasped. "Bronmore's talking through her."

Thomas lay Samantha's head down carefully and jumped to his feet. "The bastard!" Out of the cracked and crushed remains of the booths and tables in the other room, he grabbed a knife and put it in his pocket.

Thomas had never acted forcefully or heroically in his life, had never had the need to. The closest he had come to it was when he felt Bronmore's hump at the dinner. He had also risked his own life to try to save his partner's at Parmenter's but he wasn't thinking about that now. Instead he was rushing down the corridor toward the door to the sidewalk. It had stopped raining. Before Eustace and Franklina could stop him he was racing across the street to where Bronmore stood staring and smiling. Thomas reached out his arms; his hands formed claws that would squeeze the life out of Bronmore, tear out his throat and—

SLAM!

Suddenly Thomas found himself falling backward; his rear hit the cobblestoned surface of the road and the breath whooshed out of him. He had hit something—a wall of solid force and substance. He couldn't see it, but it was there. Was that it shimmering like a curtain of heat in front of Bronmore? A force field of some kind that the miserable old man had erected? Well, Thomas would find a way around it if he had to. He got to his feet and started punching the transparent, solid barrier, unmindful of his bruised and broken knuckles, or the pain and the blood. He had to get through!

Bastard, bastard, bastard, bastard!

Just then Bronmore dropped the energy field protecting him from Thomas' blows.

But not before beginning to change into his intermediate form.

Thomas stood there in abject disgust and horror as the man literally burst from his clothes, elongated, grew claws and fangs and a dripping, hideous snout that hissed and slobbered. If he turned into the Gargantosaurus again, Thomas knew he was finished. But Bronmore hadn't the strength for a complete change. He opened his mouth wide and charged at Thomas.

Thomas dodged the enraged half-beast and in his own rage jumped up onto its back as it twisted around in the middle of the street. He tried to ride it as if it were a bucking bronco. At least behind the animal he'd be safe from its tusks and claws. He nearly slid off the foul, greasy flesh, but his fingernails dug into the flanks and held on. When he thought it was safe to do so, when he was secure enough on the back, he grabbed the knife he had put in his pants pocket earlier and thrust it again and again into Bronmore's mutated skin.

The knife cut through the flesh very easily.

The Bronmore-beast screeched and stretched to its full height, but Thomas held on with one hand and dug the knife, ripping and tearing, into Bronmore's neck. Blow after blow after blow. The wounds issued an odorous green fluid like a combination of sap and vomit. Where it touched Thomas' own wounds, it burned.

Thomas could tell the Bronmore-beast's energy was nearly depleted. It dropped down on all fours and did nothing to prevent Thomas from hacking at it again and again with the knife. Thomas wanted it dead.

But Bronmore thrust upwards once more when Thomas' guard was down and managed to fling the man off his back and almost all the way across the street. He landed in the gutter at Eustace's feet. As he tried to pull himself up to once more enter the fray, Thomas saw the thing galloping away toward the bay, becoming human as it ran. Franklina stepped past him and her mother and darted after the naked, bleeding form of Gareth Bronmore. Her eyes speaking volumes, Eustace put her hand up to her lips and watched the girl go.

"I...wanted...to...kill it," Thomas said. For a moment he blacked out.

Eustace was at his side, holding him. "Shhhh. You're badly injured. Very badly. They've called for an ambulance inside."

"Must get up...go after it."

"No, no. You must rest now."

"Then tell police...to go...after it."

She shook her head. "Bronmore has reached the water by now. Don't worry. He will die tonight." She looked over toward the water and tears formed in her eyes. "Her psychic powers were no match for his, but Franklina had an alternate plan. I objected, but she's young and headstrong." She looked down at Thomas again. "Bronmore has been badly wounded.

He will be easy prey. Franklina will kill him and get my revenge. Franklina, the dear child, will finish what Bronmore started those long years ago."

Thomas wept, remembering Samantha, Roderick, Joseph, all the others. His mother and father. So many others.

He let Eustace hold him and care for him while they waited for the ambulance, as if he were a child and she his mother, the earth mother who could protect him as his own mother had and see that he was always warm and happy.

She brushed his forehead and stroked his hair with her fingers.

"I don't really care," he said, "if I die. I've lost my restaurant. Samantha. I don't know what to do, how to go on."

Eustace's voice was stern. "You will go on," she said.

"Why?"

"Because it is natural. You cannot give in to despair. I nearly did when my husband died, but I kept going. Bronmore has killed many people over the years. You must live out your full life scheme. You must live for all those who wish they could have. You must live for all those who didn't. Life is too precious to just throw it away. I know."

She was crying now, too, and Thomas wondered why.

"Franklina," she said, and the wind carried the word away, following her daughter down the street and around the block where she'd gone on a mission, Thomas realized, that she might never return from.

And he knew why The Mistress was crying.

EPILOGUE

She came to him an hour later.

"I knew you were not like the others," Bronmore told her. "I could sense it even when you were probing my mind. I could have destroyed the others, easily, but I held back and played with them. I didn't want to harm you, my dear. Not you. I knew you were not acting under your own will."

He was very badly injured, but he would survive. Already he was using a modicum of his power to seal the wounds, to let the ooze fill the holes and tears, replace the missing skin and repair the damage.

"I've been so lonely," he told Franklina. "You are like me, I can tell. Finally, near the end of my life I have found another who can understand, who can do what I can do. Come to me, my dear."

She had homed in on him again, having tracked him since he left the restaurant, listening with her mind as he ran to the river, as he let the sea water bathe his injuries, as he swam to his own boat in the harbor which his Beast form had not destroyed. Franklina followed him to the boat, climbed aboard, walked down into the cabin where he lay comfortably in his bathrobe, drinking brandy to warm his body and lift his spirits.

She sat beside him. He poured her a brandy. They drank; they toasted.

He ran his finger along the hidden lump on her back.

"I love you," Franklina said. "I thought I was the only one, but I'm not."

He kissed her tender lips. She was beautiful in his eyes.

"Do we have to remain among them?" she asked. "I don't want to walk among men. I've always felt my destiny, *our* destiny, is in the ocean."

Bronmore, enraptured, set sail. He would do anything she wanted, anything. He needed no crew. If there were any mishap he and Franklina would hardly be in any danger. He basked in her affection, her admiration and infatuation, while she shared her young, pretty flesh with him and spoke of all the things they would do together. To have someone young like this, who was like him, to share in and enrich his declining years was a joy he would never have imagined. His heart sang and he felt young again himself. And wait until they were deep out to sea and could change and swim, together. He cared nothing about revenge, about Bartlett or the others! Cared not at all if Gareth Bronmore went missing forever. Let them think him dead.

He had gone on his rampage, he thought, because he had subliminally identified with that long-dead Gargantosaurus dug up in Arizona, been reminded of his own mortality and had to prove he was more capable and powerful than ever. Instead he'd proved just the opposite.

And that fossilized beast had not even been a hybrid. It had been intelligent, more so than its descendants, but not capable of metamorphosis. Yet in some way it was an ancestor. Either one of its still-intelligent children had been a hybrid, giving birth to mammals, or one of Bronmore's direct descendants had adopted the ancient form of a Gargantosuarus for his own secret purposes.

Centuries ago, Bronmore's father had told him, hybrids could choose the beast forms they desired, could transform into just about anything. Now it was all locked into the genes and they had to content themselves with the form they carried in their chromosomes. He knew his children would also look like Harriman's Gargantosaurus.

His children? And then he thought of an heir. Perhaps he could have an heir! With Franklina and him as the parents the child would undoubtedly have their gifts, too. His race would go on; his spawn would flourish. He could always go back and settle his affairs once the child was born, make sure it would have every advantage both as human and beast.

Bronmore was happy.

Nestled together, he and his ladylove went to sleep.

* * *

Franklina thought it was too bad that Bronmore had to die.

She had come to understand him these past few hours, even to like him a bit, and there was so much he could have taught her. But her mother had taught her better. Franklina hated Bronmore for abusing his gifts, for abusing his power. Franklina had grown up fatherless, a captive audience of her mother's loneliness and torment. Her mother knew of Franklina's abilities—hybrid traits were apparently carried in their recessive genes and were normally latent—and did not object to her transforming now and then to revel in the joy of it. But she had taught her daughter well. *You are not to prey upon man. You are part human, and must have respect for life, all life.*

Poor Bronmore. He had no respect. She enjoyed the simple luxury of swimming through the ocean where no man could go, communing with the deep sea creatures, exploring the vast depths, seeing things no human could see. But what had this old man done with his gifts but pervert them, use them to make money and build buildings, to cause death and destruction. So much misery, her mother's misery! How long would it be before he got bored with their life at sea, turned on her, and returned to the world of men to plunder and consume and cause more misery? Not long, she suspected. He had turned something wonderful and blessed into something terrible and obscene. She was glad she'd fooled him, got his guard down, by coming here and making love to him.

She lifted the knife she'd taken from the galley and began to plunge it toward his heart.

Bronmore grabbed her wrist in his hand. "What's this?" His eyes glimmered with pure hatred. He wasn't sleeping. "So, you have decided to betray me! Then you've asked for what's coming."

He started to change, but so did Franklina. The form she took was quite different from that of a gargantosaurus, more sharklike, with a much bigger jaw, more teeth, enormous crashing flippers that pounded and battered him all over. He was bigger than she was, of course, but she was younger, more rested. She had not received the injuries he had, had not expended all her energy and power.

The boat fell apart around them as they enlarged, twisted, wrapped together, teeth and limbs intertwined, biting, gouging, bloodying.

The Beast, as ever, was silent.

But Bronmore roared.

Blood foamed through the thrashing water as the two, still entangled in their fight to the death, disappeared beneath the waves.

Neither of them reappeared.

Hours later the sharks and other scavengers were still feasting in the blood-red water.

AUTHOR'S NOTE

Although the Gargantosaurus is only the product of the author's imagination (hopefully!), the Seismosaurus and Supersaurus mentioned in chapter seven were real and their remains were discovered as described in the text

Nowadays the great "thunder lizards" are the objects of amused contempt—extinct creatures worthy of being pondered only by wide-eyed children, foolish romantics, and what few paleontologists are left. But the dinosaurs dominated this planet for over 160 million years, and modern day man had been around for less than 30,000 years! Hardly the twinkling of an eye. Food for thought, eh?

Luckily there are people who are still interested in this planet's former rulers, people who know how much humankind can learn by studying the past. In recent months there has been much controversy concerning what caused the extinction of the dinosaurs, as new theories and evidence thereof are introduced. This book makes use of the popular cosmic catastrophe/climate change theories, but only the future will reveal the true answers to one of this planet's greatest mysteries.

I found several books immensely helpful in researching

this work of fiction. The authors of the following nonfiction works cannot be held accountable for whatever liberties I may have taken:

The Dinosaurs. William Stout, William Service, Byron Preiss. Bantam / 1981.

Monster Dinosaur. Daniel Cohen. J.P. Lippincott / 1983.

When Dinosaurs Ruled the Earth. Dr. David Norman. Ezeter Books / 1985.

I would also like to thank my parents for their help and advice, and Caroline Schoell in particular for her expert proof-reading of the original typescript.

ABOUT THE AUTHOR

William Schoell is the author of over 35 books, including celebrity biographies, books for young adults, tomes on the performing arts and popular culture, and novels, especially in the thriller-horror genre. He has been a radio producer and talk show host, worked for Columbia Pictures, is an activist and blogger, and playwright.

Schoell is a native New Yorker, born in Manhattan, where he resides.